Advance Praise for *Lady Sunshine*

"Amy Mason Doan creates a whole world and mood with her exquisitely crafted novel, *Lady Sunshine*. It's replete with late-'70s nostalgia, and Doan masterfully renders the lives of musicians and those who are drawn to them, no matter the price. A delicious daydream of a book."

—Elin Hilderbrand, *New York Times* bestselling author of *28 Summers*

"With a winning combination of lyrical writing and a page-turning plot, Amy Mason Doan chronicles the evolution and mysterious demise of the friendship between two young women at the California estate-cum-commune of a renowned musician. A tone-perfect evocation of the free-spirited late 1970s and a riveting coming-of-age story, this sun-dappled book has it all: heart, smarts, and an irresistible musical beat."

—Karen Dukess, author of *The Last Book Party*

"This gorgeous book is part gold-drenched, nostalgic dream, part ingeniously spun mystery, but what I love best is the female friendship at its heart. Loyal, loving, and fiercely true to each other, Jackie and Willa will remind you of the times in your life when friendship was everything, when two girls together could make an entire world."

—Marisa de los Santos, *New York Times* bestselling author of *I'll Be Your Blue Sky*

"Amy Mason Doan dazzles in this epic story of a family torn apart by secrets. Haunting and vivid, with complex characters and a setting that sparkles with detail, *Lady Sunshine* will stay with me for a long time."

—Julie Clark, *New York Times* bestselling author of *The Last Flight*

"*Lady Sunshine* is shot through with free love, hope, and all the magic of the '70s, but under the sun and music lie dark secrets. It's a thrilling ride, a beautiful evocation of an era, and a story that will keep readers entranced from the first page to the last."

—Rene Denfeld, bestselling author of *The Child Finder*

"In *Lady Sunshine*, Amy Mason Doan has crafted an engrossing tale of secrets, memory, music, and the people and places you can never outrun. This novel will transport you to the '70s and summertime magic and a long-overdue reckoning. A fantastic summer read."

—Laura Dave, bestselling author of *Eight Hundred Grapes*

Also by Amy Mason Doan

The Summer List
Summer Hours

Lady Sunshine

A NOVEL

AMY MASON DOAN

GRAYDON
HOUSE

ISBN-13: 978-1-525-81154-8

Lady Sunshine

This edition published by arrangement with Harlequin Books S.A.

Graydon House
22 Adelaide St. West, 40th Floor
Toronto, Ontario M5H 4E3, Canada
www.GraydonHouseBooks.com
www.BookClubbish.com

Printed in U.S.A.

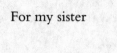

For my sister

Lady Sunshine

June

1

A Girl, Her Cousin, and a Waterfall

1999

I rattle the padlock on the gate, strum my fingers along the cold chain-link fence.

I own this place.

Maybe if I repeat it often enough I'll believe it.

All along the base of the fence are tributes: shells, notes, sketches, bunches of flowers. Some still fresh, some so old the petals are crisp as parchment. I follow the fence uphill, along the coast side, and stop at a wooden, waist-high sign marking the path up to the waterfall. It wasn't here the summer I visited.

The sign is covered in words and drawings, so tattooed-over by fan messages that you can barely read the official one. I run my fingertips over the engravings: initials, peace symbols, *Thank you*'s, *I Love You*'s. Fragments of favorite lyrics. After coming so far to visit the legendary estate, people need to do something, leave their mark, if only with a rock on fog-softened wood.

Song titles from my uncle's final album, *Three*, are carved everywhere. "Heart, Home, Hope."

"Leaf, Shell, Raindrop."

"Angel, Lion, Willow." Someone has etched that last one in

symbols instead of words. The angel refers to Angela, my aunt. The lion is my uncle Graham.

And the willow tree. Willa, my cousin.

I have a pointy metal travel nail file in my suitcase; I could add my message to the rest, my own tribute to this place, to the Kingstons. To try to explain what happened the summer I spent here. I could tell it like one of the campfire tales I used to spin for Willa.

This is the story of a girl, her cousin, and a waterfall...

But there's no time for that, not with only seven days to clear the house for sale.

Back at the gate, where Toby's asleep in his cat carrier in the shade, I dig in my overnight bag for the keys. They came in a FedEx with a fat stack of documents I must've read on the plane from Boston a dozen times—thousands of words, all dressed up in legal jargon. When it's so simple, really. Everything inside that fence is mine now, whether I want it or not.

I unlock the gate, lift the metal shackle, and walk uphill to the highest point, where the gravel widens into a parking lot, then fades away into grass. The field opens out below me just like I remember. We called it "the bowl," because of the way the edges curve up all around it. A golden bowl scooped into the hills, rimmed on three sides by dark green woods. The house, a quarter mile ahead of me at the top of the far slope, is a pale smudge in the fir trees.

I stop to take it in, this piece of land I now own. The Sandcastle, everyone called it.

Without the neighbors' goats and Graham's guests to keep the grass down, the field has grown wild, many of the yellow weeds high as my belly button.

Willa stood here with me once and showed me how from this angle the estate resembled a sun. The kind a child would draw, with a happy face inside. Once I saw it, it was impossible to un-see:

The round, straw-colored field, trails squiggling off to the woods in every direction, like rays. The left eye—the campfire circle. The right eye—the blue aboveground pool. The nose was the vertical line of picnic benches in the middle of the field that served as our communal outdoor dining table. The smile was the curving line of parked cars and motorcycles and campers.

All that's gone now, save for the pool, which is squinting, collapsed, moldy green instead of its old bright blue.

I should go back for my bag and Toby but I can't resist—I move on, down to the center of the field. Far to my right in the woods, the brown roofline of the biggest A-frame cabin, Kingfisher, pokes through the firs. But no other cabins are visible, the foliage is so thick now. Good. Each alteration from the place of my memories gives me confidence. I can handle this for a week. One peaceful, private week to box things up and send them away.

"Sure you don't want me to come help?" Paul had asked when he dropped me at the airport this morning. "We could squeeze in a romantic weekend somewhere. I've always wanted to go to San Francisco."

"You have summer school classes, remember? Anyway, it'll be totally boring, believe me."

I'd told him—earnest, sweet Paul, who all the sixth-graders at the elementary school where we work hope they get as their teacher and who wants to marry me—that the trip was *no big deal*. That I'd be away for a week because my aunt in California passed away. That I barely knew her and just had to help pack up her old place to get it ready for sale.

He believed me.

I didn't tell him that the "old place" is a stunning, sprawling property perched over the Pacific, studded with cabins and outbuildings and a legendary basement recording studio. That the land bubbles with natural hot springs and creeks and waterfalls.

Or that I've inherited it. All of it. The fields, the woods, the house, the studio. And my uncle's music catalog.

I didn't tell him that I visited here once as a teenager, or that for a little while, a long time ago, I was sure I'd stay forever.

2

4 Sea Cliff

1979

As the black town car hurled me north from San Francisco to my uncle's house near Humboldt County, I sat in the back seat, staring out the window at the roiling blue-gray waves. Awed by what my anger had accomplished.

I was seventeen, and about to spend ten weeks at a place where I knew no one, with relatives I'd never met. And I had nobody to blame but myself.

My father and his new bride were spending the summer in Europe. An overdue honeymoon in France and Italy. Patricia had floated the idea of me joining them, but the prospect of staying in San Francisco, just me and Thea, our housekeeper, was bliss.

Thea was the only person I still acted like myself with. She wouldn't put up with anything less. Then Thea's mom broke her hip trying to change a smoke detector battery in the middle of the night, and Thea had to fly home to Tucson, and my summer plans were shattered along with that seventy-two-year-old coxal bone.

I'd proposed my coming here as a test for my father, a dare. I was sure he'd veto it immediately. To him, rugged Humboldt

County, on the coast hours north of San Francisco, might as well have been the Yukon Territory.

He'd said, "Fine," and turned up the volume on the golf. Now he and Patricia were somewhere over the Atlantic, toasting their clean getaway.

"How much longer?" I leaned forward in my seat.

"About five minutes, miss."

"Thank you."

We pulled off the coast highway, passed a boarded-up frozen custard shop, a surf shack, a house with burled-wood animal sculptures for sale in the front yard. Then we turned inland, climbing up a steep, bumpy gravel road.

The driver slowed, stopped. "We're here, miss."

I got out, certain my father had tricked me and sent me to camp. And not a good one. My punishment for how I'd acted all year. The multiple calls from Headmaster Dietz about the "reputation" I'd earned, the doors I'd slammed...

I looked around—a weedy, windy field. Picnic tables, a circle of stones and split logs ringing a stone firepit, an outhouse, a wooden outdoor shower with a single filthy towel flapping on a peg. Scattered in the trees on either side, flanking this open, sunken area, were a dozen or so brown cabins.

I clenched my fist around the five-dollar bill I'd been given for the driver's tip.

He must've noticed my confusion because he said, a little defensively, "This is it. 4 Sea Cliff." Pulling my yellow suitcase out of the trunk, he said, "Need me to walk you to the door?" Then he looked at the far-flung buildings, surely thinking what I was—*Which damn door?*

"No thanks, it's not far," I chirped, Patricia-like, as if I'd been here dozens of times. I handed the driver the crumpled five and took my suitcase, and the town car coasted back down the hill behind me, gravel pinging its undercarriage.

This was my uncle's house? I knew he was a folk singer whose string of hits had ended long ago, and that my father disliked him. I knew little else. On the few occasions I'd probed him about my mother's side of the family, he'd dismissed them alternately as "perpetual infants" or "freaks."

I don't know what I expected. But not this ghost town. The only sounds were the flapping of the towel by the shower—a fitting flag for this grimy, abandoned place—and the wind sighing through the trees.

I could hitchhike back to San Francisco and hole up in the house, where at least I'd have my piano and record player. At night, I'd go to Teena's DreamTraxx and obliterate reality with the jug of Gallo Ruby shared in the alley with strangers. My body, jotted in rainbow lights, could whirl and Hustle away the summer with all the other bodies.

But in the distance, up the hill, something flashed. A luminous white point in the sky. And it drew me closer.

The spire topped the tallest structure, a wide, sand-colored stucco building that I guessed, because of its size and piercing adornment, was the hub of this strange encampment. When I reached it, I set my suitcase on the grass and shaded my eyes with my hand. What had looked like a spire from the field was actually the tip of a chimney in the middle of the roof, its sides built up into points to mimic a turret. The top was covered in a pink-and-white layer of mismatched pearlescent tiles. Or… could it be?

"Shells."

I turned to a broad, pink-faced woman in a denim work shirt, long white braids wound on top of her head like a coronet. She was way too old to be my aunt Angela, but offered no introduction.

"He mortared them onto the old chimney a dozen years ago, to celebrate when they wrapped *Three*. Frank Lloyd Wright was rolling in his grave. Not to mention he could've broken his neck up there."

"It's pretty, though. I'm Jackie." No recognition in her faded green eyes. "Pierce. From San Francisco? I'm staying here for the summer?"

"Oh? Kate." No last name, no explanation of her role or relationship to the household. "Well, your timing's good," she said. "They're still in the dungeon finishing up. Weeks late, as always. Wills is camping down on the beach, and everyone else knows to stay away 'til they've wrapped. So you have your choice of squats. Personally, I'd grab Slipstream."

Wills would be Willa, my cousin. A few months younger than me, I'd been told. Every other part of this speech raised more questions than it answered.

"Slipstream?"

She pointed across the field to our right. "The last cabin down on the north side of the bowl. The bed's good, and it's the quietest. Turn right at the tall spruce with the split crown. Then left at the stump that looks like a guitar pick, and you're there."

So I wasn't staying in the main house with the family? Or was this how they all lived, hiding in the trees like squirrels?

I was ten yards away when she called out—perhaps taking pity on me, banished to the woods in my ironed white culottes and I. Magnin flutter-sleeve blouse—"Grab it before the hordes descend!"

"What hordes?" I yelled back.

"You'll see!"

3

The King of the Castle

It was after nine, and I was in my cabin, in bed, eating Fun Dip I'd bought from the gas station down the highway and reading by flashlight a 1960 *Vogue* I'd grabbed from the Rec Room in the main house. There were piles of old magazines there, and a stereo, and stacks of albums and 45s in low cubbies along every wall—but the house felt so deserted I didn't like to stay there long.

I'd been here for three days, and still no sign of anyone but Kate. Sometimes she let me tag along as she filled the aboveground pool and staved wood hot tub, or picked blueberries, or clipped sheets to the clothesline.

"Tell me about the hordes," I asked her, daily.

"You'll see," she said, always.

I'd never had so much freedom. I could have hitched a thousand miles by now and no one would have noticed. But mostly, I stayed in my ten-foot-square cabin. Kate rose and slept with the sun, so my nights were long. Lonely.

Slipstream—a burnt wood sign hung over the door—held a sagging double bed, a child's low dresser under a speckled mirror, a braided rag rug, a pile of hatboxes for a nightstand. Its limp white curtains had been cut from flour sacks, and the quilt was sewn of old men's dress shirts and ties. No electricity, no water.

I'd decorated as best I could, arranging my things artfully on the beat-up dresser: stationery and stamps for letters to Thea, a tub of Noxzema and Coty CornSilk powder to battle my oily skin, my watch, green pearl eye shadow, wands of lip gloss. I propped my favorite albums and 45s on their sides against the mirror.

Not that I had anything to play them on in my cabin.

I'd brought a rolled-up Blondie poster but had forgotten tape, so I'd stuck it to the door with four well-chewed gobs of gum. That project killed twenty minutes.

On the nightstand I'd set only one possession. I picked it up now, gently polishing the frame with my blouse hem—my favorite picture of my mother. She was pregnant with me, in a billowing white smock over bell-bottom jeans. Her feet were bare, her long, honey-colored hair tucked under a red bandanna. She was fixing up my nursery. Laughing at the camera, arranging children's books on a white shelf. With a magnifying glass, I'd been able to make out one title: *The Important Book* by Margaret Wise Brown.

I set the picture back, carefully swiveling it to face my bed, and grabbed another magazine, turning the water-rippled pages. *Jane Fonda's No Daddy's Girl... Sophia Loren, (Oscar's) Golden Girl...*

Are you a summer, spring, winter, or fall? Whoever'd taken the quiz before me was a Summer, but she'd crossed out her results and written, "I AM *ALL* SEASONS. I WILL NOT BE TRAPPED IN ONE!"

I liked this girl. I wished she was here in person, instead of only scribbles.

Pop-pop! Pop-pop-pop!

An engine. Old and sputtering. I switched off my flashlight

and looked out the window above my bed. A single headlight at the top of the driveway: a motorcycle.

After a minute, a yellow flashlight beam descended the hill to meet it, like a fairy greeting another in the dark.

Not Kate. I knew her brisk walk, and this welcoming glow of light was moving too slowly, swinging back and forth too languidly. The engine stopped and the motorcycle headlight went out.

"Who's that, the king of the castle?" the man on the motorcycle called. He was laughing, but his voice sounded tired. "Come out to greet the dirty rascal?"

"Your words, good sir, not mine. Pray, how was the journey?" This voice, from the man with the flashlight, was an appealing, resonant baritone, booming and wide-awake despite the hour.

So this was my uncle. Anyone else talking like that, in Old English witticisms, would have annoyed me. But his velvety voice saved him from sounding obnoxious, and it was clear this routine was a familiar joke to both men.

"I hauled ass," Weary Voice said. "Haven't stopped since the city."

"You must be famished. Would sir care to partake of our local delicacy before he passes out in his cabin?"

"Man, I've been drooling over Kate's chili since Sacramento. Mitch and Sooz here yet?"

"You know Madame Suzette. Friday might mean a week from Friday." My uncle paused. "She's bringing a new beau." Then he dropped the fake formality and went on in a regular voice, sincere and tinged with pity. "Mitchell's coming tomorrow. Alone."

A dramatic whistle. "Poor Mitch. He's got it bad."

"He'll survive. This is the best rehab west of the Rockies for the brokenhearted."

"You include yourself in that group?"

"Easy, there."

"Daddy!"

I hurried to my front steps for a better view of the field. My cousin, here at last. But I was too far away to see more than a mass of lamplit yellow hair.

"We need help carrying tables," she called.

"Coming, boss!" my uncle yelled up to her, laughing. "Let's get you fed. Wait'll you see my Willow. She's taller than you. And I've got to show you this tape gadget someone sent me from Japan. It's a trip. Makes the music sound like an underwater kazoo, but what the hell do I know…"

I strained to hear more but the voices faded, and my uncle's swinging flashlight beam crossed the field, climbing back up the hill.

I stayed on my dark porch, observing. For hours I watched, behind a curtain of leaves, as the hordes came. Three cars, another motorcycle, and something long and groaning—a bus or camper. Once they parked, the visitors ascended the hill, heading for the main house. These were happy invaders; their calls, as they got out of their cars, stretching after their long drives, were full of joy.

Laughter rang out across the field, car doors plunked, names were tossed.

"Put on a few pounds, Kip!"

"Hey. Hey, take it easy."

"April here yet?"

"…coming with Max tomorrow night…"

"Seen Kingston?"

"Yeah, up at the house. In fine form…"

I was curious whether Suzette would arrive with her mysterious *beau*, and if Mitchell's voice would sound as broken as his heart, but I didn't hear their names again that night. I heard many others—and many fragments of other dramas.

It wasn't simply entertaining, listening in the dark to strangers. It was mesmerizing. An intoxicating feeling of control—

because I chose when to turn the drama on and off, unlike in my own life—and escapism—because I was out of my head, away from my own problems. Hovering over another world. I was a veteran eavesdropper at home and at school. But I hadn't heard anything as interesting as this before. These were adults, yet they sounded like kids on the first day of summer camp. Anticipation was the undercurrent. I imagined faces to match the disembodied voices, stories to fill out the hints.

My uncle didn't reappear; he stayed up at the main house. The traffic flowed uphill, to him. Footsteps tromped in the gravel, beer tabs *plink*ed in the night air, more fairy flashlights danced in the field, and bursts of laughter rang out from the main house.

Around midnight the cars stopped coming, around one I heard splashes and hoots in the pool, and by two most of the cabins were aglow.

From Plover, the cabin nearest me, a baby's wail soared high over the trees, but it stopped almost immediately, the desperate sound replaced by a man's soothing bass singing "Mockingbird."

I couldn't see my new neighbors, but the father's voice was clear, and lovely:

And if that diamond ring don't shine...

I went inside and curled under my quilt made of old shirts and neckties.

In the morning, I crept outside in my nightshirt, peeking out at the field from the trees. Color everywhere—bright beach towels and picnic blankets, print dresses, sun hitting hennaed hair.

Back inside, I brushed my hair with my round brush, coaxing it into the neat curled-under Dorothy Hamill style I usually wore. Then I remembered where I was and messed it up. My clothes were a bigger problem. Everything was too new, too tailored. Matching blouses and culottes from the Young Miss department at Saks, which kept my measurements and family account number on file. I wished I'd armed myself with Levi's so worn they were nearly white, prairie skirts, concert T-shirts aged to limpness.

I crumpled a dry-cleaned green blouse and knotted it at my waist, rolled up my white Jordaches.

Time to study the hordes up close.

But first I pulled my suitcase from under my bed. The only things I hadn't unpacked—both gifts from Patricia—would be good insurance. I needed something to do with my hands, the only decent advice I'd heard in therapy. Everyone else's seemed busy with guitars and berry baskets and other hands and other people's long hair.

The first prop was a yellow hat Patricia had found antiquing and framed for my room. She wanted me to rip down my concert posters and let her "spruce up" my walls in proper Nob Hill frilly style. Instead, I'd hung it right between Donna Summer and Debbie Harry to bug her. But when I was packing and Patricia passed my doorway to offer a train case she wasn't bringing to Europe, I'd impulsively grabbed the frame off the wall and pried out her gift. She'd watched this impromptu surgery in shock.

"It'll be *perfect* for the beach this summer," I'd said, smiling.

I'd planned to throw it away, not knowing it would come in handy here. I could tilt the brim down, fan myself with it, tilt the brim back up. But I drew the line at baby's breath; I plucked it off the hatband and threw it out the window.

My next prop—the other gift in Patricia's "yellow series"— was a diary. Patricia thought that buying me cheerful yellow objects would transform me into the sunny stepdaughter she deserved.

I grabbed the diary, threw on the hat, and ventured outside.

4

BlueHour

1999
Late, the night of Jackie's arrival

I wake with a jolt.

Music. The sweet sound of a guitar, someone playing far away, outside. The tricky run at the end of Graham's "Three," the last song on the album of the same name. I'd been humming along with the melody in my half sleep, my right hand tapping the piano accompaniment on my left.

I'd been dreaming about the Kingstons. The three of them sitting together in the sunny field. Graham, playing, with Willa on one side and Angela on the other. My uncle was like a lion, so hulking and proud. So adored. Willa was smiling at him but reaching out to me, inviting me over.

But it's quiet now. No sound except the rustling leaves. Even Toby, draped over my feet on the stiff parlor daybed, is silent. He seems as content as he is at home in Boston.

Unlike me.

I don't know what I'm doing here. Or why Angela chose me as her heir.

We hadn't spoken in decades. Surely there was someone else

she could have picked. One of her old theater friends, or Graham's music people. She must have known how hard coming here would be for me, that I wouldn't want the money. And Angela was never unkind. At least not back then. It doesn't make any more sense now than it did when the FedEx deliveryman rang my bell in Boston, asking in a bored voice for me to sign. As if its jaunty orange-and-white "Tear Here" strip wasn't an explosive fuse, about to blast apart my carefully constructed life...

I shiver, wrap the blanket tighter around my shoulders. It was probably a car stereo blaring outside the gate. One of the *fanatics* the estate attorney warned me about on the phone. That's the word he'd used to describe my uncle's devotees, the ones who leave flowers and engrave the waterfall sign with their messages. Not fans, *fanatics*. A few have tried to trespass over the years.

Maybe it was simply a trick of the wind.

But the next morning, as I'm unlocking my rental car, parked just outside the gate on the wide swath of gravel, I hear it again.

I squeeze the key chain. It's real. It's no radio, no dream. Someone's strumming the same fragment of song I heard last night. So beautiful—and so familiar. Graham's sound remained consistent from song to song, decade to decade. A tiptoeing start in the key of G, the abrupt shift from major to minor a full two minutes in, later than you'd expect.

"Hey," I say. It comes out barely above a whisper.

The sound gets richer, more intricate. Mesmerizing, fast as sudden raindrops against the window.

A neighbor? No. The playing is too close. The nearest house is half a mile away, down the hill on Gull Lane.

Of course. They're in the meadow. The little poppy meadow just outside the fence, to the left of the road. I run across the gravel and scramble up the muddy, root-tangled path through the trees, toward the music.

A man sits cross-legged, guitar on his lap. His eyes are closed. Mussed dark brown hair, stubble, black jeans, a faded black concert T-shirt under an old black suit jacket. He's younger than me, maybe not even thirty. Lanky and angular—half the width of my uncle. His face is what Kate would have called "pretty before the first beer." He's got to be one of the many interested parties who have crowded my voice mail over the past week, one of the "intriguing offers" the lawyer said I should definitely consider: "Magazine walk-arounds, fan club visits, photo shoots."

I wonder which of these three this guy wants.

Sensing my shadow looming over him, the stranger opens his eyes, hands frozen on the strings. His face cycles through emotions, expressions coming as quick as his playing—startled, confused, sheepish, worried. The worried look sticks. He knows he's hurt his case, whatever it is.

Like the sliver of cliff holding the trail to the waterfall and beach, this is officially state land, not the Kingstons'. (Correction: *not mine*.) But even without breaching the fence, it feels like he's trespassed.

He scrambles to his feet. "Jacqueline Pierce? I'm sorry. I left you a bunch of messages at your house. Nobody at that law office would give me your mobile number."

"Probably because I don't have one." I exhale slowly, still trying to control my ragged breathing from running. "Were you playing here last night?"

"You heard that? Shit. I didn't think the sound would carry. I'm really sorry."

"It's okay." I'm not sure if I'm more relieved or annoyed by the unasked-for serenade, but it explains my ability to replicate Graham's song down to the eighth note in last night's dream, even though I've avoided his music for two decades.

"I'm staying at the campground down the highway and there's not much to do, so I couldn't resist hiking up... The field's still exactly like the picture, the one inside *Three*, with the crew... in the liner notes? It must've been shot from a ladder or—of course you know it."

He frowns, unstrapping his guitar and setting it inside the case at his feet, as if it alone was responsible for offending me.

"Mr....?"

"Oh hell. I haven't even introduced myself? I'm not normally so obnoxious, swear. It's Shane." He pats himself down for a business card, finds one in his pocket and hands it to me:

Shane Ingram
BlueHour Music
100 Capitol Dr., West Hollywood, California

"I'm sorry about Angela," he says, looking me in the eye. "We were sort of friends."

It's the first genuine condolence I've received since I found out my aunt had passed away. "Thank you."

"So. I've got this…interesting project I'd like to talk to you about. I sent the details to that lawyer but…look, can I buy you breakfast somewhere and explain? It's kind of complicated."

I'm hungry—the remains of my ham sandwich from the airport didn't do much for me this morning—but I don't need West Hollywood breakfasting across from me. Turning on the charm, working on whatever it is he's working on. Me, it seems. "Thanks, but I have a lot to do and not much time. I'm sure you can explain your project here."

"Right. Of course." He breathes deep and gives me his pitch. "I'm hoping to record an unusual sort of…tribute album to your uncle. Here, in his old studio." He turns to face the house.

I follow his gaze; the white tip of the shell spire is just visible over the tree line.

His voice is reverent: "Where we can do it right. A special album for the thirtieth anniversary of *Three* coming up next year. Something really beautiful he would have been proud of."

"Covers?"

He turns back to me. "Yes, a few. But most of the tracks

would be new. Eight brand-new Graham Kingston songs after all this time."

With the pride of someone presenting a VIP ticket, he reaches inside his guitar case and hands me a pale yellow notebook. "His unrecorded lyrics."

My breath hitches—Graham's idea book. It was always tucked into his jeans. He was never without his guitar and the notebook, the way I was never without my diary, the summer I spent here.

"Angela gave it to me. I visited her to ask if we could do some *Three* covers, and she offered this, too. Look, she inscribed it."

I flip the notebook over and there on the back is Angela's loopy handwriting:

Dearest Shane,
With my love and gratitude,
A. K.

"The thing is, Angela went downhill so fast at the end… I don't have anything else in writing."

Relieved, I hand the notebook back. Ticket denied. "I'm sorry, then. It won't be possible."

"Don't you even want to look inside?"

I shake my head.

"Just to see one or two songs? Why not? Angela *loved* the idea."

Because this is hard enough. Coming here. Opening the gate, opening the door.

He continues his pitch, something about how these lyrics are poetry and can't stay buried forever, but I've tuned out. He needs to go. Every minute I spend here in the field listening to his pleas is a minute I should be packing this place away. Saying goodbye for good.

He stares at the sky, searching there for the perfect words. "… Graham even put in some chord progressions…and the unfinished music practically wrote itself. I'm not kidding myself that what I'd make is anything more than…a…a frame."

At last, he's done talking. In spite of everything, I pity him, standing here holding the notebook gently as a sacred text.

And even though I don't want to, I believe him. Angela was always mercurial and trusting. This seemed just like her.

But that didn't mean I had to go along with it. "I'm sorry," I say. "I can see that you care about my uncle's lyrics. But I really have to go now."

I head back down the narrow path through the trees.

A minute later he's at my heels, a sharp *snap-snap-snap* as he hastily shuts his guitar case. "Please!"

I pick up my pace, trying to block out his voice by running through a mental list of everything I need to do this week, when I hear skidding sounds behind me, twigs cracking. He mutters, "Shit."

Shit.

I slow and look back at him. "You okay?"

"I'm fine." He emerges from the bushes unhurt, mud on his jeans, a cluster of salmonberries on his chest like a boutonniere. "Please let me buy you a coffee," he says.

"I don't have the time. I only have a week to pack up the house."

He stops in dismay. "So you're selling. You've already decided. By fall this place'll be some god-awful housing development."

This stings. I've been trying not to think about what will happen after I hand the keys over to the real estate agent Saturday. I can't let him see. "Maybe you should buy it. Then you can keep every stick in place. Interested?"

"I don't have that kind of money. I'd buy it if I could."

He sounds so disappointed that I can't look at his face. I turn away and continue across the gravel to the car, faster now, though I feel myself softening despite how much I resent his judgment, and his presence. I should go up to the house and find some me-

mento to hand him as a consolation prize. A button pried off of the dusty mixing board. A knot of fringe snipped from a studio rug. He could put it on an altar and worship it. And then leave.

I don't want any Kingston music memorabilia. It can all go to fans like him, to people whose link to this family is as uncomplicated as it is imaginary.

I pull out my car keys. "I'm sorry, Mr. Ingram. Careful walking back down to the campground. That T intersection on the coast road can be dangerous this time of year."

"Wait, Jacqueline. Please?" His voice breaks. He sets his guitar on the gravel, trying desperately to slow things down. "Okay. I get it. You're worried I'm a leech. But it's the last chance to do this right."

He paces between the fence and my car. Faces the house, hooks his fingers in the chain-link and arches back, gazing up at the house. He looks for all the world like a kid locked out of an amusement park.

"It would take eight weeks, nine, tops," he says, then glances over his shoulder at me. "To honor your uncle's memory?"

I'm already in the car, but when he comes over and stands by the door, I give in and lower the window.

He bends so we're eye level and says it so softly I'm not sure I even heard correctly: "You don't have to do it for me. Or Graham, or Angela. But what would *she* have wanted?"

She.

Willa.

I start the ignition, press the automatic window button. He jerks his hands from the fast-rising glass and hops back.

Even with the window closed and the engine rumbling, I can hear how his voice cracks again with regret: "Jacqueline, wait! I'm sorry I said that! Let's start fresh, just talk…"

He's still pleading, reaching out to the car as if to draw it back, as I drive off.

At the bottom of the hill, where no one can see me, I park under a thick stand of coast redwoods.

And only then do my hands begin to shake.

I'm down at Glass Beach; it's late afternoon and I've been here for hours, walking back and forth along the water. After driving aimlessly up and down the highway, I dialed my Boston machine from a pay phone:

There was a hurt-sounding message from Paul. "Just checking that you arrived safely, sweetheart." I'd forgotten to call him last night.

An excited one from the estate lawyer. He's received a proposal for the recording studio. The project—Shane Ingram's, I take it—could be "quite lucrative" if we draw up the right agreement, and he'd be more than happy to oversee things this summer so I can get back to my life in Boston.

And a kiss-assy one from some reporter at *Rolling Stone*: "We've all heard about the anniversary album that's happening at the estate this summer, and I understand Bree Lang is attached. It sounds absolutely *phenomenal* and I'd *love* to set up an interview..."

Fuck, fuck, fuck.

There's a new tribute to Three *for you, Shane Ingram.*

I hung up the pay phone in shock and somehow ended up here, gathering sea glass—trash made pretty only after tumbling in the waves for decades. There are fewer pieces glinting in the sand than when I was last here, when it could take a whole morning of hunting to get a decent haul. But the small beach still holds a smattering of treasures, still deserves its name, derived from local legend that it was completely blanketed in the '40s and '50s. I sit at the tide line, my bare feet numb and pruned up, my collection of three cloudy pieces, two the pale yellow of Vaseline and one the color of cola, before me. I don't remember where I left my shoes, and the hem of my gray dress is drenched from ankle to knee.

I pick up a piece of the sea glass and turn it over in my hand. So. I'm supposed to let a pack of strangers spill bourbon on Willa's window seat, screw in Angela's garden, snort blow off of Kate's beloved marble pastry counter? Talk to reporters who'll probe me for dirt on the tragic family? All for the sake of Graham Kingston's art? His nascent fandom?

I could have the attorney write a cease and desist letter, or whatever legal jargon would scare Shane Ingram away. I could say that he stole intellectual property from Angela. Except I know in my heart that's not true.

His question comes back to me.

What would Willa want?

Nothing else matters. Not money or listing timelines or logistical hassles. Not what Angela may have agreed to at the end of her life, sentimental and lonely, or stoned out of her mind on painkillers. Not *Rolling Stone* printing stories that make me sound like a villain if I say no, a hero if I agree. Not how the teachers back in Boston will talk about me when I return. Certainly not what this Shane Ingram thinks.

And not how hard it would be. Staying here. Inviting visitors in.

It's Willa I'm here to serve. I'm only her custodian.

What do you want me to do, Willa?

"Are you okay?"

I glance up, shading my eyes with my hand. It's him, drenched from sweat and fog, like he's just washed ashore. He's tied his nice black crepe suit jacket around his waist as if it's an old sweatshirt.

But the worry in his eyes hasn't changed; it's still convincing. His eyes are old-looking, wide-set, large-lidded, under expressive brows. They amplify his every feeling, and I have to look down.

I examine the sea glass in my hand. "I'm fine."

"May I?" He unties his crumpled jacket and offers it to me but I wave him off.

"Come on, you've got to be freezing. Your teeth are chattering."

"It's refreshing."

"Well, I'm boiling. I ran all the way to the top of the water-fall trail to look for your car. Then when I finally saw it parked on the highway I ran down even faster so I wouldn't miss you. I think I need to work out more."

He sits next to me, tents the ruined jacket over his knees. "This was supposed to impress you. Make me look professional. Thirty dollars, secondhand. I haven't spent so much on a piece of clothing in years."

"I thought you music industry types spent thirty dollars on a bottle of water."

"Maybe I pick the wrong projects. I let my sentimental nature cloud my judgment. Actually, I've been thinking about that all day."

The wind whips us and I catch his scent. Mixed with the smell of the ocean, it's strong but not unpleasant.

I pick up the rest of the sea glass, piece by piece, and drop each onto the sand between us, forming a little pile. Each piece makes a sweet *clink* as it strikes the others.

"So, I got a message from *Rolling Stone*," I say. "But that's not a surprise, is it?"

"What?"

He seems genuinely mystified, but I can't keep the bitter edge from my voice: "*Rolling Stone.* They left a message for me about the album. Everyone's talking about it. Everyone's really *psyched* about it. So if I don't agree, I'll forever be the bitch who killed the great Graham Kingston's legacy. Somewhere on the spectrum of music villains between the town council that bans dancing in *Footloose* and that purple octopus in *The Little Mermaid.* That was part of your plan, right?"

"I—" He sighs. "Jacqueline. I didn't tell *Rolling Stone.*"

If he's lying, he's masterful at it. "I guess someone else put the word out, then."

"I guess. I haven't exactly kept it a secret. And I'm not the only person who thinks Graham's lyrics were…exceptional, and not meant to be hidden away."

This hurts. Like I'm one of the "suits" Graham despised. The industry people who heard only his numbers, not his words. "I don't think that. I've never thought that."

But there are hundreds of other places he could record this album.

"And I don't think you're a villain for saying no. It must be overwhelming for you, being back here with them gone."

"I didn't know them that well."

"No? Sorry, I thought… Because you and your cousin were around the same age. I was wrong."

We sit in silence for a minute, facing the ocean. The fog is thinning, and the sun peers through the clouds at last. I stretch my legs out so my chilled, pickled feet can catch its precious warmth.

Shane breathes deeply. "Well, listen, I'm truly sorry about how this morning went."

"I am, too." And I mean it. So he'd overstepped a bit in his excitement. He couldn't possibly understand how complicated this is for me.

"No, it's not your fault. I blew it, tramping around like that so close to the fence. And coming at you so hard. Mentioning your cousin. Making assumptions. And the embarrassing thing is, I rehearsed talking to you a *ton*. I probably should've gone only through your attorney, like all the rest."

"You have a single-minded obsession about a project that's important to you and you're trying to do everything in your power to get it done."

"That sounds awfully sterile."

"It's not a bad thing. You could take it as a compliment, actually. I respect focus."

"Because you're a teacher?"

Ah. So he'd done his homework on me.

"I've always respected focus," I say.

He examines the small pile of sea glass between us. "Nice little collection you've got."

"Hmmm. There used to be a lot more here in the old days. It was practically wall-to-wall. Is it the same in LA? Is that where you grew up?"

"I... No. I never noticed much of it down there."

I pick up a yellow piece and brush sand from its smooth surface.

"Diamonds are made by nature and polished by man," I say. "Sea glass is made by man and polished by nature."

Willa told me that. Twenty years ago, sitting not far from here. The wind whipping her hair so it escaped the lace she'd always used to tie it back, tendrils blown across her cheeks, her gentle smile.

She also told me this: *It starts out ugly, but after a long, long time, it turns into something beautiful.*

And I know what I have to do.

"So, here's what's going to happen, Shane Ingram of Blue-Hour Music. I've decided that you can make your record. You've got your eight weeks."

"You're kidding," he sputters, joy animating the taut planes of his face. "Really? I mean, you were so against it just a few hours ago. Was it the *Rolling Stone* thing?"

"It doesn't matter why. I'm not going to stand in your way. Your people can even crash here this summer, if that'll help you wrap it up faster. There's plenty of room."

"That's wonderful, just perfect, I can't thank—"

"The place goes up for sale soon, and I'm donating the studio equipment, so I'd appreciate it if you'd be careful."

"Of course—we won't wreck anything. I'll make sure every-one treads lightly. But... I don't want this to be weird for you. I don't want any...friction."

"There won't be friction. You and your crew do your thing, and I'll do mine. I'll stay for a few weeks while you get settled." My voice sounds more certain than I am, but I can't hand the keys over to the realtor. Not yet. I have unfinished business here, no matter how painful it may be. "After I fly home, my real estate agent will keep an eye on things for me. But I have some conditions."

"Shoot."

"One, all the profits go to charity. Not 'a portion' or 'a ma-jority.' Every cent. A charity I select." I watch his face carefully, expecting it to collapse in disappointment.

But his expression doesn't change, and he says, "Of course!"

"Two, if someone lets my cat escape into the woods this week, I'll kill them."

He waits for more.

"That's it? Those are your terms?"

"That's it."

He smiles, offers me his hand. "It's a deal."

"Don't make me regret it."

5

Lady Jane, Lady Jane

1979

As I walked through the trees to the sunny field that first morning after what Kate gruffly called "the invasion," I held my head high, my shoulders back. I was determined to pass as an adult, coolly unfazed by the overnight transformation.

I registered two things as I reached the center, flat section of the grass: smiles and skin. It was hard work, not gawking. Two women sunbathed topless by the pool. Three shirtless, bearded men tossed a Frisbee near the campfire circle. A crown of gray hair and a thin bare arm peeked above a hammock, its owner wielding a joint like a conductor's baton, swirling graceful figure eights in the air. A gust of wind carried the sweet, skunky cloud to me.

A boy of three or four, fresh from the beach and wearing only a wet T-shirt, with dried sand sugaring his tiny bottom, marched in front of me with his mother, dragging a long, olive-green whip of kelp.

"Morning!" his mom said as I passed them, carefully stepping over the fat green rope. "Great hat."

"Morning! Thank you."

"You see we've caught a dragon's tail," she said gravely.

"It's a beauty."

I walked in a straight line across the sunlit grass, my eyes on the house. But I was secretly seeking out my cousin. As if I was in the middle of an invisible radar line, sweeping it around and around in hopes of locating her. I glimpsed at least a dozen clouds of blond hair, but my cousin's wasn't one of them.

It was my uncle I found first. He was large and round-shouldered—a lion in repose. Wild silky yellow hair, sideburns, and beard circling a round face, which was both large and large-featured. He wore a tasseled Mexican pullover the color of burlap. The kind the young surfers down at Stinson wore, the hoods pulled over their dripping heads. But his hood was down.

He sat on top of a picnic table—a bunch of them had been shoved together in a long line perpendicular to the front porch, and he perched on one near the center—demonstrating something on the guitar for a small cluster of people on the grass below.

I settled on the grass by the front steps. Hiding behind my hat and diary. In an hour, I filled only one page.

But at last my uncle glanced my way. He slowed his hands on his guitar strings, so that the fast song he had been playing became desultory...*dtung, dtuuung...dtuuuunng.* He stopped playing, stood, stretched.

Then, fast as a wild cat, he leaped off the picnic table, walking up the field, toward the north side of the house. He was headed back to his studio, and in a second he would pass me.

I tipped my hat low and scribbled furiously:

The time has come for all good men to come to the aid of their country.
The quick brown fox jumped over the lazy dog.
The time has come for all good men to come to the aid of their country.

Sandaled feet on the grass near me. Moving fast. Foolish to think my uncle would realize who I was and hail me with his pseudo-medieval formality, the way he'd embraced his friend on the motorcycle last night. He had no idea who I was.

I propped the diary higher on my knees, my head so low that my hat brim touched it.

The quick brown fox jumped over the good country...

He stopped. As his huge body cast mine entirely in shadow, he began playing his guitar again. Something familiar. The same four full notes over and over. It was as simple as a children's song, but catchy and strangely insistent:

D, B, D, B,
D, B, D, B

"Good Day Sunshine." He'd read the words on the outside of the diary. I looked up.

I'd guessed that he was big from a picture I'd seen of him in the house. But he was a wall of a man. Tall, thick, wide. His gaze swept from my absurdly large straw hat down to my absurdly expensive Pappagallo sandals. But I refused to shrink, sitting up straighter, pulling the diary close to my chest so he couldn't read my nonsense entry.

He unslung his guitar and set it down on the grass. "What, no applause? I was sure it had to be your favorite song since you chose that diary."

"I didn't choose it, and it's not a diary. I'm just using it as a workbook." I sounded defensive. Not to mention the fact that this was a lie. But I couldn't help myself. He was such an overwhelming presence up close, and I didn't want to be the silly kid with the diary. I wished I had a book from the house to use as a prop instead. Philosophy, or medieval Celtic folklore. The stuff in his songs.

"Man," he said, shaking his head. Then he whispered something unintelligible to himself, his voice low and disbelieving. It seemed like, "Day to day. Day to day."

He smelled of weed. How high was he?

"Don't scare the poor kid, Graham," Kate said, walking down the front steps with a stack of towels. "Cut the drama. This is obviously your niece, Jacqueline, from the city, and this is your unmannered, unwashed uncle. You'll have to make allowances for him. He's been holed up in his dungeon too long to act civilized."

"Unwashed?" he boomed over me at her. "I'll have you know I scrubbed every inch of this fine form at the waterfall at five a.m., Kate. Look at these fingernails!" He splayed his large hands in front of me, inches from my eyes. I saw scars and nicks, calluses, springy hair, a little darker than that on his head. And yes, his fingernails were surgeon-clean.

"Well?"

Something made me want to prove he couldn't intimidate me, so I said playfully, "Immaculate."

"See, Kate? You'd have this girl thinking her uncle is some kind of derelict."

"Your word, not mine," Kate humphed, walking past us down to the field to distribute her towels.

He grinned after her. Then, resting his heavy hands on my shoulders, he said in a lower, private voice, all joking gone: "Forgive me. It's just that you look exactly like her, and sound like her. Man." Another, smaller head shake.

Before I could react to this he pulled me up, gathered me in a hug, squeezing any protest out of me. My hat and diary fell to the ground. My cheeks were pressed into his burlap-rough pullover. He spun me. So fast and so suddenly that I had to close my eyes and hold on to his voice, like clutching the safety bar on a Tilt-a-Whirl.

"Lady Jane, Lady Jane," he said into my ear.

He set me down and I reached for the porch banister to right myself.

"But you need your own title, of course. What, what?" He

glanced around, noticed the brilliant orange-and-yellow rays of the diary on the grass. "Lady Sunshine?"

I smiled, accepting the honor. Then he turned from me and yelled: "Angel! Willow! Come meet Jane's little girl! Hell, where are they?"

He turned back to me. "Willa's surfing, and Angela's trodding some board somewhere, no doubt. Well. Man. It's beautiful that you're here. Beautiful. Are you settled into our little wilderness okay?"

"Oh, yeah."

"Where are you bunking?"

"Slipstream cabin, down there."

He picked up the diary from the grass and I stiffened, fearing he would read my page of *quick brown fox*es. But he closed it without a glance and handed it to me. "You didn't want to stay in the house, with Willa?"

It wasn't an option.

"Oh, no, I have tons of work to do this summer, so the privacy'll be good." *Work?* Where did that come from?

"What are you, sixteen? What the devil kind of summer homework have they got you doing at sixteen?"

"Seventeen. I'm writing an extra-credit report for next year's social studies class. On communal living. That's why I'm here." I held up the diary, my "workbook," as proof. "My school is kind of intense. Didn't my father say anything about it when he called?"

A funny half smile passed over my uncle's face, disappearing as quickly as it appeared. "I didn't speak to him, sweetheart." Fathoms of information were contained in this admission. He hadn't spoken to him, didn't speak to him. Wouldn't speak to him.

I'd pieced together a story regarding the two men's differences and history, friction over my mother's medical treatment during her difficult pregnancy with me. But I didn't know everything.

I pressed on with my lie. "Is it okay, then, me taking some notes about your home this summer?"

"You scribble away, sugar. Study this motley crew all you want." He looked at the cover of the diary, the happy, melting cursive of the words. He said, gently, "We're just awfully glad you're here."

He scooped me up again, crushing the diary between us, and twirled me around higher than before. This time I was more prepared, and had enough equilibrium to look up. And over my uncle's massive shoulder I saw that Willa was up in her bedroom, the window raised, staring down at us. Not surfing, then.

One spin: her pale, gold-aura'd face was there. By the next revolution she'd vanished.

But I knew she'd seen everything.

Ray,
That's what I'm going to call you, in honor of your hideous kin-dergarten finger paint sunray cover. Because you're not dear, you're a stranger.

I'll bet you were expecting hearts, and a girl pining away for Chad in homeroom, and doodling "Mrs. Chad Somethingorother" in pink bubblegum-scented ink all over your Tang-colored pages, and consulting with you on if she should let Chad feel her up over or under her bra after pep club. I'll bet you just live for that stuff, you pervy little thing. Well, get over it. I'm not that kind of girl...

So, I'm settled, I guess. It's pretty here, but strange. Strange that these people are related to me.

My uncle. Not what I expected. In his old album picture he was thin, almost starved-looking, like James Taylor and Jackson Browne. Now he's hulking and round-shouldered, with a full beard. He's not at all handsome, but...arresting.

My aunt Angela. She shares Debbie Harry's birth name and hair color, but that's about it. Long fair hair pulled into a loose, high bun, the old-fashioned '60s style called a "Psyche Knot."

Gentle and pretty, with a vague smile. I've only seen her once, from afar. She's away a lot with some theater troupe.

Willa.

A real hippie, not like those fraud ones who buy feather hair clips at Stern Grove on Saturdays, all free love and do-your-own-thing, then call me Supertramp an hour later. She disappears into the woods, or goes camping down at the beach. The kind of girl who sketches fairies, who perfumes herself with neroli oil from the Nature Shed and survives on nut butter and sprouts. I wear Coty Nuance and my favorite food is French dip. Prob we wouldn't get along.

But there's something about her. A calm that floats around her like her cloud of hair. I envy that calm.

But she doesn't want me here, and I can't figure out why.

6

No Stalling, No Skipping, No Exceptions

1979

I waited for my cousin to approach me. Nothing. She didn't show for meals at the long line of shoved-together picnic tables, either.

And I was certain it was because of me.

But a couple days after I spoke with Graham, I met my aunt Angela, who'd just returned from a touring outdoor Beckett production. She was in her garden, an expertly plotted space in the flat clearing behind the house. Rows of vegetables and herbs, a neat shed, a stone well. She wore a straw hat that dwarfed mine, a big newspaper delivery bag slung over her narrow body, brimming with weeds. When she saw me she sat back on her heels.

"Are you Angela?" I'd show these bumpkins some city etiquette. "I'm—"

"Jacqueline." She stood and embraced me; her slender arms tentative, loosely circling me, the weed-filled newspaper bag between us keeping our bodies far apart. Nothing like her husband's whirlwind, wind-knocking hug. "You came back here looking for some peace and quiet, I'll bet. Well. You find a nice shady spot and I won't bother you. No one bothers me here.

You can eat here, if you like. You come any time it gets to be too much."

"Too much?"

"The visitors, the noise."

"I don't mind it."

"I value quiet time so much, myself, when I'm home. So I understand. Sometimes it can be a bit…" She nodded at the house, indicating what was on the other side—her husband and their guests. Forty or fifty summer visitors of all ages, representing a couple dozen states and the province of British Columbia; I'd surveyed license plates.

My aunt offered me iced tea made from her own mint, running down to the kitchen and returning with two tall glasses. As we sat in the shade and sipped, she asked gentle questions about my hobbies, the drive up here, my home in San Francisco. "And do you like your school?"

Vaughn Academy. I'd transferred in last year because Patricia "wondered if" my public school was challenging enough. I pictured the pink stucco arches and chilly courtyard, the quotes by dead men engraved in the pavers, the classmates I messed around with just to watch their eyes flutter closed. Public school kids called it Vomit Academy behind our backs (I knew because I used to do it).

"It's a good school, I guess."

"Is there a theater program?"

"Probably. I haven't had time to check it out yet." The truth— each day I bolted the second the bell rang, stuffing my gold-crested blazer into my backpack and rolling down my navy uniform socks, rubbing at the grid of pink, knee-high grooves they left in my calves. "You're an actress, right? Kate said you're really good."

She waved this away. "Just a bit of fun. Amateur productions. They get me out of the dirt. I almost forgot, I made something for you as a little welcome gift." She flitted to her little slate-covered shed and returned with several bundles of dried lavender tied with black grosgrain ribbon. She smiled shyly and held them out to me. "For your cabin. I saw the baby's breath decorating your windowsill so I know you like dried flowers as much as I do."

I took the pale purple bouquets, breathing in their clean smell. I couldn't correct her about the baby's breath I'd chucked out the window, not when she'd been so thoughtful. "I love them, thank you."

"Well, I'm just so happy you're visiting. If you need anything, you let me or Kate know."

And your daughter?

I wished she'd mention her. Ask if we'd met, or apologize for her absence, her lack of manners. Anything to clue me in to why Willa had taken an instant dislike to me. I was no stranger to girls not liking me. None of my female Vaughn classmates did. My public-school-transfer-student stigma plus a reputation for blatantly tugging people's belt loops upstairs at parties had taken care of that—the hypocrites called me Supertramp in the halls, as though the same upstairs recreation was acceptable if the girl was more discreet. My preference for sharing *Saturday Night Live* impressions with the guys at the "goober" lunch table didn't help, either.

But I hadn't done anything to put Willa off, at least not intentionally. For all she knew, I was the companion she'd dreamed of. A fellow fairy buff.

Angela went back to her weeds, loosening them with a long-tined fork, setting them in her grass-stained *San Francisco Chronicle* bag.

I was about to leave when she said with a small smile, a nervous quiver in her voice, "Jacqueline? Don't feel like you have to go to their campfires when they start up. I never do."

Later, much later, I would remember my aunt's choice of words: *their* campfires.

Dear Ray,
Campfire

That's what it's called. No "The." Just campfire.

Campfire is what we do here every night after dinner. You're pic-
turing marshmallow-roasting and singing, and a bucket of water for
safety, and a circle of a few dozen people smiling and talking around
snapping flames, warming their hands against the night, watching
sparks spiral slowly way up to the sky. And all of that is accurate.

But I can tell you that your idea of campfire is completely, epi-
cally, fantastically wrong. Because you're imagining the feeling of
a normal campfire. Casual, winding down before bed, relaxed.

And there's nothing peaceful about campfire...

Campfire always started the same way.

At dusk, that evening after I first met Angela, I was with Kate
in the kitchen, stacking the mugs I had wiped dry onto the wire
racks, when I looked out the window and noticed a growing
imbalance in the field. It was subtle, but unmistakable: bodies
moving to one side of the big open circle at the center of the
property. People emerged from their cabins, or hiked up from
the beach, their hair still damp, or wandered over from the picnic
tables or Rec Room or pool. They held their children's hands,
or their long-necked yellow Uno D'Oro beer bottles, or both.

There was a feeling of expectation in the air, like before a
concert or school assembly.

Kate glanced out the window and said casually, "There's your
uncle's flock gathering for his nightly service. He's officially in
session again."

In the space of a few days, Kate had become, whether she
wanted to be or not, my local guide and interpreter. Kate was
paid but had no title. She was simply Kate—she kept things running while Angela roamed with her acting troop. *Kate* was the

syllable you uttered if you had a headache or found a wounded bird. She was bouncer, carpenter, chef, nurse.

"You're not serious about it being religious, are you?" I asked.

She relented. "No, it's just campfire. Go. Record all in that diary of yours, Margaret Mead."

"Are you coming?"

"I work for your aunt, not your uncle."

"Is it work to sit around a campfire? I thought it was supposed to be fun."

"You have it all figured out."

When Kate said, "You have it all figured out," I always knew I was dead wrong.

I joined the rest. The circle of seats around the firepit was around twenty feet in diameter, made up of stumps and stones and split logs. My uncle sat on a large stump on the east side of the circle, his back to the house. His seat was as rustic as anyone else's, but because the field sloped up there, his was the highest point of the circle. I chose the low stone directly opposite him: if he was twelve o'clock, I was six.

After a few minutes my uncle rose, his beer dangling from his large hand, and started the fire himself, his large body crouched over the small ring of stones in the center of the larger circle. Pausing to take casual swigs of his beer, he stacked kindling into a cone and used a flint.

"Matches are for pessimists," he boomed. I would hear him say this often throughout the summer.

My uncle added to the kindling, blew on it, coaxing the wood until it smoked and caught. Meanwhile, the circle around him filled in.

By the time it was dark, the fire was roaring. And only then, only when the crackle of anticipation in the air had become as strong as the snapping fire, did he sit.

My uncle took one long, final slug of beer, tipped it to empty the last, pale gold drops, set it in the dirt in front of him, and spun.

Until tonight I'd encountered twelve bare breasts, plenty of alcohol and weed, some dazed-looking smiles that surely came from a substance other than alcohol or weed. But nothing too shocking, nothing I hadn't seen in junior form at high school parties.

But now, I thought, *This is it. Here is where things start to get freaky.*

People are going to have sex in the middle of the circle. Threesomes. Foursomes. 'Somes I'd never imagined, lit by the flickering fire in front of kids casually roasting marshmallows, under the innocent stars.

But I was wrong. The person the bottle pointed to was not expected to perform acts of love. They only had to *perform.*

The first person chosen was a rail-thin man in a jean jacket. He stood and ad-libbed a limerick about Skylab falling down, elevated above silliness thanks to an elegant, deadpan delivery and the fact that he walked with a cane. He'd had his right leg blown off in Vietnam, Kate had told me.

If this had been *The Gong Show,* a program I'd watched devotedly since it first came on the air, someone on the panel would have picked up the giant mallet and walloped the gong before he'd completed his first stanza. But the man delivered his bad poem with panache, and when he finished, Graham bowed so low that his hair touched the dirt.

As I sat on the bench that first time, I was too rapt to even pretend to record notes. But if I had, I'd have written that you couldn't worry about how you came across. You got picked and you sang for your supper. (And lodging, and food, and, perhaps most of all, Graham's infectious, booming laugh.) Anything would do, as long as it was served up boldly. A limerick, a joke, a card or yo-yo trick. A woman did the splits. A lot of people sang.

"No stalling, no skipping, no exceptions!" the circle of revelers would chant if a newcomer hesitated, or tried to claim lack of talent or a hangover. Other than that, there were no official rules.

There were plenty of unofficial rules.

They could be read on Graham's broad, expressive face, how bored or pleased he looked during the proceedings. Confidence was good. Weaving a mention of Graham or his home into the theatrics somewhere—also good.

Hesitation and fear were bad. Looking too polished—not ideal, there was a little sheepishness in it, but it wasn't disastrous.

I summed up campfire like this in my diary later—*Silliness is fine, if delivered with confidence. The fatal mistake is* shame.

That entire summer, I saw only one person skip their turn, and she was six. The little girl, who was hiding her eyes behind the curtain of her straight black hair, turned shyly toward her mama and the pass was granted.

The formal entertainment portion of the evening always went on for the space of ten bottle-spins, and then Graham left for his solo evening hour at the top of the waterfall, while his company roasted marshmallows, drank, talked, smoked, carried the little ones to bed.

At my third campfire, I realized two things: 1. Graham never performed. And 2. Willa never got picked. Even when the bottle was clearly pointing straight at her, her father would call out the name of the person to her right or left.

I wondered if this bothered her, but her face, lit soft gold from the fire, always remained tranquil as she smiled, clapped, played with kids, who all seemed to be drawn to her.

I needed that bottle to land on me, so I could do one of my *Saturday Night Live* imitations. I was a good mimic, and would show them I wasn't the rich priss from the city, the interloper from the stiffest branch of the family tree.

And prove to my cousin I wasn't someone to ignore.

But the beer bottle hadn't chosen me yet. And when campfire broke up, Willa always floated off, serene, into the woods behind the house before I could confront her.

"Last one," Graham announced.

It was my fourth campfire, and I was starting to believe it was a trick bottle, rigged to avoid me.

The bottle whirled, slowed, stopped. Pointed a few inches to my right. If anyone had wanted to get official and whip out a surveyor's marker to extend its true line across the fire, it might not have touched me, and we'd have watched the new girl to my right belly dance or do backbends or something.

But it was close enough. My uncle said, "Lady Sunshine," and I stood.

I was quick, confident. Fearless. Not too rehearsed, though I had a general plan. I did Gilda Radner as Judy Miller, the girl who produces a TV show from her bedroom, and got...polite claps. Jane Curtin as the wry "Weekend Update" newscaster— no better. Everyone smiled kindly at me, but they hardly seemed wowed like my lunch mates had always been. Why had I thought this was a good idea?

The one genuine laugh I got was right before I sat, when I said dryly, "I'll work on my card tricks." I'd been so cocky, thinking I'd figured out the rules here. Some phony anthropologist I was.

My uncle clapped, though. "Brava for committing, Lady S."

The only person who hadn't watched me was Willa. The entire time I'd performed, she'd looked down at her feet as if I wasn't there.

When the campfire broke up, she stood, stretched, then walked, graceful and unhurried, out of the stone circle, up the field, and toward the woods behind her house.

I waited a minute and followed her. No flashlight, no jacket. It wasn't a conscious choice. I simply had to know where she went every evening.

I hung back so she wouldn't see me, tried to step lightly on the carpet of dead pine needles so she wouldn't hear me. I tried to keep up with her light, but it grew smaller and smaller, and once it disappeared before, thankfully, appearing again, small as a firefly in the greenish dark. I rushed through the trees, scraping my right elbow, until the light was bigger, about thirty feet ahead of me. We were high on the steep, wooded ridge behind the house.

What was this? Did she meet a lover here? A boy from town, someone Graham wouldn't approve of—a kid who played an electronic keyboard or worshipped Glen Campbell?

Willa knew this land far better than me, and there was no path. She was as graceful and strong on this hill as I was awkward and out of shape.

Then the light vanished completely, and this time I couldn't find it again. I paused to listen for Willa's crackles ahead of me, and heard nothing but the wind whistling through the trees.

I'd lost her.

I was cold and turned to leave. The moon had swum behind the fog, but the lights from the house down below were bright, the voices in the field beyond still loud enough to guide me back. I started down the hill.

"Why are you following me?"

The voice came from high up.

It was my cousin. It sounded like she'd climbed a tree. Not ahead of me, but behind me, closer to the house. Somehow she'd slipped from my sight, doubled back, and begun following *me*. But where was she? I scanned the trees against the starry sky, trying to make out a human silhouette, but saw nothing except the fluffy vertical zigzags of a thousand branches.

"I'm not," I called back into the darkness, unnerved. "Where are you?" I hated people watching me without my permission. I preferred to do the spying.

"First tell me why you're following me." The disembodied voice again, from up high.

"Screw this." I marched down the hill toward the house.

I walked fast, stumbling.

Soft thuds, crackles, then—"Jacqueline, wait." Willa, so close behind me I could smell her perfume, a musky-peachy scent.

I turned, my entire body juttering with surprise. "What are you, half *puma*?"

"Sorry. My dad says it creeps him out when I steal up on him like that. I'm sort of known for it."

"I can see why."

"So, you weren't looking for me?"

"Why would I be?"

"I'm not sure, it just felt like it. But it surprised me…because your stepmom told me that you prefer your own space. That you like to keep to yourself and came here to…convalesce after a difficult year."

Patricia. Goddamned Patricia. What the hell had she said? She'd made me out to be some kind of invalid?

But there was relief in my rage; Willa'd avoided me because of Patricia.

"You're the one who talked to her? What, exactly, did she say about me?"

"Well, she said…" My cousin stopped, bit her lip.

"I can handle it. Tell me."

"She said you need *plenty of alone time*. That sometimes you…"

"I what?"

"That you *explode* if people try to deprive you of that."

I hoped Patricia would fall in the Seine. Eat a bad *moule*. Get lost, permanently, in a wine cave.

"Maybe I misunderstood," Willa said, seeing my reaction. "Or maybe your stepmom thought she was only looking out for you?"

"I doubt it," I said. "But I don't need space."

"You mean, unless it's…"

"Between me and my stepmother."

"Ahh. Is she wicked?"

"*Wicked* would be way more interesting than what Patricia is. She's oblivious. Perky to the point of derangement."

Willa smiled, a dazzling sight even in the weak yellow glow from the garden lamp.

I imagined Patricia offering "safe handling" instructions for me, thinking she was doing everyone a favor. She lived in a fantasyland where there was a clinical reason for the fact that I couldn't stand her. All spring, when I'd come home from school to find Patricia's travel agent perched beside her on our new yellow sofa, I'd pounded the piano in an earsplitting double forte until they grabbed their brochures and fled for the back patio.

If I'd *exploded* at my father, it was only because he'd replaced my mother, seventeen years after her death, with this birdlike but hugely disruptive person.

"She really said *convalesce*?" I asked.

"It might have been *recharge*."

"Well. I'm charged. Thanks for telling me." I turned, but Willa touched my elbow.

"Wait. I'm glad she's wrong about what you wanted." She smiled again. "It means we can hang out, right?"

She'd been warned by a close relative that I could detonate at any time, but she was still up for spending time with me? I knew it for sure then: my cousin was braver than me.

"I liked those stories you told at campfire," she added.

"Stories? Actually, they were—" I wouldn't correct her. Not now that she'd offered an olive branch. "Thanks."

"Want to see something?" she asked.

But I was already following her billowing, spangled yellow skirt back up the hill, and into the trees.

7

2000 Encroaching

1999

It's so quiet. So strange to be here without Willa. Her voice, her ambergris-peach scent. Strange to be here without Graham's strumming and laughter, Kate's *hmph*ing and dinner-bell clatters. The soft trickles of Angela's watering can in the garden.

I've been staring through the dining room window out at the deep green woods off and on all morning, but I force myself to turn away and focus on my task—clearing the walnut sideboard. As I empty each drawer, I run my hand along the felt bottom, the back, to make sure I haven't missed anything.

It's become a habit. I double-check under beds and sofas, peer between cushions. *Just being thorough*, I tell myself. As if I'm not looking for anything in particular. As if my hand isn't anticipating the feel of it.

As if I didn't hunt for it everywhere frantically, while the town car waited to return me to San Francisco on my last day here. After I had to cut my stay short.

It was quiet that day, too.

I worried about Shane's crew screwing on countertops, popping pills, desecrating the place, that they'd be immature session musicians only here for quick cash and a free roof. But since they arrived a few days ago—about a dozen of them, from what I can gather—they haven't left so much as a cigarette butt. They use the back entrance to the studio, tiptoe in and out. They're true fans, artists.

The only thing I hear is the occasional suppressed giggles of the two kids staying here with their parents. A girl with purple glasses and a boy in a Dodgers baseball cap who watch me through the Sandcastle's windows. They love that game—*Spy on the weird lady we're not supposed to bother.*

I'm folding a lace table runner when a car honks way down at the gate. *It's one already?* I've only filled two boxes today.

"Why don't I fly out and help?" Paul asked, when I called him last week from the beach pay phone to say I was staying for three weeks instead of one, as I'd initially planned. "Mo'll cover my summer school classes."

"You're sweet," I'd said. "But I can handle it."

"I just hate to think of you rattling around some old house all alone for two extra weeks…"

I haven't told Paul about the album, or my guests. He wouldn't understand the hold this place has on me. Why should he, when I've kept it secret from him?

Vivienne DePuis, Estate Specialist and Platinum Key award winner for Windward & Associates Realty five years running, waits for me outside the gate by her cream-colored BMW. Her suit is cream, too.

"Sorry I'm a little late," I say. "Time got away from me."

"So *good* to get this checked off of our punch list!" she says, striding toward me, her manicured hand outstretched.

This doesn't make sense—wouldn't you *punch* a punch list instead of checking things off of it? But I nod. Vivienne loves to talk about "our" punch lists, and every time she uses the term,

I picture her sitting in her office down in Mendocino, a much-perforated piece of paper in one hand, a shiny punching device in the other. In my imagination, the tool is like those pointy silver rotary-phone dialers women use in classic movies.

"We've already had *major* interest in the property as a pocket listing, Jacqueline. I think we're looking at a *very* quick sale. This is Louise, photographer extraordinaire. She's our *absolute* best."

Louise is young, curly-haired, and silent. Clearly not the cream-suit type. She's in cargo pants and a sleeveless black sweater, a camera around her neck and a serious-looking tripod case on her back. I can smell the french fries from her lunch when she shakes my hand.

Louise clicks away capably, taking exteriors of the main house and grounds from various angles.

But when we ascend the field and she starts shooting King-fisher cabin on our right, Vivienne shakes her head at her. "We won't be featuring that. Too specific." She says the same thing near the shed, and when I show her the shell-covered chimney, and Angela's garden.

Apparently a lot of the Kingstons' cherished improvements are "too specific."

"You really don't think the history of this place will interest anyone?" I ask, taken aback. I've seen two of Graham's devotees since I arrived—one coming down the trail to the beach when I was coming up, and another placing flowers by the gate. But they stayed respectfully outside of the fence, and seemed blissed out simply to be here.

"Well, frankly, Jacqueline, that's not the way we should go here. It's *highly* unlikely to remain a single-family residence. So we can't limit ourselves."

"Oh. Right." I'd hoped some wealthy fan or musician might want this land, might even keep the studio in place, but maybe I'm biased, overestimating the property's importance.

"Now, what about this waterfall overlooking the ocean I've

heard about? It would be perfect to show the tranquility of the location."

"No." It comes out fast. Surprising all of us. Willa wouldn't want her father's falls on a sales brochure. It would be a violation, sacrilege. "I don't want that in any of the materials you send out."

"Not even a file photo? If we want to get top dollar it only makes sense—"

"No."

Louise, who still hasn't said a word, busies herself changing lenses.

Vivienne has expanding ovals of sweat under her cream silk jacket, and they give me a perverse flutter of joy. Maybe that's cruel. She's only acting in my best financial interests.

"I have an idea," I say, to make up for it. "There's another pretty view of the ocean from this overlook I know, on the other side of the property. I can take you there instead."

"Well. I guess that would be all right. Is it far?"

"It's north of here, about a half-hour walk." I check my watch. It's barely two, so Shane and his crew won't emerge for hours. I picked this afternoon for the shoot because I knew they'd be safely down in the studio.

It's no secret that I'm selling, but I don't want the album people meeting Windward & Associates Realty's finest. It would feel wrong, somehow.

We hike up the narrow path and stop at the first clearing. "There's a good place for an ocean shot twenty feet up," I say to Louise, who preps her camera.

"This *is* pretty," Vivienne says. "Absolutely stunning country up here. What do you think of leading with this for the brochure—*Perched high on a tranquil ocean cliff, this pristine—*"

"Butt face!"

"Dude, stop calling me that. Be a little creative in your insults, at least."

"Wait up. Hey, Fee. Did you know *dude* means a pimple on a donkey's butt?"

"No way."

"Yeah way! I read it in this book we have at home…"

It's the kids who spy on me. The tween girl in purple rhinestone glasses scrambles up the trail, breathless, followed by the younger boy in his blue baseball cap. They stop short when they see us. They know who I am—not Lady Sunshine, but the lady they're not supposed to disturb.

They probably think I'm some kind of witch, in my black-and-gray clothes. I wish I'd packed more, but I'd been in such a daze, getting ready for this trip. And I thought I'd be alone.

There's whistling and adult laughter behind the kids. Shane and Bree Lang come around the bend, five or six others not far behind.

"Oh," Shane says, stopping. "Hey."

"Hey."

"I thought you'd be in the house."

"No, I…" Miserably, I introduce Vivienne and Louise as *friends*, hoping to avoid telling the group why they're here.

But Vivienne hands out business cards, explaining to them all about the morning's photo shoot for Windward Realty, the buyers salivating over this land.

Shane makes his introductions, and I shake hands with everyone, pretend I'm taking in names. But I already know most of them. I've eavesdropped on the kids whispering on the porch.

Mat's short for Matui. He's the sound engineer, the big, good-natured guy, born in New Zealand but a Californian for a long time. Mat's wife is a pathologist in Reseda, where they live, and she's coming up for a visit soon. Their little boy is Kauri, one of my spies. They're staying in Kingfisher cabin. Piper's the blonde bassist, and her wife is April, and their daughter in the purple glasses is Fiona—*Fee*. They're staying in Painted Seal.

And of course I know Bree Lang. I've owned her CDs for years. Over the last week, I've seen her, briefly, from behind windowpanes: a tall, friendly-looking woman in bright clothes. Her long silver Airstream trailer sits in the old gravel parking lot like a glamorous UFO. Two satellites landed on either side the same day she arrived: one for her chef, one for her personal assistants. Each time I catch a glimpse of Bree or her shiny trailer, I'm in awe that she's here. My guest.

"Nice to meet you all," I say. "Gorgeous afternoon."

"Yes, isn't it?" Shane says. "Well."

Worlds colliding. That was from some sitcom. *Seinfeld*, maybe. It was played for laughs on the show, but in this moment it's excruciating. Especially when Vivienne goes on and on about how terrific the listing is. That's what she calls the Kingstons' home: *the listing.*

Shane winces when she says that. Though the group is polite, asking about the photo shoot, now I *do* feel like that mean purple octopus lady in *The Little Mermaid*. Demolishing music history for my own greedy ends.

They don't know that I'm not keeping the money. The sale money or Graham's royalties.

After the pleasantries, everyone clumps up on the narrow trail between the ferns. We're poster children for unsafe hiking practices.

"You're not working today?" I ask Shane. His black T-shirt has a dark sweat triangle on the chest and he's plucking at it, trying to cool off. Or else—like me—uncomfortably aware of how close we have to stand to each other because of the tight quarters on the trail.

"We busted an amp tube. Won't have a replacement 'til tomorrow."

"Oh. I'm sorry. Is that a tough part to replace?"

"Only when your engineer's the biggest amp snob of all time," Shane says.

"Hey, *Chook*," Mat says, clapping him on the shoulder. "You'll thank me later. Don't listen to anything he says about me, Jackie." I like the easy way he says my nickname, and how he never asked to use it; his cheerful Kiwi accent makes it sound like *Jaaay-kee*.

We're all looking at each other awkwardly when Fiona boasts, "Shane's taking us up to a really cool swing he knows about."

"It's supposed to feel like flying," Kauri dares, his eyes shining.

"It's in my 'Off the Beaten Path' guidebook," Shane says to me, quickly. "It's supposed to be in a big tree on state land just over that way. Do you know about it? I thought you'd be in the house, so I'm sorry if we—"

"No, it's fine—"

"Last-minute plan...you know."

"Sure. The swing over Triangle Point. It's worth the hike, if it's still there."

The Flying Swing, we'd called it. If you looked straight ahead, it felt like you were swinging out a thousand feet above the ocean, when really you were a few feet above a gently sloping hill covered with silky ferns, giving only the illusion of great height and danger. Willa could swing without looking down, but I always cheated. I needed to see where I really was.

"Can you be our guide?" Mat asks. "I don't trust this joker to navigate. He'll probably take a wrong turn and send us all into a ravine."

"You'll find it. Just stay left at the fork in the trail fifty feet up, then go right, then left."

"Jacqueline, come with us," Bree Lang urges me.

I didn't know she even knew my name, but the expression in her eyes is playful and welcoming, as if it'd be the most natural thing in the world for our two hiking parties to merge.

"Oh, that's nice, but I need to get these two back to their car."

"No, we'd love to come along! We can take some shots of the swing for the brochure!" Goddamned Vivienne.

The swing is still there, a quarter-mile north, up the squiggling trail. It's perfectly safe, the cliff hasn't eroded, and should anyone fall off, they'd only tumble onto the soft grass-covered hill, which drops off gently here for ten feet, before a steep vertical cut in the cliff.

Fiona goes first, of course, and she's fearless from the start, not looking at her feet or the hill, but instinctively straight out at the horizon. It's the only way to maintain the illusion of soaring over the waves.

When I was seventeen, it had taken me three visits to get up the courage to do that. Willa had taught me to memorize *Jonathan Livingston Seagull* as she pushed me, her hands featherlight on my lower back. The length of each swing was perfectly suited to the lilting rhythm of the book, the part about birds "touching perfection" in flight, how that was the most important thing to each of them. Willa had been so proud when we discovered *Jonathan* had an *important thing* in it, like the Margaret Wise Brown book in the picture of my mother, the book I'd told her I loved. She'd thought it was a sign that she and I were meant to meet.

Fiona won't stop swinging. "The ocean goes on forever!" she yells. She yodels, she sings, she screams greetings at gulls. Gravity's no match for her; her feet dance effortlessly on the cliff to keep her momentum going whenever the swing threatens to slow down.

"I'm sorry. She's a hopeless ham," Piper says.

"Kinda like her mother?" Mat says, and Piper jumps onto his back as easily as little Kauri does.

Piper yells over Mat's head as he spins her, "Fiona Janis, hop your butt off that swing this second and give Kauri a turn."

The kids get their fill, and then the adults. Mat, who's surprisingly graceful for a big man, soaring out over the blue. Shane, who can't seem to keep the swing from twirling and slides off so dizzy he has to stand in the shade for a minute, his head down. Even Louise goes for a ride, taking one-handed pictures midair.

I'm stuck with Vivienne DePuis. Now that she's *punched off* the photos, she's making the most of her time with me. I'm trapped nodding to her about comps and zoning and top-dollar results. Shane's on the shady grass behind us, listening, looking more miserable than me. He's thinking about this place changing, turning into everything the Kingstons hated. What did he say that day we met? *By fall it'll be some god-awful housing development.*

"Jacqueline, take a turn?" Piper calls.

I want to know if it's as wonderful as I remember, infinite blue space in front of me but somehow no space for worry. I want to fly, to show the kids that I'm a good witch, not a bad one. Leave Vivienne and our grim business behind me, if only for a minute.

But it would feel empty without Willa standing behind me, her small hands tapping my lower back on each descent, less a push than a simple reminder that she was there.

"Another time," I say.

"Then, your turn," Shane says to Vivienne, holding the swing for her.

"Oh, no." She smooths her crepe skirt.

"You sure? It's such an *important part of the listing*. Hop on. I'll give you a push."

I study his face. Yes. He seems like he wants to give her a good push—straight off the swing and into the Pacific.

"Thank you, but it's time I got back to the office." She waves her mobile phone around to show us that there's no reception here, that we're holding her up.

We all troop down the trail, our backs to the sun.

"Thanks for having us here," Bree Lang says to me, skillfully pulling me away from Vivienne as we walk. "I've been trying to thank you for days, but you've been somewhat hard to slow down. A gray streak shooting across the field."

I wonder if that's a dig at my drab wardrobe. I've only seen Bree in jewel-toned dresses and caftans and shawls. But she doesn't seem unkind—just observant.

"You're more than welcome here, but it's not really my place."

"No?" she asks.

Piles of paperwork say I'm the owner, but that's meaningless. It will always, only, belong to the Kingstons. "I mean, it doesn't feel like mine."

"Aaaah. I get that."

"Um. Jacqueline?" Kauri edges over to me, with Fiona behind him, giggling.

"Can we play your piano sometime?" he asks. I can tell by the mischievous flash in Fiona's eyes that she's dared him to approach.

"Yes, whenever you want. If you like, I could show you this triple-part song I teach my kids back home."

"You have *kids*?" Fiona asks.

"I do. Seventy-two of them." Their eyes widen.

"I'm a music teacher at an elementary school in Boston. I had seventy-two students last year."

Kauri giggles at this, and even Fiona allows herself a half smile.

"You're in for it now, Teach," Bree Lang says. "Those two won't give you a minute's peace."

"I've been to Boston," Fiona says. "My mom had a job playing in a band there when I was little."

"I wish I'd seen her. Your parents have probably taught you a lot on the piano, huh? You know middle C?"

"I do!" Kauri, proud.

"Of course I do!" Fiona, haughty. "That's baby stuff."

"I thought you'd know it. I was just checking."

"Will you teach us really soon, Jacqueline?" Kauri asks.

"Yes, and you can call me Jackie."

What's the harm in a lesson? I need to stay sharp. And I miss my students. I hope they're practicing this summer, that the ones I was able to get into summer music camp on scholarship are attending.

Shane comes up from behind me and walks on my right. "You don't have to do that. We're intruding on you so much already, and now we're crashing your real estate meetings."

"Is that sarcastic?" I hate being lumped in with Vivienne. One of the joyless number-crunchers.

"What?"

"Well. I've picked up on some hostility." I nod at Vivienne, who's ahead of us on the steep, green-flanked trail, chattering at Bree.

"Oh. Sorry. It's just sad to think about everything changing." He gazes down at the house, the point of the shell spire just beginning to show through the leaves. "The real world encroaching. The year 2000 encroaching. I don't know what I mean."

"I do." I recall something Angela told me. "These woods are walls. Keeping out the present."

He pauses in surprise, gives me a curious look. "Exactly. Graham liked everything old-fashioned, didn't he? Those funky medieval-looking tapestries in the studio, weaving his Irish ballads into his songs, giving everyone titles. Lady Sunshine and all that."

"Angela told you he called me that?"

"Oh. Yeah. She did, sorry if…"

"It's okay. It just—it's fine."

"She mentioned it when she was telling me you'd be interested in the project. Because Graham was fond of you."

"Ah. Of course."

We both go quiet for a minute. Shane's the only guest sleeping in the house—he wanted to be near the studio, and I'll be gone soon, anyway—but we haven't exchanged more than a few words until now.

"It's not your fault," he says. "It can't stay the same forever. And I'll be on my best behavior with your *lovely* real estate agent from now on. Swear. But I can't let you give piano lessons when you're so busy packing. On top of everything else you've done for us? No way."

He's being the polite guest I asked for, but he's overcompensating. "It's nothing. Really. I like them—they crack me up."

On cue, Kauri and Fiona duel with saplings in front of us. With their long hair and big, fierce eyes and dirty knees, they're like feral children out of a medieval tapestry.

"Little beasties," Shane says. But he likes them too, I can tell.

The piano dealer is supposed to come tomorrow to haul the old Rec Room upright away. I make a mental note to reschedule him.

8

Nest

1979

I followed Willa back up the steep hill where I'd been secretly trailing her—or thought I had—minutes earlier, and we re-entered the thick inland woods.

She moved slowly this time, so I could catch up and find my footing on the sharp slope, but I was afraid of losing her again and stayed close, my eyes fixed on her skirt's gold sequins. Hundreds of them glittering in the dark, twinkling from waist to hem. I was a sailor navigating by synthetic stars. But still she disappeared; she abruptly snapped her flashlight off.

"Willa?" I whirled, reaching out blindly, my fingers finding only leaves.

"I'm up here…just a second…stay right where you are…" Her voice came from up high again. Branches rustled and scraped, the sounds rising, growing fainter. Then a circle of light appeared at my feet: she'd flicked her flashlight back on.

I followed the beam up, up, up…to Willa, who sat, casual as anything, fifteen feet above me, in a tree.

"Come up!"

"How?"

"It's easy, look." She shifted her flashlight to show me where she sat: a wooden platform about seven feet square, nearly hidden by leaves, built into the U-shaped cradle of the tree's fat upper branches. She spotlighted the way up: a long white rope hanging near the trunk, knots spaced every two feet. It ended at my waist and was still swinging gently back and forth from Willa's climb.

I wasn't afraid of heights. I *was* afraid of human error. The rope ladder could be rotten, frayed, attached to a flimsy branch. But Willa waited, eager for me to join her in the air, her *It's easy* so matter-of-fact I couldn't question it.

I reached, grabbed the rope with both hands, and clamped my thighs around the lowest knot. As I dangled, my hips and butt took turns slamming the tree trunk, but the rope held, and I grunted my way up to the next knot.

"What was that? Are you all right?" she called down to me.

"Sure," I panted.

Twirling and swaying back and forth, scraping my knuckles on bark, and feigning more confidence than I felt, I climbed up to my cousin. Willa had grown up scrambling around these seaside hills, while my exercise routine had consisted entirely of turning seductively during The Hustle at Teena's DreamTraxx and pounding *Space Invaders* buttons in the Fillmore Street corner arcade.

"You're doing great! Almost there!"

Willa would love Vaughn Academy's indoor PE days. When it rained, Ms. Binny relied heavily on the gym rope climb. I'd never ascended more than a couple of feet, while other kids shimmied up like monkeys in purple polyester uniforms, dinging a little brass bell on the ceiling. I was only ever rewarded, once I'd slid down and thudded on the basketball court in defeat, with Ms. Binny's delusional "Good effort, Pierce!"

"Just a little more!" Willa called.

She'd tied the top of the ladder to a large branch. No bell

here: only my cousin's outstretched arm. I clasped it, held on for dear life, and let her drag me to safety.

"It's nothing once you get the hang of it, right?" she asked, standing over me.

"Nothing." I was limp and sweaty, facedown on plywood. "How much weight can this thing hold?"

"Oh, I don't know. But we can't be much more than two hundred together."

Cautiously, I rolled onto my back. Willa bounced, laughing, circling her flashlight above her head so it illuminated wood, leaves, a length of spangly scarlet fabric draped on branches.

"Can you not do that?"

Anyone else would have laughed. Jumped higher. Willa stopped immediately. "Sorry."

She sat, setting her flashlight beam-down on the wood so it softened into a night-light.

"So, what is this?"

"It's sort of…my secret place. I come when I want to get away."

So, like her mother, Willa sometimes needed to separate herself. But maybe that was *why* she always looked so tranquil. Even when her home was overrun, she knew that her hideaway waited for her.

"Did you build it?"

She shook her head. "I found it when I was seven, the year we moved in. It was already here."

"Kate must know about it. She doesn't miss a trick."

"Kate never hikes this high on the hill. She says anything past the garden is too steep and uncultivated for her old-lady knees."

I stood and explored, tentatively at first. Holding on to a branch for safety, I peered through the leaves on the coast side where we'd entered. There was Angela's curving glow stone path in her garden, two bright upstairs windows. Beyond that, the lantern down by the pool. Someone was having a night swim.

"You can see all the way down to the pool."

"Oh...you can see way past that." Willa came to my side, leaning forward to look out, fearless. "You can see headlights in the parking lot, over that way." She pointed down the hill. "And when the fog burns off in the afternoon, there's a long triangle of ocean right there. My dad's waterfall is behind those trees." She nodded at a spot left of the house, on the southern ridge. Then she pointed to the right, north. "And you can see people hiking up to the Flying Swing over there."

"Flying Swing?"

"I'll take you."

I inched closer to the edge. We were at the top of the Kingstons' sprawling property. It was the perfect lookout. "It's incredible up here."

"My mom told me when I was little that these woods are like walls, holding back time. She's the one who found this land. My dad wanted to live in the city."

This surprised me; my uncle seemed so much a part of this place, so in charge of it. "It seems like it's grown on him."

I crossed to the other side of the treehouse, facing inland, and Willa followed.

"That's our closest neighbor on this side, down the east hills," she said. "The goat people."

I peered into the darkness. "*Goat people*. Satyrs?"

"They aren't goats; they used to raise goats. But we can call them satyrs. You can just make out their barn light down there, see?"

In the charcoal light I picked out a distant, orangey glow.

"I wish they *were* satyrs... They don't like us much. The little boy is cute. He comes over here sometimes to watch us, like our own little fan club. But Kate says the parents don't like the idea of us—of Daddy's friends. And my mom's *plants*."

"The neighbors behind us in the city filed a complaint because my stepmother had the gardener prune too many branches from their gum tree. They were blocking her greenhouse."

"How weird, to live in a city," Willa said dreamily. "Don't you feel trapped?"

"I never thought about it."

"Daddy said you're rich… But you probably think the way we live here is boring."

"No." I meant it. Willa had room to ramble and explore. I had lived, I realized, an embarrassingly compact life compared with hers. Grand-looking from afar, but narrow. My narrow, elegant home, my narrow, prestigious school. The walls between households, between the grown-up world and my own, were so high back home. I'd tried to scale them, with my messing around and my disco nights. But my attempts now seemed childish.

I picked up a pine cone from the plywood floor and tossed it out into the night, waiting a second for its faint *thud*.

"Oh, no, Mr. Bill!" I cried.

"What?" Willa looked at me, baffled.

"Mr. Bill."

"Who's Mr. Bill?"

"It's a joke. You know, from *Saturday Night Live*? He's that little clay man who's always getting dropped off cliffs and…" Nothing. "Willa, have you really never heard of Mr. Bill?"

"We don't have a TV," she said, simply. "I've never watched it. Look up."

So that's why my campfire act had been a dud, why Willa called my impressions "stories"; no one had a clue what I was doing up there. In that case, their laughter wasn't stingy, but charitable.

I was still trying to process the TV thing, pitying my *Saturday Night Live–* and *Mork and Mindy–* and *That's Incredible!–*deprived cousin, when the view above stopped me short.

Stars, framed by leaves. A sight that put the butter-yellow portable RCA TV set in my bedroom to shame. Willa didn't pity herself. She couldn't, not here.

We stood side by side, silently looking up at the sky, for a long time.

Something happened to me then, next to this relative I barely knew. A girl I'd have dismissed as spacy or immature a week ago. In that stretch of still, quiet minutes—I couldn't say if five or fifty passed—I felt calmer than I had in a long time.

"Hey," I said quietly. "Thanks."

"For what?" she asked, eyes still on the sky.

"For inviting me up here."

"You're family."

I didn't know how to respond to such a simple, generous proclamation. But I stored it up to savor later. I would think about those two words many times over the years. Long after Willa vanished from my life.

Noises came from below—the scrape and burst of a match, then the short, barking coughs and breaks in conversation that meant people were sharing a joint. It sounded like they were right under us.

"I hate to say it, man," Graham said, his voice tight. A long pause, then, full and relaxed: "The heart's missing from that one. I think it's dead weight. Here."

"Thanks," a woman said. Silence, a drawn-out exhale. "I hear you. And it's your dime, but…" *Cough.* "What does that leave me with?"

"Maybe we can thicken it up, I don't know…"

"This is amazing," I whispered.

"Don't worry, they can't hear us," Willa said. "They wouldn't unless we yelled. Sound carries up here, but not the other way."

So she'd tested this—I liked her all the more for it. My cousin and I were different in almost every way, but we had this one secret, taboo pleasure in common.

I said it with complete understanding and admiration: "Willa, you spy!"

9

You Show Me Your World and I'll Show You Mine

One week later

Squeeeeeeeak.

Willa's bike chain outside my cabin. Next would come her gentle knocks.

Tap, tap, tap. "Jackieeee…"

As she opened the door, I closed my eyes and breathed heavier. I liked to prolong my wake-up ritual. The questioning soft-ness with which my cousin said my name, the way she almost sang it, made me excited for the day, no matter how obscenely early it was.

"Jackieee… Are you up?" She sat at the bottom of my bed and I could smell her hair, wet from the ocean. A salty-kelpy freshness. She'd come straight from the beach; she always surfed from five 'til eight.

"Hmmm. What time is it?"

"I have no idea. But c'mon. I'm taking you to the swing this morning, remember?"

I pulled on the cutoffs I'd made from my Glorias under the shirt of Willa's I'd slept in, not brushing my hair. Patricia would have taken one look at me, pursed her lips at the sight of my unruly ends, and whisked me off to Giovanni's Salon.

"Url, eez," I said, through a mouthful of toothpaste, circling my index finger in the air. *Twirl, please.*

Willa turned, modeling today's costume: a lacy lavender blouse, a red scarf as a belt, and a mustard-yellow peasant skirt, knotted at the hip so it wouldn't catch on her bike chain. I never knew what Willa would be wearing when she showed up at my cabin, only that it'd be bright and floating and something I'd have looked absurd in. I'd been here for sixteen days and hadn't seen her in the same outfit twice.

By the time I hopped on my bike she was far ahead, sun flashing off her chrome fender.

We ditched the bikes when the trail got too steep, hiking the rest of the way up to an ocean-facing cliff, to the Flying Swing. It hung from a tree so wind-battered that every limb was horizontal.

"This isn't our land, it's the state's, but hardly anyone else knows it's here," she said, holding the plank seat for me. "So it might as well be ours. Our magic little scrap of earth, Daddy calls it."

I stared up at the ropes, knotted to a limb so high I couldn't tell how secure it was. At least I didn't have to climb again—only sit. I settled myself, gripping the ropes.

She pulled me back slowly, dramatically, and I felt it, the *creak-creak-creak* anticipation in the pit of my stomach, the delicious dread of ascending a roller-coaster hill. "Did your dad put it up?" I asked nervously.

"A friend did, when I was a toddler." She always referred to Graham's summer visitors as "friends."

"That's far enough," I said. She'd pulled me so far back I couldn't see anything but the ocean, hundreds of feet below.

"Okay. But don't worry, even if you fell off, you'd just land on the grass. Promise not to look down, though...it spoils the illusion. Watch the patterns of sun on the water, try to find words. I do that sometimes."

She didn't push me, only released her fingers so I could fly. The first swing was terrifying, and I peeked to find a gently sloping hill cushioned with soft ferns. Even a bad spill wouldn't be fatal. I relaxed, but exhilaration made me admit it—"I looked!"

"It's okay..." *Whoosh*, as I lost her voice under the wind in my ears. "...time!"

I knew what she'd said. *It's okay, you'll do it next time.*

Willa hopped on easily then, and never looked down, never hinted that she was tempted. She gazed straight up at the sky, her long hair flying behind her in a bright mass, its ends hiding the swing's seat.

After my swing initiation we retrieved our bikes, crossed the Kingstons' makeshift parking lot, and headed to the beach, as we'd done every day since our détente. The first time I'd followed Willa down this trail on one of the Kingstons' battered, brakeless cruisers, I'd dragged my feet. The route was rutted and bumpy and full of dicey turns, and ended in a hair-raising trip through a metal storm drain under the road. But I was learning the way, trying to memorize every switchback and dip and low-hanging tree limb that required a perfectly timed duck.

We spent our morning kicking foam, collecting sea glass, talking.

"Tell me a school story," Willa said, bending to pick up a struggling baby crab, settling it gently closer to the water.

"Hmmm. Once I stole my calculus teacher's mint wrapper box because of Tina Alverson's period." This was how I always began my stories for Willa—with something outrageous and true. My version of *once upon a time.*

Delighted: "What?"

"So there was this girl named Tina Alverson..."

As we sloshed through the shallows, I told Willa how I'd stolen Mr. Stengwatts's prized box, the one it had taken him years to make from hundreds of Andes mint wrappers. Payback because he'd shamed Tina Alverson at the blackboard for the rusty stain on her pants.

"Justice with Her Flaming Sword," she said dreamily. Willa enjoyed my school stories so much that I was tempted to embellish. But the truth impressed her plenty. Apparently, I'd spent most of my time in San Francisco avenging wrongdoing. I hadn't realized. I'd thought I was just messing around.

But I liked this reflection of myself in her clear blue eyes.

"He *was* nicer to Tina after that," I said. "I suppose if I was really noble I'd have confronted him."

"You're too modest. Tell me another—"

"Look!" I'd spied something deep blue between my feet, a telltale stillness in the restless tide. I scooped it up, showing it to her in my palm. Indigo sea glass—the rarest color, and the hardest to spot underwater.

She was next to me in a heartbeat, so fast my palm was still sieving water. "It's gorgeous," she said, brushing her windwhipped hair out of her eyes to inspect it. "Almost a perfect circle."

"For your collection." I tried to hand it to her.

"No. You keep it. Start your own collection."

I put it to my eye like a monocle. The fog was burning off, and the dark blue glass gave the bright beach a moody, vintage tint. I held it over Willa's eye to show her.

"Not rose-colored glasses, but…what?"

"Sky-colored glasses," I said.

"You always put things the exact right way."

When our hands were full and our feet were numb, we walked our bikes back uphill and lazed in Willa's bedroom. I loved looking at her pictures on the shelves next to her sunny window seat. A family photo taken last spring, with Graham between Willa and Angela in the sun, on the field. One of Willa at seven, standing between Angela and Graham at Woodstock, helicopters in the background. Graham with his long arms slung casually around various muddy but intense people.

"He didn't *play* there or anything," Willa'd said. "He only went to see some friends."

I was slowly making my way through her albums—two book-shelves full—and today I reached *C*. She organized her albums by first name, not last, as if the rows of gods and goddesses were old friends. I'd brought a dozen of my favorite LPs with me, and while Willa had taught me about her *J* singers—Joan Armatrading and Joan Baez and Joni Mitchell and Judy Collins—I'd introduced her to Blondie, Andy Gibb, Shaun Cassidy, and Hot Chocolate.

I wasn't always sure it was a fair trade, but Willa analyzed the lyrics of "Da Doo Ron Ron" and "Shadow Dancing" as seriously as the poetry woven by her folk geniuses. She said all songs were stories.

"Willa, are you kidding me?" I said, picking up a copy of Cat Stevens's *Tea for the Tillerman* signed *To little Willow, grow up strong*, above an actual sketch of a willow tree.

"Oh, that. Some guy at my dad's label arranged it years ago. It's not like we met. But that was neat of him."

Neat. Just *neat*. I slid the album back into place between Carole King and Donovan. Willa was always like this, blasé about things other kids would've bragged about.

"Do you miss that stuff?" I walked to the window and watched Graham laughing in the pool below, the center of a small circle of friends. I held my indigo sea glass over my eye, and the sky turned dark blue. Instant storm clouds.

"What stuff?" she asked.

"Your dad traveling, the big shows?"

"No," she said firmly. "He's happier here. Apart from all that."

"You're a nicer person than me. I'd miss it."

We were so different. If we weren't cousins, would Willa and I be friends? If she'd gone to Vaughn Academy, would she have been like the rest, and called me Supertramp?

"What's that taste like?" she asked, about the Coke I'd bought at the gas station and snuck up here under my shirt so the Kingstons wouldn't spot it. They had strong opinions about the Coca-Cola company.

"Hmmm?" I asked, watching the scene on the field below. A woman had joined Graham's small group on the grass with her dog, a little shaggy thing, and it was running wildly from person to person inside the small circle, enjoying the hands and bare feet outstretched to pet it.

"Your Coke. What's it like?"

"Umm. Sparkly liquid caramel."

"That sounds like one of your K-Tel disco albums," she said.

"It does, actually."

She came and stood next to me at the window, leaning close. "So can I maybe try just a—"

"I don't know."

"Just a teeny bit would be fine… You know I regulate my blood sugar better than most adults. I pay attention to my body."

True. She bought gallons of custard from General Custard's but always let it melt, untouched, into yellow soup. I suspected she bought it only because she liked Liam, the surfer who worked in the shop part-time. He flirted with her, too; last time she'd ordered a sundae, and he'd cranked the radio up on "Sunday Girl" as a little joke (and got points with me for being a Blondie fan).

"I'm not worried about your blood sugar," I said. "I *am* worried about tempting you into supporting the military-industrial complex. Your parents'd have a cow if you touched it."

"They've never made an official rule against it. They just *assumed* I'd think like they do. I only want to see what the fuss is."

I yanked the bottle away fast, joking around, and a few fizzy drops spattered onto her arm. I knew what was next.

"It's a sign! I touched it! No, *it* touched *me*. Even better."

I laughed, knowing it was pointless to argue now; Willa saw signs everywhere, even in a few wayward drops of soda. "One sip, Wills, I mean it."

She took a small mouthful, pronounced it "gross," and handed the bottle back. But she was excited, I could tell.

"What've you never tasted?" she asked.

"Hmmm. I never ate a carob brownie before I came here, and we know how well that turned out." I'd spat the chalky brown mess behind a tree when no one was looking.

"Tasted...or done. What've you never ever done because your parents... I mean, your family assumed you'd be a carbon copy?"

"How long do you have?"

"Well, what's the first thing that comes to mind? Jackie Pierce has never ever ever..."

"Slept on the beach."

"That's perfect! We'll do it tomorrow night, it's a full moon... You'll love it. What if..."

"What?"

"We write down things we've never done, but want to...and check them off. It'll be so much fun! 'You show me your world and I'll show you mine,' like in my dad's song."

Oh, Willa. She'd never been taught to conceal her excitement, to act cool. It seemed obvious to me that everything about her was a hundred times cooler than me, even—no, especially—her innocent ideas of fun. Cool rhymes with fool, as the song said.

But Willa was convinced that *I* was the sophisticated one. I wasn't about to disabuse her of this idea.

"Let's do it," I said.

After an hour of scribbling, we had this—

Willa
Try Coca-Cola X
Eat at a McDonald's

See a horror movie—Amityville?—in a theater
Learn The Hustle
Go to a real disco (and do The Hustle)

Jackie
Spend the night on the beach
Get up on surfboard
Memorize Jonathan Livingston Seagull
Recite JLS out loud, alone, on the tide pools at sunrise
Train myself to not look down on the Flying Swing at the cove

Willa approved of my list immediately, though at first she was convinced I'd chosen the *Jonathan Livingston Seagull* reciting one—something she did all the time—just to flatter her. I hadn't. I admired Willa's ritual and picked it because the prospect of being out there by myself on the vast outcropping of rocks scared me. So much aloneness. No one within kissing or arguing distance to fill the void.

I was less flattered, reviewing her choices. "Coke and McDonald's and horror movies? Is that my world? Is that me?"

"They're not the important things."

10

Mashup

1999
Fifteen days after Jackie's arrival
Two a.m.

At home when I can't sleep, I play the piano—happy pieces. Mendelssohn, the overture to *A Midsummer Night's Dream*. Fairies and harmless mischief and young love, and everything turning out all right in the morning. I may live in a dark basement apartment, but at least I can play whenever I want without disturbing my neighbors.

But here, one chord on the Rec Room piano would wake Shane. My new housemate—how odd.

Instead I stare at the ceiling, picturing the second floor. The main bedroom, hall, linen closet, powder room. And, right above me, Willa's bedroom. Lavender quilt. Dried flowers on the walls. Posters of her *J* singers: Joan and Joan and Joni and Judy.

Jackie's a J, she'd said to me once, thrilled.

Well, unfortunately I don't have a J voice, I'd told her.

But you have a voice...

I try to imagine ripping those posters down, offering up

her gauzy blouses and flowing skirts for strangers to paw. The thought alone of walking upstairs has me anxious.

What will I find up there?

But my piano craving is a physical need, strong as hunger, and there's another option, besides the battered Rec Room upright, that I know I won't be able to resist.

I creep down the hall, past Kate's dark room off the kitchen, where Shane's asleep. Down the cramped stairs to the studio, through the first door. I close it behind me, feel my way in blackness to the second, soundproofed door, which I push behind me until I hear it click.

The winking mixing board lights act as a beacon as I move toward the live room and the final door. Three doors, total.

I never came down here, never saw Angela or Willa visit, either. It was Graham's domain, and still looks like him—the saturated colors of the rugs, the faux-medieval needlepoint tapestries on the walls, with patterns of deer and castles. But many of the instruments and mics and stands are new, and there's evidence of Shane's obsession everywhere—papers, books, liner notes he's studying. Someone's left her purple shawl on a chair.

It's a relief; I prefer it this way.

In the dim light, I sit at the piano and play the *Midsummer Night's Dream* overture I've been craving. Then a lullaby, a lazy riff on Brahms, or something I dreamed up. Sometimes I can't tell the difference.

I transition to "Mockingbird," and I sing. My thin, raspy voice has not improved much with time or practice, but I don't mind anymore. Next up: "More Than a Feeling." When I was in college, playing supper clubs for spending money, I always made good tips with Boston. I was on a merit scholarship, and I'd stopped cashing my father's checks by then. I play the theme song from *Fame.* "Pop Muzik." I play louder, pounding out "The Love Cats." "This one goes out to you, Toby," I say, pointing at the ceiling. My laugh turns into a yawn.

It's miraculous, how much better I feel. I stand, instinctively open the bench seat to look inside. Sheet music, pencils, a busted metronome—nothing else.

I shut the lid.

"That. Was. Awesome."

I spin around—Shane. Clapping. Grinning. Sitting behind a long Orange amp like it's a café table and I'm the live entertainment. He's in a rumpled T-shirt, his hair standing on end.

"I'm sorry. I didn't know what to do. At first I didn't want to scare you. Then I didn't want to stop you. You're good! I've never heard anyone mash up Boston and Brahms."

"So you fell asleep working down here?" I finally muster. Wait. He's wrapped in the blanket from Kate's bed. He's got his pillow and book and everything in a little alcove behind the amp, on a neatly folded Persian rug he's made into a sleeping mat. He didn't drift off while working; he *planned* to crash down here.

"Oh, yeah…" He pulls his blanket tighter around his waist and tucks it in like it's a bath towel. I don't see any pajama bottoms—he must be down to his boxers under there. Or his briefs.

The absurdity of the situation hits me and I can't help smiling. "I came down here to play so I wouldn't wake you up. I'm sorry."

"I'm not," he says, grinning. "I enjoyed the show. I mean it— you're really talented."

I roll my eyes. "I haven't won any prizes."

"Lately. Ms. First Place in the All Massachusetts University-Level Classical Tournament, 1984."

"How'd you find out about that? It was a lifetime ago."

"Your bio's on your school internet page. Anyway, who cares about prizes? That was a thing of beauty." He gets up and sits to my right on the bench. "And you can sing, not just play. You've been holding out on us. Interested in joining our little venture?"

I shake my head more quickly than I intend to. "You don't want my voice on your album. I wish you could've heard Willa's. It was—" I stop myself.

"What?"

I answer with a soft trill of minor-key notes on the piano. I was about to blurt something I've never said to anyone, except her. That her singing was *unearthly*. It's the only word I could ever find to describe it properly.

"You two. You *were* close, weren't you?" He peers at me from the side.

"I *thought* we were close, the summer I stayed here," I admit, looking at the sheet music.

But perhaps we weren't. And maybe Willa wouldn't even like the adult me. She'd be happy about my teaching. She'd say she always knew I'd end up working with kids. But she'd scold me, in her soft way, if she saw how I was living in Boston. The fact that I only spend time with people like Paul, who I can keep at arm's length. *What's happened to you?* she'd ask.

I go on. "Everything was so intense back then. You know?" I glance at Shane.

He nods. "Angela only talked about her once. One afternoon, after I played 'Angel, Lion, Willow.' It was stupid of me. I was showing off, not thinking how it'd make her feel. I apologized, rambled on awkwardly—I've been known to ramble on awkwardly, if you haven't noticed— Anyway, she got this distant look and she said… I remember what she said exactly. That Willa *wasn't meant for this world*. It's very sad, what happened to her."

"Yes." I stare at the sheet music again. *Oh please, Angela.* How trite, how convenient. How wrong. Willa was more a part of this world than most people who live to be a hundred. But who was I to question what a mother had to tell herself to keep going after losing her child?

Her only child, who couldn't imagine living anywhere else, who planned to live here until she was an old lady with wild white hair—who'd run away without a goodbye and died two years later. Drowned off the coast of Mexico. Official cause of death: severe diabetic reaction coupled with surfing too far out given the day's conditions.

We hadn't spoken once since that summer.

I've never quite accepted it. Certainly never understood it. The Willa I knew managed her diabetes expertly, and she was as strong as a channel swimmer. The girl swallowed up by the bright water off of Rosarito wouldn't have drowned if she didn't want to...but why would she have wanted to?

I'll never get to ask her.

"You know," Shane says. "I play in the middle of the night, too. When I'm in that jangly mood."

I turn to him, grateful he's changed the subject. *"Jangly,"* I repeat, liking the sound. It describes how I felt earlier perfectly. "So, how's it going down here?"

"I don't know. Not great," he says, downcast. "Maybe I'm trying to force it. Force what's in my heart on them."

I'm surprised by how much it hurts to hear this. All the tiptoeing around they're doing so they don't disturb me can't be helping their work. And I'm sure they'll be just as cautious, as deferential, when I hand the keys over to Windward Realty. I feel like the resident killjoy. The suit. Like my father.

"Anyway, Mat says I'm getting obsessive. I feel like we conveniently bust a part whenever he thinks I need a break."

I smile at this. "I'm on his side. Breaks are healthy."

"Maybe. But I can't help thinking he's more concerned about the fact that I keep forgetting to shower than my mental health."

I laugh. Though he smells good. Like Angela's lavender-mint Castile soap, the way we all smelled back then. There are still bars of it everywhere. I must smell like it now, too.

"You know," I say casually. "If Mat thinks the group needs to relax, they can spread out. Use the place more. The hot springs, picnic tables, whatever they want."

"You wouldn't mind?" He angles his head toward me.

"I wouldn't mind."

"Well. We may take you up on that. Hey, play some more, will you?" He shifts on the bench to give me room. "Please? I like how you play."

"Any requests?"

"Hmmm. Give me a medley. Or…were you looking under here for some more sheet music?" He knocks the glossy wood between our bodies.

"Oh, no. Just trying to take an inventory of everything that'll need packing. Just being thorough," I lie, not willing to share the existence of this sacred relic from the past. "Okay, black-tie concert audience." I play, jumping from Joni Mitchell to Styx to Mozart's devilishly fast "Turkish Rondo," anything that comes to mind.

He grabs his guitar to teach me a song—a love song he wrote in college that no label wanted. I haven't played a duet with anyone except my students in a long time. But it's easy with him. He's gifted on the guitar, his fingers fast, notes and chords twining casually around mine.

I'm facing the piano and he's got his back to it now so he can play, but our hips are separated by only a little space on the bench. A foot, maybe ten inches of glossy cherrywood—the smoothest of surfaces, perfect for sliding closer to someone. For a moment I wonder what would happen if I did.

He sings, and I know why he's got Bree doing lead vocals on the album. His voice is worse than mine, growly and even more narrow in range—it struggles on anything above the lowest bass. But it's unapologetic, and even if his voice isn't pleasing, his joy in the music is:

Let them rush over and surround us
Let their colors blur around us…

I play my best. I realize, as we finish, just how much I want to impress him. I like the fact that he read my school bio on-

line. I like his bad voice, and his beautiful song. How his right
elbow grazes mine a couple of times.

I like how he nods, anticipating my choices, encouraging me
as I fudge my way through this unknown tune. He's attentive,
sensitive. Everything about his playing says—*trust me.*

It's after one by the time I settle on the daybed.

"Tk, tk, tk," I summon Toby. He's a spiral of fur in the moonlight, curled on the rug. I wish he'd stretch and hop softly onto
my feet like he does in Boston, but he only lifts his head sleep-
ily and blinks at me.

He's been like that for days; he only wants to stay right there,
on that small patch of rug.

I get out of bed and lie next to him, stroking his warm flank.
"You okay, buddy? You miss home?"

He's vibrating. Not purring—vibrating.

No, the floor is. There's a steady throb from below, from the
studio. So Shane's still awake, playing. There must be a post or
beam that transmits vibrations up to this particular spot. I press
my ear to the rug and close my eyes.

Mystery solved. So that's why Toby favors this patch of floor
to my feet. It's a comforting feeling, that sustained temblor from
below. A diffuse massage. I hum Shane's sweet, rejected song
and nuzzle my cheek against Toby's soft back.

It seems we'll stay like this for my remaining time here. Shane
and his group will lay down their songs, and I'll fill the rest of
my boxes, and we'll work on our separate levels of the house
until I say goodbye in a week.

But this place has other plans.

Just like Willa once said.

July

11

Outside of Reason

1999

"So you *are* coming back," Paul says. "I was worried I'd lost you to the Moonies."

Decent, sweet Paul. He sounds so far away that I close my eyes and rest my head on the warm Plexiglas of the phone booth by the custard shack. (Though I shouldn't call it that. General Custard's is now a frozen yogurt shop. Twenty flavors, fifty toppings.)

"The Moonies are up in Oregon, Paul. Not California."

"Well. I was able to change the dates for Cape Cod to next weekend."

"Cape C— Oh, right, great."

"You forgot," he says flatly.

A tall, touristy-looking man in a straw fedora is waiting impatiently for the phone booth, glaring at me, and I feel doubly scolded. I turn my back to him, nervously clinking the change dispenser. "No. Well, okay, I did, but I've been so busy, finishing up."

"Sure. Well." Paul sighs. "I'll see you at Logan tomorrow night at nine. Flight 646, right? Maybe we can grab a bite if you're not too zonked."

"I'd love it!" I try to make up for forgetting about our long-planned trip.

I cross the highway and hike up the trail to the house. Fast, until my heart's pumping and I'm sweating. I don't want to think about Paul in the shabby teacher's lounge, looking wounded. It's strange. I've only been gone for three weeks, but it feels like so much longer. This place is a riptide pulling me from everything sturdy and clear—Paul, my real life in Boston. The sooner I get back, the better.

It's my last day.

This morning, I bumped into Shane in the hall and asked how it was going.

"Better," he said.

Over the past week, the group's made themselves at home. They've dragged the picnic tables together, not far from their old spot in the center of the "face" Willa imagined. Beach towels get strewn farther afield each time I venture outside. I saw some near the hot springs late last night. I found someone's underwear, too. Vivienne will purse her lips at the clutter when I hand over the keys tomorrow morning.

The campfires have started, too. A second surge of life after the sun goes down, when they finish their work in the studio. "Join us!" they call if they see me hurrying past. I always smile and shake my head.

Bree calls from the fire circle now as I'm crossing the field from the parking lot. "Jackie!"

The "come join us" is unsaid, but evident in her tone, chiding me for trying to sneak past them again. She's poking the fire, and there's an unclaimed stump to her right, and her broad smile tells me it's my seat, waiting for me. Shane's on the other side of it, looking up hopefully.

"C'mon, one goodbye drink?" Mat says.

I don't have time to socialize. Since I've procrastinated so much on the second floor, my plan is to pack it all night, all morning before my noon flight—the boxes are ready, at the foot of the stairs. I'll be a zombie by the time I arrive at Logan tomorrow night, but I'll be done. Maybe it'll be less painful this way. No time to think.

"C'mon, Jackie, take a break!"

"One teeny break!"

Kauri—"Please, Jackie?"

"For the kids, Jackie," Piper says. They all echo her in a raucous chant: *For the kids. For the kids.*

I know what waits for me in the house. Upstairs bedrooms that feel like museums. Cold and lonely and full of things I haven't had the courage to touch.

Here, by the warmth of the crackling fire, they all look so happy and excited. So eager to make me laugh.

I sit.

Bree Lang smiles, satisfied, but doesn't speak. Mat, who's directly across the fire, opens a beer, and it quickly makes its way around the circle to me.

Piper speaks first. "We knew we'd lure you to our nightly fire ritual in the end."

"Did you have a bet on it?" I sip the cold microbrew.

"Yes," Piper says. "I think I had the evening of July 2 at 8:06 p.m., right? I win the pool! Pay up, losers."

Everyone laughs. Everyone except Shane, who looks at me, concerned. He's worried that I'm only socializing to be polite.

It's okay, I mouth.

Bree introduces me to the ones I don't know. Two rhythm guitarists here for the week, someone helping Mat out with the finicky analog mixing equipment, someone else who just sat in on drums for the day. There are fourteen of us total, staring at the fire as it begins to catch and grow. There is something about campfire that frees people: you don't have to look at faces. Only the fire's constant changes.

No pressure to perform at this campfire, though. I must be

giddy from my first swallow of alcohol since Boston, because I smile to myself, imagining what they'd do if I suddenly busted out my teenage *Saturday Night Live* bits. It would be worth it to see their shock. I wonder what Shane, sitting next to me picking at his beer label, would think.

"So you're leaving tomorrow, huh?" Mat asks. "Long flight?"

"Yeah. Middle seat, too."

Sympathetic groans; these are middle-seat veterans.

Bree tilts her head at me curiously and I realize I've goofed. Now they'll wonder why I'm not living like an heiress, with first-class plane tickets, and I don't want to get into that. How I'm not keeping any of the money.

Why I'm not keeping the money.

"How's the recording?" I ask no one in particular, to change the subject.

"Magic," says Mat. "Finally, after the standard nightmarish, tear-your-hair-out, puke-under-the-mixing-board-when-no-one's-looking beginning, magic. Come down for a listen tomorrow before you go."

"No time," I say. "Thanks, though."

The conversation moves on to food, movies, the Y2K bug that may or may not throw the world into premature Armageddon on January 1. A music festival down at Shoreline Amphitheatre that someone wants to check out.

"You're still selling right after this circus leaves town?" Bree asks on my other side.

"That's the plan."

"Well, good for you, giving this old place one last hurrah. It's pretty country here. I needed this. Feels like I've been indoors for two years." She looks up at the stars, and I do, too.

We fall into an easy silence for a minute. I appreciate the lack of judgment in her tone, about me selling.

"I've been thinking about your uncle a lot this summer, trying to figure him out," she says, her chin still uptilted as she stargazes. "Living inside his lyrics too much, I guess. In one song, he's generous and openhearted, and then in the next he's…" She looks at me as she searches for the right word. "Inscrutable. Almost bitter. Sometimes he's holding your hand, and sometimes he's this cold, superior being casting his wisdom down from on high. I can't figure it out."

I keep my voice light. "I doubt my lyrics would make a tidy package, if I were a songwriter. Would anyone's?"

Bree smiles. "No. Hell, no."

She changes the subject to my job back home, my students. "You miss them," she says.

"I do."

Bree is so open, so surprisingly approachable, that I raise the question that's been needling me since I heard she was coming. "Can I ask *you* something?"

"Ask away."

"I know your music pretty well, and this seems…well, like sort of a departure. Why are you involved?"

"*Sort of* a departure?" Laughing, Bree rummages in the purse at her feet and hands me a miniature photo album, open to the first page. "This handsome gentleman is the reason for the departure. My dear departed daddy. Gone for twenty-two years now. He was once a session musician, never quite made it. He played rhythm guitar on *Three*. That was his only major-label work before he gave up. He used to sing the songs to me at bedtime when I was little. Playing that album became a habit. It's good, don't get me wrong. But the intensity of my love for it *lies outside of reason*, as they say. So here I am. You ever have anything like *Three* is to me, that you love outside of reason?"

I tilt the picture toward the firelight and stare into it. Something—little-girl-Bree's yellow yarn ponytail bows, the way she's looking up at her father—makes me want to meet her honesty with my own.

"Yes. This old children's book. My mom bought it for my

nursery, when she was pregnant with me. Do you know Margaret Wise Brown?"

"*Goodnight Moon*. Sure. And now I'll have it in my head for days."

I smile. "She wrote another one, it's not famous, called *The Important Book*. So I have this habit of saying, 'The Important Thing about X is Y.' 'The Important Thing about Y is Z.' I've done it all my life."

"And now you'll start *me* doing it. Ever tell her about your important habit?"

"Oh, no. I never got the chance to do that. I wish I had."

"She's with my daddy, you mean?"

"Yes."

"I'm sorry."

We listen to the wind sighing through pines, a charred log scraping against another as it settles lower in the pile. "Well, anyway," Bree goes on. "That's the reason I'm here. Aside from Shane over there being an absurdly talented and *persuasive* producer."

"Who's absurd?" Shane asks, swiveling on his stump-chair to face us.

"We're not talking to you." Bree waves him off until he turns back to the conversation on his right. "And a nice guy, to boot," she says to me, privately. "Anyway, I thought I might find a little piece of Albert Bossou Lang down in your uncle's studio. Call me a sappy old broad."

I hand her back the picture. "No. I understand it completely."

"It's a shame you're leaving tomorrow," Bree says.

"It is," I say. Tomorrow at this hour I'll be breathing the stale, chilly air of an airplane, surrounded by frazzled strangers. Then I'll be in my dark apartment, alone. Or in Paul's light-filled apartment. Feeling alone.

Now that my departure's so close, my return to real life imminent, I'm sorry I've taken in so little of the warm fire, crisp seaside air, and easy smiles here.

I sip my beer and listen to them talk, sing, joke. Then the music starts, and I'm relieved they don't sing anything by Graham. Instead, it's a hodgepodge of bar songs, Woody Guthrie, a summer camp round Piper remembers fondly called "Black Socks."

Black socks, they never get dirty
The longer you wear them the stronger they get…
Soooometimes, I think I might wash them
But then I decide…not yet, not yet, not yet…

They'll sing tomorrow night, too. And I'll be three thousand miles away.

Fiona plays ukulele—she's good. I wonder how my kids are doing back home. This is the first time I haven't taught summer courses in more than a decade. On the last day of school, before I knew I was coming here, I gave them plastic marimbas as end-of-year gifts. Their upturned faces were so astonished, so sweetly in denial when I said, *Yes, they're yours to keep!*

I'll be able to give them way more than $4.99 plastic marimbas now. The other teachers don't understand why I live in my cheap basement apartment; even on my pitiful paycheck I could afford something better. No one knows that I donate as much as I can to keep the music program limping along. That now I'll be able to fund it for years—I only glanced through Graham's royalty statements, but I was shocked by his resurgence. His postmortem popularity would have pleased him, despite his insistence that he didn't care about numbers.

Bree hugs me. "Goodnight, moon. Wish you could stick around."

We all say our good-nights, the campfire's breaking up, and Shane and I are walking side by side to the house, when Mat

and Piper, poking at the fire to separate the embers, begin singing softly—

She has all the answers
To the questions I never ask…

I stop. Concentrate on breathing.

It can't be. But I know this song. Every bar.

"Shane. That song. Where'd you guys hear it?"

"What? Oh, it's gonna be the second-to-last track, or maybe
the last. Mat and I can't decide if we should end on a ballad or
not. Pretty, isn't it?"

"It's from Graham's notebook," I say.

"Yeah. One of the few with decent chord marks, really good
ones, actually, so we didn't have to fill in many blanks—"

"What's it called?"

"'Sky-Colored Glasses.'"

I clench my fists. "Graham's notebook. Where is it?"

"The studio, on the stool. What's wrong? Hey—"

Up the field to the house, down the stairs, door, anteroom,
door, door. Shane's footsteps pound behind me. "Jackie!"

It sits in the live room under the main mic, lit by a single lamp
beam like it's on an altar. I grab it, flip through it fast.

There. Willa's handwriting. Twenty pages later, more. And
a third section, near the back.

Most of the notebook is a mess of scribbled-out words, chord
and time markings, sideways writing. Fragments, rejected
bridges, ideas for titles and choruses that didn't lead anywhere,
circled—*perfect!*, then crossed out, the pen digging deep from
frustration—*worthless!*

But three of the completed songs in the notebook have no

markups at all. Squeezed into the blank spaces, they're the only ones transcribed cleanly, start to finish, without any changes.

There's no doubt: among Graham's songs are three that Willa and I wrote together.

I sink to the rug, staring at Willa's writing. Touching the indentations her pen made decades ago. It wouldn't have taken her long. Five minutes, ten. She must have done it sometime during our last, awful week here—the week after I'd completed these lyrics and Willa had polished the music.

But why?

Did you know you were never coming back, Willa?

Was this your goodbye?

12

Unearthly

1979

It wasn't until we were biking to the beach one day that I heard Willa sing for the first time.

As we flew down the hill, she thought I was well behind, as always, able to hear only the chattering birds, but I was in better shape by then and had entered the storm drain before she exited.

Her voice floated back to me: "Song for David" from Judy Collins's *Whales & Nightingales*. She owned three copies. She wasn't singing loud, but the tunnel acted as a giant amplifier and her voice bounced off of the ribbed walls, the acoustics better than any shower's. Not that she needed the help. Her voice was sweet and searching, but there was force in it...power. So much power, coming out of delicate Willa. The roundness of Judy Collins, the jazzy swoops and scampering of Joni Mitchell. But no, that was wrong, to try to compare Willa's voice to anyone else's, even her beloved *J* singers'. It was just hers.

I pedaled furiously to keep up. It was slippery in the tunnel, drippy and dark, mud on the ground. It would serve me right if I wiped out. My punishment for eavesdropping.

But her voice balanced me, pulled me along, and I didn't let the space between us lengthen until she was done.

I didn't bring it up right away.

I waited until that afternoon before dinner, when we were alone in the treehouse. I was idly watching Graham and some new musicians he was working with milling around outside the studio door, while telling Willa another of the "school stories" she loved.

This one was about what I used to do at the Marina Club pool. How I'd taken classmates to the hidden, shady strip of grass behind the spool of rolled-up lane markers and messed around. They'd become a blur of lips, hands, landscapes of bare chest glimpsed from below. Fourteen boys and four girls...that I could recall.

"...and what I remember most is how different everyone's sweat tasted. Salty. Sweet. It really varied. Sometimes I went back there alone, though. I could hear everyone gossiping, all of the Vaughn kids' snooty parents. Hey, Willa?" I turned.

"That's the end?" Willa, lying faceup on the plywood floor, spoke as groggily as someone yanked from a dream. "That can't be the end."

"I've told you everything I remember."

"But why'd you take all those people behind the lane-marker wall, if it made things complicated at school...and with your dad, and you didn't enjoy the actual messing around? If you were just doing things *to* them, and not letting them do anything to you?"

I was trying to get my father's attention. I was lonely. I was acting out. I'd had no adequate female role model during puberty. I was testing boundaries. These were the acceptable answers, I knew from therapy.

"I guess I needed it. There."

"But not here." It wasn't a question.

No. Not here. For a minute, we listened to the crickets, the splashes and calls from down in the field, the other soft, friendly nighttime noises that had become so familiar.

"Willa? I have a confession."

"Hmmm?"

"I heard you singing, back in the tunnel this morning."

"Oh."

"I'm a hopeless snoop. I hope you don't mind."

She extended her legs and wiggled her feet nervously. "It's no big deal. Wow, you're getting fast on the bike. I knew you'd get the hang of it. Same with surfing, you'll see."

"But your voice. I've never heard anything like it."

"It's not Judy's."

"It's wonderful. It's—" I strained for the perfect word "—unearthly. Why keep it secret?"

"I sing all the time."

"No, you don't. You hum. And you play your guitar, and you have records or the radio on constantly. You *breathe* music. But you never sing when anyone's around. And you never sing at campfire."

Your dad never picks you.

"I guess I never thought about it."

"But does Graham know how good you are?" I looked toward the studio door again, but everyone had gone back inside.

"I guess... Maybe... Hey, we should fix this place up."

I let her change the subject, but now that I'd heard her sing, I knew I couldn't let it go.

Over the next week we picked up trinkets for the treehouse; sometimes one of us bought an item in secret and installed it in place as a surprise for the other. She found me posters of Blondie and the Knack, I got her Laura Nyro and Nico.

At the thrift store, Willa found a box of fabric remnants in a bright marigold-and-purple butterfly print, and we spread it around the floor as carpet. A yellow quilt, a red Igloo cooler, which we filled with my sodas and her herbal iced tea. And a few glass tubes of Willa's insulin. Though she never tasted more than a bite of candy or custard, or a sip or two of soda at a time, and hadn't had a reaction in three years. I contributed an orange velour beanbag chair. It was a bitch to get it up; we nearly broke our necks, like what Kate said about Graham, affixing his shells to the chimney long ago. But it was worth it; we'd made a lovely little bower.

Our favorite addition came from the "Boy Toys" bin at the thrift shop. That day, as I sifted through it—cheap cereal-box prizes? A pamphlet on weight lifting? Plastic slingshots? I felt sorry for boys—a kid was digging across from me. As he tried to rake something closer using a long box, he looked at me suspiciously, like I was his competition. I pretended to examine a slingshot, but in his patched shirt three sizes too big, struggling to reach the elusive toy, he was so pitiful that I reached in to help.

"Is this what you wanted?" I handed it to him—a plastic *CHiPs* motorcycle with a helmeted man astride it. "Do you watch that show?"

I took the tiny man off of his bike and made him do a little boogie, one arm up, John Travolta–style. The kid seemed terrified, so I took a quarter from my pocket. "Here, he's on me."

He grabbed the bike and figurine and quarter, threw the coin on the counter, and bolted out the door, shoving past Willa, who came over with an *a-ha* look, like she'd busted me. Busted me being nice. "You're so good with kids! That's the boy who lives over the ridge."

I laughed. "He fled, Willa. Kids *hate* me."

"I saw how you were. And your voice… It got different. And you bought him the toy."

"Whatever." I inspected the long box he'd been using as a shovel. *Boy's Spyglass Kit*, it said. A freckled kid in a sailor cap on the outside, a cartoon thought bubble: *Wow—20x Magnify-*

ing Power!! The "kit" was only a gold-painted tin spyglass and booklet of "Tips for Pirates."

But the spyglass worked. From the treehouse, we could now see the zinc on people's noses in the pool. The plumes from musicians' smokes, as they loitered by the studio door on breaks. Their expressions, too.

"Pretty good for a quarter," I said, sweeping our new toy back and forth. "Hey, sing for me?"

"What?"

"A pirate song. A spy song. A lullaby, or a ballad for our little friend at the thrift store. Anything."

She hesitated. But I'd kept my request casual, and my back was to her. She thought I was occupied with the spyglass.

She sang.

13

Just Hum

Late afternoon, a few days later

Dear Ray,
I can't believe it. It's her. Her.

I shut my diary, grabbed the magazine, and ran across the field to look not for Willa, but for Graham.

He was near the lower pools, the ones fed by his waterfall, talking and tuning his guitar in a group of a dozen people, including the new visitor Willa and I privately called Bicentennial Woman. (She had piles of red, white, and blue T-shirts and knee socks and visors for sale in her VW; she and her last boyfriend had gotten stuck with them after a 1976 moneymaking scheme, and it's all she wore. She also had red hair, pale skin, and blue eyes: she matched her T-shirts.)

When I approached and saw that her eyes were closed—Graham's tuning was apparently that mesmerizing—I hesitated.

"What's that?" Graham called.

"Oh, I'll... I'll show you later. I don't want to interrupt." I turned to go.

"Guys, give us a sec?"

When they'd scattered—Bicentennial Woman looking miffed—I handed it to him. A 1958 issue of *Posy* magazine. Inside was a numerology game where you entered your first, middle, and last name, and totaled up the number of letters, and it told you your character traits.

The girl who'd filled out all of those magazine quizzes, my unknown, time-traveling companion, was *Strong, Creative*, and *A Loyal Friend*, according to the quiz. She'd tallied up the total carefully—21, based on the 4, 9, 8 values of her name:

> *JANE*
> *ELIZABETH*
> *KINGSTON*

My mother.

She'd died having me. *Preeclampsia...seizures...systolic blood pressure of 180...magnesium sulfate...* I'd found the medical file in my father's study one rainy October afternoon, detailing what he'd already told me.

A miracle to have hundreds of silly magazine quizzes to off-set those sad documents.

"I just thought you might like to see it," I said to Graham.

It took him a few seconds to understand, and then his face softened. "Sweet Jane," he said. "Where'd you find this?"

"In the Rec Room. There are piles of them."

"Man," he said. "Trippy. Now I know why I hauled those old magazines down here. I was clearing them out from the old family place in Evergreen. I tried to throw them out but some-thing stopped me. I guess Janey stopped me."

Janey. I liked the way he said it.

"And now we know why you came to this crazy place. It's because she wanted you to meet her." He patted the grass. "Sit for a minute."

"There are lots more, if you want to see them," I said, settling next to him. "There's one where she took a diet quiz, and it told her to switch to half a grapefruit and black coffee for breakfast."

He smiled at that. "Jane liked pancakes."

It sounded like a line out of a Dick and Jane book, but I treasured this scrap of information. I pictured a sunny breakfast room, a tall stack of pancakes topped with a golden square of butter, place mats, a book bag by her penny-loafered feet, the smell of bacon and coffee, a younger, much slimmer Graham teasing her with an older brother's affectionate ruthlessness. My mother's hair brushed, the side of her fork slicing through the gold-and-white layers.

Graham's expression clouded. "When our folks had to move to Evergreen, she made herself pancakes for dinner. I was in the Village then."

A new picture replaced the old one, fast as a slideshow: my mother sitting alone, no eggs left, no syrup, no butter. Dark outside, parents off at their night jobs at the paper mill, her older brother living in New York, pursuing his music dreams. The radio playing for company.

He set his hand on my shoulder; it was so big it spanned to my collarbone. "I wish I'd come around after you were born. Me and your dad…"

"I know."

"I wasn't sure how much you'd want to talk about her. But you ask me anything you want. Okay?"

He looked at me like we had all the time in the world, though someone was calling to him from up near the house.

"You don't need to get back? We can do it another time."

"I'm busy, Christian!" he yelled over his shoulder. By the trickling lower pools, he told me all about her. Everything he could remember.

"She was so much younger," he said when he was finished. "I wish I had more for you, I really do."

"I know."

"I wrote a song about her. Only one. But don't think because I only wrote one that I don't remember her all the time. It broke my heart, writing that one song."

The 45 record was on my cabin step when I came out the next morning.

It looked homemade, the label askew and gummy. It was a song called "Evergreen," and it was about growing up in Washington state. A game they had, playing in the rain with boughs from a tree down the street, snapping it so drops of rain would fly at each other. It was so simple and straightforward compared with Graham's later songs. Though of course I was biased because it was about my mother, I liked this one best.

I stayed up until three, scribbling a poem by flashlight in my cabin. I'd dabbled in poetry, inspired by the Anne Sexton we'd studied in English class last year, but I'd never finished anything until now. I called it "Janey."

In the morning I read it over, wishing I'd captured my mother more completely. She deserved it.

I wrote the poem onto my palm in permanent marker so I could read it during my surfing lesson—an hour of exhausting paddling on my dinged-up, borrowed longboard next to Willa on her sleek one, pondering the poem on my hand while she dismissed nearly every wave as too big or too small.

When at last she cried, "Hurry, this one, this one!" she sounded so sure I'd succeed that I tried my hardest. But I wiped out immediately, sputtering and spitting salt water.

All for the still-elusive dream of standing upright for one second.

"You were close today," Willa said. "You'll get there."

I peeled off my borrowed wet suit and followed her not over to the dunes as usual—it was too windy today—but up to what she called the Far Pond. A warm, peaceful place, protected from the wind.

I collapsed on the grass a few feet from the bank, sunning my chilled, exhausted body, as Willa, not tired at all, told me about the monarch butterflies that only laid their eggs in milkweed plants, and what the pond was like in winter, and the big album cover shoot Graham had done here when she was little and he was still on the radio.

"He floated on this... Look." She showed me a crude wooden raft he'd made for the shoot. "I hated all the people I didn't know tromping around, the equipment, the serious man from the label shouting instructions," she added dreamily, lost in the memory. "That's what I remember most, hiding behind these milkweeds and wishing the mean strangers away until they left."

"Please don't ask me to do anything physical for the rest of the week. I think you may have to carry me back to my cabin as it is." I raised my hands as if she'd need to drag me.

She laughed, took my wrists. "Okay, you don't have to get on the raft, but your nose is burning. Come to the shade... What's this?"

I pulled my hand from hers. "Nothing. Sort of a poem about my mother that I wrote last night."

She sat next to me. "Because of those magazines you found."

I nodded. I'd told her last night, elated, after confirming my suspicions with Graham.

She was so silent, so accepting that the writing on my palm might be too private to share. And it was so quiet and warm here on the bank, I held my hand out to her.

She read the lines, spreading my fingers so she wouldn't miss a word. "It could be a song."

"I just mess around with poems sometimes. That's different."

"Is it?"

I shrugged.

"If you were going to hum this first line, how would it go? You've memorized it, right?"

"Yes," I admitted.

"So close your eyes."

"Willa. I haven't even finished it."

"I know... C'mon, no one's around but the butterflies, and they're too busy to listen. Just close your eyes and hum."

14

Stowaways

1999
Midnight

Shane and I lie on the studio floor, on the overlapping Persian rugs, islands surrounded by a sea of paper. Notes, album liners, zoomed-in copies of the notebook he made as backups. We've been analyzing them for hours.

And I've been rereading the same three songs: "Sky-Colored Glasses," "Answers," and "Janey." Shane has selected all three for the anniversary album.

"I can't believe I didn't see it," he says, rubbing the back of his neck hard, more as if to punish himself than to relax tired muscles. "Some super fan."

It's not his fault. "Their handwriting's similar. He's the one who taught Willa cursive."

"Still. God, I feel like such an idiot… I mean, it's so obvious now that I'm looking for it. But how are you feeling? Do you want to hear the songs?"

"Answers" and "Sky-Colored Glasses" are already laid down, and "Janey" is nearly mixed. But I shake my head; I can't bear to listen to others singing in Willa's place. Not yet.

"They're beautiful songs, Jackie. You two… Do you think you'd have worked on more together, if things had turned out differently?"

"We weren't planning that far ahead. We never dreamed they'd have an audience beyond the two of us. That wasn't why we wrote them."

I stare across the room at one of Graham's tapestries. Leaping stags and turrets and moats. No. It was just something we enjoyed doing together, like trading opinions on *Important Things*, or digging a sleeping nook into the dunes on Glass Beach.

I've wondered about these songs often, even hummed parts of them, in unguarded moments. I dismissed them as girlish, shallow. But, looking over them now, I can't resist a surge of pride. We *made* these. The songs started life in my head. Then I wrote them in my diary, or on my hands, or flattened custard cups, on anything, if I had an idea that I feared would blow away. Then, once I was ready, I showed them to Willa, and she set them to music. Since then, they have sat, waiting patiently in these cold pages. Little stowaways from the past.

"So why do you think she put them in there? Did you ever see Willa writing in the notebook?" he asks.

"Never. And Graham nearly always carried it with him. The notebook and his guitar."

Except for the last week.

I remember every detail of that week—the cups of tea Willa wouldn't drink, the drab clothes she wore.

I remember everything. But there's so much I don't know.

"So, maybe she was proud of the songs," Shane says. "And she wanted to show them to Graham, but she was too shy to ask. It could be as simple as that."

"It could be." But I know that's not what happened. The timing makes it impossible.

He shakes his head again, still upset with himself. "I should've realized…"

I read through the last stanza of "Janey" again. The song I'd written about my mother, and how she'd filled in those magazine quizzes. I'd been so thrilled to discover what those silly, glossy magazines hid.

Circles and check marks and a few precious words in her youthful handwriting. Handwriting...

"Shane. Angela would've recognized Willa's handwriting if she looked through here. Do you think she knew?"

"You think... She always referred to it as *my late husband's music*. You think she *knew* some of these songs were yours and Willa's?"

"It's possible. And if Angela did know, maybe it was the reason she said yes?"

"Said yes?"

"To your project. You know, when you first approached her about recording Graham's covers, and she agreed and offered up the notebook, too?"

"Right, I..." He flips through the notebook yet again, as if we haven't scoured through it over and over. "Maybe that's why she..."

"What?"

"Nothing. She was just sort of cagey now that I think about it. Or, not cagey, but drifty. I mean, she'd sort of conveniently float off whenever I asked her too many questions. I don't know what I'm saying. This whole thing... I don't get it. So Angela knew Willa wrote three of these, and she wanted her dead daughter immortalized on the recording, fine. Why couldn't she just tell me? And arrange for her to get credit?"

"I don't know." And this part is true. Maybe she didn't know. Maybe, like me, she'd been too scared to look inside.

"So, what now?" Shane says.

"You mean, with the album?"

He nods. "I guess you'll want to call it off, huh?"

"I'm not sure. I have to think about it."

Except I don't want to call it off. I want to be on that album. Me and Willa, holding our own with her legendary father. The way I always dreamed we could.

I want to be on the album, but would she have wanted that, after everything?

That question leads to a hundred others. So many questions, after so many years, that I can hardly breathe.

"Maybe we should take a break, clear out for a few days. Give you some space to decide what you want to do... You all right?"

I drag myself back to the present. "Hmmm? Yes. I just..."

"Hey, we'll figure this out." Shane touches my hand, smiling sadly. He's sure I'm going to kill the album. "Try to get some sleep."

"You, too."

But I don't try. I go upstairs and walk out to the porch to gulp in fresh air.

The lyrics have brought Willa back in a way no mountain of her family belongings could.

You show me your world and I'll show you mine.

And Willa had kept her promise. But I never imagined that once she showed me her world, invited me into it, she'd leave it.

Gripping the porch railing, I gaze out at the soft night. Willa's been dead longer than she was alive. It seems impossible.

Why did you leave your beautiful home, Willa? I've wanted to ask her that for so long. That, and another question.

Why did you leave me?

It wasn't our fault, what happened.

I need to accept that I'll never find the answer.

But when I go inside, I can't help myself—I recheck the hall closet I've already emptied. Which leads me to the kitchen, where I run my hands inside the drawers and on the high pantry shelves I've already searched. I give the empty dining room sideboard one more look.

By the time I enter the Rec Room, I'm a wrecking ball. I toss orange corduroy cushions and LPs and 45s everywhere, destroying my planned genre organizational system for the donation boxes. I rip into the beanbag chair to root inside, knowing it'll be fruitless, but in the moment it feels good, tearing into it so it bleeds foam pellets across the carpet. It's not here.

I'm torturing myself, looking. Hoping. But if I could only find it, maybe it would tell me something new. Offer me some clue I was too self-absorbed to understand back then, at seventeen.

There must have been a word, an inflection in a voice, a look on a face that would have prepared me for how my time with the Kingstons would end. A sign of what was building, what we were speeding toward that summer, when all I'd paid attention to at the time was my own happiness.

"Morning," Shane says on the porch, handing me a coffee. "You look like you need that as much as I do. Rough night?"

I nod. "But I decided. I want you to finish the album. The way you planned it."

"With your and Willa's songs?"

"Yes. And I'm going to stay until it's done."

"You can think about it awhile."

"No. I'm sure. Willa would like it." And I'm surrendering. To the Sandcastle's hold on me. To this admission: I want to stay longer.

Time making something beautiful out of something ugly, like how she described sea glass. That was always the plan for this project.

I just didn't know until now that some of the beauty on the album would be Willa's and mine. Our songs. Pretty survivors of violent seas.

Should I have seen just how rough they would get?

Or was it something that started so gradually, so far below

the surface, I'd have had just as much luck trying to pinpoint the second a shard of glass, whirling in the waves, became completely smooth?

15

A Small Favor

It started so casually. An afterthought, it seemed.

"Hey, could you girls do me a small favor?" Graham said by the picnic tables, one windy day after lunch. "That kid who came today. Can you play with her this afternoon? Her folks're exhausted." He meant Dylan, the daughter of his session pianist. She and her mom, Serena, had come up to surprise her father.

A couple days after, Graham asked if we would mind "entertaining the wild things," since we'd been so good with Dylan. He handed Willa some bills so we could take a group of kids for custard. I hadn't technically agreed to do it, but who could say no, when he needed us, and put it so nicely?

Before custard, we took them to Glass Beach. Dylan wouldn't wade out to the tide pool, a rite of passage an older, much bigger kid had come up with, since it was no challenge for him.

"The important thing about Dylan is she needs to feel proud of something," I said to Willa as we watched her. "What if she was the first to try the Flying Swing? Then we could give her a super special bravery award."

"Brilliant," Willa said.

"It's brilliant, if she'll do it."

I'd found the reward in the treehouse, getting the idea from the *Superman* movie posters I'd seen everywhere—one of the marigold-colored fabric remnants we used as carpet.

At the swing later that week, when we presented Dylan with the cape, for her bravery, she turned positively drunk with happiness, the bright, butterfly-print fabric streaming behind her in the sun. She wore the cape night and day after that.

That's how it began—our informal day camp. One afternoon became every afternoon. It became expected, that we would corral the littler kids while their parents lazed in the grassy bowl or at the beach or in the springs, restoring themselves after the morning's work, the night's revelries. It was only a few hours a day, and helping felt like an honor since it was for Graham. I'd have organized his guitar picks if he'd asked.

"They listen to you," Willa said in astonishment, when a little boy refused to come into shallower water at the beach and I lured him using a "redirection" trick I'd learned from an old book I'd bought at the thrift store. *Parenting with Compassion*, written by a wise-looking woman named Barbara Fairwhistle, Licensed Clinical Social Worker.

They didn't always listen to Willa. She overindulged, and they climbed all over her. Still, together we made a good team, and Graham showered us with praise about how wonderful we were with the children, how clever.

Angela helped sometimes, when she was around. She taught the kids how to make daisy chains, how to hold their hands flat to offer apple slices to the goats she'd adopted, after they wandered over, neglected, from the neighboring property Willa had showed me from the treehouse.

One day after lunch she emerged from the house in thick stage makeup. We were making pine cone birdfeeders at the picnic tables, and the sight of her garish, painted face—the left side happy, the right sad, like mime masks—was a shock, at first. I think Willa and I may have been more startled than the kids.

But then Angela pulled an old tweed train case from behind her back and revealed its treasures: sticks and pots of old Max Factor greasepaint. The real stuff. She held the kids in thrall, as I imagined she did in the touring plays I'd never seen, demonstrating how a few stick-paint swipes in the right places could transform them into witches or fairies.

Like Willa, she was gentle and serene, murmuring confidentially to a little girl as she made her detested freckles vanish with a few strokes of her ancient Max Factor stick.

Graham wandered by and stood over Angela. "Can I be next?" He reached over her shoulder for a red stick and painted a sloppy clown smile over his own, making the kids laugh.

He leaned down to kiss the crown of Angela's head, just above her old-fashioned gold bun.

Angela closed her eyes to receive his kiss as she spoke gently to the little girl beside her: "This stuff can hide anything, see? I've used it for decades. But you may decide that you miss your freckles. You know, my favorite flowers have freckles..."

I would remember this afternoon later, how Angela helped us "entertain" the little kids, showing us all how to try on new faces. And how even under greasepaint, she and Graham looked more natural and happy together than my father and Patricia ever had.

The morning after Angela's face-painting lesson, as Willa and I crossed the parking lot from the beach trail—now that we were busy with the kids every afternoon, I got up at dawn with her for my surf lessons—I noticed the Sandcastle's latest arrival.

"Who's that?" I asked.

"Who?"

"That guy over there. Prince Valiant with the truck."

I watched the tall, shirtless man unloading crates of fruit from his truck bed. His blond hair was pulled into a ponytail, and his shoulders were slick with sweat. "He must be delivering supplies for Kate."

"Oh, that's just Colin. He crashes here a few nights every summer, on his way back from picking. He's an old friend of my mom and dad's, he's nice, you'll like him. Colin!" She flung her bike to the gravel and ran across the parking lot. They exchanged a friendly hug and Willa waved for me to come over.

I fiddled with my bike, propping it against a tree. This *old friend* seemed a lot younger than Graham and Angela. Maybe twenty-five or twenty-six. And good-looking. Wearing brown sandals, Levi's faded almost to white, and nothing else.

I tucked my salt-stiffened hair behind my ears and crossed the parking lot, wishing I'd put anything but *Get up on surfboard* on my *Never-done-but-want-to* list. Willa was a patient and creative instructor, but my lessons made my nose run and my eyes red.

"This is my cousin, Jackie," Willa said.

"Named after *the* Jackie? My folks were wild about all that Camelot stuff, too. My little brother's name is Kennedy."

"Actually, I was born in '61, but it's just a coincidence. I was named after a great-great-grandmother from France named Jacqueline." In one swoop, I'd pointed out our exact age difference and shifted the conversation to the supremely unsexy topic of great-great-grandmothers.

But he didn't seem to mind. "You have her eyes. Wide-set brown eyes. Hey, you two mind helping me carry these up to the house?"

"Sure!" My worn-out muscles had, miraculously, gotten a second wind.

As we lugged the berry boxes up the field, I watched a rivulet of sweat progress down the valley of tanned skin between his shoulder blades.

I would always associate the smell of fresh berries with Colin.

16

New!

He installed himself in Plover cabin, next to mine. The family with the baby had just left for LA—*thank you, family.*

He was twenty-six and, I learned from grilling Willa, had met
Graham and Angela back when they were students at UCLA and
his mother was their sociology professor. He didn't have a fixed
address, preferring to roam with the seasons. Cannery work in
Alaska, picking in Washington and Oregon, working concerts
or the Country Fair or the wine crush down in Napa. He slept
in the back of his truck and sometimes crashed on the beach.

He'd worked as a roadie for Graham in his late teens. But he
wasn't a musician. And, unlike the rest of Graham and Angela's
visitors, he liked to repay the Kingstons for their hospitality.
First were the crates spilling over with fresh Oregon raspber-
ries and strawberries. Then, the next night at campfire, he gave
Graham a gift. A small stack of new albums.

My uncle took one look at the flames and satin on the covers
and said, "You've been out there too long, my boy."

"Just for fun." Colin's smile seemed innocent, but he had to
know that Graham loathed this kind of music. It was the stuff I
adored, even now that I had a newfound appreciation for folk.
I kept my passion for pop and disco between me and Willa (we
held her Hustle lessons in the woods or my cabin).

The albums were still in cellophane, emblazoned with round yellow Tower Records *New!* stickers. That meant they were at least $3.99 apiece. A lot of money for a poor wanderer, for a joke.

"My contribution to the Rec Room," Colin said. "But only if you give your blessing, of course. Otherwise we'll toss them in the fire. A ritual purification." Colin snatched the top album from the stack in Graham's hand and stood. He held it over the snapping flames, looking right at Graham and smiling.

He had a great smile. I was besotted enough to register the thought, though it was a strange moment.

"They're just teasing," Willa whispered, sensing my tension. "They're always like this, because Colin says my dad is a music snob. Watch, it'll be fine."

Sure enough, Graham held his hand out for the album, smiling indulgently. "Always good to know what the kids are twitching to these days. Thank you kindly, lad."

It was the first time I'd seen someone come close to disrespecting Graham. But the moment passed so quickly. Graham smiled at me, cracking open a new beer. "We don't burn albums here, do we, Lady?"

I shook my head, honored to be singled out.

The rest of the night went as normal.

Colin got picked by the bottle and sang a raucous sailors' tune he'd learned canning. Graham clapped louder than anyone.

When Colin and I were walking down to our cabins that night, he said, "So, Graham seems to be in good form this summer. I'm glad, for Angela and Willa's sake."

"What do you mean?"

"Oh, that he can be…you know."

"What?"

"Oh. Nothing. I've known Graham and Angela forever. I'm like the son they never wanted. And you? Known them long? You and Willa seem tight. You're always disappearing together."

I shook my head, but this pleased me. "I hadn't met any of them before this June."

Colin nodded thoughtfully. Then he smiled, looking up at the sky. "Weird to think of it watching us."

Skylab—he didn't need to say the name. We were all aware of Skylab that summer. You could be talking about it in broad daylight and you'd still have to look up at the flat blue sky. It was always up there. A threat, a joke, a shining symbol of governmental arrogance and human fragility.

"It's not coming down in our part of the world," I said.

"No?"

"I saw it on the news."

"Well, okay then. I guess I can sleep soundly tonight, Jackie of the trustworthy eyes."

I was halfway up Slipstream's steps when he called, "Hey. Why *do* you and Willa disappear all the time? You always look so eager to get away."

"Oh, you know." I jiggled the right handrail; it was loose, but I kept fixing it with gum. "She's teaching me about local flowers, berries. Stuff like that." So much for *trustworthy eyes*.

"Ah, right. Well, sleep well. If you get any updates on space debris, you'd better knock on my door first."

"I will!"

I liked Colin. I half wished I'd tugged him up my cabin steps; I'd almost done so.

But the fact that Willa and I stole away to work on our songs every chance we got was our secret.

So were the spots where we found our privacy—the dark treehouse, the warm hollows in the beach dunes we carved behind sheaves of seagrass, the buzzing, milkweed-shaded banks of the Far Pond.

She had her budding flirtation with Liam from the custard shack and I might soon have Colin—he was hard to read.

But those places were only for me and Willa.

17

Lovedrenched

1999

Shane keeps asking me how I'm doing. How I feel, knowing about the songs.

It's a reasonable question.

But the answer changes hourly. Sometimes I'm overcome, in disbelief that Willa has reappeared after so long in such a strange form. Sometimes I'm proud of us. Of what we made together. Then I'm furious with her for disappearing, for throwing away her voice, her talent. Her life. For leaving so many mysteries behind, and turning her back on me. Just as quickly as it comes, my anger dissolves into sadness.

And then simple gratitude—to Willa, for transcribing our work so it wouldn't be lost forever, for the fact that she must not have hated me during those minutes. She wanted to be close to me inside those lyrics and chords and melodies, at least.

Shane and I told everyone about the music. I was worried that they'd think it was some kind of trick, that maybe I'd even been in on it, sneaking our work in with the great Graham's.

But they were all so full of compliments about the songs, how much they add to the album, that I felt ashamed I'd worried.

Bree had sensed all along that the songs were written by more than one person—"inscrutable," she'd said of the collection at campfire—and now we all know she was right.

They asked me this morning, yet again, to come down and listen.

"Not yet," I said. I'm not ready. Whether I'm grateful Willa included them or not, it won't be easy to hear them.

Instead I'm in the Rec Room, organizing the albums I tossed during my rampage last week. It may be in worse shape than when I arrived, but I have time on my side now. A little more than a month to pull myself together. I have a lace kerchief on my head made from an armchair doily, and my bare arms flutter with Post-its I stuck there so I'd be ready to sort—*garbage*, *recycle*, *Goodwill*, *Pop Culture Museum*. I thought if I looked like a serious organizer I'd act like one.

I'm doing the classical albums first—they're safe, impersonal. Heaped in a corner where I'm unlikely to come across a song title I remember from campfire, or a radio tune that Willa and I danced to at the beach.

Then I turn to my right, and *pow*. A picture of seven-year-old Willa, playing in the mud at the Far Pond, right at eye level. Propped against an orange corduroy cushion on top of the waist-high cubby shelf, like it's the featured title in a record store display.

Or a viper waiting to strike.

It's the back cover of *Lovedrenched*, Graham's third album, written in the glow of the year he and Angela first moved here, when Willa was a toddler.

I take it and sit back on my heels, setting it on my lap. Willa's in black and white, but even so her smile is dazzling. Her thin legs are streaked from knee to toe. She'd been looking for the butterflies that lay their eggs in milkweed leaves, by the pond's rich soil, she'd told me. She looks so happy. So young and free.

The room's a mess, but I'm sure I didn't leave *Lovedrenched* like that, upright, on top of a pile. Someone's been poking around. The kids, maybe.

I turn the album over. There's Graham, lying on his back in the pond, holding his guitar with his eyes closed. He looks like he's levitating, a god. The sunlight's rainbow bubbles hide the raft under his back, so it seems like an act of great faith and daring, a miracle: my uncle trusting that he and his dear Gibson won't sink into the opaque green water.

I wonder if the raft is still on the bank, waiting patiently for a passenger. It's probably rotted to splinters by now. I wonder if it still feels like magic at the pond, if the milkweed butterflies still cluster there, laying their precious eggs.

Windward Realty would want me to clean the raft up…

I set the album down, peel the Post-its from my arms, and go outside.

I remember the way: Willa showed me. Start at the old logging road north of the house…

From there I head farther north, the afternoon sun on my left. Spruces and evergreens cool me as I walk; it's shady on this side of the property, shrouded in mystery. I remember these soothing sounds. The high chatter of crickets, even in daylight. The chirps of the small birds that nest in the inland reeds. They're more gentle-sounding than the shore birds.

The Far Pond is where Willa and I became fledgling songwriters. A whole afternoon could pass without more than a scrap of music we liked, but we didn't care. It felt so good to team up—me in charge of lyrics, Willa the music—and make something that hadn't existed before. After years of feeling weak, worthless, songs were little worlds I could control, but they didn't leave me hollow like messing around with my classmates had. And after saying things I didn't mean for so long—to my father, Patricia, whoever—the words poured out. Words that matched the inside me. Willa accepted all of them without judgment. She didn't just *hear* me, she transformed the scattered outpourings of my heart into music. Into things with strength, structure. Things that were lasting.

Magic, isn't it? Willa had whispered to me when she first led me to this pond so that we could write without anyone knowing, or bothering us. She'd closed her eyes, tilted her chin to the sky.

When I'm almost there, something snaps sharply to my right. I stop and fiddle with my shoelace, listening for Fiona and Kauri.

But I hear no one. I keep walking, alert to every sound.

Twenty feet from the pond, where I can catch glimpses of the water's shine, a little blue interlaced with the green foliage, there's a series of cracks. Right behind me. I freeze. "It's okay, guys," I say. "I'm not mad. C'mout, c'mout, wherever you are. Kauri. Fee, c'mon."

Nothing—odd. Now that we're friends and I'm their unofficial summer piano teacher, they usually giggle at this point.

A ridiculous thought. If I turn, I'll see her familiar gold hair, and she'll emerge from the trees and smile and explain that it's all a mistake. She's been here all along, she left out the album with her picture on it so I'd come here and find her...

And she'll say that it's the third sign. Angela choosing me as sole heir, our lyrics neatly transcribed in the notebook twenty years ago but not reappearing until recently... They're not coincidences. They're calls.

Calls from her.

I hold my breath and turn, but of course there's no figure haunting these waters, no gold hair. Nothing but green.

I'm angry at myself. A little frightened by what my mind is capable of here. I'm thirty-seven, a teacher, a reasonable person. Yet out of no more than an album placed where I don't remember leaving it, I'd concocted a magical scenario in which Willa had left me greetings from the beyond.

"Motherfuh... *No no no no...*"

I spin back toward the pond and it's Shane. In the middle of the water, flailing, his frantic slapping noises making a steady backbeat to his shouts: "No no... Fuuuhuuck!"

I run to the shore. His back is to me as he straddles the sinking raft like it's a horse and holds his guitar over his head and kicks, leaning wildly this way and that.

I have to laugh as I slosh in. I can see the problem—one of the life vests Graham nailed under the crude raft has come loose and drifted off, so the raft's sinking.

Of course, I realize as I surge toward the capsizing craft, the cold water a whole-body shock. Shane was snooping through the Rec Room albums, found *Lovedrenched*, and, naturally, got inspired to hike here to re-create his idol's legendary cover. The pond's hard to find, a half-hour walk on the northeastern edge of the property, but he's probably been roaming the grounds for days.

There's always a logical explanation.

Shane's muttering an impressive stream of profanity. "Fuck this fucking slime pit... Ow!"

"Is that an official vessel distress call?" I yell as I sidestroke forward, now just a few feet from him.

He looks over his shoulder in shock, eyes wide. Surprise gives way to relief that I've appeared, a miracle. But his sudden shift has thrown him off balance and he's off the raft and trying to tread water with only his legs, his guitar hoisted overhead like a barbell.

I swim up. "Here. I've got it." I grab the neck of the guitar while he holds the other end.

"Well," he pants. "This isn't. Embarrassing. In the slightest."

We kick our way to shore, each paddling with one arm, the guitar shaky above us.

A minute later we're on the muddy bank, dripping, wringing water from our clothes. I yank off my head kerchief and rub at the spattering of drops on the guitar. "There. Is the inside okay?"

"I think so... Just feeling ridiculous."

"Don't. I've always wanted to try out my ocean rescue technique from Girl Scouts. I'm just disappointed we didn't need to blow up our shirts into flotation devices."

"I think you deserve a badge, anyway."

Glug, glug, glug—we turn at once. We survey the scene of the disaster, just in time to catch the raft becoming vertical, then bobbing valiantly. A second later, it's gone. All that's left are bubbles. And one ancient red life vest, floating like a dead fish.

"I drowned the raft," Shane says, his hand to his forehead. "I'm so sorry."

"It's okay. Hey, you're bleeding."

"Am I?"

I hold his elbow to inspect the V of blood on his right bicep, blot it gently with the kerchief. "I don't think you need a tourniquet. Darn, another scout skill I can't bust out."

"You're ruining your pretty hat..."

"It's nothing. Let's get you cleaned up. There's first aid stuff in the kitchen."

He looks back once more at the spot where the raft was, and I know what he's thinking.

"Shane. Leave it."

"I can probably still find it. The raft's part of this place. I feel horrible."

"It's a bunch of two-by-fours and a rotting life vest. You did me a favor by sinking it."

We sit on the sunny porch steps, wrapped in musty quilts I unpacked from a Goodwill-bound box in the hall—his, yellow-and-white check, mine, purple paisley. Though the long walk back was warming and now only our tennis shoes, lined up side by side on the grass in front of us with the tongues lolling out, are still wet. We were both quiet on our return hike, but it was an easy silence, one that gave the forest's big and small glories—evergreen trees so triangular they looked like children's drawings, chittering squirrels spiraling up trunks, holding still until we passed—their due. I was glad Shane didn't feel the need to fill the time with chatter.

We're dry and warm, but we linger, lazy and comfortable after our adventure.

Shane adjusts his quilt around his shoulders. "So," he says, mischievous. "Aren't you going to ask?"

"Ask what?"

"What I was doing in the pond?"

"I already know. You were re-creating Graham's raft stunt from the *Lovedrenched* cover."

"Yeah. I saw the album in the Rec Room this morning. Sorry, did I mess up your system? I didn't mean to—"

"No, don't worry about it."

"Anyway, I bet I looked pretty foolish out there," Shane says.

"A little." I think of him flailing in his sopping green shirt and laugh. "Like a frog whose lily pad betrayed him."

"So. She *can* laugh. It's a nice sound."

I'm defensive: "I laugh all the time."

"At home, maybe. Hard for you to laugh here, I guess."

His comment has stopped my laughter instantly. I brace myself for what's to come. He has an anxious look in his eyes that tells me he wants to talk about the Kingstons.

"*Stunt,*" he says.

"What?"

"You said Graham's raft photo was a *stunt*. Interesting choice of words. I guess he could be a little much, huh?"

I stand, tighten my quilt around my shoulders, and go up the steps to the porch.

I reach high to touch a little brass hook screwed into the roof beam. It's the hook that held Kate's dinner-bell triangle. I haven't found the triangle itself, which hung on a leather strap.

I remember that sound. Solid, commanding, comforting, like Kate herself. Dear Kate, who decamped to become a state park host in Arizona in the eighties after everything fell apart here, then died peacefully in her trailer at age eighty-one a few years back. She and I wrote for a long time.

It's probably about six o'clock right now. Willa and I would be dashing across the field from wherever we were writing. The pond, the beach. "Cornbread!" she would shout to me as we ran. "With lemon-marionberry tarts and zucchini fritters!" Her sense of smell was as keen as an animal's.

A little much. Yes. Graham was everywhere. He took up all the space here—the great songwriter. His genius and struggles and needs left no room for anyone else's. Willa and I hid our songwriting away, tucking it into corners. I bet Graham had never written or played a single word at the pond before that photo shoot; the album cover was a fraud.

Finally, I answer Shane. "Sometimes he could be a little over the top." I turn to him and lean against the porch railing. "So, was your field trip today worth it?"

"Hardly. I clearly wasn't able to re-create the cover. But to be fair, that photo shoot was so elaborate. Really big-time. Graham was ecstatic about it." Something passes over his face then—embarrassment about how much he worships my uncle, I imagine. How he's inserted himself into the past like one of Graham's intimates. He quickly amends: "*Looks* ecstatic on the cover, I mean. I read that in an article. About how happy he was, wrapping *Lovedrenched*. I sound like a fanatic."

"Not at all."

"I'm lucky you found me. Though I have a confession to make."

"What?"

"This is only my second-best guitar." He thumps it and grins. "If I'd been a true fan, I'd have brought my best onto that raft."

I think for a minute, then beckon him to follow me. "Come on."

Inside the Rec Room, I hand him the album.

"Oh. No."

"Take it. Please. You're doing me another favor. One less thing to catalog."

He holds it up carefully, reverently, by the edges. "God, he's so young here. But he looks immortal, doesn't he?"

My eyes avoid the back cover. I've had enough haunting images for one day. Instead I come around to his side of the album and show him how the light bubbles obscure the sides of the raft on the cover, and make it seem as if Graham is closer to the water than he is, that he trusted magic to hold him aloft and keep his favorite guitar safe. "The raft used to be much wider than when you got to it. So don't feel guilty about not bringing your number one guitar."

"I *do* feel better, even if the illusion's somewhat shattered. Ever the teacher, huh?"

"I guess. Though my classroom feels a million miles away. I miss them, my kids."

He looks at me, nods. "I'll bet you're a good teacher. You were so calm today."

"Thank you."

"Well, thank *you*. I'll treasure this. It was Angela's favorite of his, she told me at Arbor View."

I'm so glad to know this that I beam at him. So his outing wasn't about the great man, the immortal Graham. At least not entirely. It was also for Angela.

"What?" he asks.

"Oh. I like the way you talk about Angela. How fond you were of her."

"Ah."

"You know, she's the one who found this place. Not Graham."

"Was she? I'll bet not a lot of people know that." His voice… He may be a lousy singer, but when he speaks, it's smooth and deep.

I force myself to hold his gaze, moving my hands in the finger stretch that's become a nervous compulsion around him. Widening them in front of me. It's an exercise designed to stretch the finger span. I have the kids say *Abracadabra* when we do it during warmup. They love that.

He reaches over to me, but before his hand can touch my temple, I dodge.

"Sorry. You have a little pond gunk there, over your right ear. That's all."

"Oh." Embarrassed, I swipe at the wet leaf stuck to my skin. "Well, I should go change."

"Me, too. Sorry I keep inflicting personal injury on you. Shock, that first day. Now glacial water exposure..."

"Not quite glacial," I say, smiling. "We're only a little above sea level. But you did expose my ear canals to pond amoebae."

"That's a risk people seriously underestimate. Thanks again for rescuing me."

"Any time."

18

Slipstream

A few days later

Paul isn't happy about my sudden decision to stay here through August. He's hurt and confused and he has every right to be, since I've given him no explanation. Just a hasty message a week ago, the day he'd planned to pick me up at Logan. I'd left it at ten a.m. Boston time, when I knew he'd be teaching summer school.

"What's going on?" he asks quietly. "Just what kind of pack rat was this long-lost aunt of yours?" He tries to laugh, a sad little sound.

"I'm really sorry, Paul. I'll send you a check for the Cape Cod deposit."

I wait, the receiver cold against my ear, the crackle of our bad connection as loud as the skids and whacks of the skateboarders doing their tricks outside the phone booth. Two cars pass on the highway before he speaks again.

"A *check*. Great. You do that. I'll look forward to receiving your *check*." He hangs up—Paul never hangs up first.

Funny. I keep trying to picture him, but it comes out as mental lists. Paul is tall, lean. He plays handball. Paul has blond hair and a silky blondish-red beard. He reads detective novels and his favorite food is shrimp fried rice. Once last year, after our hundredth fight, when I told him I needed space, he left a coffee table book about comets on my doorstep. Paul has blue eyes. But I can't remember what it feels like to look into them.

I buy a frozen yogurt for my lunch and carry it to the dunes, but it melts into chocolate chip soup, like the custards Willa used to buy only so she could talk to Liam. Liam. Angela's detective tried to track him down after Willa ran away, but couldn't. Someone thought he was surfing and teaching English in Bali.

I sit, watching surfers, tourists picnicking, the slow rightward progress of a tanker far off at sea.

"Jackie!" Kauri runs up to me the second I'm through the gate. "We found something important!"

"*I* found it," Fiona corrects him. "He was scared of the raccoons."

Proudly, Kauri waves something like a homemade maraca, releasing a high, bell-like sound, and hands it to me: it's cold and smooth in my hand. A small mason jar with the lid rusted shut. The smallest of Kate's jars, the size she used for her strongest relishes and chutneys.

I shake it, rattling the key inside, echoing the music Kauri made.

"It was under the steps of one of the big cabins no one's using," Fiona says. She points to the trees flanking the field downhill on our right, on the north side of the property. "There's a whole raccoon *fam*ily living under there. A *colony*. We saw a baby go in…"

I nod and look where she's pointing, though I don't need her explanations.

I'm the one who hid the key under the steps of Slipstream cabin. Twenty years ago.

"We thought it might be important," Kauri says. "Like a key to someone's safe."

"It's too teeny for that," Fiona says to him. To me: "Do you know what it opens?"

I trace the raised grape design on the smooth glass. "No. But I really appreciate you braving the raccoons and getting it for me. Those raccoons must have known you were people to trust."

"Can we show you where we found it?" Kauri asks.

"Please."

I let them lead me. I've avoided it, but I'm ready now, and it'll be easier with these two along.

Into the trees, *left at the stump that's like a giant guitar pick*. It doesn't look like a guitar pick anymore. It's crumbled, hollowed out in the center.

"Giant's Cup," Fiona says as we pass.

So they've found their own favorite places here, made up their own fairy-tale names.

At Slipstream, we peer in at the darkness under the porch steps: eight sets of yellow eyes peer back. I make the expected sounds of appreciation, commend them on their bravery for grabbing the key from the raccoon's compound.

I gaze up at my old cabin. Padlocked. Windows boarded up. The right handrail, the one I was too lazy to nail in place and fixed with gum, is gone now.

"It's abandoned," Kauri says with relish. He must not realize that his family's cabin on the other side of the field looked just as forlorn a few weeks ago, until I unlocked it, pried the boards off with a crowbar from the shed, swept and cleaned.

"Should we go in?" I ask.

"How?" Fiona says.

I reach into my back pocket and pull out my big key chain, shaking it. A rattle of the sticky doorknob, a hip-bump against the thick wood like it's my disco partner, and we're in.

No condoms or drug needles on the floor, thankfully. Nothing on the walls but bare pine. I wonder what happened to the Blondie poster I stuck to the door with yet more wads of gum. No more dresser, and the bunches of lavender Angela gave me the first day we talked have been removed from the mirror frame, too, or crumbled to dust. No sign that I was ever here.

But the bed frame is still by the window, covered with a tarp, and as the kids are looking out the window, I feel behind the chunky wooden bed's legs. Of course there's nothing. I may have the key now, but I haven't been able to find what it opens.

So many nights I slept here. At first it had felt unfamiliar, being the only one under this little roof (though eventually Willa had crashed here sometimes after we'd had an evening beach outing). But gradually I'd come to love my solo cabin, surrounded by the sounds and life of so many other families.

And then Colin had come, and he'd joined me on this bed, or I'd joined him in his. Angela and Graham, technically, temporarily, my guardians, had seemed unfazed by how much older he was than me, or what he would tell me. They didn't care where Willa and I slept or if there was a roof above our heads. I look out the window at Plover—no more sign on that one. How Willa and I had howled when a branch had dipped over it, transforming the name to "lover." Colin runs a small organic farm in Maine—I saw his ad in a newspaper circular once, and he looked happy.

Fee and Kauri are chattering about what a fine playhouse the cabin would make, about who might have lived here once.

"The giant!" Kauri says.

"It's too small," Fiona says.

"Maybe it can be the giant's dollhouse," Kauri says, with less conviction.

I'm about to tell him what a good idea this is—Fiona can be so harsh—when she says, "That's a good idea, Kaur."

They exchange a look of disappointment when I lock up, but I pretend not to notice.

When we're back at the main house, drinking lemonade on the porch, I say, "Tell you what. Want to trade keys?" I pull Slipstream's off the ring and hold it out. "I'll take the teeny one and you can have this one. Then you can visit any time you want. But promise not to go near those raccoons again, 'kay?"

"Okay!" they chorus. Fiona hands me the jar and they fly down the field back to their giant's dollhouse.

Shane and Mat come around the corner.

"So the kids showed you their latest discovery," Mat says. "Kauri's convinced it's the key to Thumbelina's treasure chest." He's proud of his son's imagination.

"Maybe it is," I say.

Mat laughs, but Shane's quiet, watchful. As they eat their lunch and talk about the afternoon's session plans, he keeps glancing over at me, and the jar with the little brass key inside.

In the parlor, with the shades drawn and the door shut, I struggle with the aluminum lid, trying to wrench it open to get at the key. I wrap it in a T-shirt, hitting the top with my hairbrush like it's a stubborn mustard jar lid. I have red welts on my palm, but the lid is stuck tight.

Do you know what it opens?

No.

It's been a long time since I lied to kids.

19

The Giant

1979
Six days after Colin arrived

Dear Ray,
Colin helped us build a slide for the kids this morning. Entertaining them cuts into our songwriting, I guess, but maybe I'm becoming like Willa—I need less sleep. This place gives me energy. We find time for everything important...

We built a waterslide running down half the field, taking advantage of the slope from near the house down to the center of the bowl. It was my idea—I'd always wanted a Slip 'N Slide after seeing the commercials, but hadn't grown up in a Slip 'N Slide household.

"It was more of a *Sip-n-Sigh* household," I told Colin and Willa after lunch, as we staked the huge roll of Angela's gardening plastic in place. Willa laughed appreciatively along with Colin, but mouthed *Sip and Sigh* to herself when he'd turned his back. I knew she was thinking that "Sip and Sigh" could be a song.

"Poor Jackie," Colin said. "At least you're making up for your deprivation now."

We slicked the plastic with detergent and water and took turns shooting down, and within five minutes every kid there was begging for a turn. The angles of the bowl did the work for you. You started out slow, and then you picked up speed, then you were flying, and then, just before it got too scary, the field leveled out.

Even the hordes used it. Even Graham.

"Every castle should have a slide," he said, launching his huge body onto it, singing one of his obscure English ballads all the way down, something about the *castle keep, dark and deep.*

I could just imagine how Patricia would've wailed if I'd tried something like this in our patch of groomed side garden in the city. *Robert, we'll have to resod!*

As we watched Colin climb back up the hill after his third ride, dripping and laughing, shaking his long hair, Willa murmured, "He never stays this long."

"Never?"

"Never. I'm telling you, it's because you're here."

True, he sat by me at meals and campfire, talked to me, sought me out. But we hadn't kissed.

Willa thought this was irrelevant; she had decided it was preordained that Colin and I would come together. I dismissed this, but yesterday morning, when she and I were in Slipstream talking about Colin and Liam—with whom she'd had three private surfing dates—we'd looked out the window at his cabin. A branch had dipped over the burnt wood sign that said Plover, covering the *P*, and we'd burst out laughing.

Now Willa said casually to him as he walked up to us, wet from his slide, "Hey, Col. Me and Jackie and Liam are camping on the beach tonight. Want to come? The stars have been amazing lately."

"Sure!"

When he left to buy food for our camping expedition, I turned to her. "Why, Willa Kingston, you crafty girl."

"I think you're rubbing off on me." She laughed and flew onto the slide, graceful as an arrow.

I watched her. I didn't want her to change too much. I liked her dreamy, gentle ways, her honesty. But she'd said it as if this talent of mine—for nudging and plotting—was so obviously a good thing. I couldn't help but savor the compliment.

Before nightfall, the four of us had built a fire at the beach and set up our skylit beds.

Willa and I had spent the night on the beach, just the two of us, five times now. First to check it off my list and then just for fun. I understood why she loved it—the steady surf washing away every worry, big and small. The contrast between cold face and cozy body, wrapped tight in a sleeping bag. My dreams on campout nights were vivid and expansive and restful, not the fitful, crowded dreams I often had indoors. "High-Ceilinged Dreams"—I'd played around with a song about them.

But I'd only experienced these new pleasures with Willa next to me on the sand. I had no interest in sleeping outside completely alone, like she sometimes did.

After the four of us set up our little camp, Willa and Liam went for a night swim and Colin and I sat by the fire, passing the last of his strawberries and one of Angela's joints back and forth, listening to Wolfman Jack's friendly rasp on Colin's radio.

"She should enter this crop..." he said, holding the weed so deep in his lungs that his stomach became concave under his jutting rib cage. He exhaled: "...in the county fair. Bless you, Angela. An invention born of necessity for Mrs. Graham Kingston, I guess. Here."

"Why do you say stuff like that?"

"What?"

"Hint that Graham's so hard to live with."

"What? Oh. Just that Graham isn't always such a jolly gold giant. Pass that back, will you?"

I handed him the joint. "You mean he can be moody? All artists get moody once in a while. If they spent every second worrying about etiquette, what'd be left for creating?"

"Sorry, but that..." He took a long drag, held it, blew a slow plume up at the sky. "...is grade-A horseshit. I hate that *indulge the stormy artiste* garbage. You wouldn't be so quick to defend him if you hadn't seen something interesting. Spill."

"But I *haven't* seen anything. Honestly. The only time I've seen him moody is when you tease him."

"But he's got you babysitting for him."

"I don't mind it," I said, too quickly. "It's fun."

"Hey, I'm sorry." He nudged me. "Jackie?"

I shook my head, staring at the fire and refusing to look at him, but he tapped my knee with one gentle finger, speaking more quietly.

"He's a *brilliant* man. I wish I had a hundredth of his talent. Maybe I'm a little jealous. And he's helping people, offering up his studio, opening his home as a...waystation. It's a kindness, really generous of him, I don't deny that."

"How generous of you to admit it."

"Is this a fight?" He touched my hand. "Hey, look at me. I'm not trying to be a know-it-all. I like you. I just don't want you to be...disillusioned. If you find out he isn't perfect. He gets something out of playing the host, too."

Willa and Liam came in from the water then, dripping, laughing, shaking their hair on us, unzipping their wet suits. They exchanged a long kiss before sitting together across the fire.

"Just be careful with the hero worship," Colin murmured. "That's all."

I watched Willa through the wavery air above the fire; she was preoccupied with Liam, winding one of his wet curls around her finger. "I know Graham's not perfect," I whispered.

I thought we'd dropped it. We finished another joint and roasted marshmallows, and I taught the other three dances to the kind of pop radio music I loved and they pretended to hate, Willa and me sneaking a glance during The Hustle, which was on her list. Her Hustle was as good as it was going to get, but she kept putting off our disco outing, insisting she could improve. But prescribed group dancing didn't suit Willa. Her body wanted to float free, to do its own thing; it rebelled at the mechanized twirls and claps of The Hustle and The Hot Chocolate and The Bump.

Liam, usually so reserved, had the brilliant idea to make our own disco lights by bouncing a flashlight on a shard of abalone shell, through a pine cone. It wasn't Teena's DreamTraxx, and the sand made it hard to slide and hip-bump, to drop into a "dishrag" in Colin's arms. But this felt better. Teena's hadn't been about connecting with other people, not really. Not for me. It only looked that way.

We collapsed onto the sand after "MacArthur Park," and when we'd stopped laughing, Colin said, staring up at the hills, "Who's up for a little hike?"

"Where?" I asked. The sky had gone hazy, but maybe that was only thanks to Angela's blue-ribbon crop.

"The falls. I've never gone after sunset."

I glanced at Willa; we all knew this was the hour Graham would be up there. Right after campfire, which we'd skipped tonight.

"Let's go on the swing instead," I said, shooting Colin a fierce look.

"C'mon, I want to see genius in action," he said. "Willa, you've watched him up there before, haven't you?"

I was sure she'd object. But instead she didn't answer, just stood. And, without a word, led the way up to Graham's private ritual spot.

It was a steep hike, and the four of us hiked silently: Willa, Liam, Colin. Me.

I'd never been higher on this hill than the fork where the path up from the beach split—the left trail heading to the Kingstons' gate, the right looping up past the ponds to the falls.

The climb was steep and I was winded, but I kept the others in sight as we got closer to Graham's special place, winding around the wooded hills in the fast-fading light. I heard the falls before I saw them. First a whisper, then a trickle, then a rush.

And then I glimpsed him through thick branches in twilight. Graham. Sitting shirtless, with his back against the falls. His hair was wet and he was soaked, but his notebook sat on a dry rock nearby. Closed. His eyes were closed, too, chin tilted up, and his ring fingers were pressed to his thumbs, his hands raised shoulder-level in front of him. Like he was a vessel waiting for inspiration to pour down from above.

This was *genius in action*? It was too absurd. The water had parted his hair down the middle and pasted it on either side of his head so he looked more like a grade-school kid about to take a bad school picture. I'd expected to find him scribbling in his notebook. Ripping out pages, fighting through ideas, fighting to master his doubts and write something brilliant. But he looked so…passive. I had to clap my hand over my mouth and nose to keep from snorting out loud. I hated to give Colin the satisfaction, even foggy from pot and worn out from hiking.

But then Graham rose and left the falls pool, walked to the ocean-facing cliff. He stood between two thin young tree trunks near the edge, held them, and leaned forward.

I was about to burst through the greenery and pull him back, but Willa stopped me. She shook her head, pressed her finger to her lips. So this was normal. This was part of the ritual. Now I had the answer to Colin's question. She'd come here many times to spy on her father.

Graham, tilting thirty degrees over the ocean, had stilled

himself; his wet hair, whipping wildly, was the only part of his body that moved. I felt as I had once at an elementary school field trip to the de Young Museum, when the docent had ushered my class into the sculpture hall, and I'd stared, mesmerized, at a marble of an Etruscan man charging into battle. His mournful eyes made it clear that he would fail, would die, but his body soared forward anyway.

If Colin had brought me here to show Graham up as a fraud, someone not worth worshipping, he'd failed.

I looked at Colin and found, to my relief, that his expression was serious, that the moment had moved him, too, in spite of his fondness for needling Graham. If he'd still been laughing, I would have resisted my attraction to him. Colin faced me for a minute, contrite. Then we both turned our attention back to my uncle.

A twig cracked under someone's foot, Graham turned his head sharply, and we scattered.

It was disorienting at this elevation. You couldn't distinguish the roar of the waves from that of the falls, and I got separated from the other three. I looked up—Willa had tried to teach me stars—but I'd been a distracted pupil and the sky told me nothing. Blurs, blinking lights, blobs that could be airplanes or nebulae or Skylab leftovers—it all looked the same.

I glanced down and noticed a bright mound gleaming in the dark, at my feet. Twenty feet away, another. Graham's shell cairns. Everyone knew about them—piles of white shells that marked his path. Once, years ago, Graham had stumbled, high, off into the thick woods, and it had taken hours for him to find his way home. He added the cairns so it would never happen again, completing the project the summer before he got the idea for the Sandcastle's shell spire.

The trail was cut into the hillside in a long, gradual spiral, and it was astonishing how helpful the little shell piles were, guiding me in the falling dark, like neon. Like magic.

The hill had helped me, Graham had helped me; by the last hundred feet, when I could hear the waves and my friends' voices, I was ecstatic.

I made it to the beach only a few minutes behind them.

"We were just coming back for you!" Colin said. He sounded sober, and genuinely worried. A little repentant, too, after his failed mission to dethrone Graham. He hugged me and kept his arm around my waist.

"I followed the cairns." I was still amazed that I'd made it.

We talked late into the night, passing a jug of Almaden, cheese, two entire loaves of bread. Willa told us what it was like here in fall and winter, when there were fewer guests, when it rained, and sometimes snowed.

"It's perfect," she said. "The deepest quiet."

Liam opened up about his favorite surf spots and secret camping spaces and the food in Costa Rica. Colin described everywhere he'd worked over the past year—five states, a dozen jobs.

And I, who usually told the stories, this time mostly listened.

Tired, relieved that Graham hadn't seen us and that the hill had guided me back safely, I reclined against Colin's chest, letting the others' voices wash over me. When the wine jug came my way I didn't sip, but pressed its cold neck to my hot one and passed it on. I wanted to hold on to my exhilaration, to the sense of clarity I felt tonight.

I kept picturing how regal and brave Graham had looked, leaning forward between those two trees, trusting that they'd bear his weight. I knew why he stood on the edge of his cliff. It wasn't just a cheap high, or ego. He did it to remind himself that there were scarier things than trying to make music.

Li and Willa went quiet, except for the occasional rustles and muffled sighs from their shared tarp.

Colin bent over me, dipping his head low to kiss me upside down, his hands on my knees, trailing up my thighs. A few months ago I'd have taken his hands in mine before it started to feel too good, led him behind the grassy dunes. Looking for reversal, control. But I was braver now. Here, I found I didn't want to do that. It felt all right with him, to lie back, to be the one tended to.

To let fate take its course.

20

Running a Pound

1999
One week after Jackie found the key

"Beer break?" Mat lifts the lid of the cooler. "You've been working hard all day, and it's a hot one."

I smile but shake my head. "It's two, and a beer'll make me so sleepy I won't get anything else done today, but thanks." I'm on the front porch, labeling the boxes of kitchenware I've filled for tomorrow's Goodwill pickup. My doily head kerchief has become a sweat mop, wadded in my back pocket.

Mat's relentless: "It's five, East Coast time. C'mon, Jackie." Mat has taken charge of the cooler, an ancient green metal Coleman from the pool equipment shed. He's the only one who can lift it. "Okay, if you don't want beer, there's also a local pear cider I picked up. Oregon pears. Only six proof, pure fruity refreshment, excellent work fuel."

Shane, who's marking up some sheet music in the porch hammock, says, "Leave her alone, Mat. Not everyone has your tolerance."

"You're just jealous, Cuzzy Bro," Mat says good-naturedly. To me: "'Cause I'm pure muscle."

"I'll take one of those ciders," I say, figuring I'll have a few polite sips before returning inside to work.

Mat sends Shane a triumphant look, cracks the cider open barehanded on the porch rail, and offers it to me.

I take a sip, then a long swallow. "That's really good," I say, surprised.

Mat toasts me with his beer and Shane laughs. "You're a corrupting influence, Mat."

"Who, me? I'm a force for pure good, Chook."

"Then give me one of those."

I'm laughing at the two of them, pressing the cold neck of the beer against my own damp neck and surveying the busy field. We all fixed up the Doughboy pool together yesterday during their break, scrubbing and cleaning it. I personally taped the rusty ladder. It's an eyesore, but it's a pool again.

Piper and her wife, April, and their friends who've come up from LA for a few days are in the water doing a synchronized swim routine to the Radiohead blaring from the speakers. Mat always drags them out on Sunday afternoons, transforming the bowl into a giant stereo.

Fiona and Kauri and some other kids someone brought are at the picnic table, working on the old Farrah Fawcett Glamour Center head I found in a closet. They're striping Farrah's hair green and purple with homemade dye—Jell-O powder and water made into paste.

Three bare-chested guys and a bikinied woman are playing a whooping game of Frisbee around the campfire circle. Another woman is sunbathing, facedown, lazily throwing a tennis ball for her yellow Lab.

Other visitors, farther off, are engaged in their own Sunday afternoon diversions. Sketching, reading. It's like a picture in one of those Richard Scarry books I loved as a child: happy activity everywhere. With more skin.

That's when I see him.

He's walking up the center of the field, in a navy sweater vest and navy button-down and black pants, a suitcase in his hand. The sun glints off his light hair and beard. He's squinting. Of course he forgot sunglasses. Does he own sunglasses?

I take in the scene through his eyes. The shirtless Frisbee players, the barebacked sunbathers, the raucous swimmers, the kids with their rainbow Farrah bust.

And me. Standing on the porch barefoot, in a short yellow sundress I found in the sauna changing room this morning. Drinking at two in the afternoon and laughing with two strange men.

"Who's that, a traveling salesman?" Mat asks. "Census taker? *Unnnnder*taker?"

Shane turns to see who he's talking about.

"No," I say. "That's Paul."

"So you just forgot to mention that you're managing some sort of...what? *Commune* here this summer? Boy, when I asked if you were running away with the Moonies, I had no idea how close I was to the truth."

"Paul. It's hardly a commune."

We're alone in the parlor after an awkward group dinner, the door and windows shut. It's stuffy, but though everyone moved tactfully away from the house hours ago, I don't want to take a chance on them hearing us.

Mat and Shane may look shaggy, but they showed better manners than me. They offered Paul a beer and a seat on the porch swing, asked about his flight, tried to make warm conversation. At dinner, everyone tried to include him, tried to keep the shop talk to a minimum. Compensating for my halting explanations and obvious shock, my fumbling hostess job.

Paul got the address from the school office; I'd given it to them so they could mail my lesson plan forms and fall class lists here. Instead he'd brought them personally, as a surprise. He took a red-eye with two hideous layovers. The cheapest possible flight, but a splurge on his teacher's salary.

"Not a commune," Paul says. "Compound, then. On your dead aunt's property. Which you now own, if I understand what your friends were saying out there?"

"Yes."

"Were *you* ever going to tell me?"

"Yes, of course. It all just happened. I didn't plan it, Paul. Like I said. There's an old analog studio down in the basement. It's a big deal to some people."

"And that's who all of these people are, your houseguests. Musicians."

"Not all of them. Some are friends of the musicians, and, I don't know, sometimes people just show up."

"Strays. So, not a compound. A pound." He laughs bitterly.

"That's not nice."

"I know it isn't. I'm sorry. And they're making a record out of your uncle's music."

"Yes." *And mine.*

Paul sighs and reaches down to scratch Toby's chin. "Hey, buddy. Toby missed me, at least." He's trying to joke, to lighten things up, but it comes out childish. Paul is the most mature person I know. I hate seeing him like this, knowing it's my fault.

"I'm sorry, Paul. I should have told you." I squeeze his arm. "And I'm really glad you're here."

He pulls away and turns his back on me, touching the pattern of nudes on the stamped velvet wallpaper. "The house is quite something. It's not what I pictured."

"You pictured a small house. An old-lady house."

"Yes."

"And you pictured me alone."

He nods and turns to face me, rubbing his beard thoughtfully the way he does.

"Tell me about summer school," I say. "How's Rae Simmons, have you seen her?"

"She's been coming to the Bridge program."

"Good. Good! I've been thinking about her."

A pause. "Should I tell her you'll be back by September?"

"Paul. Come on. Of course I will. That's why I asked Frances to send my papers. I've already got my ticket."

"So much for the Cape, huh."

"I'm sorry about that."

His silence is long and heavy with accusation. He clears his throat and says quietly, "Well. You just tell me your flight number in August, then. I'll pick you up at Logan. If you still want me to."

"Of course I do!" I come to him and wrap my arms around his neck, squeeze him. After a minute, he kisses the top of my head.

"So, where are we sleeping? Upstairs?"

"No. I don't sleep up— It's a mess up there." Though of course I have no idea if this is true or not.

I still haven't gone up there, to the main bedroom. Or Willa's.

I'm behind schedule. Every day, I wake up freshly determined to go upstairs and get it over with. I tell myself I'll work fast, be ruthless and decisive. But then I don't. I can run up and down the beach path all day, clamber around the bowl and the hilly grounds with my visitors. But I can't seem to climb those fourteen carpeted stairs.

"You've been sleeping in *here*? On a sofa?" Paul says. "Not even on a real bed?"

"It's been fine, see? It's really comfortable."

But there's no way the two of us can both fit on the daybed, so I drag some orange velour cushions in from the Rec Room to make myself a floor pallet. Paul, selfless Paul, insists on taking it, of course.

I don't even try to sleep. Paul tosses for an hour and then gathers his pillows and blankets.

"You can still sleep in here, Paul. Even if you're mad at me. Which you have every right to be."

"That's not it. The floor's shaking too much in here. I think you have plumbing problems. I'll sleep on that porch hammock."

"No, I will."

"I'll be fine. One of your new friends told me we should all be sleeping in hammocks, they're good for the spine. Apparently the American mattress industry is one giant conspiracy against the spine. Anyway, I want to get the flavor of the place."

"You're a good sport, Paul. I'll make it up to you tomorrow. I'll cook you a big breakfast. Your runny fried eggs and everything. The works. Even if we can't go to the Cape, we can go on a little road trip around here somewhere. Mendocino, or Fort Bragg? Would you like that?"

"That sounds heavenly." He kisses the tips of his fingers and presses them to my shoulder before he heads to the porch.

I watch him out the window. A long, agitated lump in the hammock—a restless chrysalis. He's in a *jangly* mood. But finally his body stills.

He came all this way to get treated like a party crasher. I *will* make it up to him tomorrow. Show him the grounds, take him on a romantic beach picnic. My real life is in Boston. Not in the netherworld I've created out of twenty-year-old memories. Paul has flown three thousand miles to remind me of that.

But I pause on the rug to feel for Shane. The sweet, secret shaking has stopped; he's finished.

What am I doing? I kick the leg of the daybed, the wooden lion's paw, in frustration.

The little jar with the key inside rolls out.

I cross the garden, the damp soil cold under my bare feet. I'm in only my nightshirt, but I'll be warm soon enough, after climbing the hill.

Creeeeaaak.

The studio door.

I duck behind the stone well. It's Shane. Not asleep, then.

He's come out for air. To puzzle over the grace notes of whatever track he plans to record tomorrow morning.

He enters the garden, no more than twenty feet from me. In the orange circle of the garden lamp, he looks around, rubs his hair. He touches a tomato stalk so neglected I can hear its rustle from here.

He pulls a flashlight from his shorts pocket and heads uphill, behind the garden. Purposeful; he has a destination in mind. Ten feet. Twenty, thirty.

I follow.

I have no flashlight, but it's a full moon and I can see well enough. I track his bobbing light, just like Willa once tracked me. And though I've avoided these fir thickets behind the house until now, they're still familiar.

But he doesn't slow as we pass the treehouse. I stop and glance up—it was always well-hidden, and there's not enough moonlight in this spot to see if anything's left of its base. I trail my fingers along the bark. How many pink-and-white scrapes did it leave on my clumsy legs and hands that summer? By July I could climb up the rope ladder without worry, but I was never as swift or graceful as Willa.

Shane's clambering faster now and I press on, trying to keep my panting under control so he won't hear me. We continue straight uphill, to the ridge that marks the eastern edge of the Kingston land. There he stops, his back to me, looking down over the neighboring property. He rubs his left side, under his T-shirt; he has a stitch from hiking so fast.

As I watch from behind a trunk, he picks up a rock or branch—it's hard to tell—and throws it over the ridge. He throws another. And another.

Then he turns and walks slowly downhill.

When it's safe I creep up to the ridge and look for what might have incited his rage. But it's only rolling hills and trees sloping down, down, down for acres. Toward a few distant roofs, silvery in the moonlight.

I follow Shane's flashlight downhill.

This time he stops at the treehouse. Right under it.

Against its thick trunk, he sits. Rests the back of his head on its bark, his neck stretched long. He's looking up at the dear old hideout—or, if its simple plywood frame has been battered to nothing in a storm, where it used to be. He reaches up with both hands and strums his fingers along the bark. A little washboard-music song.

What is this? Why here, of all the square feet on these 416 acres?

My head's pounding—I was too tense to eat today, nothing but that gulp of cider on the porch. I should go back for a glass of milk, bed, forget this madness. Shane has an artist's temperament and keeps artist's hours. The live oak's trunk is an inviting place to sit. That's all.

Crack.

The glass jar, slick with my sweat, has shot from my fingers and smashed on a rock.

"Hey!"

I duck behind a tree and freeze, hold my breath.

"Hey. Who's there?" Shane's up, walking in my direction. Any second his flashlight will reveal me.

I could creep away. I still know these woods. But the broken jar—I can see it from here. Big, broken pieces like cups of moonlight, waiting to give me away.

"Jackie?" His voice is softer than before. Surprised, but not angry.

I move toward him. For a minute, I stand in my white night-shirt in the beam of his flashlight.

How did we get to this point? The day started so relaxed. Me and Mat and Shane on the porch joking around, enjoying cider. And now I'm out here in the dead of night like a ghost, sneaking around…

He lowers the beam to the glass between our feet, bends to pick up the miniature key. He hands it to me, then goes for the glass, carefully wrapping the shards in a Kleenex from his pocket and setting them on a stump.

I wait for him to ask what the key opens, what the hell I'm doing out here in the middle of the night spying on him, throwing jam jars.

"Can't sleep?" he asks.

"Didn't even try."

"Jangly night."

"Yes."

"Been out here long?"

"Awhile."

"Oh." He nods.

"You can tell me if you want to be alone," I say.

"Actually, I'd very much prefer not to be alone. If you're not needed elsewhere."

"I'm not."

"Then sit with me a little while?"

We sit at the base of the giant live oak tree on Shane's spread-out sweatshirt, our backs against its massive trunk. I try not to look up. Try not to show how hard it is for me not to look up.

"So, how's your packing going?" he asks.

"I haven't been upstairs yet," I confess.

"It's hard, letting go of stuff."

"Yes." It's a relief to say it. "If I don't pick up the pace, I'll be ready to sell by *next* Labor Day."

"Terrible shame."

"Oh, right. I'm sure you're devastated by my lack of progress."

He smiles a little, and I smile back.

"I could help you if you want, on breaks. That's the least I could do. Since you're our belatedly credited songwriter and all."

"Thank you. I may take you up on that."

"So. Your guy's here. Been together a long time?"

Paul. Alone, dangling on the porch.

"I'm not... Paul is... We have a lot in common. Both teachers, same age."

"He seems like a really good guy."

"He is! He is. And he played in a garage band when he was in high school. They were called the Bananas Foster. Because his last name is Foster."

We let that hang there for a minute, let it congeal and harden into full absurdity.

"I didn't know he was coming," I admit. "It's a little awkward."

"So I gathered."

"Thanks for being so welcoming to him. That was nice of you."

He looks me in the eyes. "Not really."

I glance down at the key in my hand. Then—I can't help myself—I look up.

"It's still there," Shane says softly. "If you were wondering."

I stare at him. "You know. You know what's up there?"

He nods.

He hands me the flashlight and I shine it straight up. There. Plywood floor. The pale rope ladder looped on a high branch.

So it is still there. I wonder what it's like inside, if any of the homey touches Willa and I worked on together so happily remain.

"When did you notice it?" I ask. "You were on a hike and happened to look up right here, or what?"

Nothing.

"Shane?"

He touches my knee. His hand is warm. "Jackie, I need to tell you something."

21

A Race

I was watching the kids on the slide. Willa was in the garden talking to her mom and Colin was gone for the night, visiting some friends in Humboldt.

I was about to round the kids up for the beach when Graham came over with a metal disc in his hands.

"What's that?" I asked.

"Trash. A year's worth of trash. Who wants to race?" he yelled.

Alice, a fearless little girl from Sausalito, ran over.

"Ready, set, go!" He set the disc on the hill and watched it roll, gathering speed.

Something was flapping from it—a shiny tongue of brown-gray plastic—and it hit me. This was a recording reel. What was Graham doing?

Alice jumped on the bright yellow slide belly-down, easily outpacing the tape spool. It made it all the way to the bottom of the bowl, bouncing and skidding, the ribbon of shiny brown tape behind it, before it stopped.

"Your music's not on there, is it?" I asked gently.

He stalked toward his waterfall trail as if he hadn't heard me.

I sat on the grass and smiled blankly at the kids playing. Beyond them, the neighbor boy—the skittish one from the thrift shop, the one Willa called "our fan club"—was spying on the happy scene from the trees. A minute ago I'd have tried to coax him from his hiding spot, invited him for a slide. But all I could do was swallow the tears that threatened.

It was the first time Graham had been unkind to me. I tried to focus on that day he'd neglected his work to tell me about my mom, about "Janey."

Maybe he *hadn't* heard. If he had, he was entitled to one bad mood.

But I was glad Colin was gone for the night. It would confirm his opinion that Graham was overindulged—a spoiled *artiste*.

"Theatrics."

I looked up. Kate.

"I saw from the kitchen window."

"Is he okay?" I asked.

"He's fine. Once he threw an entire master in the ocean. This is nothing."

"I didn't know he was recording his own music again. He said it has a year's worth of stuff on it."

"It might. Then again, it might not. Take my advice and don't waste another second worrying about it." Kate gathered up the tape and rolled it back up on the spindle. "I'll leave it in the basket outside the studio door tomorrow, with the doughnuts and coffee. He'll have forgotten all about it by then." She pointed it at me. "And you should, too."

Willa came up then, with a canvas bag of new toys—Angela's old trowels and rakes and tin pots.

"For sandcastles," she said, excited. "Let's take the kids down to the beach."

"Beach, guys!" I yelled. I thought about mentioning the incident to Willa, but Kate certainly seemed nonplussed, and I didn't want to worry her over such a silly thing. So this was my moment of crushing disillusionment that Colin was so concerned about? It was nothing. Merely proof that I was in Graham's inner circle—he'd let me in enough to show me how he struggled. How he hurt.

Maybe by the end of the summer we could even talk about it, about how painful it could be when your hopes for a song were dashed. Willa and I hadn't told anyone about our dabbling, yet, but maybe we'd write something good enough to share.

By dinner, Graham was back to normal. Buoyant, in fact.

We all ate together at six, summoned by the rusty dude-ranch triangle Kate rang from the porch, crowding onto the shoved-together picnic tables. The people gathered at the tables changed constantly, but family dinner was a constant.

I was sitting across from Graham, and Willa was filling her glass up at the water urn on the porch.

"So, I have a little gig in August," Graham announced. "If it doesn't fall through. I'm playing the Gate benefit in Golden Gate Park."

"That's huge, man!"

"Neil Young and Jerry Garcia headlined last year, right?"

"It's no big deal," Graham said. "But they're giving me a bunch of comp tickets. If any of you bums have nothing better to do."

"You know I'll be there, man…"

"It's about time!" said some new guy a few feet down the table to my left. A greasy-haired man in a black T-shirt that said "Skylab Collection Crew 1979," with drawings of blood dripping down the shoulders.

Skylab guy got elbow-jabbed by the woman next to him, and he quickly added, "You know what I mean." He looked around for help, got nothing. People were suddenly intensely interested in their farmer-cheese-and-sprouts-on-date-bread sandwiches. "It's been too long since he…since you were onstage, that's all.

I mean, I get why you'd want to stay here... It's 'a magic scrap of the world.'" This was from one of my uncle's songs. "A clean corner of the dirty world, you know?"

I wished Willa was here to translate for me, to say it was nothing. I knew it had been years since Graham had performed in a real show, but was he actually *ashamed* to be purely behind the scenes now, donating the studio so selflessly, helping others make their music? The awkward silence made it seem like he should be.

The guy tried to recover: "I only meant I'd pay to watch him play live every night."

Graham nodded and swigged his beer, then directed his response, inexplicably, to me. Smiling. "I'm only an unbilled guest, it's nothing. An old friend from my Fillmore days set it up. As they say, I'll believe it when it happens... I didn't even decide to do it 'til today."

I nodded, proud that he'd distinguished me above everyone else. I wished Colin was here to see it.

Angela, who'd been eating quietly by Graham's side, got up and left, drifting behind the house. To the garden, surely. It struck me as odd that she wouldn't share in her husband's excitement, but that was Angela. She was always doing that, disappearing to tend her garden, disinterested in music-business talk. She preferred long hours in the woods with her newsboy bag, collecting interesting pine cones, or flowers to press.

Someone switched the conversation to Kenny Rogers and Glen Campbell, how their popularity *said something* about the country. Something grim.

"I'm telling you, man," a woman down the table said. "It *means* something. We're going straight back to the '50s. Cowboys and bar fights and defending the little woman's honor."

Then everyone got into a long debate about who was more painful, Kenny or Glen Campbell. That was the word my uncle always used for music he didn't like—*painful*.

I finished my sandwich, glad that the easy dinner conversation had returned. Equally glad that I'd left *The Gambler*, which I knew by heart and loved fiercely, back in my bedroom in San Francisco.

Out of nowhere, my uncle faced me once more. "Hey, Lady Sunshine. I've been meaning to tell you. Don't let that dreamy daughter of mine make you fall behind on your summer research project."

I stiffened and stared down at my plate, waiting for the rest. For words that would lay bare my lie about my diary.

But the blow didn't come. And I realized that there hadn't been a trace of mockery in the way he'd said *summer research project*, though he knew perfectly well that had been fictional. When I looked up at him, his expression was friendly.

I have thought about this moment a lot in the years since. About how good it felt to count him as an ally, so unlike the adults I'd known in San Francisco. To learn that he wouldn't use my lie to diminish me or entertain his guests. If he had, maybe I'd have kept my wall up.

And so much would've been different.

But there at the table, on that sunny midsummer afternoon, with my uncle's glamorous, shaggy friends all around, I was grateful to find warmth in his eyes. He knew why I'd tried to hide behind the "research notebook." That I'd been afraid to admit the truth—that I was lonely, and wasting away in San Francisco.

Here was everything I craved—family, warmth, noise, freedom.

My uncle had plenty of flaws, but he understood pride.

"I can take a break," I said.

"Right on. I'd hate for you to waste all summer working, Lady." He lifted his beer bottle. "To breaks."

Willa returned and squeezed next to me. "Breaks?"

Graham finished his second beer and wiped froth from his mustache. "Skylab. They should've given it brakes." He joined another conversation on his left.

We never talked about my diary lie again, my junior anthropologist disguise.

But maybe I had a trace of archaeologist in me.

Because when no one was looking, I slid an artifact into the front pocket of my culottes: the cap from my uncle's *cerveza*. I taped it into the diary, after the lyrics to "Superman."

Dear Ray,

Hope you don't mind a little Scotch tape. Or beer fumes.

I'll be gentle...

If my Vaughn Academy Spanish from Señorita Miller is correct, "Uno D'Oro" means "One of Gold."

I'm not sure why I took it. Am I regressing to thirteen instead of seventeen? Or maybe it's my marker, like in that story I read about gamblers? And... I took it because I feel indebted to him, and I don't want to forget that I owe him?

Oh, I'm lying, Ray. I'm making it so much more complicated than it is. I took the beer cap because I'm a fan. Not of his music. It's pretty, but I'm a disco girl, not a folk lady.

But somehow...look at me. A groupie. Can you be a groupie of someone's existence? Of the world they've created?

There's the evidence, undeniable, laminated under Scotch tape for you. I'm like that kid I saw in the alley behind the Dead show in Oakland last year. He pocketed some roadie's cigarette butt like it was a splinter from the True Cross.

Next thing you know, you'll be a big fat fan sandwich, stuffed with more junk that I can't resist grabbing—busted guitar strings, Black Jack gum wrappers, pulp from the pages he throws in the pools.

Watch out, Ray.

I know he's not perfect. Colin thinks I'm setting myself up for disappointment.

But I'm not perfect, either. I know what it's like to lash out. We have that in common.

I locked the diary. Hid the key in the mason jar under my cabin stairs as always. Then, instead of putting it under my mattress, as I had until now, I sought out a safer hideaway for the diary. I hiked up to the treehouse and stored it in the fat crook of the limbs on the east side.

The next entry was—

Ray, you have a better hiding place, under the treehouse. Don't get a big head.

22

Satyr

1999

"I need to tell you something," Shane says, leaning his cheek against the tree trunk.

I'm afraid. Because he looks afraid.

"I used to live here. Just over that ridge. I guess you could say I grew up next door."

I echo him: "You grew up next door."

"Yes."

"You lived next door to this place." If I keep saying it, maybe it will start to make sense.

"I did. From when I was born 'til I was twelve."

"Back when Graham was alive."

"Yes."

"And you just forgot to mention it."

"No."

I think back to the microsecond pauses in our conversations. A distant look here, a stiffness in his shoulders there, the occasional, slight reshuffling behind his features. Words chosen too carefully. How he found the pond so easily. His bitterness about this place being sold, hurling rocks over the ridge only minutes ago. I should have seen it.

"You're one of the satyrs," I say. "Willa's satyrs."

"What?"

"Willa called your family the satyrs. The goat people."

He breathes deep and nods. "Goat people. Yes. We kept a few. And sheep, for cheese. We tried alpacas, a couple of summers. Minks, one disastrous winter…not much else. Never enough to make a decent living, anyway. The bank repossessed in '82. Too bad. If my pop had been able to hold on, he might have made a lot of money. His mistake was falling in love with this land a little too early." He massages his left side again. "I'm out of practice on these hills. God, I used to run up and down as easily as…"

"Willa."

"Yes. Willa. And Angela."

"You knew them back then?"

"I knew Angela. We were sort of friends." He goes on slowly, anxious to tell the story right. "Angela and I had a special stump."

It's a cryptic, arresting opener, like the ones I favored when I used to spin my stories for Willa.

"I was a lonely kid," he says. "I used to hike over here to the Kingston land and hide in the trees to spy on everyone. The family, the never-ending parade of visitors. But especially Angela, in her garden, and the woods.

"She looked like such a nice mother. My own was… Anyway, there was always so much laughter, so much music on this side of the ridge. I thought this place was heaven."

"They wanted it to be heaven."

"Yes, and I wanted in. But for a long time, years, I watched from afar. Not *afar* enough, because Angela was on to me from the beginning. Maybe she wouldn't have noticed me if I'd used a spyglass." He waits.

"You're him. You're the boy who used to spy on us!"

"You knew?"

In spite of everything, I smile. "Yes. Willa called you the fan club."

He smiles to himself, shy. "I thought no one could see me. You were nice to me, remember? The toy motorcycle you bought me that day in the thrift store? With a tiny rider."

I hug my legs close to my body and concentrate, strain to remember until I can see it: the inside of that store. Dusty shelves, big bins, and wooden fruit crates packed with time-worn goods. I can picture a boy there. But I don't know if it's memory or imagination, if he's painted the scene for me and I'm only a spectator after the fact.

"I still have that motorcycle," he says.

"Do you?" I'm lost for a minute, dreaming, half in the past.

"You were kind, Jackie. A good person. You still are." He touches my hand.

A twenty-five-cent plastic motorcycle I bought you when you were a kid, and you think I'm a saint. You don't know me at all.

"Tell me the rest," I press. "About Angela. About why you lied."

"So... I used to spy on Angela," Shane says. "And I guess the whole time she was totally aware that I was sneaking around these hills watching her. Because one day when I was seven she said, 'Is there a little squirrel over there behind that tree? I wonder if it'd come out and make friends with me. I'm kind of lonely today.'

"She started leaving me gifts in a burned-out stump behind the hot springs. Little surprises. Cookies. Clothes. Books. My family didn't have much. One Christmas it was a portable record player and a stack of 45s. Talk about *heaven*."

"Did anyone else know?"

"It was our little secret. Angela kept a lot of secrets." He bites his lip. "So. After I left here I sent her a few of my band CDs over

the years. But I hadn't seen her since '79, same as you. She'd…
withdrawn. After Willa took off."

As I'd withdrawn from everyone I'd known here. Except
Kate, who I could never disobey; I'd taken her occasional calls.

"Go on," I say.

"Then, a year ago, right after moving out of here into the
assisted-living place, she calls me in LA. Out of the blue." He
pauses. "Jackie. The idea for this album. It wasn't mine."

"It was Angela's."

He nods. "She says she has a special project for me and I need
to come see her at Arbor View. I drove up that night.

"She says she's sick and not going to get better, and offers up
this idea. A last wish. She gives me Graham's song notebook.
But she refuses to put anything in her will about it, and has me
promise I'll tell you it was my idea, not hers. And that I won't
say I grew up here."

"But why?"

"She wanted you to decide on your own. She said, 'If it's
meant to happen, it'll happen.'"

I close my eyes.

"You don't believe me. Jackie, I know it sounds *nuts* but I
swear—"

"No. I believe you." I sigh and open my eyes, look straight at
him. "It sounds exactly like something a Kingston would say."

"I wish, god, you don't know how much I wish I'd told you
everything from the beginning. I tried a few times."

"A for effort," I say softly.

"I'm so sorry."

"That's why you knew Graham's nickname for me." *Lady
Sunshine*.

Shane nods.

It hurts. I'd thought of us as two people thrown together ran-
domly. Equally confused to find ourselves here, in this strange
place. When all along, he's had the upper hand.

"Jackie? I was trying to keep a promise to Angela."

We're both quiet, and I'm sure he's thinking the same thing—
And now it's broken.

"So it was some kind of test, whether I would agree to the album or not?" I ask. "I wonder if I passed or failed."

"I think you passed. Angela wanted it to happen. That's the only part I know for sure. I could see it in her eyes."

And maybe she did know Willa would be on the album. Willa and Graham.

And me.

A happy ending. One big happy family. On CD and vinyl, at least.

We lean our heads against the tree trunk, not speaking, for a long time.

"I don't know what I'm doing here," I say quietly.

"Here, at the house this summer? Or here, out in the woods in the middle of the night with me?"

"Both."

"I'm glad you're here. Both."

"Thank you." I squeeze the little key tightly.

"Well. Feel like going back for some midnight pancakes? I'd say we've earned them."

"Tempting. But I may stay out here a little longer, if you don't mind."

"Sure." He stands, stretches, and I watch him go, trying to get used to the fact that he grew up here. That he knows these hills as intimately as Willa. And that he lied to me.

A few feet away, he pulls his flashlight from his pocket, comes back.

"In case you need it for anything." He glances up at the treehouse, presses the flashlight in my left hand. He knows I'm clutching the key in my other hand.

And he must have guessed what I've been looking for so obsessively.

I wonder how many times he watched me here writing in it.

Locking it up. Stuffing it down my waistband before clambering up the rope ladder after Willa.

And I wonder what else he saw, spying in these woods.

I listen to Shane go. When the studio door creaks open, then
shut, I stand. I flick on the flashlight and sweep it around the
ground. Searching.

There, five feet away. The perfect branch. Long enough,
curved at the end. Not Willa's old shepherd's crook limb, but
it'll do. I reach up with it, poking at the rope until it swings
free. I tug it. Tug it again. It feels secure.

But still my heart thuds. I know where this ladder leads.

I hold the tiny key under my tongue and the flashlight in my
teeth, reach up, and climb. It's not easy, barefoot. After the first
difficult hoist, my body, though twenty years older, remembers.
Cling, grab, cling, grab.

It's dank in the treehouse. Creaky. The floor, never perfectly
level, tilts away from me at a ten-degree angle, a funhouse. But
as I edge onto the platform, it holds.

I take the flashlight from my mouth and cast the beam around.
The fabric remnants from the thrift store are still on the platform, but they've stiffened. The posters stuck to the stripped
branches are torn, rippled, faded.

What would Patricia think if she knew how much I wanted
to get my hands on the diary now, after the way I'd acted when
she gave it to me, the four-beat pause before my *thank you* a masterpiece of teenage condescension? She and I developed a decent
relationship over the years, after everything. She and my father
live in San Diego, enjoying their plush retirement. She's always
said that I came home to San Francisco at eighteen—"after that
unfortunate summer"—more "mature." I was certainly more
respectful toward her and my father. The truth is, I returned to
them pliable, quiet, little fight left in me, and this suited them
both. It seemed pointless to torment them, to waste time on

jealousy, small hurts and slights and losses, when I'd lost everything that mattered. Maybe that is maturity.

Gingerly, I cross the plywood floor and sit near the eastern
edge, set the flashlight down. I take the key from my mouth
and wrap it in a piece of fabric, placing it in the center of the
platform so it won't get lost. Lying on my stomach, I reach over
the platform, fumbling blindly, plunging my hand down into a
damp crevice where two big branches split off.

I looked here before. I looked everywhere, that last awful
day, before I returned to San Francisco. But maybe, in my grief
and rising panic, I was careless. Even if the diary has decayed to
near-nothingness, a bit of yellow plastic and moldy paper with
smudges that were once my thoughts, at least I'll know my secrets are safe in it…

But it's not there.

I wake at dawn, aching after an hour of sleep on the treehouse
floor. I take the key bundle and the flashlight and climb down
the rope, my body sore in so many places I feel like I have the
flu.

Paul is still out on the porch, snoring lightly, his long legs
splayed over the hammock, a beach towel scrunched on top of
his face as a makeshift eye mask. He must have had a miserable
night. I gently pull his blanket up over his shoulder and go inside to cook him breakfast like I promised.

Fresh orange juice, sliced bananas, sunny-side-up eggs. I'm
chasing a shard of eggshell around the bowl with my index finger when the upper studio door creaks softly. A second later I
look out the window and Shane's in the garden again. Rumpled, hair unbrushed. He looks like hell, like he hasn't slept any
more than I have. As I pour the egg in the pan and start making coffee, he stretches and turns toward the kitchen window.

Keep your head down. If you keep your head down and act busy until he's gone, he won't come in.

Remember Paul. He flew three thousand miles for you. Breakfast. Paul. Paul has never lied. It's all easy and clear with him. The way it should be.

All smooth edges, nothing to snag on, nothing to cut you.

Nothing to hold on to, either.

I look up. Shane smiles at me, waves. I can't help it—my arm moves on its own, lifting the coffeepot in invitation.

"Saving me once again," he says as he comes in through the back door to the kitchen.

"Not much sleep?"

He rolls his neck and yawns in reply, settles on the stool across the butcher-block island from me. I pour us each a big mug of coffee, and we don't speak until we're on our second.

"Thanks. So. Was it there?"

He means the diary. I shake my head. I'm still processing the fact that Shane grew up around here. That he watched Angela, and me and Willa, too, sometimes. It's unnerving, but there's comfort in it, too.

I thought I was the only one left who knew just how special this place used to be, who remembers what I was like here at seventeen.

"I'm sorry."

"I think Willa took it with her when she left for Mexico."

"If so, then she wanted you with her, in a way?"

"I guess. But maybe that's wishful thinking. Maybe she threw it in the ocean." As soon as I say it I wish I hadn't—I'm tired and it slipped out. It makes me think of her in Rosarito, sinking into the sun-strewn water. That's how I picture it—a clear, beautiful day, though I wasn't there.

"Why would she do that? I used to watch you two together, and you looked happy. I would've given anything for a friend like that."

"But at the end, right before she left, things changed. She'd barely speak to me. I don't know why. Those last days here were...chaotic. Confusing."

He nods, sips his coffee. "Natural. Where's...you know?"

"Paul. Still asleep."

"Red-eyes are the worst. They screw me up for weeks."

"You travel a lot, huh?"

"This is the longest I've stayed in one place in months. Started the year in New York, helping a friend out with an EP. Then London, a fill-in thing. LA. New York again. Chicago, somewhere in there. Are you and...?"

"Paul."

"Paul. Are you two going on any trips while he's out here?"

"I'm not sure."

He nods, a little too rapidly. And I think he knows Paul's name.

"And you two are...it's serious?"

I hesitate. "I'm not sure about that, either," I murmur.

Paul comes in. Not still asleep, then. He's dressed, his hair and beard hastily combed, but there's a diamond hash mark pattern on his forehead from the hammock. It looks like he got beaned by a waffle iron.

I'm not sure if he heard, but he's a gentleman, and probably wouldn't show it if he had. He kisses me on the cheek and I try not to shrink from him. I try to banish the unkind thought that comes with the first whiff of his Pepsodent and wintergreen rinse—*He's performing. Marking me his.*

Shane rises, his voice too loud, his smile too fixed: "Well. You two have fun today! Back down to the dungeon for me!"

"Don't leave on my account," Paul says.

But Shane goes, fast. As if we've done something wrong.

"You poor thing, Paul." I force a laugh, hopping off of my stool. I touch the grid pattern on his damp pink skin, trying to summon tenderness instead of pity. "Coffee's ready, and the eggs won't take a minute."

"Jackie."

"And we don't have any rye bread, but there are some sour-dough English muffins. Then, after breakfast, I'm going to show you the prettiest spot on the beach."

"Jackie." He shakes his head. "Don't."

I toy with the twist tie from the English muffin bag, straightening it on the butcher-block counter, fitting it into one of the deep knife marks that scar its top.

His voice is flat. "Say it. Say what you're going to say to me at that pretty spot on the beach."

I shake my head.

"Say it. It's no good, is it? You and me?"

I look up at him.

He nods. Leans down over the countertop, pressing his forehead to it.

I touch his shoulder. "I'm so sorry, Paul. I'll pay you back for the flight."

He huffs at this, waving me off.

"I knew," he says, looking up. "Maybe I came out here because I knew. So this Shane. You're with him?"

"Oh. No."

"Then what is it? You want to play groupie for the summer with these…" He gestures wildly at the window behind me, at the empty field. "These *musicians*?"

If he'd lain awake in the hammock all night thinking up how to make this easier on me, he couldn't have landed on a better way than choosing these dismissive words.

"That's not how things are," I say quietly.

"Then what? What are you looking for out here?"

"I don't know."

I walk Paul to his airport van down by the fence. When I hug him goodbye, the tenderness I couldn't summon in the kitchen comes rushing back. Especially when he squeezes me and whispers in my ear: "I hope you find whatever you came here for."

After, I wander down the trail to the beach, kick off my shoes. It's a warm afternoon, but the water's ice-cold. I wade in knee-deep, until my legs are numb. I hunt for sea glass but it's high tide and I can't find any.

I walk back at dusk, uphill through the trees on the left side. I avoid the field, but when I exit the trees, hoping to slip into the house without them noticing, Piper calls, "Jackie!" She and Fee are playing with the hose they've attached to the porch faucet.

They all summon me. "Jackie!"

"Come swimming!"

"It's too hot to work!"

"C'mon, the water feels amazing!"

Shane's voice, as usual, is not among those calling me. His silence, his cautious handling of me, stands out. But he's watching me from the pool. I can feel it all the way from the porch. He knows Paul's gone. I can feel that, too.

The day's shot, anyway. I won't get any packing done.

I turn toward them, anticipating the feel of cool water on my skin.

Fiona is chasing after a squealing Piper with the hose, her thumb making a long jet, and the mist from the arcing rope of water creates a shimmering wall in the center of the field. It's a rainbow curtain of light, a slight warp in the air. Like the waves you sometimes see on a hot day at the gas station. It gives everyone behind it a dreamy, iridescent appearance. Even no-nonsense Piper, in her big nylon shorts and clunky sandals, seems to move as gracefully as a spirit.

Behind Piper, the woods seem half-enchanted, too. It's still beautiful, this place. Still magical. *A magic scrap of the world.*

What are you looking for out here? Paul asked.

I don't know.

Liar. Because I know.

Who are you looking for? he should have said.

As I observe my houseguests from across the bowl, at the sun dancing on ferns behind the hose's fine spray, as I squint just so, I see flax behind the leaves. Gold hair moving through the woods, a young, peaceful face. Willa.

Watching from afar. I wish for it. She'll cross the field and take my hand and explain everything. Why she left, why she wrote our songs into Graham's notebook. If she took my diary to remember me, or dropped it in the sea because she wanted to erase my existence.

A second later, Fiona redirects her hose straight up, drenching herself under the shower, and the illusion is shattered. "Jackie! Come be on my side!" Kauri calls from behind the pool.

"Yeah, c'mere, Jackie!" Fiona hides the hose behind her back. She's already twitching with excitement; I'll get it full blast if I join them.

My heart lifts, and I kick off my shoes, and walk toward the pool.

I wish Willa could see that there's joy here, again.

23

"The Ballad of Ben and Rose"

1979

Willa and Colin and I huddled together in the dark, behind a stump, entranced by the pool we'd transformed with an otherworldly blue-and-gold glow. We'd stuck candles on little rafts—cork coasters from the thrift store—and set them afloat. Ten flickering votives—one for each year Rose and Ben had been married.

Ben and Rose were general favorites at the Sandcastle. Both extravagantly beautiful and small, with matching long, dark hair and long-lashed brown eyes. They'd driven their beat-up brown Datsun here from New Mexico, where they ran a pottery studio, and had seemed so happy when they first arrived back in June.

"They'll come. I feel it." Willa, always so dreamily confident that things would turn out the way they were supposed to.

"Any minute," I said. "Patience."

"A marriage hangs in the balance, you two. How can you be so calm?" Colin asked, half joking.

Willa sounded proud—"She's done this kind of thing before. She does it all the time."

I knew what she was thinking—Justice with Her Flaming Sword.

Her grandiose title for me, because of my little revenge plots at school, like the one with Mr. Stengwatts's Andes mint wrapper box. And the other day, when she and Liam told me his co-worker at General Custard's was stealing his tips from the jar. (I'd remedied that in ten minutes. One "I Know What You're Doing & Will Contact State Labor Authorities!" note in the jar from "An Anonymous Observer," written on a Monopoly ten, and tips were now, miraculously, split fifty-fifty.)

This was the first plan I'd hatched at the Kingstons'—there was little need, when the atmosphere was so idyllic.

"It's just something I do for fun," I said. Though Willa and I both knew I was lying.

"Well, good luck. Let me know how it works out." Colin caressed my bare shoulder as he left; he was seeing a college friend in a bar band in Eureka tonight. He'd invited us, but Willa and I preferred to monitor Ben and Rose.

"He's right over there," Willa whispered. "Don't move."

I thought for a second that she meant Ben, our unwitting target, but she was looking not at the pool but past me, into the woods at my right.

I mimicked her, turning my head ever-so-subtly, keeping my body still so he wouldn't know he'd been spotted. I could just make out a sliver of white T-shirt, a thin arm. The little neighbor boy again. Always on the fringes. I wondered what he thought of the unusual games we played here.

Footsteps in the dry grass. "They're coming!" I whispered.

There, from opposite sides of the field. Ben on our right, Rose on our left. Walking toward the pool.

Willa took my hand and we waited, suppressing laughter, to see if our elaborate plan would pay off.

It had started a few nights ago, as campfire was winding down.

"I'll come to bed soon, baby." Rose, at my right, had reached up playfully, expecting Ben, passing behind her, to lean down for a kiss.

But he'd muttered, "Don't bother," and stalked away. We all watched him disappear into the dark.

"And, *scene*." Graham swigged his beer and left for the waterfall.

"Sorry, everyone," Rose said. After a minute, she got up and left.

Conversation resumed, but Willa and I slipped off to the treehouse.

"Her hand was shaking," I said. "Did you see?"

"No. But he kicked a stump when he left. I know that sound."

"I wonder why they're fighting?"

We got our answer soon enough. They decided to have it out behind the stone well in Angela's garden, believing, as so many others did, that no one could hear them there.

"It's time to go back," Ben said. "Enough. Aren't you sick of it here? When's the last time we had a meal alone? One god-damned meal."

"I like it here. Taos is dead right now! What's waiting for us there?"

"The shop. Tourists, with money to spend."

"Just another week or two and we can leave together."

"I never see you, anyway. Maybe I'll go by myself."

"I guess you should, if you hate my friends so much. I'll hitch back."

But after he left, Rose's shoulders crumpled and she sobbed like an animal in pain.

"This business is murder for couples," Willa said softly. "I can't even tell you how many breakups we've had here…"

"Let's help them," I said.

"How?"

We'd laid a trail of shells and flowers from the pool to the van, which had a radio playing KGLD, *Slow Gold*, and a picnic basket from Kate waiting—she'd outdone herself, despite how sour she'd acted to our faces, how she'd said we were being busybodies and shouldn't play with other people's lives.

"There!" I cried.

Ben and Rose, crossing the field from different directions. They came to a stop by the ladder, but we couldn't hear what they were saying to each other; sound didn't carry here as it did when we were up in the treehouse.

"Do they look happy?" Willa asked.

"I can't see. He's blocking her face."

"Let me look. Don't bogart the spyglass."

I passed it.

"She's smiling," Willa said. "They're following the trail!" She handed me the spyglass, but there was nothing to see by then except the trail of shells and flowers we'd laid.

The next day at breakfast, Rose and Ben appeared smiling, hands in each other's back jeans pockets.

We'd received Graham's blessing for the plan, and he told them what we'd done. *My cupids*, he'd said, swooping his arm toward us at the picnic table.

Up in the treehouse after, basking in our success, I tried to write a song called "The Ballad of Ben and Rose." But the lyrics wouldn't come. Maybe I wasn't tortured enough to write anything great.

I grabbed the spyglass and wandered over to our window as Willa, still on a high, continued to rave about what we'd accomplished. "That was perfect. They just needed a little nudge..."

I moved the instrument around—I could now position it where I wanted with a few wrist flicks. The green blur of trees, blue sky, trees again, bright garden, the pale stucco house. There. People taking a break from the dungeon.

Rose and Graham.

Rose stood with Graham outside the studio door, smoking. A regular cigarette—nobody let Angela's perfect joints burn out between their fingers like that. Graham said something, pointing at Rose playfully, and she ruffled his hair, standing on tiptoe because he was so much taller.

It was nothing. Except the gesture looked so confident. And everyone knew Angela'd left for Marin for a few days, for some festival. Would Rose have done it if Angela was yards away, spraying her tomato leaves with tea tree oil?

But people got close in the studio. The long hours, the intensity.

"What are you looking at?" Willa asked.

"Nothing." The answer came out automatically as a breath.

And I could make it true. A slight shift of the spyglass to the right, and Rose was gone, so it looked like Graham's hair was only blowing in the breeze. A slight shift to the left, down a little, and all I could see was his smile, as if he was recalling an amusing incident from their morning session.

"Jackie?" Willa asked. "C'mon. You haven't budged from that spot."

Just your dad and Rose joking around. For all I knew, Angela had a theater pal who tousled her hair the same way. I didn't know what the rules were between Angela and Graham—if they had any. It would be naive to compare their standards of behavior with the ones on Snob Hill. Their marriage wasn't like any I'd seen.

"Who're you staring at, 'fess up."

"Just that session guy who came here yesterday," I said.

"The bassist? Have you replaced Colin already? Give me that for a sec."

I stalled, pretending I *was* obsessed with the new arrival. I held the spyglass out of her reach. She tussled, grabbing it.

"Darn, he's gone back in," Willa said, hanging the spyglass back in the little fabric-scrap hammock we'd made for it.

"Darn."

The next day, Ben and Rose took off for home, Rose cuddled against Ben's arm. We didn't know what they'd done in the van—fight, make love, both—but all that was missing was the "Just Married" sign on their bumper.

And I was glad I had lied to Willa about what I'd seen through the spyglass.

24

Adam's First Wife

1999

Bree and I lie by the pool on rusty, avocado-green chaises, soaking up the sun. Piper's in the water, drifting around on a raft, her Discman, protected in a Ziploc on her stomach, giving off tinny beats.

This is an unscheduled break. Shane and Mat told everyone they needed to "have a discussion" so everyone should take five.

That was five hours ago.

Bree is going over contracts facedown, using the missing rubber slats in her chaise as a reading window, and we're talking idly about music. Favorite album, favorite song, favorite album cover, favorite live recording of a duet, favorite song to slow-dance to...

"Favorite song to regular-dance to?" I ask.

"Marvin. 'Got to Give It Up.' What's yours?"

"Hmmm... 'I Feel Love,' Donna Summer. It's got that one a.m. disco sound, with a little danger in it, you know? I've spent *years* practicing the synth bassline. It's like a racing pulse."

She mimics the baseline with her highlighter on her stack of papers, beating out the rapid *dum-dum-dum-dum, dum-dum-dum-*

dum. "Fast as a pulse while making love," she says, low, so no one else can hear. "I've heard you playing it. That piano in the Rec Room is standing in for a person, Jackie. Poor thing, getting worked over night after night."

I laugh. "'Heart of Glass' by Blondie would be a close second…"

We discuss artists, artistic temperaments. The conversation comes around to Graham.

"You get this sort of *smeared* look around the eyes whenever anybody mentions him," she says. "Like you're intentionally wiping off any expression. Didn't you like him?"

"I love how you put things. You should make that into a song. 'The smeared look around your eyes…'"

"You're changing the subject."

"Am I?"

"You've done it before."

A white cloud-bank like a puffy figure eight floats toward the sun. "When I first met him, I liked him very much. Everyone here treated him like a god. But he was just a man. I guess he had his selfish side, when he got frustrated about not being popular anymore."

She says nothing in response and I lie quietly for a minute, listening to Piper's splashes and metallic beats from the pool, the kids calling happily to each other, far off. "No. I didn't like him."

"Thank you. I know it wasn't easy to say."

If only it was that simple. *No, I did not like my uncle.*

For a minute I listen to Bree's highlighter squeaking confidently across her pages.

"Bree?" I say.

"Hmmm?"

"How do you and James do it? Keep your marriage healthy while you're traveling, or obsessed with a new project, and working night and day with other musicians?"

"James is a saint. You'll see when he visits. There's nobody to touch him."

"So you've never been tempted?"

"I'm human." *Squeak, squeak. Squeak.* "But I don't buy into that tortured artist bit. I mean, the torture is real, but it's not an excuse for bad behavior."

"But so many people can't handle it. Even enormously gifted ones. Did you ever consider walking away?"

She stops marking up her pages. "Not in a long time. I guess I'm one of the lucky ones. It hasn't sunk me, not yet."

I think of Willa, how she never had any interest in singing professionally. How much was because of her discomfort with crowds, and how much was because she'd seen how ugly the business was, how it had swallowed up her father?

And yet the business had managed to sink her anyway, through him. I'm grateful for the songs she left in Graham's notebook, a treasure, a miracle—no matter why she put them there. I know Bree'll do them justice on the album. I just wish I had a recording of Willa singing them.

"It's a loss, though," I say softly. "When someone gifted decides to keep their talent to themselves."

"A loss for who? Maybe they get plenty of joy from it, all alone."

"No, it's useless!" Shane moans to Mat. Their "discussion," which started as a private talk down in the studio, then moved up to the garden, has spilled around the house, onto the front porch. And it keeps getting louder.

"It's lousy, Mat. I wish we could start from scratch."

I can't make out what gentle Mat answers, but it's got to be something reassuring because Shane snaps at him. "Then you need to have your ears checked, Mat!"

The fight surprises me. Shane's seemed so confident about the work until now. Full of praise for how my and Willa's songs came out, and on the rest, so sure that he was merely a conduit of decisions that the great Graham Kingston had already dictated from the beyond. That he was just shading in a few blank spots in the notebook. Like a lowly tech doing art restoration on a masterpiece.

But he keeps changing his mind on the "pivot attitude," whatever that is. He's wrestling with how the album should end, if the second half should be big and happy or stripped-down and tender. It's hard to get a sense of what the problem is. He says different things on different days.

He and Mat move around to the back of the house, so I can't make out their words, only yelling.

"This sounds serious," I say from under the damp white *Bree Lang Magical Sistery Tour* T-shirt shielding my face from the sun.

Bree chuckles, undisturbed, and continues squeaking away with her highlighter. "Shane'd better get it together or he'll lose his chance."

"Chance with the album? It's that terrible?"

"The album's genius. I mean the other chance."

"Bree. Please. He's barely out of his twenties."

"Well. Forget it. Forget I said anything, a thousand apologies. I didn't know about the ironclad rule that someone who's thirty-five can't date someone thirty-one."

"I'm thirty-seven."

"Got it. Practically on Social Security, aren't you? James is four-and-a-half years younger than me, you know, and I've never heard him complaining."

"You're different. You're Bree Lang."

For a few minutes the only sound is wind and the tinny beat through Piper's earphones. When I think the subject's closed, Bree says casually, "I had the same conversation with Shane a couple of days ago."

"Jesus, Bree!"

"The age thing didn't come up. I just said I could tell he had an itch for you."

"I hate that expression."

She makes me wait.

She'll make me beg. *Sometimes people need a nudge.* Or a shove.

"Okay. Tell me what he said."

"He said you were *gorgeous, of course.* His words—down to the *of course* part. Exact words. He said you were just his type. But that you'd made it clear you had zero interest beyond friendship. In case you were wondering."

"I wasn't."

"I know. You have too much to do here. How's the packing going, by the way?"

Mat and Shane have circled to the front of the house again.

"We should just junk it," Shane says. "I'm sorry I got you all roped into this mess."

"You're breaking my heart. Have some faith, bro…"

"*Is* the album going to be junked?" I whisper. Starting from scratch is not an option, not if Shane wants Bree on the record. She can only stay for three more weeks.

She laughs at my worried tone and flips a page. "No cause for alarm. Your boy's just having a regulation freak-out. We're right at the murky middle. Five tracks laid down, five to go. So I figure he's right on schedule."

"*Please* stop calling him *my boy.* He sounds really worried. He keeps quoting the Bible and Winston Churchill. This morning I heard him tell Mat that he'd been 'weighed in the balance and found wanting,' and he 'thought he was up to the task but he'd failed miserably, alas.'"

"Like I said, your standard freak-out."

"Shane saying *alas* is standard? It was kind of disturbing."

"It means the work's going beautifully. Too beautifully."

"Huh," I say, doubtful.

The rubber straps of Bree's chair bounce as she flips over, and I remove the wet T-shirt from my face to look at her. She faces the sky, gesturing with her pink highlighter, as she explains in a whisper, "It's like this. He loves it so much he's afraid to finish."

I think for a minute. "You're saying he's stalling?"

"She's got it now." Bree stretches, her bare arms, shining with coconut oil, intertwined above her head. She's got one of Angela's old royal-blue kilims twisted in a turban, covering her hair.

"Then you think the album's going to be good? It's coming together?"

Bree looks at me sideways. "*Awfully* curious for someone who's insisted for weeks that she has less than zero interest in it. Or in the person producing it."

She's got me, and I say, knowing how lame it sounds, "I just don't want the summer to be a waste, that's all."

"It won't be."

But Mat and Shane are really getting into it now. They've come near us again, apparently unconcerned about everyone listening.

"Brother, you've got to get a grip," Mat says. "Better yet, get *your* ears tested." For good-natured Mat, this is the height of rudeness.

"We tried, buddy. We tried and we failed." Shane's grandiose summing-up of months of work, and a lifetime of fantasizing about his dream project, would be funny if he didn't sound so pitiful.

"What's with the *we*?" Mat says.

"Okay, *I*! I've blown it! I'm stuck!"

"Go for a swim, buddy. Run down to the beach. You need to cool off."

Bree groans. "This is getting *ti-yer-some*."

"He respects your opinion," I whisper. "If you convince him the work's good, maybe he'll see reason."

"I have a better idea. A little dose of just the right medicine for what ails him. Pretty boy!" she bellows up at Shane on the porch. "Mat! Pipes! All of you fools! Get over here!"

They obey. Bree's chef, Martin, comes out from the kitchen. Even the kids swim over.

When everyone's assembled in front of our lawn chairs, Mat and Shane pointedly standing at either end, Piper still dripping from the pool, Bree orders, "Pack a bag and be ready in an hour."

Seven p.m., four hours later
Shoreline Amphitheatre
Mountain View, California

No big deal. This is what it means to be Bree Lang. One phone call and she can whisk people into the air on a friend's private ten-seater Cessna, leaving the earth's petty arguments and frustrations six thousand feet below. By the time we start our descent, Shane and Mat have hugged and Shane has told everyone he's sorry for acting like an ass. When we're backstage getting bracelets around our wrists, he apologizes to me directly.

"I'm sorry about my little…outburst. You took a risk for me, opening up the place. I guess the pressure got to me."

"It's okay. Bree says it'd be abnormal if you didn't have a freak-out. She says it means the work's going well."

"I'm still sorry."

"Apology accepted. So, have you been to this show before? I tried to get tickets for the Great Woods Center in Mansfield last summer but it was sold out. I really wanted to see Patty Griffin." *Lesbo-Palooza*, some idiot had chortled to his buddy, passing the nearly all-female ticket-buying line. We'd booed him.

"Actually, this'll be my third. I saw it in Pasadena last year and Irvine two summers ago."

"I'm impressed."

Lilith Fair: named for the legendary first, wanton wife of Adam in Jewish folklore. Conceived because Sarah McLachlan was sick of Lollapalooza's macho vibe, of hearing that festivals could have only one token female act, that radio stations couldn't possibly play songs by women back-to-back. I can't believe Bree initially turned down a guest appearance because she was committed to our little project.

Bree leads us into a VIP tent, and I can see her transform into performance mode. She's still herself, talking to people warmly, extricating herself, signing autographs with a smile, extricating herself.

But there's a shield up, a desire to keep moving that I've never seen in her, during our long, lazy talks in the field. It must keep her sane, keep her feeling in control, like herself, doing this all the time. It must keep her from feeling that all of these people who want something from her are picking away at what makes her Bree.

"I saw Bree giving you quite the talking-to on the plane," I murmur to Shane, as we watch her in action, giving an impromptu interview to some reporter.

"The upshot is she said I was acting like a damn fool. Which I have been. Don't argue—you know I have."

"Who was arguing?"

"She said one more thing. That *this* would remind me why I started the project in the first place. Not *this* this..." He indicates the VIP tent. "*That* this." Meaning the real concertgoers outside the tent.

We look at *this*. Thousands of people, dancing, lolling on blankets, strolling, or crowding the stages.

A jumpy woman across the tent makes a beeline for Bree the second she finishes with the reporter. Her press pass says *Hailey Allen, Rolling Stone.*

"Look," I say to Shane. "Our friend from the many voice mails."

We eavesdrop. "I understand that you canceled your summer performances to work on the Graham Kingston tribute album. Care to comment?"

"Write that this album is *important*," she says, with a wink at me. "And that it has some surprises on it. Shane and Jackie here can fill you in on the rest. If they want to." She slips away.

"Wait, you're Jacqueline Pierce, the new owner of the Sandcastle?" the reporter says, flipping to a new page in her notebook as if we've already agreed to an interview. "I've tried reaching you a bunch of times through your attorney."

"Oh, really? I'm sorry. This summer's been pretty hectic."

"And Mr. Ingram, this is your baby, of course. Nice to meet you both, finally."

I'm happy to see that they clearly haven't spoken before.

"What kind of release date are you looking at?" she asks Shane.

"Most likely June 2000," he says. He throws her a few bones about the recording process, shaping the album. Not giving away too much. Just enough to make her feel like she's getting a scoop. Like Bree, he's good at this, in control. It's attractive, seeing him in work mode. What did Bree say by the pool? *Gorgeous, of course.*

The reporter swivels to me. "Ms. Pierce, just fact-checking a few things…"

I tense, but say, "Oh, sure." Just a few answers, I can do that. I owe it to Shane, to the group. Piper and Mat and the rest— this album could be a huge career moment for them.

"So, you were Graham Kingston's niece on your mother's side, and you've inherited the property and his catalog. Have I got that right?"

"Yes."

"So you're the only one involved with the project who's actually a family member. That must be meaningful."

"I'm not really a family member." Why am I so quick to insist on this, to quibble? I'm throwing blood in the water for the journalist.

"Oh? I thought—"

"I mean, not a close one. But, yes. It's meaningful."

She nods, her eyes warm with understanding and compassion. But her pen never stops moving.

"How are you liking what you've heard so far?"

"I… What I've heard so far is brilliant. They've all been working so hard, really pouring themselves into it. This is a rare break, this show today."

"I'm sure…" She scribbles, checks her notes. I begin to relax. Observing Bree and Shane has given me some crash media training. It's not so hard. Give them something, anything, steer the questions where you want them to go. And, in a pinch, just lie.

"So, do you think the deceased relatives would approve of what you're doing?"

Her big brown eyes are impossible to read.

It's okay. Be like Bree, with an invisible shield…

"I think they'd approve," I say. "I'm trying to do what they would've wanted."

"Though your uncle was fastidious, quite controlling about his work, correct?"

"Yes. The group here has been true to his style. It's respectful, a loving tribute." I look at Shane and he nods, comes close, gives me a secret, reassuring hand-squeeze.

"Great, great… So, I understand that you lived at the Sandcastle in…" She flips through her notebook. "1979. Right before your uncle's death."

"Yes."

"I'm so sorry. It's quite a valuable property now, and I understand it's going on the market, that you're listing it with a real estate agent up there?"

"I— That's correct."

"So, the studio will likely be demolished soon. How do you think your uncle would've felt about that?"

"Not great, of course. But it's a difficult situation."

"Yes, his death was such a tragedy," she says. "Such a loss."

"It was."

Scribble scribble. Way more scribbles than the words *It was* would require.

I feel queasy. The tent's unbearably crowded with bodies, smelling of sweat and ambition. Hailey Allen's concerned look feels inescapable. Endless.

She fiddles with her earring, casual: "And of course, your cousin's death, a few years later. Such a tragedy."

She wants me to sob. To give her something I don't want to give, to spice up her article with my tears about the tragic Kingston branch of my family.

I won't show her how much her questions hurt. Won't give her the satisfaction of explaining that the Kingstons weren't simply tragic. That there was so much beauty there, before.

We're trying to save a tiny bit of it. Aren't we? But now I'm not sure. Maybe she's going to convince everyone that the album is in poor taste. I don't know what I can say that will end the interview so I can get fresh air, get away from that scribbling pen and notebook.

"Look, Ms. Allen," Shane says. "I've got another quote for you. Can you write this down? Ready?"

"Shoot."

"Here you go—'Everyone on the project is beyond grateful and humbled that Ms. Pierce has generously welcomed us into the studio for the summer.' And you can call her publicist, Melva Peachtree, to set another interview time with her. But right now, we really don't want to miss the show because Bree's going on soon. You understand that, I'm sure."

"Of course. Ms. Peachtree's number?" she asks me.

"617-555-4646," I say.

Shane and I shake her hand goodbye, all smiles, and bolt outside.

"Thank you," I say. "Melva Peachtree?"

"My first-grade teacher. What's the phone number you gave her?"

"My burrito take-out place in Boston."

He hoots in delight. "You were great. Are you okay?"

"Yeah. But you'll have to do press and stuff to promote the album next year, right? I don't want to piss her off."

"Believe me, it'll make them want more. I'll keep the beast fed. Want to get out of here?"

"Yeah."

We work our way to the side of the main stage, and then, edging and slithering around bodies, to the front. Until we're only a few people back from the stage. Bree is coming on soon, but we've lost the others.

"Better?" he shouts.

"Yes!"

I can breathe here, packed in with tens of thousands, more than in that tent of thirty. Someone passes me a joint and I take a couple of drags, pass it to Shane, who refrains.

"Bree said this was *medicine for what ails you*," I shout. "Is it working?"

"So far!" he shouts back.

I'm thinking about the other teachers at school. How they think I'm so removed, so antisocial. Paul and I never joined them for happy hour karaoke, though they asked all the time; they think we're stiffs. They imagine I'm home with a cup of chamomile tea, a classical record playing, Toby a still, furry spiral on my lap. When I'm dancing with strangers.

"What's funny?" Shane asks.

"I'm home drinking chamomile tea!" I say, laughing, but he can't hear me.

Hot from dancing, I take off the jean jacket he loaned me and tie it around my waist.

"You're a weird girl!" he shouts.

"I know." I close my eyes.

Then Lhasa de Sela introduces Bree, who jumps right into two songs before stopping for a little patter.

"And I'd like a special guest to join me now," Bree says. She sounds as relaxed as if she's only talking to a single old friend across the lunch table. "A good friend of mine, a new friend. She's flown here all the way from Boston to play for us... Where are you, lady?" She searches, finds me, locks on me like a radar gun.

"She's not," I say to Shane, backing away. "She wouldn't."

"She would. She is."

Oh, sweet fancy Jesus... No, Bree.

I scowl at her, which only makes her go on more enthusiastically. "She thinks we hit thirty and nothing new happens. Hell, I'm fifty-four and something new happens to me every day. We don't agree with her, do we?"

"No!!!"

"We can give her a good welcome, right?"

"Yes!!!"

"Ms. Jacqueline Pierce, accompanying me in her West Coast debut. She's going to help me out with a little piano backing on an old favorite of hers by Donna Summer." There's a roar—for Donna, of course. Not for me.

Phew. At least she doesn't expect me to sing. Twenty thousand strangers encourage me, probably convinced that this is all planned. I'm hoisted up to the proscenium by unseen strong, friendly hands, hauled up onstage by a roadie.

I shake my head at Bree, but I turn to face the crowd and wave. This, this right here, right now, is what Willa didn't want. What she found so unappealing that she kept her gift of a voice to herself.

I sit, trill a few notes, then nod at Bree and start the bassline of "I Feel Love." A racing pulse, like lovemaking. Bree's gorgeous mezzo voice winds around it, finding lovely new highs and lows and sideways trips, detours. Her voice romps, then slows, then flies free again.

I glimpse Shane for a second before I lose his smile in the crowd and myself in the music.

I wish I could bottle this air, this atmosphere, and breathe it in when the world seems too cruel for me to get out of bed. I wish I could share it with my kids, so they could breathe it in, too.

As we finish, and sweat's rolling down my temples from the hot lights, I close my eyes and think of Willa. *This is for you, Wills. I know you hated crowds, but I sure wish you were alive so I could come home and tell you about it.*

On the way home, everyone else sleeps, lulled by the plane's buzz. I curl against the cold window, stare out at the fog. As exciting as it was, being onstage, it's also a relief to be away from the packed-in bodies and applause, to return to our tranquil hideout in the woods. I wonder what it feels like to do this all the time. To go from strutting to dreaming, and back again. Over and over. Graham was bitter about what he called "the circus"—at least when it lost interest in him. Willa never wanted any part of it.

"May I?" Shane. He has two drinks, and hands me one as he sits in the aisle seat next to me. "Ginger ale spiked with honey. The perfect cocktail to protect your voice after a performance. It's a little post-show ritual that I read Nina Simone swears by."

"Thanks." I take a sip. "It's tasty. Of course, I didn't sing. The reason we know that is I'm not scrubbing tomato stains out of my shirt right now."

He laughs, then reaches high, his fingertips touching the cabin roof, and pivots his spine back and forth in a stretch. "Your voice isn't so bad. I heard you in the studio, remember?"

"I do. Spy."

"Guilty. But really. You were a good sport tonight. And you were beautiful up there."

I circle my cup rim with my index finger, around and around. "Thank you."

He starts to speak, pauses. "You are beautiful."

I have no answer for this. I'm too drained to come up with a change of subject, too happy to shoot his compliment down with another joke, an eye roll. I turn to face him, rest my cheek on the seat cushion. *You, too,* I mouth.

It's nearly two and we linger in the hall. Everyone else has gone to bed but we've been standing here for ages, dawdling.

"Well," he says. "Remember the little people, now that you're famous."

"Of course I will. Shawn."

He smiles, brushing at a nail hole in the wall where I've taken down a painting. "I've heard toothpaste works on these. White toothpaste. Not Crest."

"I have putty."

"Ah, good. Well. You're probably exhausted."

"Yeah. I'm going to crash."

"Me, too." He stretches, circling his arms as if to demonstrate how tired he is, but it's the gesture of an early-morning swimmer standing on a starting block, ready to race a thousand meters. Not someone about to dive into bed.

And neither of us moves.

"Well," I say.

"Well. Fun night!" He reaches his arms around me, wide, a too-careful hug.

"Yeah!" I pat him on the back—*'Night, bud!*

One gesture, one word from either of us to acknowledge what we really want. That's all it would take. A finger. A syllable. But we separate and go inside our rooms on opposite ends of the hall.

I scratch Toby, who's asleep on the parlor floor, hoping some quality mystery-massage action from below is imminent.

I change into my souvenir Lilith Fair T-shirt. I pace.

The look Shane gave me in the field, as everyone else hugged and called out their good-nights and dispersed for bed. He looked at me that way again as we stalled and small-talked in the hall. I can't stop seeing that look. Remembering it sends my thoughts to places I don't want them to go. To his warm lips, his skin, his smell. His long arms and skillful, fast-moving fingers.

I press my hand to the rug by Toby's right front paw but don't feel anything. Shane must be sound asleep by now.

He'll have come back to earth, and he'll be relieved we didn't do anything. I get in the daybed and flick out the light.

Sounds from the kitchen. Footsteps, then the suction-y *thcks* of the fridge door opening, closing, opening again. Someone getting a midnight snack. No, a two a.m. snack.

I know it's him. For one thing, he's the only one besides me who sleeps in the house. Everyone else wants a little space from the studio, or has kids, and has taken over cabins and yurts.

I know it's him because the same adrenaline that's keeping him up is keeping me up.

"Stop me, Tobes," I whisper to my oblivious cat.

I slip out of the room, walk down the hall toward the kitchen light.

He's got his back to me. The counter in front of him is covered in food—rye bread and ham and turkey and chips. He has a tub of rice pudding out, too. He's struggling with a jar. He gives up on it, sets it down, and braces his arms on the edge of the sink, looking out at the field.

"Hungry?" I ask.

He turns, not hiding his happiness to find me here. "No."

"Neither am I."

I hop up on the counter near the window, across from him. "I've been meaning to tell you something. Toby sleeps curled up on the center of the floor in the parlor. He feels vibrations coming up from the studio in that spot, when anyone's working down there. You disappointed him tonight."

"Is he waiting in his spot right now?"

"Yeah. He's optimistic."

He laughs. "D'you think he likes what he's felt so far?"

"If he hated it, he wouldn't sleep there."

"Our first review."

I smile. "A good one."

He walks to me and stands close, between my dangling legs. I tilt my head down to kiss him, sweet and quick. But it feels like a lie to kiss him that way. He clutches my shirt, wrapping the fabric around his wrists until it's snug against my hips, and my legs wrap around him.

He lifts me off the counter, carries me out the kitchen door to the hall, heading for his room.

"Not in there," I say into his neck.

He sets me down.

"Outside." I tug him by the wrist. Through the front door, across the porch, down the steps to the field. He kicks his moccasins off as I lead him past the picnic table toward the trees.

"A cabin?" he says.

"No."

I lead him by the hand down the narrow dirt path toward the hot springs. In the moonlight, the water looks like mercury. I take two towels off the pegs in the changing shelter.

"A soak," he says. "That sounds good." Trying to hide his disappointment.

"No. After." Because we're not stopping. Just past the springs there's a small clearing in the trees. Someone has carried up lawn chair mats for lying on, dozing. Perfect for catching your breath and cooling down between soaks. Perfect for collapsing onto when you can't stand the 106-degree water for another second, when you feel faint. Cold then hot then cold—the contrast makes you feel alive.

I spread the towels over a mat, pull him down after me, already sliding his shorts off. Then his boxers. He shuts his eyes as I touch him, run my thumb over the tender, wet skin. He rubs his face against my neck, burrowing in so close that when he breathes, my throat vibrates.

He tugs off my skirt, then my underwear. I lift my hips, helping him, lifting my shirt, and the cold middle-of-the-night air feels good on my breasts, the inside of my thighs. His mouth is attentive, kissing and sucking until I'm wet above and below, shivering whenever he allows space between his face and my body. It's like going in and out of the pools. Hot then cold then hot again. His hand, below, is gentle, steady, exploring, and my pulse races faster than any two a.m. disco song. I push against his fingers and they speed up, separate. *Not something everyone can do…easy for him, though…and for me. There's a word for that…temerity…dentellity…no…whatever the word is, musicians always have it…*

I take his wrist, stop him before I come. We roll to our sides, I hook my leg behind his, digging into the back of his thigh with my heel until he buries himself in me.

Contrast. Slow, fast. Hard, soft.

Yours. Mine.

The last thing I see before I have to close my eyes, before all thought ebbs away, is the curve of his shoulder against the purple sky.

After, we soak. The sun's coming up behind us, but it's still so early that the trees are more black than green. I'm sitting on his lap, my right arm extended in front of me, my right index finger dancing in the air.

"I can't figure out—" he kisses my left shoulder blade "—if you're casting a spell or conducting an invisible orchestra."

"Neither. I'm tracing the tree line. See. Close one eye."

He copies me, making an invisible zigzagging line over the treetops with the tip of his index finger.

"Isn't it wild?" I ask. "In a month that line will be completely different. Some trees will grow a little faster than others. One might die because insects have gotten a little too comfortable, or maybe it's struck by lightning. Some might bend slightly in another direction to reach the light."

"Already thinking about fall?"

"No." I don't want to think about fall. I don't even want to think about tomorrow. "Just about how much things can change when you're not paying attention."

"It's true. You hated me a month ago."

"*Hate* is a strong word."

He laughs. "When did the tide turn? Because you had to've known I've been gone over you since that first day in the field."

"Who said the tide has turned? What if I'm just using your body? Plus, you had all those singers onstage tonight to soften me up. Maybe they seduced me, not you."

"Ouch."

I turn to face him. "No. Your playing would've done it for me, too. I like it." I nuzzle against him.

"And I'd like you, even if you didn't play a thing last night."

"So it *was* me, not just Sarah and Beth and Lhasa and Lucinda?"

"It was you."

Judy and Joni and Joan and Joan. I gaze off into the trees behind him as if Willa's out there, watching me, forever a teenager, envying me because I've had so many years to love. Except she was never envious.

I push the thought away and bring my attention back to this living person, who's here with me now, warm and close.

"I think that may be the best show I've ever been to," he says.

"Second-best for me."

"What's your number one?"

"Blondie. Is, was, always will be."

"What show? I saw them in LA in '85."

"'79. Sonoma Fairgrounds."

"Ah. Not too far from here."

"Yeah."

Shane squeezes my hand. "Do you remember what they opened with?"

"I remember the entire set list."

"Go. And don't think I won't look it up on the internet."

"'Dreaming,' 'One Way or Another,' 'Hanging on the Telephone,' 'Look Good in Blue,' 'Youth Nabbed as Sniper,' 'Sunday Girl,' 'Heart of Glass,' 'Rip Her to Shreds,' 'In the Sun,' encore of 'Heart of Glass.' Impressed?"

His answer is a kiss, slow and sliding, that turns into another hour of lovemaking, of bobbing and crying out in and along the edge of the hot water. Someone could come by and catch us; I don't know if it's six a.m. or eight. After, we kiss again, the steam making everything nearby a blur, until we both feel too woozy to stay in a minute longer.

"Prehistoric," he says as we crawl out, too tired to finish the reference. But I know what he's trying to say: we're like two primordial creatures, crawling from the ooze. Nothing but instinct left.

Our wrung-out muscles tangled up, we lie in the clearing. Too spent even to lift a finger and trace more tree lines.

"Dexterity," I manage, panting.

"What?" He tucks a strand of wet hair behind my ear.

It's a few minutes before I can speak again. "I was trying to remember the word. Last night. The word for skills. With your hands."

He laughs. "If you're trying to remember words while making love, maybe the dexterity is lacking."

"No. Not lacking at all. Not one little bit."

"We need something to revive us," he says.

"Two options. Coffee or beach?"

"Beach. Then coffee. Then bed."

"Don't you have to work today?"

"Change of plans. I'm giving everyone the day off."

25

Fade Away and Radiate

1979

Almost three weeks after Colin arrived with his strawberries and albums, he presented his best gift. This one was for me. Four Blondie concert tickets. I'd known about the show coming up down in Sonoma, but it had been sold out for months.

"They're your favorite, right? I saw that poster in your cabin." He was standing to reach for the honey, and his voice carried down all eight picnic tables. But no one seemed to care that he visited Slipstream as often as I visited Plover.

"What's this?" Graham called.

"I'm taking Jackie to a concert as an early birthday present," Colin said, dripping a long stream of honey into his tea.

"Dead show? Dylan?"

"Blondie."

I braced myself. Would Blondie be as offensive as disco or Kenny Rogers? They were too young, too high on the *Billboard* chart, and too TV-savvy to meet with Graham's approval. But Graham clearly had no idea who they were, and quickly lost interest.

During the three-day run-up to the concert, I could talk of

little else. When we were in my cabin getting ready—Willa braiding the left side of my hair, above my ear, so that I could secure it with a glittery ribbon clip—I said, yet again, "I can't believe we're going."

"I know," she said, trying to smile.

"What is it?"

"Oh. Nothing."

I turned. "Wills? Is something going on with you and Liam?" In my excitement, I'd offered him the fourth ticket without consulting her.

"We're fine. Look at this masterpiece." She held up my hand mirror so I could inspect my braid.

Colin drove us down to the Sonoma County Fairgrounds in the Kingstons' temperamental old Dodge Streaker van, Rip Van Winkle—named for the psychedelic mural of a bearded old man airbrushed on one side. It usually sat on the logging road as extra housing. On the way, I gave the other three a crash course on the band. "And the guitarist is Chris Stein and the drummer is Clem Burke, and they're getting branded as disco because of 'Heart of Glass' but they're really not. They're sort of new-wave-slash-punk."

"I can't believe we're going! Thanks again, guys!" Liam. He was as guileless and pure as Willa. The two of them, snuggled close in the second row of the van behind me and Colin, looked like they'd stepped out of *Surfer* magazine. Except for Willa's tense expression. What was causing it?

I didn't understand until our hands were stamped and the four of us were on the lawn inside the fence. As she watched everyone streaming in, Willa looked increasingly nervous, but the opening act wasn't even onstage yet because I'd insisted on getting here hours early. When Blondie came on in two hours, fifteen thousand people would be surging toward the stage.

Way too late, I realized why she was unhappy. This was a girl who'd hidden behind a milkweed stalk when she was little because of her dad's photo shoot. She kept putting off our disco outing, pretending it was because her dancing wasn't perfect. But it was the crowds, of course.

I whispered in Willa's ear. "I'm sorry. I feel so stupid. I was so excited I didn't think about how much you'd *hate* this. Let's go."

She turned to me and spoke more fiercely than I'd ever heard her—"No!"

"But you're miserable!"

"I'll be okay."

All through the opening act, I stayed near the back out of respect for her.

But as the time for Blondie to come on ticked closer, and the crowd's energy revved up, my body longed to be up front, and Willa knew it.

"Go!" she shouted to me over the roars.

"I'm fine back here!"

"I'm not fine with you back here! Go!" She shoved me.

"I'll stay here with her," Liam said. He wasn't paying attention to the music, anyway; that had been clear since the first song. The only thing that held his attention was Willa.

Colin and I worked our way forward. A few feet from the others I turned back. Liam had lifted Willa onto his shoulders back against the fence line, safe from the crowd.

Go! Willa mouthed.

Expertly, with Colin behind me clasping my hand, I snaked us up front toward the infectious beat of the opening act.

"You're good at this!" he shouted when we were ten rows back.

"I've been to a lot of shows!" I'd snuck out to the Warfield and the Cow Palace, Shoreline Amphitheatre and Mo's. I had an album of concert tickets at home.

The group was leaving the stage and roadies were changing out instruments, checking equipment. I knew from experience that the lull was our last chance to make forward progress.

Five people back. Three. Then we hit an obstacle; the man in front of me. He had a narrow body, but a dance style that was so distressingly *wide*. Every time I tried to get around him, one of his limbs blocked the route.

Colin laughed each time I was thwarted. "He's a human guardrail! I think this is as good as we're going to do."

"No, I can get us up there! It's like a video game!"

The guy in front dropped his beer can and bent to pick it up.

"Now!" I said. Colin and I seized the moment, passed. Two rows back.

"You think Willa's okay?" I asked.

"Sure! She's always been like that."

"Has she?" But my question got lost in the roars, whistles, stomps of thousands.

Weaving and slithering, holding hands, we got all the way to the front row. And then, when the shared anticipation was so feverish I didn't think I could stand another second, Debbie was right in front of me. Belting out the opening bars of "Dreaming." Debbie, close enough that even though I was jumping up and down like a kid, I could see the light flash on her pink cat-eye sunglasses. I could see her forty-five-degree-angle razor-cut bangs, her snarl, her small hand on the mic. Nothing between us except a little air. She'd stepped straight out of my poster and into a California vineyard.

"Thank you!" I shouted to Colin, whose hands were up in the air along with mine.

"Happy?"

I nodded, wiping a tear away.

"Because, you see, she's soft underneath the toughness. She wears both so easily," I explained to Colin, after.

We'd parked the van on the logging road, where it would be quiet in the morning and we could sleep as late as we wanted, undisturbed. Liam and Willa had conked out on the drive but Colin and I were lying on the roof under a blanket, staring up at the stars, me in his flannel work shirt because it had gotten chilly. I was way too wired to sleep.

"Huh," Colin said. "It's a mystery to me. Why on earth would *you* relate to someone like that?"

"You've only known me a few weeks. You think I try to act tough?"

"Only sometimes. Hey, I wish I didn't have to go tomorrow."

"Me, too," I said.

He looked at me with real regret, stroking my hair. "I wish I could stay. But I should've been on the road ages ago. They need artichoke pickers in Castroville. Gotta go earn some cash."

Money. Of course, money. But he was so careless with it. He must've blown twenty dollars just on the concert tickets.

"Hey, I know what you're thinking. But seeing your face tonight when you were dancing was worth every penny. I'd pick a whole choke field myself to see that again."

"How do you pick an artichoke? Do they grow on vines?"

He laughed. "They look like giant reefer plants."

"My stepmother has a whole set of special silver dishes for artichokes. Twelve place settings. Different bowls for the hollandaise sauce, and tiny tongs, barely bigger than tweezers, and these fancy, individual wire baskets for the scraped-off leaves. We use them maybe once a year."

This seemed horribly sad all of a sudden. I shivered, and he carefully buttoned the top three buttons of the shirt he'd lent me.

I turned to my side and curled up against him, touching his cheek. We kissed for a long time, and then I unbuttoned his shirt again.

I woke before dawn, to a mist-swirled sky. No Colin. For a minute I thought he'd taken off already. Off to his field of chokes.

"Pssst." A gentle tap on the van ladder. Willa's voice—"Can I come up?"

"Of course."

She climbed up and settled next to me under the blanket. "Colin and Liam went to get us all breakfast from town."

"Breakfast in bed. I like this date."

"So. Did anything new happen last night?"

I lowered the blanket to show her I was wearing Colin's shirt.

"Does that mean… You're officially a…*recipient*?"

I laughed, nodded.

"Wow. Was it…"

"Yeah. It was. Yeah."

"Better than the Marina Club pool?"

I hadn't told Colin about my past experiences, how lopsided they were. How they were my lovers, but I wasn't theirs.

I'd just bitten his shoulder at the fateful moment.

"It was as different from the Marina Club pool as it could be."

"Good."

We got quiet, staring up at the stars, listening to the crickets.

"What was that song, last night?" Willa said. "'Fade away… fade away…'"

"'Fade Away and Radiate'?"

"Yeah. I liked that one. What d'you think she means?"

"It's about TV."

"Oh. I thought maybe she was saying we don't have to live a noisy life. I kind of liked that."

"It can mean that for you. I don't think Debbie would mind."

"Thanks, Debbie…"

"But I'm sorry you suffered through the show for me," I said. "All the shoving, the crowds. I should've realized how hard it'd be for you. Next time, I'll just go and tell you about it."

"I'd like that… You see all the shows and come home and tell me about them. But it's all right, I survived."

"Because Li was there to be your personal treehouse."

She laughed.

"Hey, Wills? That's why you started camping on the beach, and going up to the treehouse, isn't it? To get away from crowds."

She nodded. "I used to hate my dad's shows, back when he had them. They took us away from home. And I never wanted to leave home."

"Think you ever will?"

"Never. I'll stay 'til I'm an old lady with long white hair, and I have to haul myself up the treehouse with a pulley." She laughed. "Anyway. The shows...all those bodies packed in, and how...revved-up they made him, then bitter if things didn't go how he... I just hated the whole scene. I used to think maybe it was only because I was little. But now I'm sure...big crowds just aren't for me."

"But campfire."

"That's different."

I thought, *Yes.* Not a huge crowd of strangers packed close, but a circle of gentle people in the dark, friendly faces lit softly by firelight, and acres of space in every direction for Willa to go, before or after, if she needed to be alone. And a father who understood why she never wanted the spotlight, who kept her safe from his twirling bottle.

I hadn't recognized at the time what a compliment it was, that day Willa'd flung the treehouse ladder down—inviting me into her sanctuary.

"This is enough of a crowd for me," she said. "This is..."

We watched the tipped-over bowl of sky, a bird crossing a cloud. She did that sometimes, trailed off, faded away. Let nature make her point.

But when I was sure she'd fallen back to sleep, she pointed at the sky and said, "This is all I need."

It was a beautiful thing to hear, but it pained me. Because what I needed would soon be out of reach—the different kind of life I'd found here, thanks to her.

Maybe, if I was a different girl, I would have visualized returning to San Francisco a new person. Taking the experience
of this summer with me and offering my newfound peace and
contentment to everyone I touched. Bringing some of Willa's
softness back with me, an invisible souvenir to share with my
father and Patricia.

All summer they had sent postcards. Patricia's elegant handwriting detailed lodgings and meals and the dazzling purchases
she'd made for me. (I imagined her visiting shops across Europe,
asking, "Do you have this in yellow?" in various languages. *Am-
arillo*, *jaune*, whatever it was in Italian.)

My father wrote the same thing on every card. A small, meaningless observation about whatever city they were visiting, and
"Hope you're well."

Juan-les-Pins is stunning. Hope you're well. Father.
Milan is elegant. Hope you're well. Father.
Madrid is lively. Hope you're well. Father.

The thought had started coming in quiet moments like this,
as we sped toward the day I'd go back to San Francisco. The
thought I kept trying to push away, because I didn't want to
spoil the days we had left. I whispered it—"Wills?"

"Hmmm?" She held my hand and waited for me to speak, as
we listened to the morning birds hopping around their branches.

"I wish I could stay here forever."

August

26

Zig and Zag

1979

Colin was gone, leaving me wistful but not wounded. We were going to write. He came to the city sometimes.

The city. I knew, objectively, that it was one of the most beautiful in the world. But it loomed large and ugly and lonely to me now. I had a little more than three weeks left—though I tried to resist tallying my remaining days here, I couldn't help it.

I longed for the nine wasted days from the beginning of my stay, before my cousin and I spoke. How I wished I could reclaim them. Fill them with her, with our rituals and confidences. I'd never had a friend like Willa.

"You'll visit me all the time," I told her.

"Of course I will."

But even if my father and Patricia allowed this, I knew it wouldn't be the same.

We sat around the fire circle, waiting for Graham and his bottle. Willa passed the joint that was making the rounds; I'd only recently broken the habit of keeping it low, out of sight, like I'd done at home, in disco alleys and parks.

I inhaled deep, holding it. I took a second puff before passing it to the woman on my left.

"Let's go surfing," I said to Willa.

"You mean, tomorrow?"

"No. Now. It's the only thing left on my list." I'd become fixated on finishing. We were going to a disco next week, to check off Willa's last thing—she insisted, though I'd promised her there was no shame in backing out now that I knew what crowds did to her. Liam was going to stand by, like he had at the concert. Run outside with her if there were too many people.

But I hated that my last thing was uncertain, that I might leave without standing up on a surfboard. I'd learned how to stay out of the way when we tandem surfed—which meant Willa stood and I clung to the front of the board for dear life. I'd even come close on my own a few times, so close I was sure I had it, but promptly wiped out whenever I took more than five fingers off the board. That didn't count.

"Why don't you work up to night surfing after you master the day surfing?"

"I think daylight's holding me back. I have a good feeling about it. Tonight's the night."

"You're tired. You must've run five miles playing with the kids this afternoon. I don't know…"

"Please, Wills? I'm running out of time."

She nodded. "Okay. But if the break's not good, we'll save it 'til tomorrow morning."

"See?" I said, zipping up my suit. "Nice rolling sets."

"Don't go too far out…or too near the rocks. Just try a baby wave first."

We tandem surfed to get things started, and for the first time, I didn't immediately wipe out after separating my hands from the board. No wonder Willa was addicted to this.

I stood perfectly still, my posture as straight as if someone was pulling me up by marionette strings from the crown of my head. We only stood for a second or two, but it felt endless.

"You're doing it!" she cried behind me.

Then we were under, the world topsy-turvy.

"You're so close," she said. "We'll paddle out first thing in the morning, if it's calm."

But I wanted to try it alone, now, while Willa watched from the sand. This was the night—it had to be.

"Look how bright it is," I told her. "If I wipe out, I'll swim for the stars."

"Okay. Baby wave…"

Her voice, calling encouragement from the shore, sounded so close. I felt safe, paddling out. I felt like I could do anything. For a second, maybe less than a second, I stood.

And then I tried to duck under a wave with Willa's beautiful seal-like motion but my timing was off and I got a throatful of salt water.

I was under, like the thousand other times I'd tried. But unlike those other times, it was dark. And I didn't bob up right away. Something was missing besides the magic and the sun, something else was wrong… It hit me, and panic quickly followed. We'd forgotten the leash.

Liam's suit, overlarge, felt like it would drag me down to the sea floor. The legs had gotten unrolled and I thought—if only I can unzip it. But I couldn't find the pull.

The board… I swam for it but it was heading for the rocks.

I was close enough to shore that I could see someone's distant fire, hear their radio, but I knew no one could hear me over the waves, and the certainty terrified me.

I popped up again and again, gulping, but couldn't spot Willa.

"Help." Pitifully weak, swallowed up by a wave. Water down my throat.

For just a second, I imagined letting go. Patricia and my father sobbing. Would they sob?

But Willa. She'd never forgive herself if I drowned. I couldn't leave her onshore, blaming herself forever.

Swim parallel to the beach if there's a riptide or you're in trouble, she'd told me. *Even if it feels wrong. Zig and zag, nice and easy, until you get closer.*

Zig and zag, like the foot-tickling game I'd seen the other day in the field. Six people tickling each other's feet while lying down in a chain, their bodies forming a jagged up-and-down line, trying not to laugh...

I zigged and zagged. Made my way closer. And just before my arms gave out, my toes touched bottom and I crawled onshore.

"Jackie! Jackie!" Willa, coming closer with each lapping wave. So that's why I hadn't seen her as I'd desperately scanned the beach; she'd been in the ocean with me, trying to help.

She stood above me, holding something white-and-red, long as an Amazon's spear. Then reality pierced the fog of Angela's pot. It was Willa's board. Her cherished board, split on the rocks.

"Oh shit." I reached up, too limp to stand. "I'll buy you a new one, Wills."

"I don't care about that, silly... I was trying to get you to grab it but you wouldn't look back. Promise you're okay?" She gave up on tugging me closer in, to dry sand, and lay next to me in the foam, holding my hand.

"Perfect. Just worn out. The edge. My own edge, except water instead of sky."

"What? You're not making any sense..."

It had made perfect sense in my head—Graham had his waterfall ridge. I'd skirted danger tonight.

"It's my fault," Willa said. "You're high as a kite."

"Heavy as an anchor. Wet as a herring. But I did it!"

"You did." She fumbled in her hair and handed me something sopping. "Here's your Super Special Bravery Award. Sorry it's not a cape."

I held it up, squeezed the water from it, laughed. It was one of the lace scraps she always used to tie her hair back.

We lay on the wet sand, limp with relief and gratitude, staring up at the stars and listening to the distant growl of Wolfman Jack signing off on someone's radio down the beach.

"His signal's so strong. I read his radio tower's all the way down in Rosarito, Mexico," I said. "Or maybe he's back now, I forget. But they keep trying to shut him up and they never will."

"Ow-ow-owwwwwh," Willa howled, imitating him.

"Owowhowhhhhhh!"

27

Sticky

1999

Nearly every morning for the past week Shane and I have gone to the beach. We swim, and after, we wrap ourselves in towels and huddle close if it's overcast, lie on each other's stomachs to soak in the sun if it's clear.

We've agreed to hide it. Us. Shane doesn't care either way, but I don't want anyone to know yet. It's hard, though. We try not to look at each other too much, not to touch. We walk to the beach separately, meet in an unoccupied cabin, sometimes twice a day, timing our exits, like thieves. Sweaty, successful thieves.

Today it's sunny, and he's got his head on my lap. I play with his wet hair, twirling sections around my fingers.

"Jackie."

"Hmmm?"

"You know how I lied. About growing up here."

"Yes."

"We haven't talked about it much since."

"Did you want to?"

"I just… You know why I did it, right? That I'd never lie to hurt someone?"

"I know that. I've forgiven you." I lean down and kiss him. I can't fault him for honoring Angela's dying wishes. In a way, it's a relief—knowing his bond is with Angela, not Graham. That this project is for her. I like that Angela is in charge of the studio at last.

Wishing we had more time, we head back.

We have a routine down: we take the beach trail together, but walk quickly and don't hold hands. Then I slip up the left side of the field. He'll dawdle, then slip up the right side, and we'll enter the house at different times. He thinks such games are foolish, that we should tell everyone, but he indulges me.

That night, Bree's husband, James, arrives for his visit, and seeing how they can't keep their hands off of each other, how they feed each other roasted marshmallows at campfire like honeymooners, makes me smile to myself. Then, furtively, across the circle at Shane. If a smile could swoop someone up, the secret one he sends back over the fire would carry me in to bed.

"I'm going inside to wash up," I tell Bree. "I'm all sticky."

Before I can put my hands under the kitchen faucet, Shane's behind me, his chin on top of my head, hands trailing down the backs of my arms. I shiver and turn, splaying my fingers and holding them away from us. "I'd wait if I were you. This marshmallow's worse than superglue and I wouldn't want to ruin your heirloom T-shirt."

"I'll risk it." He takes my fingers in his mouth, scrapes his teeth gently up and down the white ribbon of marshmallow on my thumb.

"Someone might come."

"Exactly."

I look out the window at the group, at the bright campfire, but nothing seems important except the warm mouth around the fingers of my right hand, and I lean against the counter so I won't buckle to the floor.

Shane concentrates, finishes his task, twining my wet fingers with his. "All clean. So why are we keeping it secret again?"

"I don't remember. Because it's more fun?"

We slide to the ground. My left hand is still marshmallowy. It's all a mess, a sticky-sweet mess, but right now I don't care.

We average three hours of sleep a night. Shane works feverishly in the studio, coming to me at midnight or one a.m., and the two of us make love and talk all night, catching a few hours of sleep before the gang starts stirring. I'm too excited to sleep. I'm in constant motion, wandering the grounds, biking down to the beach to wander some more. I don't realize I'm smiling until an older woman strolling on the sand, clutching her young male caregiver's elbow, beams back and me and says, with great effort, "P-pretty smile."

"Thank you."

"P-pretty. Day."

"Yes, it is. It's gorgeous."

I know that it's madness, the exact wrong move, to get involved with someone I barely know, here, at this time. For so many reasons, it's wrong. What kind of person would do this, in such a sacred place? But happiness lifts me above shame, and the things that have worried me for so long.

Five days later

A long morning at the beach. Longer than we intended to spend here—Shane's late.

We're at the fork on the trail, about to go our separate ways. I try to unlace my fingers from his but he squeezes my hand.

I laugh. "You're supposed to be in the studio in twenty minutes, remember?"

"Let's go for a quick walk," he says. He looks anxious.

"Where?"

"Up to the falls. I thought we could... We've never gone up there together."

He must've realized by now that even the sign marking the falls trail pains me. That I have no interest in going there. I told him how I shut down the real estate agent's request for a photo of the "picturesque waterfall."

And every time we hike up from the beach trail I make a sharp left turn here, not even looking at where the path continues uphill, curving into the shadows.

"Please?" he says.

I shake my head. "I'm too tired, but you go. I'm heading back for a shower."

"Jackie, wait. That was stupid of me. I shouldn't've—"

"It's fine." I force a smile and turn toward to the house.

Maybe he's reminiscing about when he lived near here. He liked the falls when he was younger, and wanted to share the memory with me. He needs to say goodbye to this place, too, and that's why he suggested it. An impulse.

Shane would never be deliberately cruel.

He's even throwing me a surprise birthday party. I'd kept the date quiet, but Shane snooped at my driver's license and found out my birthday was coming up. On the day, he serves me breakfast in bed, and for dinner he decorates the picnic table, picks out music, arranges for Martin to make a special punch and cioppino, a huge cauldron of it, filled with Pacific mussels and clams and cod caught that morning, a spicy-garlicky sauce that simmered all afternoon. San Francisco sourdough loaves thrown around the table and torn, family-style. There's a cake and presents.

"Mine first." Shane secretly brushes my knee as he sets his gift in my lap.

I hold it up—thin, square, sixteen by sixteen inches. "I wonder what this could be?" I say, teasing.

They laugh as I tear off a strip of wrapping paper. An album.

A mint-condition LP of Blondie's *Parallel Lines*, signed by Debbie Harry and Chris Stein and Clem Burke.

"I love it," I say, remembering just in time not to kiss Shane. But I hug him.

"This is perfect, you guys," I tell everyone. And I want to mean it; it's nearly perfect. These people feel like family.

I smile, touched.

But I can't hide from it anymore, the tug of the past. As Martin's clearing the table, I see it.

Everything's been swept away except the bowls that had been set down for our cioppino shells.

White bowls, filled with shells, spaced here and there along the long brown line of tables.

"Jackie, Jackie, Jackie." Restless calls from over at the campfire. Performances wait. They have a sweet evening for me. Against all odds, they like me. I'm a favorite in this ragtag group. They're proud of how they've won me over.

Get it together, it's nothing. I pick up a mussel shell.

"Hey, Birthday Girl." Shane secretly nuzzles my neck from behind. "You're not trying to clean up, are you?"

I touch the sharp mussel with my index finger. It's furry on the outside.

I stare at the table, at the bowls, biting my lip so hard I can feel the little scar I have inside my mouth, from my teenage bike crash. There are a dozen bowls. Not like the ten cairns. Two bowls too many. Otherwise, it's a perfect miniature.

I can't seem to escape what happened at the waterfall trail.

28

This Place Had Other Plans

1979

Dear Ray,
Willa and I have planned my birthday from sunrise to sunrise.
We're waking up early and biking down to Glass Beach. Then
we're hiking up to the Triangle Point swing for a picnic lunch, just
the two of us. Kate's cooking an elaborate, mysterious dinner, and
Willa's hinted about "a little surprise" for me that I can't open
until campfire. And then, after we've eaten my cake and watched
the stars come out and doused the flames, we're driving Rip Van
Winkle to an all-night disco down in Mendocino, where we're
dancing until the sun comes out...

I marked my place in the diary with the scrap of lace Willa had
given me, my Super Special Bravery Award like Dylan's cape,
hid it in the treehouse, and went to bed.

Our day didn't quite work out like that.

Or, as Willa put it in her airy-yet-mesmerizing way, "This
place had other plans for you."

We were coasting downhill on our brakeless bikes, bumping along the dirt trail to the beach like we'd done a hundred times. I'd never go as fast as Willa, but now that I'd memorized the most perilous bumps and turns—and identified a few handy, unofficial markers that reminded me where to duck or slow down—I'd become confident enough to relax and enjoy the ride. The wind whooshing up from the beach chilled my face, and it was so early that dew beaded the dark leaves.

There could be a song in that. The deep green leaves, how the sunlit drops clinging to them sparkled like stars. "Night for Day." No. "Almost Like Stars." I'd play around with the idea tomorrow night, alone in my quiet cabin, and if anything came of it I'd ask Willa to set the words to music. Today was for biking and surfing and dancing.

"Eighteen!" I shouted down to her.

"Eighteen!" came the reply, a few seconds later.

"Sing for an old lady!"

She obeyed, and I leaned forward to catch her voice over the birds. I'd told her that listening to her voice on the way to the beach kept me balanced, and the idea thrilled her. Really I just liked to hear it, now that she trusted me enough to share it.

Today she sang something new—a silly, personalized version of Joni's "Circle Game":

And nooow the girl is eighteen...
And her dancing is the best you ever seeeen...

I smiled to myself. Even Willa's nonsense songs could stop your heart. Her voice was so pure when it trilled on a high C.

I was focusing on Willa's impromptu song, and excited about my birthday, but I remembered to look for my safety markers. There, ahead of me, the shred of yellow nylon tied to a dying branch that reminded me to slow down ever-so-slightly on a gradual switchback. A few minutes later, on my right, the coast side—a trio of fat pine stumps right before the curve where a winter mudslide had made the trail uncomfortably narrow. A graceful lean to the left along that stretch and I was fine. I tilted and swerved, leaned and corrected like the Tour de France racers I'd seen on ABC's *Wide World of Sports*, as if I'd done this for years. Like I belonged here.

And now the girl is eighteeeen.
She is our San Francisco queeeen…
She thinks Blondie is peachy-keeeeen…

"I love it!" I shouted down.

Her voice fluttered up the hillside: "Do you think it'll be a hit?"

"Number one with a bullet!"

I could just catch her laughter over the birds and my whirring bike spokes.

My most important marker was coming up. It was nailed to a tree halfway down, about ten yards before a hairpin turn: a birdhouse.

It was wood, its roof studded with shells. Willa had made it when she was little, and though it was mossy and badly splitting—hardly a weatherproof shelter, which is why it was always unoccupied—the pearly shells that she had glued on when she was seven still stood out clearly against the dark umber bark.

Whenever I saw the birdhouse's shell roof straight ahead, I knew it was time to drag my right toe on the ground in preparation for the sharpest left turn.

I was thinking about many things. The fact that I was now an adult. The fun day ahead. A new scheme I had concocted, to get Willa to perform at a nursing home or hospital to nudge her out of her *stage loathing*, as she called it.

Still, I remembered to look for that flash of white.

By the time I realized I should have seen it already, that something was wrong, it was too late.

One second I was safely in the middle of the trail.

The next I was in the woods. Desperately gripping the handlebars, crunching over ferns and juniper bushes. I missed a tree trunk by inches. I juttered down, out of control, my mouth bouncing off my handlebar. My front tire hit a log and the bike bucked me off. I was airborne, a bright green bed of ferns flying at my face. I could make out fringed edges, individual dewdrops. *Sparkles. Stars. Stars Falling on Me. Another new song*, I thought, before I closed my eyes in fear.

Go limp, I thought. *Limp as a rag doll.* Ancient wisdom retrieved from some girlhood riding lesson. I landed face-first in the wet fronds and rolled, tumbling downhill.

Panic, confusion, the drumming command *go limp, go limp, go limp*.

Pain came later.

Branches cracked, something thudded. Me, I realized. When at last I stopped rolling and the world became quiet again, my first clear thought was that I'd been betrayed. The trail, and this land I'd grown so tender toward, had turned on me. Like it wanted to let me know that I didn't belong here after all.

My second thought was that my father and Patricia would hear of my accident from across the Atlantic, blame Graham, and make me leave early.

"Jackie!" Willa's voice. Strange. It came from above me, up the hill. It seemed impossible that I'd overtaken her. Had I fallen that far, that fast? I opened my eyes to the marigold ruffle of her skirt hem floating above me; she was frantically checking my legs.

"Oh my god are you okay does that hurt don't move your head's bleeding. Did you break anything? Don't move, you're not supposed to move."

Her face hovered over mine, eyes huge with worry.

"Hey," I said. "I finally beat you."

She didn't find this funny. She pulled off her sweater and wadded it gently under my head, tucked her beach towel over my body. "Don't move, I'm getting help." She ran uphill.

"Willa!"

"What?"

"Don't tell my father," I called weakly. Then the forest went black.

When I woke I saw green and blue. Evergreen branches framing sky. Then, eventually, the green and blue of Graham's soft plaid shirt.

Blood was trickling down my forehead and we didn't know how bad it was yet, but as he cradled me and picked me up, as if I weighed no more than the bough of a baby fir, he said, "I guess this place doesn't want you to leave, Lady Sunshine."

"The birdhouse disappeared."

Though he couldn't have understood what this meant, he said knowingly, "Ahh, child. Isn't that always the way?"

Later, after Willa went back to retrieve my bike—the contents of my basket had scattered far and wide, and my glass tube of Strawberry Kissing Potion was nestled in a branch six feet off the ground—she reported that the birdhouse had fallen off of its peg. Age and rot. Nothing insidious.

My injuries could have been much worse. Three sprained fingers, a gash above my right ear, a cut inside my lower lip, from when my face slammed against my bike bell. It left me with a permanent, private thickness that I'd run my tongue along whenever I was nervous.

I most likely had a mild concussion, according to the doctor half a mile up the highway. But he didn't think a scan was necessary. He shaved the two-inch strip above my scalp himself—apologizing because his nurse was off—gave me seven tidy stitches and a bottle of Vicodin, and made Graham and Willa swear they'd wake me every two hours.

"Better still if she doesn't fall asleep at all tonight," he said.

"Yes, sir," Graham said, mockingly, and I thought of insubordinate draftees from anti-Vietnam movies. But he added, looking at me: "We'll keep her entertained, Doctor."

I was bandaged, babied, rather enjoying the attention.

On the long van ride home—Graham driving, Angela in the passenger seat, me flat on the bed with Willa by my side—I asked Willa how my hair looked.

"It looks fine! Really punk!" But her eyes were still clouded by fear.

"I'm okay, Wills."

Angela made me wash the Vicodin down the kitchen sink drain. She offered me grass instead, something misty and gentle, for healing. Kate installed me in Willa's waterbed, with Willa on the floor. Angela put her cool hand on my forehead and promised she'd only write to my father if I got worse. All day people came bearing gifts. Records, pillows, magazines (new ones for a change). Liam presented a half-melted pint of custard. The kids clubbed together and gave me a lunch sack full of scratch-and-sniff stickers.

That night, Graham carried me to the top of the campfire ring and set me down next to him at his place of honor, decreeing that the entire community should stay awake with me.

What followed was an all-night campaign of carousing, improv, smoking, singing—some beautiful, some shockingly bad. A *Decameron*'s worth of entertainment crammed into one night.

I remember Willa's face at my right, aglow from the crackling campfire. She gave me a signed Blondie 45, a UK pressing from 1976 with "In the Flesh" on the A side and "X Offender" on the B side.

"Oh, Wills," I said, wiping my eyes, though the fire's plume was nowhere near me.

"It's nothing. Just wait for my dad's gift."

Near two in the morning, Graham handed me a small package. It was the gadget someone had sent him from Japan, the one that made music sound like "an underwater kazoo"—a Sony Walkman. I was glad to have it, but puzzled. Willa's excitement didn't seem to match this gift, expensive as it was.

Then Graham stood.

"And now my real birthday present," he said. "I told you today after your wee spill that this place didn't want you to go. And we don't want you to, either."

I held my breath, afraid to hope.

"Your father wrote back. He said you can stay here through the school year."

Most people can go their whole lives without feeling so loved.

I had sixty days of perfect happiness. Sixty consecutive days. I was needed, I was wanted, I was accepted. I was loved. I wonder if I appreciated these things more than any other visitor that passed through their gates. I was so hungry for it.

How ironic, if the person responsible for destroying their Eden had the only true taste of it.

29

W Room

It's been three days since my birthday, but I can't shake the *jangliness* that returned when I saw the bowls of shells on the picnic table. I try to hide it from Shane but he knows something's shifted between us.

The giddiness has vanished, and I can't seem to get it back. I can't run around here with him as if it's some kind of summer fantasy camp for reliving the past. A false version of that precious summer where I reenact everything good—music at campfire, unlikely friendship, infatuation, freedom from old rules, from the person I didn't want to be anymore—and pretend the bad never poisoned it.

I've been on a cloud. Happy to let my infatuation crowd out every other feeling associated with this place.

No, not *letting* it. Inviting it in to blot out the rest.

"Where've you gone?" he'd said, before drifting off beside me in bed just now. After weeks of wearing each other out until four a.m., I'd tensed when he kissed me. The first time that had happened.

"I can't stop thinking about everything I have left to do," I'd said.

"I'll help you. We'll all help you…"

I watch him sleep, trying to commit him to memory—the way his lips part in an appealing O, the curves of his shoulder under his left cheek, how he tucks his left hand between the mattress and headboard. I realize I don't know his birthday.

He went to so much effort for me… What if his is soon?

I lift his right hand from my hip and set it down gently, tiptoe out of bed. I ease his wallet out of the frayed black shorts he's draped over Kate's desk chair.

Business cards, health insurance card, grocery store club card…there, driver's license. Address the same as the one on his business cards. But he already told me that, how he's cobbled together producing work for the last few years. Money's too tight for a separate office.

His birthday's not until October. A Scorpio—now I can read his horoscope like a lovelorn schoolgirl. I'll be seven years older for only a couple of months, then six for most of the year. I can't help but be pleased by this fact, then scold myself for caring even for a second, for my vanity. So far, it hasn't bothered me except in the abstract, our age difference.

I slide the cards back into their leather slots and feel it. A folded-up paper in the big compartment, with his cash.

A love letter from an ex? His parole papers?

I can't help it: I always was a snoop. I glance over my shoulder to check that he's still sound asleep, pull the square of paper out and unfold it. It's the color of a tea stain.

A newspaper clipping from August 1979.

I wonder how long he's been carrying that sad story around.

I'd read the article back then. I'm the one who brought the newspaper up to the house, this house, the day it came out.

The story had been on the front page and I hadn't known what to do with the paper—if I should crumple it up and throw it in the water to disintegrate, the way Graham used to destroy the pages of words whose very existence pained him.

The Klamath Weekly Breeze

Fatal Accident Near Glass Beach Waterfall Trail
Local Singer Graham Kingston Dies at 47

By Sue McCafferty

Folk singer Graham Kingston, whose hits from the 1960s included "Lonely," "Meredith Lee," and "Breton Park," died of sepsis August 25 after sustaining multiple severe fractures from a 20-foot fall near the scenic North Fork Trail, adjacent to the Kingston family's 400-acre private property in Agate Beach. Kingston, 47, had lived in the area for 10 years.

"It's a devastating loss," said his long-time manager, Augustus Meade, 62, of San Francisco. "The music world has lost one of the greats."

Kingston was born in San Francisco in 1932 and studied music theory and medieval poetry at the University of California, Los Angeles, before dropping out sophomore year. He honed his musical style as part of San Francisco's club scene in the 1960s, opening for such notable acts as Big Brother and the Holding Company, Moby Grape, and the Charlatans, at clubs including the hungry i and Bill Graham's Fillmore Auditorium, before breaking through as a solo recording artist with Steel Pony Records in 1968. He was married to Trinidad Playhouse Company producer and actress Angela Swift Kingston, 50, and had one child, daughter Willa Ariel Kingston, 17.

Kingston was best known for his ingenuity and versatility on both six-and twelve-string acoustic guitar as a "sweep picker," for his ornate, "brocade-style" lyrics, which frequently mined obscure Irish and English folktales, and for his controversial 1970 experi-

mental album Three, *a commercial failure. His sprawling property in Agate Beach, the famed 400-acre "Sandcastle," which regularly attracts musicians and artists of all stripes, has been favored in recent years as a recording studio for up-and-coming performers.*

Kingston was hiking alone at dusk near the scenic trail, which overlooks the Pacific Ocean and Glass Beach Cove. Authorities believe that he became disoriented or lost his footing on the challenging terrain early in the evening of August 25. Toxicology reports were pending and Sheriff's Department officials would not comment as this issue went to press, but sources close to Kingston suggest that drugs may have been a factor.

Kingston was expected at the Gate Music Festival late that evening in San Francisco's Polo Fields, along with Neil Young, Jefferson Starship, and other headliners. When he failed to arrive for his scheduled car service and searches around his property proved fruitless, authorities mounted a 1,000-acre search and rescue operation. Kingston was found, unconscious and dehydrated, by a scent dog, concealed in a fern-covered, narrow stone crevasse on the adjacent property, only 100 feet from where he fell.

"Locals sometimes forget that these hills are still wild, and that our damp climate can make even seemingly gentle terrain slippery and unpredictable," cautioned Humboldt County Parks Health and Safety Manager Sheila Newton. "This unfortunate event is a warning both to novices and confident hikers who are well acquainted with the area. We always advise..."

Something has sprung loose inside me. Some final gate around my heart.

It's time.

I planned to deal with Willa's room while movers bustled around me, thinking it would make it easier. The organizing list I wrote the first week I came here, intending to stay only a week, is still taped to the parlor door. At the bottom it says— *W room. While movers here.*

But I know now that nothing, no distraction or delay, will make it easier.

I slip down the hall and sit at the foot of the stairs, gathering my courage.

Toby pads across the hall, looks at me curiously, then loses interest and lies on his side, batting his white mouse toy.

"Tk, tk, tk," I call, craving his silky warmth, a quick hit of comfort before I have to go upstairs.

But he's too occupied with his synthetic mousie. It's not rattling as it's supposed to and the feathers have come off, but he's ferocious—lobbing, chasing, clawing. He bats it hard and it slides far, gets stuck in the brass grill of the heating vent at my feet.

I kneel, fish it out. But it's not his toy, it's a big dust bunny. Big, and pale, with a short fuzzy tail. Toby swats at my hand as I examine it, unroll it— A shoelace? No. It's wider. With cutouts, an ornate design.

A scrap of lace. Willa's lace.

Was it the piece I'd used as my diary bookmark, the Super Special Bravery Award she gave me for a few seconds of surfing? She had so many lengths of lace for tying her hair back, and this could be any of them.

I tuck it into my pajama-top pocket and it calms me as I walk upstairs.

I'm not sure what I'm more afraid of—that the room will be swept bare or that it'll be exactly as it was—I only know that I need help to make it through.

As I climb the stairs, I picture us sprawled on her rug, playing records, laughing. Willa sleeping on her bedroom floor after my birthday so I could have the bed, my well-meaning but exhausted nurse.

And Willa hiding in her parents' room, alone, after Graham's accident at the falls.

"I'm so sorry," I whisper. "I wish I'd told you from the beginning that I didn't have all the answers."

I walk down the hall, open her door, and flick on the light.

It's the same. Of course it is. So Angela couldn't bring herself to change a thing. I guess that's why she stayed here as long as she could, long past the time when she should have downsized. She'd wanted to preserve this shrine to her daughter.

Willa's quilt, lavender with delicate sprigs of white flowers. Willa's ruffled pillow shams. The pale brown knitted bear cub with the stretched-out neck she'd called Acorn, because its eyes were made of acorn caps.

On her dresser: Ambergris-Peach Essential Oil from the Nature Shed, amber and turquoise beads strung from a miniature brass tree with stained glass leaves. Stacks of surf wax: the brand called Sex Wax, chocolate-and peach-and bubblegum-scented. Willa's thrift-store china teacups holding shells and sea glass.

On the walls are her posters, just as she'd tacked them up: Joan and Joan and Joni and Judy. All the *J*s that meant so much to her.

But no trace of this one. It's as if I was never here. I take pieces of sea glass from a cup and arrange them to form a *J* on top of the dresser.

I push aside the floral window curtain and kneel on the window seat, looking down at the field. It's a calm, cloudy day, but I remember so well that windy, bright one. I picture a seventeen-year-old girl down there, so out of place in her starched white eyelet blouse and I. Magnin culottes. She's dragging a yellow Samsonite suitcase. Her shiny brown shoulder-length hair, cut to look neat and frame her heart-shaped face, whips every which way in the wind. She chose to come, but she doesn't want to be here. And she's so angry. Her anger radiates off of her so furiously, it's as if she, not the breeze, is making the ripples in the grass.

She is angry. She is afraid. She asked to come, but now that she's set everything in motion, she's not sure she wants to be here. But of course that changed the minute her cousin invited her into her treehouse.

I open the door to Willa's small closet, brush a hand along her clothes. Her soft, flowing blouses, skirts, dresses. The rainbow of bandanna-print sarongs she favored for throwing over her swimsuit on the beach.

Gently, I push the hangers to both sides, exposing the bare lathe-and-plaster slats of the back closet wall. One board near the top of the wall is not nailed in—it's only resting on the board beneath it. I pull it out to reveal an opening, like a mail delivery slot cut into a door. But the diary isn't there. I replace the board and shut the closet door.

I look in the dresser, Willa's desk, under the rug and bed.

But the diary isn't in this room, either. Just as it wasn't twenty years ago. Willa must have taken it with her to Mexico. I suspected as much back then, and now I'm certain.

It's a comforting thought. That she wanted something of me with her.

I test the waterbed with one hand, and though by some miracle it hasn't leaked, it's half-full, so surely whatever liquid remains inside has gone brackish and fetid. But I lie on it. And I hug that deformed old stuffed bear tight for a long time. Imagining that he smells like peaches and fresh air, like Willa, instead of the mustiness of decades.

I know that, eventually, I'll have to move. I'll have to carry boxes up here, fill them, tape them shut, and label them. Say goodbye to Shane, and to all these good people, and fly home.

But for now, all I want to do is hug Acorn and lie perfectly still.

I can't start packing Willa's room yet. But the next morning, early, I go in the main bedroom with boxes.

To my relief, it's all Angela in here—nothing of Graham remains. Angela's clothes, Angela's gardening catalogs, Angela's albums of pressed flowers, her medical gear from her last weeks in the house, before Arbor View. It's a sad combination. I check under the bed.

Her desk has been cleared—the important documents are on file with the estate lawyer. But there's stationery. Stamps. Some old calendars.

My hand seizes around plastic—cold, the right width, could it be? But I know before I pull it out that it's the wrong weight. It's not the diary. It's a bundle of letters in a plastic file folder, marked *Correspondence.*

So formal. Letters from Willa? Did she write to Angela during those two years, despite what I was told?

My heart leaps, though Kate had said clearly, during her increasingly despairing calls, that Willa never phoned or wrote. Angela hunted high and low, hired private detectives on three continents, burning through money she couldn't spare back then, but they couldn't find her. Until word came from Mexico about her drowning.

I pull the letters out. No, they're not from Willa. They're only requests from music people, written after Graham got popular again four or five years ago. Asking to use the studio, to cover his songs.

Graham would find the gushing amusing—and highly gratifying. When he released *Three* in 1970, the few critics who bothered to review it dismissed it as "pretentious" and "treacly." When he came back in favor again, it was suddenly "pure" and "groundbreaking."

Some of the letter-writers are names I recognize; Shane would love to read these.

I thumb through the requests, and I realize that Angela tucked carbons of her typed responses in with the original letters. Fastidious Angela. She kept an orderly garden and, apparently, orderly business correspondence. Her responses are polite, brief, and repetitive—

"I'm sorry, I'm unable to say yes to your request to lodge in the stu-

dio, but thank you for your interest and your kind words about my late husband."

"I'm unable to agree to your request to take pictures in front of the house, but thank you for your interest." Over and over and over. She should have run off Xeroxes.

"I'm sorry, but unfortunately I've been unable to locate the lyrics my late husband was working on in 1979. But thank you for your interest and your kind words…"

Unable to locate?

There's another like that: *"Sadly, I've been unable to find the notebook of songs my late husband was working on in 1979."* And another: *"I've searched high and low but I'm unable to locate the notebook you mentioned seeing Graham with during your visit, which I remember fondly…"*

Of course Angela could be lying in the letters. But if so, why the change of heart last year? Because she knew she was running out of time? Because Shane was dear to her, and she wanted to help his career?

Shane. The source of all my information about the project. I don't want to think about the possibility that he hasn't been truthful from the beginning. But he did fail to tell me he grew up next door. He could have bought the notebook off of some black-market vintage music dealer, who'd stolen it from here years ago. Or could have stolen it himself. Maybe he forged the dedication in the notebook.

On the beach the other day, he'd tried to bring up his dishonesty. He'd said he'd never lie *to hurt someone.*

Maybe he has the diary, and I'm the world's biggest dupe for believing his stories, falling for him. Him and his pained eyes.

I run downstairs. "Shane?" I whisper, touching his arm. "Hey, Shane, wake up."

"Ahmmm? Up."

"I need to show you something."

He sits up, bleary-eyed. "Are you all right?"

"I'm fine. I found something. Look."

He rubs his eyes and reads. "'*Couldn't locate*'... What the hell...?"

He reads all of the carbons Angela kept—seven variations of the same claim. That Angela didn't know where the lyrics notebook was for years. The last letter stating that is only a year old.

"You're sure she never told you it'd been missing for a long time until recently, anything like that?"

"No way. I remember everything we talked about."

"So. Either she was lying in these letters, or she was telling the truth, and found the notebook pretty recently."

"Or I'm lying about how I got it. Except I swear Angela gave it to me. You believe me, right?"

"Of course."

"God, this is so fucked up."

He holds me as we reread the old onionskin copies together. "You think she found it when she was packing to move to Arbor View?" he says.

"Or maybe she had it all along and just wasn't ready to revisit Graham's music until she knew she was about to die."

"That makes sense. That she'd be torn about it, because of..."

"What?" Again I wonder just how much Shane saw from the trees. The little squirrel boy, Angela's secret friend.

Shane speaks gently: "Jackie. Angela wouldn't say much about the past at Arbor View. She'd...conveniently drift off...close her eyes, if I brought things up that were too hard to talk about. But she did say once that Graham could be difficult. No, *inconstant* was the word she used. She said his love was *inconstant*. Did you ever get that feeling?"

He watches me, waiting for my reaction.

"*Inconstant,*" I say. "A romantic way of putting it."

"Putting what, exactly?" he says.

"That he had a wandering eye." This is a euphemism, and

I'd scolded Shane for using one about Willa's drowning before. But it's the closest I've come to the truth.

"And that Angela...had a hard time with it?"

I nod.

"You think because I respect his music that I have illusions about him," he says. "But I don't. I did this for Angela."

"I know. Now. But why did Angela want you to? Why was she so cagey?"

He shakes his head, rubs his already messy hair. "I don't know. I don't know what it's like to be a woman on her deathbed, with a husband and daughter already gone in the saddest way. I guess we'll never know what was going on in her mind."

But however it got here, maybe the notebook's mysterious reappearance is a sign that the album was meant to be.

I'm sounding like Willa. It's the kind of flower-crown-y wishful thinking I used to tease her for. She saw signs in a gust of wind, in a skinned knee, in a song playing on the radio. She thought it was a damn sign that I'd been sent there for three months rather than two, or four. A sign that I was meant to stay here with her forever, because three was the most powerful number in nature.

I'd told her that she lived in a fantasy, seeing signs everywhere.

But now I want, more than anything, to believe in this one. That Angela found the notebook after it had been lost for many years, and I may never know how, but it has brought Willa and me together in the only way possible now.

I will try to appreciate that story. It's beautiful, even if parts of it are missing, and I have to fill them in, or leave them blank.

30

The Golden Lady

1999
One week later

It's the hour I like best. We're all outside, spread apart but linked together invisibly by our plans to rejoin soon. Family dinner.

I'm picking wild mint with Bree and Fiona in the sunny patch by the garden. We're having proper Cuban mojitos tonight at our barbecue. Our nighttime get-togethers have lengthened, often stretching to one or two a.m.

Shane and Piper are playing their guitars on the porch to escape the heat, their strumming interrupted by passionate discussions about the greats' styles, strings, humidity tricks that kept their guitars in prime sound. "Geeking out on their music history esoterica again," Bree calls it.

Mat and the rest have gone for a little hike.

"C'mon, you don't even want to hear your own songs?" Bree asks me.

"No. Not yet."

"Well. They're good."

"Of course, because you're singing them," I say lightly.

"I've heard all of it," Fiona says, her mouth full of mint. "It's pretty good. For old-people music."

"Well, thank you, Miss Fee," Bree says. "I'll take that as your highest praise.

"I'm going to keep hounding you 'til I leave," Bree says.

We go quiet. Even Fiona.

We rarely talk about leaving, though only a little polishing is left on the album, and Bree's Asian tour starts on August 25. In a week this place will be just as deserted as when I arrived.

"Jaye-kee!" Mat is calling from the woods behind the house. There's an urgent, un-Mat-like edge to his voice.

I drop my mint bouquet and hurry toward his voice. Everyone else does, too, thinking the same thing as me—Kauri's hurt.

"Jaye-kee!"

Mat again. His call is impatient, but not panicked, so Kauri must be all right. I follow Mat's voice, and realize he's not far from the treehouse. Maybe he and the other hikers have discovered it? Looked up at just the right time? I love them all, and it makes me happy whenever I see Fee and Kauri using my old cabin as their private playhouse.

But the treehouse is different. It belongs only to me and Willa.

I'm relieved when they come into view just south of the live oak tree. Mat, his wife Belinda, Kauri. Unharmed.

"Kauri thinks he saw a trespasser," Mat says.

"Oh yeah?" I kneel before him. Bree, Shane, Piper—everyone—comes up panting behind me. "Did someone scare you, Kaur?"

"No. I've seen her before. It was your golden lady."

"My golden…"

"I don't know what he's on about," Mat says. "Didn't mean to spook you. Just thought you should know, in case someone's climbed the fence."

"You saw a woman up here?" Shane asks Kauri. "Where?"

"There." He points at the base of the treehouse.

Shane and I exchange a quick look and he places his hand on my shoulder. I'm grateful for the warm, reassuring pressure, but have to will myself not to run over and look up. At the treehouse platform, the mostly hidden rope. Whatever else I might find.

Flax behind leaves.

"A blonde woman, is that what you mean, Kaur?" I sound so calm, so in command. My teacher-in-a-crisis voice. But inside I'm unstrung.

The FedEx, Willa's writing in the notebook, the album with her picture that Shane left out, the too-clean lace, Angela's onionskin copies. Each shock has softened my resistance, blurred my certainty that some things just aren't possible. Each has prepared me for this moment—Kauri announcing that a golden lady haunts the treehouse.

Kauri shakes his head. "No. It was that golden lady we saw before. That day." He points downhill, toward the ocean.

Everyone else is mystified; I breathe out slowly. "You mean that day we all went on the Flying Swing."

He nods. He means Vivienne, my real estate agent, with her gold jewelry. Of course that's what a kid would remember about her. There's always, always a logical explanation. I am relieved and disappointed at once. Perhaps a grain more disappointed— and Willa would be proud of that. Of how this place can still make the most grounded person believe in the unearthly. At least for a fleeting moment.

"And the Golden Lady was walking around here just now?" I ask. "Alone?"

"She was with a man. They were looking down at the house, then they walked up there." He points up at the ridge. "They were snooping."

"Oh yeah?"

He nods; he would know.

"I'm really glad you told me, Kaur. Thanks for looking out for this place."

I lead them uphill toward where Kauri pointed, taking a
slightly indirect route to avoid going under the treehouse.

We all troop up. Me and Kauri and Shane, flanked by the
rest of the crew.

I look over the ridge, at the eastern vista Willa once showed
me from high in the treehouse. The light is fading fast but I can
still make out the neighboring property, past the few remaining trees on this side of the property line. The land behind the
Kingstons' wasn't much to look at then, and it still isn't. A few
decaying structures, scrubby fields, downed animal pens.

But in the distance, near the road, there's a bulldozer, scaf-
folding. A pit that will soon become a swimming pool. An
expensive renovation will replace the old shack with an impressive mini-estate. This land has become *highly sellable* in the last
twenty years, as Vivienne and Rand Whitman have told me
many times. Even without views and beach access and *natural
amenities*, like the Kingstons'.

Two voices drift up from behind a cluster of nearby coast firs:

"…we could push for a fast escrow if it suits you. You'd have
six hundred acres, including ocean frontage. Impossible to find
around here now." Vivienne. The little sneak.

A strange man's voice: "And why is it we can't go on the actual property in question yet?"

"The current owner is working on some kind of *rock album*
there before vacating."

He must make a face or mutter something sarcastic, because
Vivienne says, "I know, I know, and you'll want to raze all of
those structures, of course. But the lower acreage of the parcel
is special, really incredible. I'll work on her…"

Vivienne's chatter gets louder, a little strained from exertion;
they're walking north along the hill-face, coming closer to us.
"…truly sought after, we've had a deluge of interest. Half a mile
to the north it's all state preserve. Of course you're familiar with
the egress—"

They emerge from behind the trees. Vivienne in a cream dress and her gold jewelry, and a stubby, suited man who's mopping his shining forehead with a hankie.

They spot me and the group, standing in a line on the ridge above them. Gunslingers from a Western. Vivienne, busted, stops short.

"Hey, neighbors!" Piper calls out. "Nice day for a stroll!" Piper's shooting Vivienne the kind of look old hair-band guitarists in videos give the camera right before they smash their axe.

It's how I feel. How dare she poke around here, near the treehouse, as if it's just another *parcel*. Not my sacred ground.

"Jackie!" Vivienne says, trying to recover. "What terrific luck! This is Andrew Simmons, who recently bought this parcel. Remember, I mentioned that he might be interested in yours? We were just—"

"Trespassing?" I call back.

They have a private conversation and walk up to us, Vivienne sending me *don't botch this* looks.

"No harm done, right?" The man peers downhill. "Since we're here, how about showing us a little more of the promised land?"

"Not today," I say coolly. "It's not a good time for us."

I glance over at Shane, but his attention's not on me, or the man in the suit, or Vivienne. His eyes are glassy, and he's staring down at the bulldozers cutting into the neighboring land. The *parcel*.

"Jackie, I would've called you if you had a cell," Vivienne says. "We just crossed onto your side a titch to see the parcel from above."

"Vivienne," I say quietly. "Take your visitor back. The way you came. And I'll be hiring another listing agent."

"Jackie, I know you're—"

"Go," I say. She marches back uphill with her client.

Shane hasn't said a word. Not *don't be rash*, and not *way to give it to them, Jackie*. Nothing.

He's just gazing off at the bulldozers.

"Hey?" I ask him, rubbing his arm softly. "What's up?"

He shakes his head slightly. He's got that pained look again. The look from the first day, from the field. I haven't seen it in a while. Maybe he's thinking about how we all have to leave here soon, how life after August is a big unknown, so cold and foreign that we're afraid to talk about it. Maybe he's just depressed, seeing the bulldozers carving into the hill.

The two of us stand there, silent and still. Close. And I don't realize until Fiona giggles and Piper shushes her that I've given it all away—that Shane and I are together.

"Paving paradise," Bree says. "Well, that was all very exciting, but I'm thirsty. C'mon, soldiers." I see her out of the corner of my eye, signaling to the others to leave us alone.

Long after their footsteps in the dry leaves fade out, Shane and I watch the bulldozers below the ridge. He seems even sadder than me to see them there. His jaw and fists are clenched, and I remember the rocks he threw that night I followed him.

"I'm no better than they are," I say. "I'm the pavement villain from the Joni song. That's what you're thinking, isn't it?"

"Oh. No. Oh, Jackie." He's out of his spell. He puts his arms around me and I rest my cheek on his chest. "Not at all."

"But it's true," I murmur. "I saw you throwing rocks here that night. And this time next year, maybe sooner, there'll be a fleet of bulldozers on this side of the ridge, cutting everything up. Then it'll be as ugly as what's over there."

He strokes my shoulder. "It happens. Land changes hands. Land changes. It's not your fault, you know it's not."

We turn, walk downhill, back toward the house.

Under the big old oak that holds the treehouse, we stop and gaze up. It's my first time here during the day.

"I thought Mat or someone had found it and that's why they

were shouting," I said. "You think whoever buys the place will cut the tree down?"

He shakes his head, caressing the bark. "It's a beautiful old tree. They won't hurt it."

I circle the trunk, looking up. "You're just saying that to make me feel better."

"Is it working?"

"A little, even if it's bull… Shane?"

"Hmmm?"

"Look at the rope."

High above our heads, the frayed end of the rope ladder swings gently. It's not where I left it the night after I climbed up, carefully tucked high up into branches, the way Willa and I used to hide it between visits. And it has broken off about ten feet from the ground. I hunt around…there, in a bush. The lower section of rope. I pick it up and hold it, running my hand over the split ends. They look spiky, but they're soft as baby hair.

"Maybe an animal chewed on it?" Shane asks.

"Maybe."

"Or one of the kids was swinging on it and it broke?" Shane says. "Or someone else, one of the session guys who wandered up here for a smoke…?"

"But they'd have to see the rope, then get it down, and it would've been nearly impossible to notice if you didn't already know it's up there. Even in daylight."

"*Nearly* impossible."

"A trespasser, after all. I hope they didn't get hurt." I peer into the woods to where my uninvited visitor might have vanished.

"You don't know that for sure. But we'll call the cops to be safe."

"No." I try to climb the tree but it's useless; I get only scraped palms. "There's a ladder in the shed. Angela used it for picking crab apples and plums."

"Jackie, let's talk first, ask the others if they know what's up…"

"Fine, I'll get it."

He puts his hand out to stop me. "No, I will."

When Shane's gone, down the hill and safely out of earshot, I call out softly, knowing it's madness, to see how it feels.

"Willa?"

We sit in the darkening treehouse.

There's a water bottle, a sleeping bag in a corner. The fabric scraps that were strewn on the floor as carpet have been mounded up as a bed pallet. Since the night I came up weeks ago, someone has slept here.

"It wasn't like this when you…"

"No."

"It was probably some fan," Shane says. "Or… I hope it wasn't someone I brought to the studio who didn't tell me they needed a place to crash?"

"Yeah. That's probably it."

"But why wouldn't they just ask, with all the empty cabins around? It's weird…"

"It is."

"Goldilocks," he says, taking my hand. Trying to lighten my mood. But that hits too close to home.

Like everything else, this too can be explained away. A visitor to our secret, favorite place. I know, logically, that there must be a simple answer, one that has nothing to do with my lost cousin.

I won't tell Shane about the young face, the length of flax behind wind-ruffled leaves I imagined seeing that day when everyone was playing by the pool.

"I still think we should call the cops," he says.

"No. Let's let them be. No harm done."

He comes to me, wraps his arms around me from behind as I stare out to where the ocean is. "Well, they can't climb up here again. Not after we lock the ladder away."

"That's right."

"Jackie." He hugs me, but my hands stay close to my sides until he lets go.

I have no business being happy here. For weeks, I've been acting like a teenager. Now I feel every day of my age.

How am I thirty-eight, Willa, while you're forever nineteen? Half my age…

Invincible. We'd felt invincible together. We felt like we could control things, right things, from this hidden aerie in the trees. We'd done it with Ben and Rose. Liam's thieving coworker. I'd schemed at school, recounted my little revenge missions to her. I'd loved how Willa saw me—Justice with Her Flaming Sword. Her clever, brave, cool city cousin.

I wonder, sometimes, if the closeness we had that summer was all in my head. The girl who vanished without a goodbye doesn't sound like the cousin I knew…or thought I knew. Maybe what we had for those three precious months was only a confluence of her isolation and my longing for family. I wish I understood why Willa turned her back on this place, the place she'd always vowed she'd never leave. Even after everything that happened the last week we were together, she should have found healing here. I wish I'd tried harder to reach her, to help her.

I gaze west. "You can't see as much now. You used to be able to see all the way to the water. That myrtle tree's grown like crazy. It blocks the view."

I leave Shane and cross the rickety platform. "Sometimes Willa and I would fall asleep here. It wasn't so comfortable. But it was really something, waking up high in the air. Hearing the birds in the morning, and…"

I see something in the crook of a branch outside the tree-house, near the window. Another flash of yellow. Was it here the other night? I might not have noticed it in the dark…and I only felt around on the other side of the tree, in my hiding place.

I reach out as if I'm just leaning on the tree to get a better view and touch it. Solid. Rectangular. I know the shape, the thickness, as well as I know the feel of my piano keys under my fingers.

"Jackie? What were you saying?"

"Oh." I'm aching to pull it from the branches, but I don't want to tell him yet. I'm not sure why. "Nothing. I'm exhausted. I don't know what decade I'm in."

At two a.m., while Shane is sleeping, I creep back behind the house to the garden shed, the flashlight in my jeans waistband.

I carry the weathered gray-brown ladder back up to the tree, prop it against the trunk on the far side. The east side, where it can't be seen from the house.

I climb up. Reach for the corner of yellow. *Don't get your hopes up, it could be any book.* A Bible, *Treasure Island*, an ornithology guide…

The cover is plastic, trimmed with fuzzy strips of artificial suede, stiff and cold to the touch.

I set it on my lap and examine it under the flashlight.

A cloud of batting has escaped from one corner of the diary, where the plastic cover has split, and it's dusty, but other than that it's in remarkable shape, considering. Its colors are still garish. The cover's made up of wide yellow and orange and red and pink color blocks, separated by thin borders of glued-on white Ultrasuede. In the lower left corner is a sun, bright as an egg yolk. Shooting out from it across the cover at forty-five-degree angles are thick rays, three of them, holding fat, stretched-out words—

GOOD
DAY
SUNSHINE

I remember how Graham strummed a few bars of the Bea-tles song when he came across me writing in this. He got me to crack, peek at him above the cover. He knew how much I wanted to join in.

How I pity that swaggering girl I used to be. Acting so tough, when she was aching for the Kingstons to embrace her as one of their own.

They'd won me over so easily. A kind look from Willa, Angela's cool hand on my forehead, Graham strumming a few Lennon–McCartney bars on his guitar.

And I was theirs.

31

Skipper's Fall

1979

Dear Ray,

I'm eighteen now.

And I'm staying.

Graham wrote my father, and he agreed.

Willa and I are so happy we can't close our eyes, even though we were up all night at my birthday/concussion party (more on that some other time). We keep trying to sleep, but then one of us bursts out laughing in the dark, and her waterbed rolls and sloshes like we're sailing in a squall out on the Bay, and we give up and turn on the light again.

We've got the radio on KFOG, The Top 200 Hits of Summer Countdown. They're on number 103. My old favorite, "Goodbye Stranger" by Supertramp. Three months ago I'd have switched the station at the first note of that dopey organ. But when it came on just now Willa and I only looked at each other and laughed. She knows all about the incident(s) at my school.

My former school. I never have to go back there. No more of that junk in the halls. No more of that girl, whoever she was.

Goodbye, Stranger.

*Willa's across the bedroom making space for me in her closet.
She just asked if I want the left side or the right. I told her I don't
care. I'll hang my clothes from the trees, Ray. I'll stuff them in the
pantry next to Kate's jelly jars. I'll sleep in the woods.*

I'm staying and that's all that matters.

Happy.

Happy.

Happy.

The Monday after my birthday was clear and sunny. Beautiful, but too windy for the beach, so we took the kids to the lower pond. It was lush and green, fed by Graham's waterfall.

Willa and I kept smiling at each other across the water. Basking in the knowledge that I was staying.

I was watching Dylan—of the superhero cape—and her new friend, bold young Alice. They were playing with Alice's most treasured toy, a Skipper Barbie doll. Malibu Skipper, Barbie's younger sister. Every time we went to the falls, Malibu Skipper went swimming, or the kids made her a boat out of leaves, or a jungle gym out of branches. Skipper had had so many adventures that her tan had been scraped off, but she was a hardy soul and had survived worse. Their latest game was putting her in a swing made out of Dylan's cape.

Willa was attending to a little girl with a scraped knee, and I was helping a bunch of kids hunt for Graham's paper, his song rejects, as we always did here—they liked scooping up the pulpy masses that he crumpled up at the falls.

So neither of us was looking at Alice and Dylan. If we had been, maybe we'd have advised against Skipper's latest outdoor adventure. Or made sure the cape had been knotted more tightly. Watched out for calamity.

I'd just spotted a clump of paper near some reeds when there was a wail from the other side of the pond.

Dylan. A wail of such undiluted agony that I was sure something terrible had happened.

Willa and I rushed over and were relieved to see that the victim was plastic: poor Skipper.

Poor Dylan. In their haste to get started, or our inattention, no one had checked to make sure that the knot securing Skipper's swing was secure. Or maybe the kids had dunked the doll a few seconds longer than usual, and her hollow plastic torso had filled with more stream water than the other times they'd played this game. Enough to make her a slight, tragic bit heavier. I could still see her, cruising away fast, the bright fabric bunched under her legs like a gay little life raft. Dylan could only point and wail. Willa picked her up, soothing her.

Alice was stoic—so Alice—and seemed more fascinated by this, Skipper's ultimate dare, Skipper rounding a big boulder like an Olympic whitewater paddler.

I jumped into the cold water, confident that I could reach the doll and the cape before it was too late. The drop was a good twenty feet away, with plenty of rocks to stop her. I was not worried, I swam and reached out. I caught…hair, only hair. Skipper's synthetic blond mop.

The four of us watched as Dylan's prized cape, marigold decorated with purple butterflies, whooshed off into the foam and disappeared down the falls.

Willa and I exchanged a look. Silently and immediately, we agreed—deceit was the only option. The cape would soon be soaked, tumbling in the ocean, but what poor, crestfallen Dylan didn't know was that her Ultra Special Bravery Award had a dozen copies lying on the floor of the treehouse, waiting to save the day.

"I'll just run down to the lower-lower pond and grab it, Dylan. Don't worry. I'll be back before you know it."

She stared at me in relief and surprise. A *lower*-lower pond?

No one had mentioned it before. But she was happy to believe in this miracle.

"See!" Willa crooned, rocking her back and forth. "Jackie's going to take care of things. Jackie always knows how to take care of things." This was for me, said gratefully as she looked up, with a slight twinkle in her eye.

First I went downhill, but a cursory hunt in the fast-moving stream proved what we'd feared: the cape was beyond rescue, sailing out to sea. There was, of course, no lower-lower pond.

I hurried back up the edge of the trail, slipping past the lower pond in the trees where the kids wouldn't see me. I ran across the field, turning left as if to go to my cabin, but taking my customary route up to the treehouse instead. It was adult nap time, and all the kids were with Willa, so no one would be there to follow me. But my sneaky, indirect route was a habit at this point.

I fished the rope ladder down with Willa's shepherd's crook branch, climbed up and pulled the rope inside after me. Another habit—I wouldn't be here more than a minute. I grabbed a piece of fabric off the floor, inspecting it for any telltale marks that would distinguish it from the real thing. But Dylan would want to believe this was original, that her cape had swum back to her. I counted on that.

The first piece I picked up was the right size but the wrong shape. I hunted for a more rectangular one. As I was crumpling it to simulate wear, I looked idly out the treehouse window, down at the garden. Two people stood near the fringe of the trees.

I grabbed the spyglass.

Graham and Serena stood close together near the edge of the woods north of the house, holding hands. Then Serena pulled back with a smile; Graham, heading toward the house, tugged her to him for a kiss. They had come from the woods, from the direction of Serena's cabin, which was near mine; it was obvious they were saying their goodbyes.

Serena, Dylan's mother.

Serena was wearing denim overalls with nothing underneath and fumbling to clip the left strap onto the button. Graham casually bent and rubbed his face back and forth between her breasts while she laughed. Then he clipped the strap in place for her. As if he'd done it a million times.

Serena said something to him that I couldn't hear. They were too far away. But it was playful; she was still laughing as she swatted at him, trying to leave for the woods, her cabin. Soon it would be four, the hour that Willa and I usually returned with the kids. Adult nap time would be over and they were cutting it close.

I'd never seen them speak, had only heard Graham complain about Serena "sabotaging the work," so they made a strange pair. A strange movie, framed by the gold-painted ring around the toy spyglass lens that brought me right next to them. *Wow— 20x Magnifying Power!!*

But they were as oblivious to my presence as the loved ones you're trying to save in a nightmare.

Then Serena looked past Graham, at something in the garden.

She stopped laughing.

She pushed his head away, fumbled with her other shoulder strap to cover herself.

Graham turned to see what she was looking at, and I swept the spyglass left, a blurry circle of fast-moving greens and blues rushing before my eye as I searched, moving the spyglass around, up, down to find what had startled them.

Angela.

She stood alone behind the garden shed. She wore her canvas newsboy bag, the front compartment bulging, dandelions poking over the edge; she'd been weeding. She'd told me last night at dinner that she was thinking of expanding the garden to make room for fall herbs. There was a lemon balm leaf that grew well here, if you tended to it carefully. But she was supposed to be at a friend's matinee in Forest Grove; I'd heard her talking about it with Willa.

She didn't say a word. She stood perfectly still, her face amused. *Amused.* Her actor's skill on display. I sat in the upper balcony, but even without the spyglass I'd have felt what she was projecting.

Graham said something quick and sharp to Serena and she left, disappearing into the trees.

Then he walked over to his wife. Unhurried, his body already dictating calm.

"Angel," he said.

They were closer now; I could hear them clearly. I no longer needed the spyglass but I kept watching them through it, holding my breath as if they were as near as they seemed, and might hear me.

"Have a good nap?" Angela asked. "I know how badly you've been sleeping." Her low voice was full of concern. She sounded so tender, so selfless.

So false. It would have scared me less if her voice held a trace of real emotion.

"Angel. It's nothing."

"I know, darling." She tidied her newsboy bag, carefully packing the dandelions down in the front, adjusting the yoke so that it hung more comfortably around her neck. She looked up at him, smiling sweetly. "I'm just curious about one thing. When she blows you, do you pay our daughter double time to babysit her kids?"

And then it was Angela who laughed. Mirthless, frightening laughter.

For one endless minute he stood frozen. Then his hand flew across her face. She flew to the ground.

The spyglass dropped to my lap.

I kept watching, trying to believe it. Graham was the gentle giant, everyone knew that. His van had bumper stickers that said "Choose Peace" and "Make Love, Not War." But maybe war on a personal level was a different cause. Maybe he thought there were exceptions, if you'd had a run of bad luck.

And maybe, later, he would tell himself that he had not hit her. That he'd only *slapped* her. Some other word to try to pretty up what he had done.

I hadn't seen his fingers; it happened fast and my viewing angle, from above, was not ideal for that detail. It was possible his fingers had been spread during the second they made contact with her skin. Maybe the sound of his right hand meeting her left temple was higher and hollower than it had seemed by the time it floated up to me.

But what did it matter if his hand was closed or open? There were two hundred pounds behind it. And it sent her to the ground.

And the saddest sight of all, more than Graham nuzzling between Serena's breasts, more than the casual way he had clipped her overall strap back in place, even more than his giant hand flying across Angela's face, or her small body hitting the ground, dandelions tumbling out of the newsboy bag, was this—the way she now crouched, her hands clasped over her head. A protective stance, like what they made us do in the city during earthquake drills.

He loomed over her: he was smaller, now, through my naked eyes. His hand was raised, though his wife couldn't see it.

If he does it again you'll run to her.

I hope I would have. I'm not sure.

But he didn't do it again. He dropped his hand. Shrank back into himself and collapsed to the dirt next to her.

"It's stopping, Angel," he said, his face resting between her shoulder blades, rubbing back and forth. "It's stopping this second, for good. I was nervous about the show and I made a mistake. I'm so sorry. My beautiful Angel, I don't deserve you. I don't know why you stay with me."

His shoulders shook. He had started to cry.

He picked her up and though I couldn't see her face she didn't resist, and hung limp in his arms. He carried her inside, through the back door, as tenderly as a new groom carrying his bride across the threshold.

I waited, staring out the treehouse window at Angela's tidy plantings of summer herbs and vegetables, until Graham and Angela had been inside for a long time.

When Kate clanged her dude-ranch triangle, the short signal that told us all it was time to wash up and get moving because the food would be out in ten, I folded Dylan's substitute cape into a square and stuffed it in my back pocket. Legs shaking, I made my way down the rope ladder and used the shepherd's-crook branch to push it up and hide it on a high limb, the way Willa had taught me.

I would never tell her. That much I knew already.

Except.

"Willa?" I whispered.

She was under the big cypress twenty feet up the hill and to the right, staring down at the garden just as I had been a moment earlier. As if her parents were still there. She sat with her chin on her bent knees, her long yellow flower-print sundress spread around her.

Her frozen expression told me: she'd seen everything.

I spoke more loudly: "Willa?"

She started and looked over at me in surprise, but didn't say anything. I walked up to her; the hill was so steep here that I practically had to crawl.

"Are you okay?" I asked.

She nodded, but took her hands out of her lap to hug her legs close to her body.

Her wrists and forearms were bright red.

Blood, I thought, somehow blood, she'd done the worst. It made no sense, to think she'd done that; there hadn't been time or opportunity. But that was my first thought as I dropped in front of her, fumbling with her slippery, bright red arms, examining her wrists, hunting in vain for the wound. "What did you... Where did you..."

She unclenched her hands, showing me what was inside them. Not a cut. Strawberries. Garish clots and seeds from the handful of bright berries she'd squeezed. "Dylan's cape has that big stain," she said mechanically. "I wanted to make the new one match. I was worried I wouldn't find you before you gave it to her."

Relieved, I sat next to her and tried to get control of my breathing. "That was good thinking, Wills. That was smart of you."

"I left her in the kitchen with Kate. She's giving the kids ice cream." She hugged herself tighter and began rocking back and forth.

"Yes. Good."

"We have to use a piece that's the same size. If it's not the same size, she'll know."

"It's okay, I found one." I took the fabric from my pocket and unfolded it, draping it gently over her knees. I guided her palms down to it. "Here? Show me where."

She stopped rocking and focused on the task I'd assigned her, wiping her hands on the lower right corner of the cloth, carefully pressing and rubbing the crushed berries in to replicate the stain.

"I'm so glad you remembered," I said. "Dylan's lucky that you did."

"She's frantic."

"I know." I squeezed her hands, staining mine. "But what about you? Are you okay?"

She nodded, looking down at her lap, where the berry juice had streaked her yellow floral-print dress red.

"Don't worry, we can get that out. Let's rinse it before it sets."

I led her down the hill to the pump behind the garden shed, took Dylan's cape from her and set it on a sunny patch of grass. I bunched up the stained part of her skirt and held it under the water, careful to wet only what I had to, rubbing at the red splotches with the bar of homemade lavender Castile soap Kate kept hanging inside an old stocking knotted to the handle.

"Look, it's coming out. See?" I lathered and rinsed, squeezing the cloth until the only traces of strawberry juice on Willa's dress were a few pale peach shadows on the yellow background.

I washed her hands for her, cleaning mine at the same time. The white lather turned red, then pink, then white again, the water running clear, but no matter how much I scrubbed I couldn't remove the angry U's of color from our cuticles.

"Have a drink." I caught water in the cup of my hand and made Willa sip. "A little more, Wills." Obedient as a child, she let me tip water into her mouth. I turned the rusty pump handle to shut it off.

"Wait," she said. "Dylan's cape."

"What? It's okay, it's right over there, remember?" Maybe this was shock. I should splash her face with cold water, or no, keep her warm—it had been foolish to get her dress wet. I'd take her to her room, bundle her up...

"It wouldn't be dry," she said. "You just saved it from drowning."

Relieved that she was making sense, I turned the tap back on and held the fabric remnant under it so that it would look as if I'd just rescued it from the stream. "There. See? A perfect copy. She'll never know."

She nodded.

"Willa—"

"She's waiting. We have to bring it to her..."

"Dylan'll be all right. Kate's good with her. She can wait a few more minutes. I want to talk to you."

She shook her head, a quick, clearing-out motion, totally

unlike her. It took me a second to remember where I'd seen it before.

Graham. It's what he did whenever he was disgusted with something he'd written and needed to erase it, to pretend it had never existed. He did it right before crumpling up his scrawled-on pieces of paper and tossing them into the water.

Kate's dude-ranch triangle sounded again from the front porch: a cheerful clatter of *tings* that would carry across most of the Sandcastle's four hundred acres. *Time to come together, children.*

"Second dinner bell," Willa said.

I tried to put my arms around her but she stood stiffly, evading my hug, not my floating cousin but some graceless impostor.

It was like this for six days. She pantomimed the real Willa, and no one but me seemed to notice. Maybe Angela would have seen the change in her daughter, but she was gone again. A Lillian Hellman festival up the coast. A last-minute trip.

Whenever I tried to talk to Willa about what we'd seen in the garden, she'd find an excuse to change the subject. If I pressed, she'd leave. Or she'd surround herself with kids, throw herself into entertaining and soothing them.

I tried to at least keep track of her whereabouts, but she vanished for hours. Willa knew how to shake me; she was as skilled as a wild animal in that way. I guessed that she was rambling around the woods, venturing onto the neighbors' land, over the ridge to where the family of "satyrs" lived—land where I didn't know the terrain and would get lost immediately if I tried to find her.

She went to campfire, continuing to share our low stone seat as if nothing was wrong. She watched politely. But she did not clap or laugh, and she disappeared off to the woods as soon as Graham stood and stretched, the nightly ritual that always preceded the private one—his hike up to the waterfall.

Willa stopped meeting me at the treehouse at night, claiming, mechanically, that she was too tired. She certainly looked tired; I wondered if she was sleeping at all. She didn't go to the beach or bathe, and her body began smelling different, a sour-fruit smell. Grease darkened her hair to dirty-blond, and instead of floating around her in its usual bright nimbus cloud, it became snarled, and hung in hanks down her neck.

Liam showed up one night after campfire for a date, holding wildflowers, and Willa hid from him.

"She's not feeling well," I said. "A little summer cold. But I'll give her these."

He looked crushed. "I'm leaving in a couple weeks," he said.

"I know. I'll remind her."

But when I did, she only nodded and gazed off at the tree line.

For everyone else, life went on much as it had all summer. Smiles, skin, sun. People driving up, people driving off.

We were awash in music, as always. Audible music—the constant, unhurried playing around the field. Discussions about music. The *awareness* of music being created in the dungeon, evidenced by the purposeful coming and going through the studio door—it had given me such a thrill, just a week ago, to know what was happening down there.

But for me, the joy had been drained from all of it.

Even the light had changed, making everything seem starker, shadowed. Maybe this was only because it was late August and the sun rode lower in the sky.

Maybe it was because I was alone again.

Within hours after Angela caught Serena and Graham together, Serena and Dylan had left for good. Dylan hardly got to say goodbye to me or Willa, and although there were many reasons to be angry at my uncle, and Serena could hardly have stayed after what happened behind the garden shed, her little girl's sudden and undeserved exile from paradise stood out, that awful week, as an especially vivid cruelty.

I imagined Dylan in the way-back of her mom's wheezing Pinto wagon, crying and hugging her substitute cape, pressing her chubby hand to the glass as they pulled away. She would have watched as the spire of the Sandcastle got smaller and smaller, then disappeared behind the trees.

32

The Peloponnesian War

Like Willa, I went through the motions. Six more babysitting sessions in which I added up the minutes we'd given Graham for betrayal. Six more campfires, with him holding court, laughing. The generous host, the gentle giant. It seemed impossible that what we'd seen was real.

Instead of acting contrite, he was buoyant, floating on excitement because the "little gig" at the polo fields in Golden Gate Park, the one he insisted was no big deal, was coming up soon.

"Grace is playing. I don't know who else is gonna be on the lineup, Bill's full of surprises, as always... But you shouldn't waste a whole weekend on it. It's such a haul down to the city..."

To the right of me on our shared stone seat, Willa sat stiff and mute.

Silently, we watched Graham laugh and carry on, proving with every denial and self-deprecating joke, every casual use of a legendary first name, how huge this was for him.

I looked at Willa and for once she met my eyes. The firelight danced across her face as she held it perfectly expressionless, her mouth a straight line. When she rose and walked into the dark, I went after her.

She could have lost me within seconds if she wanted to. But she stayed in the center of the clearing, heading straight downhill, and I was able to keep up. That's how I knew she was ready to talk.

I followed her across the parking lot, down not the pretty, private trail, but the gravel road. A route we never used.

When we reached the highway I stayed close, ready to yank Willa back from a speeding car. I'd been wrong about her cutting herself behind the treehouse, but this Willa was unpredictable, and no one else was going to keep her safe.

But she seemed in control. She looked left, then right, then left again, before crossing. Past the custard shack, down the steep trail to Glass Beach. Around the tide pools, past a touristy-looking older couple on a picnic blanket.

We walked past the spit, climbing over washed-up kelp and other debris to a long stretch of sand that was deserted except for a single log: this seemed to satisfy her.

She sat, leaving me space on her left. I settled next to her and for a few minutes we were quiet, watching the moonlight stippling the dark waves, listening to the wind and the slow, steady breathing of the tide. Off in the distance were a few surfers, the glow-rings around their necks floating and gliding, but I couldn't make out Liam's familiar shape.

"It's starting again," Willa said, shivering.

"What is? The night surfing?"

She shook her head, that awful clearing-out gesture of Graham's. "I guess Liam'll be hitting the road for Costa Rica soon."

"He's desperate to see you."

"Did you tell him anything?"

"No."

"Thanks." She shivered again.

"Here." I started to take off my cardigan.

"Then you'll be cold."

So I took my right arm out of its sleeve. I drew her close and folded her inside the body of the sweater, wrapping the thick wool around her, pinning the empty sleeve tight under my left elbow to keep us both warm. Now I was the one who was rock-ing, the slightest of side-to-side motions.

"That's nice." She leaned her head on my shoulder and her body softened. "I'll bet you're sure glad you came here."

"Of course I am."

"You don't want to split?"

"No."

"But your place sounds perfect...even the address. *Number Eight Pleasant Avenue.* Nothing ugly could ever go down at Number Eight Pleasant Avenue."

Continuing to rock her gently, I spoke with all the patience, the lulling, hypnotizing *reasonableness*, that we used to calm the kids. I tried to sound as soothing as she had been when Ceci-lia was howling about the wasp sting she'd gotten on the cove trail, and the time in July during one of our hikes to the mud flats off of Glass Beach, when Rhys had stumbled onto a grackle with a broken wing:

"You think you know about Number Eight Pleasant Avenue?" I said. "Let me tell you about Number Eight Pleasant Avenue. Everyone stays in their pleasant rooms, hiding away from each other. The pleasant man and the pleasant woman have twin beds and their own pleasant, separate, luxurious bathrooms with brand-new pale yellow tile. The cream-colored carpet is pleas-antly thick so no one has to hear a single footstep. The walls are thick, too. But it hardly matters because they never, ever raise their voices at each other."

"Never?"

"Of course not! They *discuss*. The father wears a tie to break-fast, even on Saturdays. The wife wears a full face of Elizabeth Arden and pearls and one of her hundred-jillion pairs of beige I. Magnin pantyhose that she keeps in her second dresser drawer, lined up on their sides. Like file folders."

This got a tiny smile out of her; I felt it in the way her cheek moved against my chest.

Encouraged, I went on. "They're always on their best behavior. It's a museum, Wills. A quiet, cold, freaky museum. The Robert Morrison Pierce Museum of Repression and Depression. I'd rather be here than there, or anywhere else. Because here it's messy, and loud, and colorful, and real. And here has you."

She became quiet for a minute, as she always did when I finished a long story. Then she said, "I don't know what I'd do if you hadn't come here."

"But I am here. And it'll be okay."

It had to be okay. Willa needed me; what I'd seen from the treehouse had made that more clear than ever. I had to hold it together for her, help her. Who else would? Angela couldn't even help herself. She'd just split.

"Now that your dad's realized how wrong he's been, and his career's looking up with the show and all, maybe things'll go back to how they were before."

"No. You've got it backward."

"What d'you mean?"

She turned to face me. Bound together as we were inside the sweater-cocoon I'd made, she was only inches from my face, so close I could feel her breath on my cheek—little puffs of warmth the wind couldn't steal.

"What, tell me?" I asked. "I mean, I'm not excusing what he did. Especially... No way. But he's been convinced nobody would ever want to hear his music anymore, I mean, outside of here. That's heavy stuff. It had to do a number on him. I'm sure that's why he messed around with Serena, and why he... What?"

Her eyes were so sad. So *cynical*.

What, Willa? What?

It finally clicked.

"Oh, Wills. I'm so stupid." That's what she'd meant by *It's starting again*. I'd thought she was talking about the night surfing. This wasn't the first time.

"You're not stupid," she said. "You just haven't known him

very long. You know *Uncle Graham*. Graham the host, the dad. You don't know *Graham Kingston*."

"So it's happened before. Other summers."

Willa's voice became dreamy, a singsong: "Yes. Other summers. Winters, too. Falls, and springs." She crooned to herself as if it was one of our sweet tunes about nature, and not her beloved, traitorous father.

"I should have seen what was coming," Willa said. "If I'd seen he was going to get a taste for it again, maybe I could've helped him."

It. I wasn't sure if Willa meant only a taste for fame, or the pain that came along with wanting it. Women who weren't Angela and long swigs of Uno D'Oro.

And what he'd done in the garden.

I was afraid to ask about that part, but I had to know.

"The hitting," I said softly. "It's happened a lot?"

Willa smiled a vacant smile, a *you-sweet-thing, you're-still-not-getting-it* expression. How weird to feel our roles reversed; in this moment I was the naive cousin and she was the worldly one, the cynic. It was heartbreaking to see her like that.

"She's good at hiding it." Willa arched her back to pull away from me and raised her hand to my face.

I flinched, instinctively protecting myself, my body fearing for a second that she was about to imitate how Graham had hit Angela.

But this was still Willa, in spite of her sadness, so of course she wasn't about to strike me. Even in her darkest moment she was a gentle creature. Slowly, she brought her index finger to my forehead, a butterfly alighting. She drew it around my left eye, tracing across my eyebrow, down along my cheek, and back up along the bridge of my nose.

She wasn't imitating her father, but her mother. Reminding me of that sunny day at the picnic table, when Angela had let us play around with her stage greasepaint, when she'd demonstrated how to make ourselves up to look like fairies and crones.

"I should have known it had started again," Willa says. "That day when she came out with the face paint. But they seemed happy…"

Angela's treasured old sticks of stage makeup, the exaggerated faces she sometimes put on far from any stage.

This stuff can hide anything, Angela had said about freckles.

The occasional black eye? The odd bruise? Yes, it could hide those, too. It could hide them, while reminding the person responsible what was underneath. *I've used it for decades.* Everyone thought the makeup was Angela's quirk, her bit of fun. It wasn't unusual in this place, where eccentricity was the norm. Anything went—though hadn't I heard someone whisper once that it was her attempt to upstage Graham? This struck me suddenly as incredibly unkind. And sad.

Angela's greasepaint, Graham's master tape spool rolling down the hill, the way she'd abruptly left the picnic tables when he announced he was agreeing to the show. They were related; it was some coded, grotesque conversation between the two of them.

I remembered the way that Angela had dropped to the ground while Graham loomed over her, his hand still raised in a threat. Her gesture had been so practiced—an earthquake drill. *Stop, Drop, and Cover!* the cheerful poster in my grade-school classroom called it.

"How long has it been since the last time?" I asked.

"Three years… Before that they were always fighting, making up. Battle, cease-fire, battle, retreat. The Peloponnesian War. Did you ever study that?"

"No."

"The tutor I had three years ago was big on it…"

I was impatient, but let her drift back on her own time. This was how Willa dealt with problems. Floating above and around them. I wanted to get in and fix them immediately.

"Once my mom was gone for a month…" She shook her head at the memory.

"But the summer after I turned fourteen, it stopped. It was like a miracle. I heard them talking in the north hot springs, and he said he'd finally accepted that he was never going to be big again. 'Graham Kingston had a nice little run but he's dead.' He promised he'd be *Graham* and focus on us…appreciate what he had and forget the rest. Radio play and sales numbers and charts and everything that tortured him. The stuff he calls 'the circus, the numbers game…'"

She went on, clenching her fists in a way I'd never seen: "He said, 'I'm going to leave the circus in the past where it belongs and be happy.' And we *were* happy! He didn't need anybody else! Or any*thing* else. There wasn't any fighting…"

She floated away to some private thought and came back to me. "You know that picture in the hall, of the three of us? It was taken after he made that promise. He looks happy in that, doesn't he?"

"Yes."

"I thought he was, and my mom was, too. She was happy, and she was *here*. And for three years, he was good. He *was*. He *was*. But now…" Her voice broke.

"But now his old friend from his Bill Graham days has come through with an invitation to play the big show at the Polo Fields in Golden Gate Park," I said.

I thought of another way I'd betrayed Willa. Add it to the list—how Angela had bolted for the garden when she heard about the show, and I hadn't said anything to Willa about it.

"I can't believe I didn't realize before…what we saw. If I'd realized, I might have… I at least could have…" She shook her head. "I've been so busy…"

She didn't say the rest.

"Busy with me," I said. "Distracted because of me."

"No."

"Yes."

And she didn't know the worst part—that I'd seen the ugliness building up in him, but excused it, and chosen to hide it from her. That reel he'd sent careening down the hill. The way he and Rose had been together outside the studio. I should have known something was simmering.

Graham seems to be in good form this summer, Colin had said. *I'm glad, for Angela and Willa's sake.*

But I hadn't told Willa about any of that.

Hadn't even cared enough to ask her about it. Not for some noble reason, not to prevent her from worrying, no matter how I'd justified it at the time. But—I knew it now—because I hadn't wanted to spoil things for myself. I loved it here too much.

Foolish, reckless. Selfish.

Graham. Willa seemed to have a little compassion for him.

I felt only rage.

All of the afternoons we'd babysat because he'd asked, had wanted Willa and me to do him *a special favor*. He'd been so charming, so skilled at recruiting us to assist him and making it seem like a whim.

And while we were playing Red Rover with June or cutting the crusts off of Dylan's sandwich or showing Crystal how to scoop a moat around her sandcastle, Graham and their moms were off screwing in some field, some empty cabin. It made me sick.

As if Graham was doing his guests a kindness, giving them energy. When it was really him, draining love from their families to keep his worn-down ego going. He'd made us accomplices in his betrayal.

And in his brutality with Angela.

"Does your mom know that you know?"

"No. The only reason I do is I saw her take her makeup off once when I was little…seven or eight… I'd been hiding in the bathtub, behind the shower curtain, and she had a purple mark under her eye. She said it was a blueberry stain."

"Oh, Wills." I pulled her back into the sweater and rocked her fast. For a long time, the only sound was the ocean's rush and retreat.

"I just want things to be like they were in that picture in the back hall," Willa whispered against my collarbone. "I want to go inside that picture and live."

"I know."

"And I wish… You know what I can't stop thinking about?"

"What?"

"Friday night. How it's going to be watching him offstage… How I'll have to clap and smile, as if everything's fine…as if it's not going to send us all back to how bad things used to be, as if, as if—"

"So then we won't go," I said into the crown of her head. "It was too much to ask of you, anyway, braving those crowds. We're not going."

Willa lifted her head from my chest and looked at me. These three short words had put a glimmer of hope back into her eyes.

"No, we're not going," she echoed.

Settled. Willa's face softened in relief that I'd made this decision for her. That there would be consequences for what Graham had done. Even if they went unnoticed by anyone but us.

Even if the punishment was pathetically mild.

"My mom's not watching, either," she said. "She asked my dad if he minded her going away for the weekend instead, up the coast to some friend's pantomime in Trinidad."

If *he* minded. As if he was doing her a favor by allowing her to miss it.

"My mom said she didn't want to hurt his feelings, but she was worried that she might make him nervous by being there. Because she hates the city and crowds. She always has, almost as much as me. And he said, 'Maybe that's for the best, Angel.

I don't want to put you through that. Go, and have fun...' But I wonder if..."

"You think by not going she's protesting, in her way?"

"Maybe. I just wish..." She looked over my shoulder into the dark, at some imaginary sight.

"What, Willa, tell me." I grabbed her hands. *Don't disappear on me again.*

"I wish *he* wasn't going." She said it so quietly. So strained and exhausted that even though she was still only inches away, I could barely make out the words over the wind. It must have taken all her reserves of courage to form them. The rest was unspoken, but I understood her perfectly: *I wish he would feel punished instead of rewarded. So maybe he would go back to how he was in the picture.*

"Me, too." *The important thing about this moment is to keep talking.* "So maybe he won't."

She looked at me.

"Maybe he won't go." *The important thing is to keep her attention.* "Remember when I was telling you about the most effective way to discipline kids, that thing I read in that old parenting book? 'Appropriate punishment is designed to show that someone's watching, and someone cares.' The right punishment says that someone has noticed."

"What are you talking about?" Horrified: "Not the police, please, Jackie. They'd just make things a thousand times worse, *please—*"

"No, shhh, I know, of course not." No, we wouldn't go to the police. Or Angela, or some social worker with a clipboard, or a spaced-out, well-meaning friend who'd just returned from an est consciousness-raising weekend. Not even Kate.

I'd seen Graham at his smallest, his most human, but even so he still loomed huge in my mind.

He would never listen to a mere *person.*

But a place? A world?

I spoke slowly. "He's not heading down 'til pretty late Saturday. I heard him say so to Augie. Maybe he'll miss that fancy car service he was telling everyone about."

"But how?"

I was formulating as I went, molding images and instinct and memory into something resembling a plan.

The important thing is to be decisive. The important thing is forward motion. "Augie was begging him to stay in a hotel in San Francisco Friday night because it's such a long drive from here, but your dad's insisting on going up to the waterfall right before he leaves. For good luck or something."

"Yes. In the old days he always went up there right before he left for a show or a trip," Willa said, remembering. "It used to drive Augie nuts, how close he cuts things."

"Yes. He cuts things too close," I said.

The whirl of images spun faster before my eyes, Willa's hopeful, trusting face a bright background. She was so sure that I could fix this. *Jackie knows how to make things right.* It was my fault. I'd come here, and I'd selfishly hidden things from my sweet cousin. I had to make it right.

She looked so hopeful that I began to hope, too, and what had a minute ago been me weaving another tale, merely a way to comfort and distract her, began to feel like a reasonable solution.

I thought of my bike crash, how Graham and Willa had both said that it was the Sandcastle telling me it didn't want me to leave.

He and Willa believed in such things. I pictured the white shell birdhouse in the trees, the missing landmark I had come to trust completely as I sped downhill. How that small change was enough to send me the wrong way. Upend me. In such a short time, I'd come to rely on a little cluster of white shells.

Graham had lost his way.

A cluster of white shells...

"How did my book put it, 'Punishment means correcting behavior'?" I spoke faster, convincing myself that it could work. "Not punishment without a hope of change, but punishment as a kindness. A reminder. What if this place did something to remind him? Showed him that he was right to leave the circus behind."

If Graham missed the show, he'd see it as a sign, and things might go back to how they should be, how they were in the hallway picture. Shameful, but that's what I wanted more than anything. I wasn't Justice with Her Flaming Sword. I didn't care much about justice.

More than anything, I wanted restoration. For Willa, and for Angela, and me. Most of all, me.

I had tossed my cousin a lifeline. I threw the plan to her, acting as confident as she had been when she'd unfurled the tree-house rope ladder down to me, back at the beginning of my stay.

Here. Trust me. Follow me.

I was desperate to give her hope.

"We'll need shells," I said. "Lots and lots of shells."

I watched her face, waiting for her to catch up. When she realized what I was thinking, relief dawned along with excitement, and she nodded.

She looked around. The tide was low and shells were dotted everywhere on the smooth sand, surrounding us, glowing in the moonlight. Sand dollars, razor clams, the spiral pink-and-white shells the kids called *whirligigs*.

Willa reached for the closest one and handed it to me. It was a beauty. A bright, intact, butterflied white mussel, already scrubbed clean from the surf.

I brushed sand from its ridged surface. "I think the beach is trying to say we have its blessing."

33

O.F.

1999

Dear Ray,
O.F.

I can't bear to turn the page to the final entry. Though I feel it, thick with the stickers the kids gave me for my eighteenth birthday. I put them there to hide it—my words from the day of Operation Fairwhistle, named for the author of my thrift store parenting book. *O.F.* Under the stickers is the entry I wrote in lemon juice, so it could only be seen if held up to candlelight. The trick of aspiring grade-school spies.

Stickers and code words and lemon juice trick ink. A tree-house. How I'd savored the little pleasures of those younger than me when I was here that summer, after acting older than my age in the city. I was seventeen, and had stepped out of that black town car cynical, wary. But Willa's innocence, her utter disinterest in whether people thought she was cool or not, had rubbed off on me. Words like *mature* and *babyish* didn't mean much here back then, even when Willa and I entertained the littlest kids, because the lines between adult and child play, privileges, sleeping hours, and conversation were so often blurred.

Our plan was elegant in its simplicity.

No, even now I'm softening facts in my favor, smudging the border between my ideas and Willa's. It was my plan. I was the leader, the general. Single-minded in a battle to keep Willa from withdrawing again. The plan gave her hope that Graham would change back to his real self.

It seemed like such a good idea at the time. How often do people say that? But Willa and I both felt it, as we went through the details over and over. I was a disciplined leader, determined to factor in every contingency. Each time we ran through the plan, visualizing, step by step, exactly what we wanted Graham to do that night, it became more vivid. Until the *wanting* part faded away, and the events of August 25 seemed as real as something that had already happened.

It wasn't just a good idea—it was inspired. We were merely redirecting Graham down the right path, like a parent taking hold of their child's elbow so they wouldn't get hit on a dangerous street.

I'd done it before. I'd succeeded in my elaborate schemes at school. Helped Ben and Rose. I'd saved one family. Why not this one, the most important one?

Checked, chastened, Graham would again become the person I'd thought he was at the beginning of my visit. The person in Willa's favorite family picture in the hall. Everything would go back to how it was supposed to be. Angela would be safe, Willa would be happy.

And I could stay.

I close the diary, carefully marking my page with the scrap of lace I've kept in my pocket since the day I found it. I must have read hunched over on the treehouse floor for hours. Near dawn, I'd climbed back down the ladder with the diary under my arm, walked, dazed, down the darkening hillside and found my way here, back to the parlor.

I wrap the diary in a clean shirt, tuck it into my suitcase. I return to Kate's room, where Shane is still sleeping, one arm flung over his head, and slip into bed next to him.

Willa. When I read the diary, it's like you're here with me, and I'm discovering you for the first time. Like you're alive again.

Three days later

"You'll come see me in Boston, right?" I say into Bree's shoulder.

"Of course. And like I said, any tickets you want. You just let me know."

She gives me one last squeeze and whispers in my ear, "You did a good thing here. You should be proud."

She climbs into her trailer and Shane and I lean against each other, waving goodbye. Clearing our throats, both of us holding back tears. It's just us two, left to close up.

Piper and Mat and the rest left this morning. We've all promised to phone, to visit. I've held it together pretty well. I didn't even cry when Fiona flung her arms around me and sobbed, though I whispered in her ear, "I'll miss you, Fee. Keep playing."

Now Bree's gone, too, only a glint of sun on silver down the hill, and I have to wipe my wet face on Shane's T-shirt. He's upset, too. Edgy, not making eye contact with me.

"And then there were two," I say into his chest, as he strokes my back. The summer is all falling apart, all ending. Again.

This morning I read about Woodstock '99, about women raped in the mosh pit, $12 bottles of water, the ugliness of it all, and I closed my eyes, trying so hard to remember Lilith Fair weeks before, and how it felt on that gently sloping lawn in the mist off of the Bay.

I want to hold on to that. To run after Bree's trailer, bring all of them back here. Go back to June and reclaim our wasted

days, the way I wanted to with Willa when my time here was
dwindling.

"Well," I say. "Back to work?"

I have the upstairs to pack. He's handling the studio; the dealer
comes from San Francisco tomorrow to pick what he wants and
haul it away. I'll donate the proceeds to charity, like all the other
money. My guilt money.

"Shane?"

He's stiff, and his hand on my back has gone still.

"What?" I pull away from his chest to search his face.

But all he says are three little words: "Come with me."

34

They'll Try to Stop You

1979
Ten a.m.

It was seven hours before Operation Fairwhistle, and we were
in the treehouse going through logistics one last time.

"Basket?" I held my pen over the checklist, looking around
for the apple basket.

"Basket, check," Willa said. "Well, I decided to use this instead. It'll be easier to carry." She held up her mother's canvas
Chronicle newsboy bag.

"We were going to use your apple basket from the thrift
store."

"I know, but…it's heavy. I'm the one who has to carry the
thing up the hill and run around moving the shells, then put
them all back in the middle of the night before anyone notices.
Don't worry, my mom'll never miss it. She won't be home 'til
Sunday."

"We'll have to clean it out before putting it back in the shed.
After."

"Sure."

"I mean, not a flake left. Not one calcium molecule."

"I'll do it."

"And you know which peg she hangs it on?"

"Um, top left, I'm pretty sure."

I stared at her.

"No, I'm sure. Look, it's all right. We're ready, Jackie. We couldn't be more ready. And…"

"And Liam's waiting down at the beach for you, huh?"

"Well…"

Willa wanted to spend the rest of the day with Liam. I could hardly blame her; he was leaving for Costa Rica in five days. He had $246 and a ride that would take him and his board as far as Cotulla, Texas. Liam had no family who gave a damn about him, no one to tell him he should stay in one place for a while. Except for Willa, and she wasn't about to hold him back.

"He can wait a few more minutes. Let's finish the list."

Willa groaned and lay flat on her back, on the mass of fabric remnants.

She'd been like this all week. She went along with my instructions—she'd done two dry runs in the middle of the night—not actually moving the shells, but pantomiming every step, every sweeping and pouring motion, so we knew it was possible. We were sure she could stealthily move the whole line of ten shell cairns to their temporary places in nineteen minutes, while Graham was occupied at the falls.

Then she'd wait, out of his sight. After he'd wandered downhill the wrong way, foolishly trusting the glowing piles at his feet—so that he got lost in the vast southeastern woods bordering the Kingston property—she'd track him until at least eleven p.m. Then she'd approach him and lead him back to the house, pretending we'd been out looking for him. Once he was safely home—mourning the loss of that Golden Gate Park stage spotlight—she'd sneak out again and replace the shells. No one would ever know about our treachery.

Willa knew exactly what to do, but there were lapses, like casually substituting Angela's newspaper bag for the basket.

More startling—she'd become affectionate with Graham again.

He was a bundle of nerves because of the show, as he'd told anyone within earshot for days: "It's going to be lousy" or "Why'd I agree to this?" or "I'll probably get bumped, anyway."

"Don't worry, Daddy," she'd said after lunch yesterday, draping herself around his neck.

"What would I do without my girl? I'm so glad you're going to ride down with me. My good luck charm, that's what you are. Better than my lucky Chet Atkins thumb pick." He lifted her up, spinning her.

When I saw her orbiting her father, her gold mass of hair flying out around their whirling bodies, I was shocked. Willa couldn't be that duplicitous.

Maybe I could, but not her.

I cornered her on the porch by the lemonade urn afterward and asked her if she wanted to back out. "Are you sure?" I whispered. "Maybe you don't really want to do it."

"I do!" She sounded panicked.

"Shhh. The way you were with him just now, it seemed like you were having second thoughts, and that's okay. But I have to know."

"No, don't you see… I'm happy *because* we're going to help him. I can be around him again because of the plan!"

"It's okay, shhh. Everything's okay. I was just surprised, that's all."

But last night I'd woken at three a.m., drenched in sweat, convinced that Willa had told him everything. In my dream he'd banished me from the Sandcastle for life. I was sitting in the back not of Serena's decrepit station wagon like Dylan had when she was sent away, but Patricia's yellow, leather-upholstered Mercedes. And I was watching the shell spire recede.

"You're sure?" I asked Willa again in the treehouse now, as we went over the plan one last time. "I won't be mad if you've changed your mind. I won't think any differently of you."

"I've decided. I promise."

"Okay."

"And what's the signal if something goes wrong and we have to cancel?" I tested her.

"I clang the dinner triangle for one minute…"

"And when are we meeting in the treehouse after?"

"One a.m."

We were ready. There was nothing to do but wait.

Dear Ray,

…so it's tonight.

I'm still not sure Willa's as committed as I am to O.F. She says she is, but she goes from being super distracted to kind of, I don't know. Weirdly giddy. But it all hinges on her. (You know why. Graceful her/klutzy me.)

All right. I've fussed over O.F. for a week, trying to remind Willa of every not-so-gory detail. But it's not super complicated. We're going to make a new path for him.

Ray, the next time I write, it'll be done.

Willa says the stars are aligned for us. She says they're on our side. I know you are, too…

If this were a proper campfire tale, there would be one of two twists. A surprise enemy, or a betrayal.

The surprise enemy: the heroines would meet some unexpected foe in the woods. Someone who, with the best of intentions, not realizing that Graham's salvation was imminent and in the capable hands of two teenage girls, would somehow destroy their plans. An old friend of the family's might have dropped in at the last minute, hoping to tag along to the big show in Golden

Gate Park. Altered Graham's schedule just enough so that he made his ride at six p.m., and strode onstage at the Polo Fields in front of forty thousand people.

Or Angela could have changed her mind, U-turned on Highway 1, and decided to come back. She'd been with Graham for nineteen years. She might have crept up to the falls to make peace, share good vibes as he prepared for the show as Willa told me she used to do. And she might have seen her daughter tiptoeing around in the shadows, carefully relocating piles of seashells.

Or, variable two—betrayal from the inside. After all, I'd braced for it for seven days. Expected Willa to tell Graham, or her mother, or confide in Liam, or someone else who would have told her the idea was deranged and shot my carefully laid plan to bits.

I waited for one of these things to happen the late afternoon of August 25, as I sat out on the near-deserted field, killing time.

Graham was playing his twelve-string guitar for a little boy. They sat across from each other, cross-legged, on top of the picnic table. It was a soft tune I hadn't heard before, and he was showing the boy how to pluck the strings with a pick.

"Maybe you'll grow up to be like me and play both ways, with a pick and without. But take this, anyway." He handed him the pick.

"Neat!"

The kid looked so happy I had to walk away. As I left, Graham began telling him one of his favorite stories about Jerry Garcia, how he hadn't let his chopped-off finger stand in the way of his greatness.

"You don't let anything stop you, hear me? They'll try to stop you…"

I don't know what got to me more. Graham's talent, or how kind he seemed in that moment, how sweet he could be when he was in the right mood. Giving away his good luck pick hours before his big show.

I knew, now, how the sweetness could vanish as suddenly as it came, replaced by fury. But I was glad Willa hadn't been there. If she had, she'd never go through with our plan.

And things would never go back to how they'd been.

35

Stars and Soil

1999

Shane leads me toward the falls trail. I know he wants to take me uphill, not downhill to the beach. I can hear it in his voice. It's still light out; the sun won't set for another hour.

He knows I don't want to be here. He knows how I've avoided the falls; the last time he tried to take me here I practically ran, and he'd apologized for trying.

I pull back at the fork in the trail. "Why are you doing this to me?"

"Because it's important. Jackie. Please. I promise it'll be okay. I'll be right with you."

Each step a force of will, I follow.

I hike slowly, but I'm panting by the time we make it up to the first shell cairn. The first of ten. It's right where it used to be. It's no longer a lovely pile of shimmering white, two feet in diameter. It's dirty, smaller, messy. But still, no one could get lost, night or day, with these to mark the direction. This, and the nine that follow, spiral slowly, gradually in a helpful line up and around, showing the safe route to and from the crest by the waterfall, which presides over everything below. It's easy to get lost here, where the trees and forest floor all look the same. Easy to stumble into trouble, especially at dusk, before the stars come out, or when it's foggy. But the cairns guide your way.

Shane takes my hand and leads me off the trail. Inland, ten feet to the southeast. Twenty feet.

"Shane, what is this? Look, if you're trying to scare me, it's working…"

"Please, just a little farther."

I don't like this. Being here, his steady march sideways into the trees, his grim tone. But I'm transfixed by his voice, and follow.

He stops in the thick woods. I can only orient myself because the sun hasn't quite disappeared. If it was night, I'd already be hopelessly lost.

"Here, look." Shane crouches, scoops up some dirt, and shows it to me.

Under the sideways orange glare of the dropping sun I see it clearly. Glittering in his hand, in with the dirt. Sparkles, mica. Like stars in the soil.

He picks out the biggest fragment and hands it to me—a piece of shell. "It took me a while to find them."

I don't understand. "So a couple of shells made their way over here, off the trail, over the last twenty years? People kick them. It rains. Kids play."

"No. That's not what this is."

His voice is tortured. Even worse than it sounded when he tried to take me here two weeks ago.

"Then, what? Why are you—"

"There was a real pile here once, Jackie. A whole cairn. But it was only here for a short time. Less than a day, actually."

I shake my head.

"Yes. The shell cairns were moved once. The night Graham died. The whole line was shifted so he'd get lost in the woods."

"But—"

"I know because I saw her move them."

He takes my hand, gently shapes it into a cup, and pours the dirt into it. Remainders of what was here for a short time, the night Graham got lost, and stumbled. And died.

Flashing remnants in with the dark earth. Brighter than sand, because Graham only chose the brightest shells for his trail markers. I'm holding points of light.

I want to get away. Up out of the trees where I can breathe, where what Shane's hinting at isn't suffocating me.

I saw her move them.

Clutching the dirt in my hand, I run. Heedless of rocks, roots, gopher holes, phantom trails and grown-over logging roads, all the perils that Willa had warned me about. All the things that can trip and confuse you. Hurt you. Send you in the wrong direction.

"Jackie!"

I have no idea where I am or where I'm going but I let instinct take over, because it knew I shouldn't have come here. I should have listened to my pounding heart the day the paperwork arrived in Boston telling me I'd inherited the Kingstons' home.

"Jackie!" Shane's calls grow faint, then disappear. But I keep running.

The trees all look alike, the sun will soon be gone completely, there's no sound of ocean or dinner bell or waterfall to orient me. It's getting foggy, though I never learned to navigate by stars, anyway.

I stumble and my knuckle meets something brittle. There's a mound of white at my feet. A shell cairn.

I've made it back to the markers. I count the little piles of shells as I pass them. Three, four…ten. I'm running so fast they blur into white streaks. Like neon. Like magic. *I'm running so fast I can make it to the top before it's too late. I can help him down, show him the way. Undo it all.*

After the last pile I come to the section of hillside that's so steep it's almost vertical. At the top, the trees huddle, like they're afraid of falling. It's dusk. Hard to see here.

But the sound of the falls guides me: a sigh, then a whisper, then a roar.

The shell cairns were moved…

I fly into the open, the ocean so bright and sudden in front of me that at first I'm blinded.

My lungs burn. And a single sentence throbs in my head, in time with my beating heart:

I saw her move them.

I saw her move them.

Shane stumbles up behind me, panting, and he almost slips on the wet rocks that border the falls pool, but he rights himself in time. He rests his hands on his knees, struggling to catch his breath. "Jackie? This isn't how I wanted to…"

I sink to the wet stones by his feet. The ocean's in front of me, the falls are behind me. Both are magical. You could go a whole lifetime and not be lucky enough to see anything so beautiful.

But instead I look down at the clump of spangled dirt in my hand.

"I need you to tell me what you know," I say numbly. *What you think you know.*

He sits and I feel him staring at me, but I can't take my eyes off of that handful of earth. The roar of the falls behind us is so loud, so steady, it mutes everything else—the gentle music of early evening I've become familiar with, fond of again—frogs chirping, the occasional, distant calls of an owl. I hear only that never-ending rush of water.

And then Shane's voice. "That it was her fault he fell that night. Angela's. She moved the shells so he'd get lost coming back from here. She kept looking over her shoulder, checking to make sure no one could see. She was wearing her green work shirt, and that green army cap over her hair. She used that old newspaper bag she carried everywhere. Swept the shells into the bag with a piece of bark, then poured them out into new piles to form a different path. Leading southeast instead of east. They were fighting...they fought a lot. I used to watch her, crying in the woods...and I didn't realize it then, but I'm sure, now, that she wanted him to miss his big show.

"Jackie? I saw Angela move them. But they were moved back before anyone else noticed. I know because I'm the one who did it... I'm the one who moved them back where they were supposed to be. After one of the sheriff's men knocked on our door looking for Graham."

My head's roaring louder than the falls. *I saw Angela move them.*

"They came over that night, asking if we'd seen Graham. Because his manager was furious he'd blown off his ride and no one was at the Sandcastle. And I didn't say anything...but before anyone could see what she'd done, I snuck up here and put the trail back to how it usually was."

"You put it back..."

"I didn't want Angela getting in trouble for tricking Graham. My dad was always complaining about the Kingstons, Angela's pot plants. He was always threatening to call the cops on them so they'd move. I'd seen her once, yanking out pot plants in a little clearing in the woods when my dad sent the cops over the ridge to poke around about a noise complaint. She'd looked over her shoulder the same way that day as that night at the falls. Like she was nervous.

"I never told her that I moved the shells. Or anyone. And Angela wouldn't talk about Graham's death, at Arbor View... she'd only talk about the album. How great it was going to be. But it was Angela's fault he got lost that night. And I know it's hard to hear.

"But I think—no, I'm *sure* she wanted to make peace before she died. *Choose Peace*, remember the bumper sticker on that broken-down orange van the Kingstons had? That's why she wanted this album to happen. Jackie? She must've blamed herself, even if it was an accident. Not just for Graham, but for Willa being brokenhearted about him dying, all of it... Are you okay?

"It's all right," he says, his hand on my shoulder. "I'm sure Angela never imagined he could die."

I stop breathing.

"Jackie? I wasn't sure if I should tell you or not. But I decided you had a right to hear the truth about what happened that night, and why I think Angela was trying to...atone. With the album."

I want to hold on to this moment. I want it so desperately, as desperately as I wish I could go back to that night he's talking about, go back in time and stop it.

But I can never go back.

I stare over at the woods that hide the falls trail.

"I know it hurts," he says, caressing my arm. "I know it's just a stupid bumper sticker slogan. But Angela deserved peace. We all do."

"Not me," I whisper.

His hand is featherlight on my arm, his voice even softer. "Of course you do."

I can't look at him.

"It wasn't Angela you saw. It was our plan. Willa's and mine."

His hand stops, clenches my elbow in shock. "I thought...because of the bag, and her clothes...the way her hair was tucked away. I was so sure it was Angela. It was you two?"

I shake my head. "Not two. One."

"You mean?"

I say it softly: "One of us changed her mind."

36

Still Time

August 25, 1979
Six p.m.

I sat in the field, just inside the gate, my diary in my lap.

I'd been down here for half an hour, and there'd been no sign of Graham. No ring from the dinner triangle, aborting the plan.

Crunching gravel—Graham's limousine pulled up and stopped outside the gate. The driver looked confused by the rows of assorted VW bugs, vans, motorcycles and woodies sloppily parked outside the gate.

He was surely thinking *what the hell is this place?* Just like my driver had back in June when he dropped me off. Just like I had.

He got out and again I was glad that Willa wasn't around. The fancy driver in his black uniform was one more thing that might have made her take pity on Graham and back out, run into the forest and find him just in time.

I walked up, casual. "Hi."

"Hi there. I'm supposed to pick up a…" He looked at a notebook. "…Graham Kingston?" Zero recognition. Poor Graham.

"It says here he's going to meet me in front of the house. Is this the front of the house?" He looked around doubtfully.

"This is where his drivers always come. You can't get up to the front door. It's too steep and muddy. I'll go find him."

"Hey, thanks!" he said, relieved. "I should cut you in on my tip."

"No problem! My cousin and I are catching a ride, too, actually. I can't wait to get down to the city. I'm sure he'll be ready soon."

I headed up the hill and darted into the trees so I could watch him.

He leaned against the car, smoking and reading the paper. I watched time tick by on my gold watch.

Ten minutes, no alarm from Kate's dinner triangle.

Twenty minutes, no bell. The driver looked around, wondering what was taking me so long.

Half an hour. Forty minutes.

No sign of Willa or Graham. No one searching for him in the field; it was deserted except for a couple of little kids playing. No one to ask what I was still doing here, or if I'd seen him, or Willa.

Everyone going to the show had left hours ago so they could catch the whole thing.

The driver tossed his newspaper into the car window impatiently and walked to the gate.

"Hey!" I waved, running down to him. "I don't think he's here. We're looking, but someone said he decided to catch a ride earlier, with someone else."

"What?"

"Sorry, he's always doing stuff like this."

He looked over my shoulder doubtfully. "Is there a phone I can use?"

"We don't have a phone. But there's a booth downhill, by the beach. Did you see that place called General Custard's?"

"The ice-cream joint?"

"Yeah. It's in their parking lot."

He stared at me, unsure. I gave him my best Vaughn Academy Chapel smile. "I guess my cousin and I will have to hitch a ride with someone else."

"Well. Okay. Thanks."

"Sure! Have a good day!"

It would take the driver fifteen minutes to find the phone booth and figure out the phone didn't work. Then, *if* he still bothered to call his dispatcher, and *if* he got lucky and headed the right way to the closest working phone booth—ten miles north at the truck stop—that was another half hour. He wouldn't be back for an hour, if at all.

I walked to the bowl and sat. Night would soon fall; we'd nearly done it.

I didn't realize it until just then: I wasn't just mildly worried that Willa could change her mind. I'd expected it.

But she hadn't. I should've been triumphant—the plan had worked. Instead I felt only jittery. Slightly queasy.

The boy Graham had been talking to at the picnic bench earlier sat in the center of the grass not far from me, yawning. Staring down at the guitar pick in his hand like it was the most precious thing he'd ever seen. *A splinter from the true cross.*

His mom collected him, carrying him away to their distant cabin, and I was the only one out on the darkening field.

I went to the treehouse to wait, even though Willa wouldn't be back for hours. I paced around inside, played the Walkman Graham gave me, tidied our carpet of fabric scraps. Seven-thirty. Eight. Nine.

And then it came over me, a cold wave like the one that had almost drowned me the night I'd gone surfing.

I couldn't do it.

But it was okay. There was still time to stop it. Still time to find him. A couple of cars in the parking lot to whisk him to his show.

I ran toward the falls trail. *Still time.* If he hadn't strayed too far into the woods yet. If we sped a hundred miles an hour down the highway, if there wasn't too much traffic. It was summer. There might not be too much traffic. The other acts were probably running long. He was supposed to go on near the end, anyway; he'd been proud of that, that he wasn't an opening act. In the morning, he'd laugh about almost missing his big comeback.

Grateful we'd saved the day, he'd hold me and Willa close, and we'd get him some other kind of help for the ugliness, recruit Kate or his friends or...

Still time.

I clambered up the trail. So dark, but there was still time, and even without the shells' help I thought I could remember the way from the one other night I'd come up here—that blissful, infinite-seeming night that Colin and Willa and Liam and I had camped on the beach and spied on Graham. How brave and graceful he'd looked, his long body arcing out like a sail in the moonlight between two tree trunks.

A flash of white at my feet. The first cairn. Right where it always was. Twenty yards later, the second one. The third, the fourth. Willa hadn't moved them.

Relief flooded through me, the sweet conviction that Willa and I were the same, that I hadn't let her down.

She had changed her mind, too.

I waited in the treehouse, snug in the quilt Willa and I had bought at the thrift store, passing the time by playing tapes in the Walkman.

There'd been no sign of Willa, probably because she was sheepish about changing her mind, afraid to face me. Or, no—maybe she'd driven down with Graham in someone's car. Gone to the concert as we'd pretended we were going to, and would stay over in the city with his friends. I wouldn't see her until morning. I wondered what she'd told him about me not going.

But I was so eager to tell her it was okay, that I understood because I'd felt exactly the same way. I hated that it might be morning before I could reassure her about her change of heart.

I dozed off around three, woke with one foam Walkman headphone stuck to my cheek, the other folding my ear back so it ached.

Near dawn I heard the familiar *scritch-scratch*ing of Willa reaching for the rope ladder with the long shepherd's crook branch. I threw the rope down to her, so giddy I almost flew down with it.

I couldn't wait to talk to her, to celebrate our joint decision. She'd say it was almost a psychic connection, a mystical event, or nonevent. Kismet.

"Don't worry, I changed my mind, too!" I said, the second her hair appeared, glinting in the moonlight. It was too dark for me to see her face.

"You…"

"I changed my mind, too, Wills." I hugged her once she got on the platform. "You're freezing. Have you been outside all night? It's okay. I know you changed your mind about the shells, too, because we're the same, I know you're worried about telling me but it's okay, we're the same and I'm so glad."

She trembled from cold.

"You're exhausted, aren't you?"

"Yes."

"Here, sit. Bundle up." I wrapped the quilt around her. "Did you end up going to the show with him?"

"Oh… No. I didn't feel like it."

"So I guess he got a ride down to the city with someone else? The driver didn't come back?"

"A ride… Yes, I think so. He must have."

"Oh, good. Did you talk to him, or…"

No answer.

"Wills?" And then I knew why she was so foggy, so quiet. I'd been relieved, thinking only of tonight.

But she was in despair again, because we still had a horrible problem to solve. That's why she'd stayed out in the woods so long, distraught. Of course it was.

I hugged her again, bundled her tight in the quilt and stroked her fog-damp hair. "It'll be okay. We'll figure something else out when the sun's up. Just sleep."

But the morning was chaos. We woke to voices foreign in their urgency, their efficiency. Willa was reluctant to climb down the rope. I had to go first, help her down the last bit.

But it was so early, so noisy, I understood her confusion, her uncharacteristic slow pace.

We made our way around the house to the porch. Uniformed men. Dogs barking. The engine of a sheriff's truck grinding up the field, right up to the house. It left hideous tracks in the grass. Apparently the sheriff had come by in the night, sent in a rage by Graham's manager, Augie, when he heard that Graham blew off his car service. But no one had answered the door at the main house. Kate and Angela were gone, everyone else was at the show except a handful of sleeping nonentities, Willa was off in the woods. I was in the treehouse listening to the Walkman.

And of course there was no phone.

Two facts took shape:

Graham had never made the show.

Graham hadn't been seen since he climbed up to his falls yesterday.

"It'll be okay," I told Willa, cradling her in my lap, as we waited in her bedroom for news. "He knows this land better than anyone. He probably had one beer too many. Or a bad joint. Maybe he just freaked out about the show and wanted to back out and couldn't tell anyone?"

She nodded, closed her eyes.

"He's probably meditating somewhere beautiful, or writing a song about spending the night in the woods. Things worked out the way they were supposed to. And we didn't even need to do anything. It's going to be fine."

"Jackie?" Willa asked.

"Yes?"

"Will you sing to me?" Her voice was so childlike it shattered me.

"You don't want to hear my lousy voice right now, Wills."

"Please."

I gathered all my strength and sang "Sunday Girl" for her, as her eyelids drooped and closed. I sang, and stroked her hair, and we waited.

It would be hours before the third fact crystallized, but not long enough so that Kate and Angela could return. Not long enough so that a loving, familiar voice could deliver the news to Willa.

She had to hear it from the deputy sheriff—Graham had fallen.

37

The Point of Pain

Willa spent the miserable week after her father's death in Graham and Angela's room with the door closed.

Willa, who couldn't stand to be indoors for too long.

During that week Angela lived in the garden. Tending her tidy rows, weeding. She even slept out there on the bench, covered up by a quilt Kate brought her when she refused to come inside.

And Kate and I spent our time hugging each other, keeping up the house, dealing with the outside world's occasional intrusions. It was understood that I was Willa's designated attendant, and Kate was Angela's.

But Willa wouldn't let me attend to her. All day, I sat on the hall floor outside the bedroom into which she'd retreated, hoping she'd emerge to cry on my shoulder, or scream.

If she'd asked me to shave her head, or mine, like those grieving women in documentaries, I'd have agreed, gladly.

"She'll talk to you when she's ready, sweetheart," Kate said. "It'll be okay."

Gruff Kate, calling me sweetheart. It made me cry.

Everything did. Graham's shirt in the laundry, his jar of sour-plum jam in the fridge. Me, the tough cousin. But I didn't hear a single sob from Willa.

I slept in her room, left her trays of food she didn't touch, and, periodically, knocked softly on her parents' bedroom door, calling her name.

"Willa?"

Not a sound.

But I listened, waiting for a breakdown that didn't come.

Willa came out only for the memorial service.

It was on the beach at sunset, and it was well attended, with a hodgepodge of readings from est and Buddhism and Judaism and Graham Kingston lyrics. The ceremony was beautiful. Someone made a design on the sand out of wildflowers, swooping around in spirals and paisleys.

Willa still wasn't speaking to me, but Kate told me she'd made a single request—that someone find her a black dress to wear to Graham's nontraditional ceremony.

"I'm wearing black, too, then," I insisted, and no one argued.

Some friend of Angela's offered a few to choose from and Kate took them in, hastily, with safety pins. At the service, one kept scratching my waist. As Graham's friends sang and spoke of him, I was grateful for the point of pain on my right side. It was something else to focus on.

Willa let me stand on her left and hold her hand. It was so cold, so limp in mine—when I squeezed it, she didn't squeeze back. But I kept it in my grip, wiping my tears with my left hand.

I could hear Angela, close on Willa's other side, crying softly. I hoped Willa felt comforted by her mother's warm body beside her, since she couldn't derive any comfort from mine.

I let the mourners' words wash over me. I wasn't interested in metaphors about waterfalls. And there were many. Time was a waterfall, life was a waterfall, beautiful and powerful, never-ending. The beauty of nature would purify us, heal us, after this tragedy, and eventually Graham's meditation spot at the falls would be celebrated for the creation, not the loss, that happened there.

I was only interested in what wasn't being said about Graham's life and death and his cherished wife and daughter.

And this fear that maybe Willa wasn't speaking to me because she blamed me.

We hadn't gone through with the plan, but I knew she felt guilty that she'd considered it, let the thought in—inviting nature to betray her father. Because I felt guilty about that, too.

After the speeches, everyone left the beach but me and Willa. We sat so close to the water, ignoring the creeping tide, that the skirts of our too-large black wool dresses were soaked to the hip.

I didn't care if my dress got wet to the starched collar. I wasn't leaving until she was ready.

Willa picked up a nearby daisy from the service and floated it in her lap, in the black pond her skirt held. "They're costumes."

"Costumes?" I thought this was a metaphor. A comment on our earthly bodies as temporary shells or something. Costumes we shed when we died, was that where she was going?

"These." She wrung water from her dress hem. "I'm pretty sure they're from a play. Wonder which one."

She meant the borrowed dresses we were in, the ones from Angela's theater friend. Grateful that she was speaking to me, I ran with this. "*The Sound of Music?* Novitiates' dresses, maybe?"

She nodded vaguely.

"Wills?" I asked.

She turned to me.

"I'm sorry. About everything. Your dad. How we… How things ended."

"I know you are."

"It just happened. You didn't cause his accident in some mystical way, by simply agreeing to the plan, by tempting nature. You know that, right?"

"But what if I had tempted nature?" she asked, so softly I could barely hear her. "Would you hate me?"

"But you *did*n't. And anyway, it was *my* plan. If anyone tempted nature, it was me."

She smiled sadly. "I feel so confused. So heavy. Like if I sat here and waited for the tide to come in, this dress would weigh me down to the seabed."

I reached for her hand. "It won't always feel like that, I promise. It'll get better. I'll help. I'll stay, just like we planned. We'll go to that school in Humboldt together, and—"

She shook her head. Stood, extricating her fingers from mine. "You should go back to the city, Jackie. Go back and be with your own family."

I was still taking this in, how unlike her it was, how uncharacteristically cold and cruel, when she said softly, "I think I'll camp on the beach for a little while."

She walked away.

I thought she meant Glass Beach. I told Angela and Kate what she'd said, and the three of us decided to let her mourn in her own way.

"It'll be okay," Kate said. "It's just what she needs."

But, sometime that night, she took off. The beach—did Willa know, even then, that she meant distant beaches? Mexico, where she drowned, less than two years later?

For once, Kate had been wrong. It wasn't okay.

38

Almost

"Oh my god," Shane says. "I'm so sorry, I never—"

"I was mad at her for so many years," I say mechanically. "Willa. Mad at her for leaving without saying goodbye after Graham's service. I couldn't understand why she was so cold to me."

I'd thought Willa was wrecked over Graham's death. But I could never understand her just vanishing, drowning in Mexico.

"She did it, and she couldn't tell me, and it's why she left. Why she…" Willa had carried the burden of the shell trail, all alone, for two years. Until she couldn't anymore. I'd never accepted her suicide, but now it made sense. "It's my fault."

I wait for disgust, accusation. For Shane to judge me, because it was my idea. I wait for him to flee.

Instead he pulls me close. "I'm so sorry."

But all I can hear is Willa's voice, up in her bedroom, small and lost, asking me to sing for her as we waited for news.

Willa's voice on the beach, when I told her she should banish any thoughts of guilt, mystical responsibility, of flinging the idea of Graham getting lost into the universe.

What if I had tempted nature? Would you hate me?

"She tried to tell me. She wanted to tell me."

And if Shane hadn't told me about the little figure he'd assumed was Angela, up here all alone carrying her mother's newsboy bag, hair tucked under her mother's green hat, doing what I'd asked her to do, I'd never have known the real reason she ran away.

She'd tried to protect me by keeping it to herself.

"I can't bear it," I whisper to Shane. "Willa. I let her down."

He says all the right things, the comforting things. That we were kids, that it was an accident, that we never planned for anyone to get hurt. That he was to blame, too, for racing into the night and covering for Angela after he overheard the sheriff tell his father that people were trying to find Graham. Instead of telling the sheriff what he'd seen, that Graham was lost in the woods.

He has a hundred reasons why I shouldn't feel so guilty.

But no words can bring Willa back.

39

Goodbye, Ray

1979

My father and Patricia sent a car for me the day after Willa took off. They hadn't been able to get back in time for Graham's service, but had shipped flowers.

Numb, I packed up Slipstream, then went to retrieve my diary.

I'd left it up in the treehouse's live oak, in the nook between the big cuplike trio of limbs. I reached down for the damp canvas. I hadn't opened it in a week, since I'd written the O.F. entry, and it had settled into the crevice. Still, when I tugged, it gave.

But something was wrong. The thick rucksack was too light. Empty. The diary was gone.

It wasn't in any of my hiding spots. Slipstream, Willa's room. Nowhere. It wasn't in any other place I looked.

I kept the town car waiting for more than an hour, but I couldn't find it.

40

Spyglass

1999

I'm sitting in the treehouse. Alone. There's no sign that anyone's been back, though I've left the ladder out in full view.
The sun's coming up. I didn't sleep, of course. I tiptoed out of
the house last night after we returned from the falls and fell into
bed, so Shane wouldn't worry.

I've been here all night, a blanket wrapped around me, rereading my diary from the beginning by flashlight. Trying to
pinpoint where it all went so wrong.

The last entry is covered completely in stickers. I run the pad
of my index finger over the smooth circles, careful not to scratch
them. A grinning peach, a 45 record with the fat, swirly words
Keep On Groovin'! That one still smells, faintly, like vinyl.

But what they hide is much darker.

Below them is the plan for Operation Fairwhistle. Stickered
over right after I finished writing the entry that day.

I don't want it in here.

I rip that page out.

On the next page, there are more stickers.

Stickers I didn't place there.

They're all flowers, with ecru backgrounds. I dig and scratch, peeling them off. The writing underneath reveals a sad, beautiful song about a girl who wants to move a galaxy.

A spiral of stars, and she gives it a little push, to right it. But then she finds, after she's done, that she can't tell anyone.

Still, there's a little hope at the end. Because she's created a new world for herself.

There are even chord progressions, the key and melody. But these don't interest me, not right now.

Because the song is called "*Spyglass*, California."

The handwriting… It's printed, not cursive, but enough like Willa's…

I climb down, run inside to the boxes in the hall. *Where, where?* The old California map from the parlor was one of the first things I packed—it was going to Goodwill. I dig through frames, chipped knickknacks, faded prints…and there it is.

I sit back on my heels, half-afraid to examine the map, bracing myself for disappointment. But I can't resist—I scour the words, starting at the top, near the Oregon border, and working my way down, down… There. Faint italic lettering that means it's a tiny enclave on the coast, not even a town. Just north of Santa Barbara:

Spyglass.

On the sunny porch steps, Shane examines the diary, the gummy handful of floral stickers I've peeled from it, the ripped map.

"You found the diary in the treehouse. Three nights ago."

"Yes."

"And it wasn't there before?"

"I'm not sure," I admit. "I hadn't been there in weeks, and I know what you're going to say. That it could've come from anywhere. Maybe our squatter found it on the property this week and stuck it in the tree. Or a fan got it on eBay. Or they're a scammer. Someone's toying with me, hoping to get a piece of Graham's royalties. I know, I've thought of all the possibilities—"

"But that's not what you believe."

It must be on my face. It feels so good, so sweet, the first hit of a new drug.

"You believe that Willa didn't die eighteen years ago. That she only disappeared and has reappeared now, and wrote this in here so you'd find her in Spyglass, California."

"It sounds ridiculous, I get it. But you didn't know her. How much she wanted to live apart from the modern world. And how can you explain these lyrics? They're about what she did with the shells!"

He nods, as if this is rational. The expression in his eyes says it's anything but. "You don't think you're reading into them because you want to believe—"

"No."

"You haven't slept, you've been forced to relive an intensely painful experience. I've thrown all kinds of new information at you, about the past. Naturally—"

"No. Not naturally. I know how it sounds."

"But—"

"I've seen her."

"What?"

"I've seen her. Here, this summer. At first I thought it was a trick of the light. You know how the light changes so often here?"

"Yes." His voice is so reasonable, it's frightening. It's how you'd talk to someone about to have a breakdown.

I'm sure I'm worrying him as I lay out my outlandish theory, but I can't help it. Can't keep the thrill from my voice.

"She looked just the same. I know how it sounds, but it was her, and she's left me clues. Not just the diary. The album out with her picture facing the room, right where I'd see it. An old piece of lace she gave me that Toby *just happened* to find. She's been sleeping in the treehouse."

"Jackie. After what you've been through this summer, it's perfectly understandable that you'd start to wish...to *even half believe* that Willa's—"

"Not half."

"Okay. Okay. I'm not saying you didn't see *somebody*. Piper's blonde, around the same size. Couldn't it have been her? Or, we had that session player in July, she was blonde—"

"No. I remember that woman. She was fifty and her hair was dyed. Practically orange. This was Willa."

"But it was...a trick of the light, like you thought. A trick of the light and wishful thinking from one cousin who misses the other very much."

"So explain this." I gesture at the diary entry with the song.

"She could've done it twenty years ago. Like with the notebook. Or, say it is new... There are grifters. Fakers. You know how psychics research people so they can offer them a few tidbits to make them believe their dead relatives are communicating with them? It's not hard to do. You find some mementos, root through a few garbage cans...a little public records research. It happens all the time—"

I say it softly: "I don't want to make this into something that happens all the time."

I've given him an out. Maybe he'll leave me the phone number of a grief counselor or therapist before he speeds off for LA. I wait for him to sigh, and go.

He sighs, but stays. "So, what now?"

41

All the Answers

Two days later
Spyglass
Two hundred forty miles down the coast

When we left, the map was a clean, starched rectangle. Now it's grubby, as limp as cotton. For two hundred thirty miles, I've gripped it with my sweaty hands, unfolded it and draped it across my lap like an afghan, refolded it and wedged it in the glove compartment. Taken it out immediately. Stared at it, just to see the word again, to confirm that it's not just a memory Willa and I shared, but a place: Spyglass.

"You doing okay?" Shane asks again.

I nod, too anxious to speak. We're close. Only ten miles away.

Shane is having second thoughts, and he's worried about me, but he's driving me where I want to go. Maybe he's only indulging me until he can figure out his next step. How to talk me out of what I believe, find someone who can help me.

He still buys the official paperwork, the official story. It's what everyone else believes. And what I never wanted to accept, but had no choice to: that Willa has been dead for nearly twenty years.

I no longer think that.

"Don't be disappointed," he says, yet again.

"I won't be." *Because I'm right. I have to be right.* But I run my tongue along the scar inside my lower lip, my old nervous habit.

He starts to say something, stops himself, and sighs. He's afraid that whoever's been lurking around wasn't Willa, but some twisted fan. He made me read blogs about Graham's death so I could see how much information is on the internet—and how many lies and conspiracy theories there are. Some of his fans think he killed himself, dismissing the detailed medical report of fractures and sepsis. One claims he was pushed downhill by a jealous rival, a sort of Salieri–Mozart scenario.

"I'm not saying there's no chance," he says. "But you can't just have someone declared dead without… There would have to be investigations… You have paperwork that says she's dead, Jackie." He grips the wheel tightly.

He saw her from afar, those years ago, on their shared hill, but he doesn't understand her the way I do. He doesn't see how exactly *like* Willa this whole thing is. How much she valued her freedom. And though she always said she never wanted to leave her home, she changed the Sandcastle when she moved the shells that night. And it was no longer her home.

"You didn't know her," I say. "Not up close. She always wanted to fade away, so she did."

"And you think Angela knew she was alive and planned this whole thing with her?"

"I don't know." I spread the map over the dashboard, but it billows and rattles from the wind rushing in our open windows, so I refold it.

"If she were alive all this time…"

"What?"

"Wouldn't she have reached out to you?"

"Except she did reach out. She has."

"Jackie…"

"There, down this road. One more mile."

"When we get there, where do we go? Sit in a restaurant and just wait to see if she shows up? Go door to door?"

"I don't know. Left there, by the lookout."

He pulls in and stops in a small parking lot overlooking the beach.

"Jackie. I want you to be right. You don't know how much." He touches my knee. "But you need to prepare yourself to be wrong. There are a million possibilities that aren't Willa, alive, prowling around for two months and playing games with your head… Where are you going?"

I'm out of the car, on the wedge-shaped overlook. Shaped, just as its name implies, like a spyglass. It juts out over the water, a long piece of land, slightly wider at the end. I lean against the guardrail and look out. It's a foggy late afternoon, but the beach is crowded. Lots of surfers. Lots of kids. Couples, barbecuers, people walking their dogs.

Shane stands to my right, scanning the beach with me. But he's fidgety, looking over at me often.

I stay there for a long time, as the shadows of the bodies on the beach get longer, and the sun drops close to the blue horizon.

Shane paces, rubbing his hair, and still I watch.

He kisses my shoulder, whispers, "Jackie."

"Not yet," I say. "Just a little more time."

He asks if I want water, food. I shake my head and pull the lace bookmark from my pants pocket again so I can squeeze it. I always did need to occupy my hands when I was nervous. He retreats to the car to sit.

I watch the beach, and he watches me from the car. I can feel his eyes on me, feel the intensity of his worry from here. But my eyes don't leave the beach. The day-trippers start to pack up their blankets and coolers, and there are just a few clusters of bodies on the sand here and there.

"Jackie," Shane calls, when I've been staring for more than an hour. "It's going to be dark soon."

"Just a little longer."

"Let's go get some dinner. We can find a hotel down the highway and come back in the morning if you want. Look somewhere else nearby, or put up flyers? What do you say?"

"Half an hour more," I say, disappointment bitter in my throat.

He hesitates. "Okay. I'll walk to town and check things out."

Maybe he senses that I need to be alone to let go. To let her die a second time, and to let my teenage self die with her. The way people in hospitals know to leave the room, because otherwise their loved one will cling to hope. To life.

The sound of Shane's footsteps grows faint. The beach below is nearly empty.

And that's when I see her.

She's in the water, riding the waves. Her surfing form is as unmistakable as her voice. She's part of the ocean, not fighting it, but always a breath ahead of it, intuiting its next move. It's a rare thing to witness, that combination of confidence and humility. It's matchless, a miracle.

"Willa!" In my head it's a shout, but it comes out faint and raspy.

I take off, flying down the trail, my heart surging. I hold my breath around every switchback that forces me to take my eyes off of her; I'm relieved each time the blue sea comes into view again and she hasn't vanished. By the time I'm on the sand, she's still there. Yellow bikini bottom, white rash guard. Not even a half wet suit. It's warmer here than in the waves of her girlhood. Long blond hair darkened only slightly by time. It's her, could only be her, the bend of her body, the space between her toes and the nose of her board, the angle of her fingers to her wrist when they dip into the water, trailing across it casually, as if she's strolling past a garden fountain. Instead of mastering millions of pounds of dangerous water, unpredictable nature.

You did master it, Willa. It couldn't kill you, not when you loved it so much. And I'm sorry I ever believed you wanted to leave this earth, because you're so at home in it.

"Willa!" I shout, but the wind steals my voice.

My shoes are soaked, my pant cuffs wet and heavy, but I walk fast through the waves, straight toward her. When I'm thirty feet away, nearly hip-deep, I stop.

This life has kept her miraculously young; she still looks seventeen as she straddles her board, peering out toward the setting sun for one more wave. Her body is lean and toned, her hair is long, wild. When it dries it'll puff up into a cloud around her head.

She notices me at last. She smiles, paddles toward me. Drops her board on the sand, rips her Velcro board leash off her ankle and strolls over. Serene, casual. As if she's not surprised to see me at all.

Willa has hazel eyes now. She's two inches shorter.

"I knew you'd come," she says. Her voice is completely different. Lower. Sharper.

Disappointment is a vise around my heart. It's not her.

"I knew it," the strange girl says. "I knew it would work. It's nice to meet you, Jackie." She laughs, delighted.

Cruel, cruel girl. A fan, just like Shane's worst fear. A groupie who read up on Graham's family. A twisted soul who doesn't care who she hurts.

"It was you," I say slowly. "You were the one…"

She nods, still smiling. As if she hasn't just shattered my heart into a million fragments, pieces smaller than the shell dust by the waterfall trail.

"Why? Why would you—"

"Mom!" the girl yells over my shoulder.

I turn.

Down the beach, there's a woman. She has short red hair, and a little boy. She hasn't heard her daughter over the wind.

She's so good with the little boy, so gentle and unhurried, crouching to show him shells or sand crabs. Or a piece of sea glass...

"Mom!"

The woman looks happy. That's my last thought before she glances up and sees me. Freezes.

Her happy expression vanishes. Replaced by shock. She straightens.

Then she walks toward me slowly. When she's a few feet away she stops.

Lines around her round blue eyes. Freckles on her shoulders, from a life in the sun. The shallowest of creases above her kneecaps.

"She's been visiting me," I manage, fidgeting with the lace in my hand. "Your daughter. She's been lurking around the Sandcastle this summer. She put a song called 'Spyglass' in my old diary and left it in the treehouse so I could find you."

"Did she?" Her voice is the same. Hoarse from shock, but still rich and musical. Still young. "I didn't know. Not about that part."

"But you knew other parts?"

"I knew my mom left you the Sandcastle. Because I asked her to. And I knew there'd be an album with some of our music in with his. Because that was my idea, too. I wrote our old songs in the notebook, a few months before my mom died."

"But me finding you. That wasn't your idea."

Willa looks over at her daughter, who's watching us from afar, and shakes her head no.

"So then..." I take this in for a minute before I can dare ask, my voice raspy from fear of her answer. "Are you sorry I'm here?"

She doesn't answer.

She doesn't want me here. She wants me to go, and forget I ever saw her again. Pretend she's just a woman with red hair, a stranger I passed on the beach.

She never wanted to see me again. Her daughter lured me here without Willa's permission and now she's upset.

Then all thought is obliterated inside the force of her hug.

42

Tilting a Galaxy

That evening

"We're going on a campout," Willa announces to everyone near their van, which is parked in a quiet, tree-shrouded spot on a hill overlooking the beach. She says this to Liam, who she loves, and who helped her vanish twenty years ago. To their four children.

Willa has three boys, including the one I saw with her on the sand. Eighteen, seventeen, and seven.

And a daughter. An untamed daughter named Avery who's fifteen, and looks exactly like Willa used to except for her eye color. A daughter who is every bit as clever and imaginative and skilled at schemes as Willa and I were.

Willa is alive. Willa has four children, and lives in a van. They move it often. Whenever they have to, if they get tickets or people they don't trust ask too many questions.

I glimpse the inside of the van, as she's packing a rucksack for us, and it's orderly, for such a cramped space. I repeat these facts in my head as she introduces me to her children, as Liam (thicker, rougher-skinned, still kind, still shy, still besotted with Willa) hugs me.

Willa is alive, and has four children, and has been living in a van, traveling up and down the sands of western North America, for two decades. They are beach nomads. They have no phones, no television, no mortgage or internet service or formal school schedule.

They make money mostly by giving surf lessons. Just enough money is enough for them.

They're happy.

"You'll be okay?" I ask Shane, who's sitting in a camping chair talking to Liam.

"Yes. I'll get a hotel or I'll wait here and sleep in the car or… I don't know. Just, go, go!" He kisses me, hugs me tight. His eyes shine for me, showing a joy that I can't feel yet. None of this feels real.

"Thank you," I whisper into his ear.

I'm steps away, following Willa as she heads uphill into the trees, when he says, "Wait!" He fumbles in his backpack, pulls out a small tape player. "In case you two want some music tonight. Tape's in it."

"It's what I think?"

He nods. "The quality's not so great, a rush copy job. But when the music works that shouldn't matter. Don't tell me if you hate it. Go, have fun."

I smile, tuck it in my bag.

Willa and I hike north on the beach for half an hour, carrying our heavy bags full of supplies, listening to the gulls and the waves and our breathing, the soft thuds of our footsteps in the sand. I'm grateful for this time to think.

She leads me to a small, protected stretch of beach against a tall dune. Far enough from the beach access road that there aren't any people around.

We roll out our sleeping bags, set out our water bottles. Collect dry wood for our fire.

We build it together, halfway between our beds and the water, kneeling close to tend it.

"I discovered this spot about ten years ago," she says, settling back onto the sand once the flames are snapping.

I sit next to her. Not too close.

"The surfing's poor because of those rocks out there," she says. "See, those shapes? But it's my favorite place to camp alone when we're staying nearby. I come here when I need a little quiet."

"Four children, Willa. Four."

She smiles at me, her face glowing from the flickering fire. "I know."

"They're beautiful."

"Thank you. Li doesn't need to get away from them, ever. I need to a few times a year."

"And no one's ever recognized you, not in all that time?"

"It's easier than you think, disappearing. Liam never had any family...not any family who'd search for him..."

"I remember."

"And this helps." She touches her red hair. "Henna," she says, making a face. "I'm so used to it, I don't remember what my natural color is anymore."

"It's their color. The kids'. But this is pretty, too." Her dyed hair has a slight crown of frizz around the top. Her aura, I used to call it. I wish I could touch it, to reassure myself that she's real, but I keep my hand in my lap.

I have so many questions for her. Did she ever think about coming back? How long had she been in contact with Angela? Does she ever miss her old home and does she worry about the kids getting taken by social services and what about all those people who were sure she'd drowned in Rosarito, and who wrote the song "Spyglass, California" that Avery put in my diary under stickers, her or Avery? And me... Did she ever want to reach out to me?

But all of those questions can wait. The important thing is Willa is alive, and well, and here next to me.

"So you did go through with it," I say. "The shells."

She nods. "How did you—"

I explain about Shane. Our fan club of one, who secretly moved the shells back in place, to hide what he thought *Angela* had done.

"What did you think when you saw the shells had been moved back that night?" I ask.

"I didn't see them. I never went up there to move them back."

"But—"

"I came to the treehouse to tell you I'd lost him, Jackie, that I'd screwed up and I'd been out all night looking and I was worried it had gone too far. I followed him as long as I could into the trees and then I lost him."

"And you would have told me, in the treehouse, but I came rushing up saying how wonderful it was that you'd changed your mind. Oh, Wills. I'm so sorry. I wish I'd known." I'm crying, the tears streaming, warm and constant, down my cheeks.

"I thought if you knew I'd gone through with it, you'd hate me," she says softly. "You were so sure I hadn't done it. I hated myself, for a long time. That's why I left..."

"I don't hate you, I never could. And it was my idea, Wills. I'm so sorry that you've had to carry that by yourself this whole time."

We sit watching the fire until I've stopped crying.

"And Mexico?" I ask, wiping my nose on my sleeve.

"I didn't plan it. Li and I weren't even in Baja that month. We'd left Rosarito way before that drowning theory started. But I'd left my backpack behind in a port locker because we were rushing for our ferry. It had my insulin in it.

"And I guess a piece of someone else's board washed up nearby, and some fisherman said he'd seen a bunch of bummy-looking kids surfing too far out that day, so the lazy private detective my mom had hired decided it was probably mine. When Li and I read about it in the paper..."

"You let everyone think you'd drowned." *Even Angela. Even*

me. This is unfathomable, still. But I won't hurt her more by saying it aloud.

"I know how it seems, Jackie. But it was the only way I could live. Does that make any sense at all?"

The only way she could live—letting the girl who'd moved the shells die. I would try to understand it.

"I know this. That you'd never hurt anybody unless you had no other choice. Not then and not now."

"My mom said almost the same thing, the first time I visited her. After the shock wore off."

"So you—"

"I started visiting her at Arbor View a year ago," Willa says. "When I heard she was sick."

"And you told her all of it? About that night?"

She shakes her head no again. "I considered it. But we didn't have much time left, and she wanted to talk about the future, not the past. I think hoping the album might happen, with our songs on it, allowed her to hang on a little longer."

"And your daughter?"

"She doesn't know about that night, either. She just thinks 'Spyglass' is a song about the way the stars look from here."

Before we left the family at the van, Avery insisted to both of us that she hadn't planned the diary part of their scheme, that it had been a last-minute impulse because she "only wanted to help." Her words were contrite; her face was gleeful.

"Okay," I say, trying to get my head around it all. "You wrote our lyrics into Graham's notebook because you wanted the album to happen. Then, Avery secretly wrote your song about where you guys were staying this summer in my diary to bring you and me together? Am I getting it right?"

"Those are the highlights."

"Well. So you're writing lyrics now, not just music? You've replaced me." I say this lightly, trying to get her to smile, but maybe it comes out wrong because she only shakes her head no again.

"Now tell me a story." I reach for her hand. "Tell me the story about everything that's happened since you were seventeen."

This makes her smile. "Let's see. How would you start? Did I ever tell you about the time I hid my old life inside a Belgian cookie tin?"

I settle in.

What's most remarkable about the first eighteen years of the story is how steady its overarching theme is. The theme is contentment.

Willa's life hasn't been perfect, not entirely free of longing, homesickness, deprivation, cravings for comfort. But Liam and Willa have been happy with their choices, as their family has moved and grown, as they've raised their children in freedom. They wanted a different kind of life, and they created it. Out of little more than their talents and decency and faith that they could do it. And their love for each other.

At the eighteen-year mark, the story takes a twist. That's when Avery found a cookie tin of mementos tucked under the back seat of the van. It held the few things Willa gathered before she fled: a letter with her old address on it. Graham's song notebook. Family pictures—even pictures of me from that summer.

And a diary. Mine.

Avery asked questions. She started hitchhiking up to the Sandcastle whenever the van was in Northern California, spying on her grandmother from outside the gates.

First it was Avery's secret. But when Angela got sick and moved to Arbor View a year ago, Avery came clean to both of them and convinced Willa to visit Angela. To tiptoe back into civilization once in a while for her dying mother.

"How did she take it, when she first saw you?" I asked. "Back from the dead…"

"She was frightened, ecstatic, furious, sad, worried. All at once."

"And you?"

"I only felt one thing. Guilt. But she didn't want me to feel that way. She was just so happy that I was okay. She'd touch my hair, convincing herself I was real." Just like I'd wanted to. "She touched Avery's hair, too, and the boys'. I brought them twice."

"You snuck in so the nurses wouldn't see you, or what?"

"We were careful. You get good at back doors, living how we do…good at saying just enough for what you need that day."

It was Avery who came up with the idea for the album as a way to make peace with the past. With Willa's blessing, she gave Angela Graham's notebook. It was Angela's idea to choose Shane as producer.

"I'm sorry Avery scared you," Willa says. "Lurking around, the diary…"

"I'm not sorry."

"We worry about her hitching up and down the coast all the time, but we can't seem to stop her. She's half-wild. I know we chose a wild life but… The boys love how we live, but she's restless. We don't know how much longer we can keep her with us. If it's right to."

"She's your carbon copy, Willa. She's going to give you away."

She laughs. "She's a strong girl. Always full of plans. She reminds me of you."

"Uh-oh."

"No. I'm so glad that she's strong. But she's become impossible lately…"

We're settled in our sleeping bags now, head to head.

"Jackie?"

"Yes?"

"Angela said something. Near the end. Something you should hear."

I hold still. Her voice has never had this quality of authority, not that I remember. "What?" I ask, a little afraid.

"That maybe it wasn't such a tragedy, what happened to him. And sometimes I'm..."

Trailing off—the commanding tone is gone and this is the dreamy Willa I remember.

She doesn't need to say it. *Sometimes I'm not sorry about what happened to him, either.*

Because of how he'd abused Angela. Because it might have gotten worse.

Because toppling Graham freed Willa to live somewhere besides his kingdom—though she hadn't seen it as only his until she'd left.

"He could be a brutal king," I say.

"Yes."

"Now let's hear this anniversary album everyone's talking about."

We play it on low, just loud enough to hear above the breathing ocean. I take her hand as we listen, and we gaze up at the stars like we used to. We're far enough from the city lights to see the cloudy glow of the Milky Way. We're part of it.

The shell trail was a spiral, a white glow in the dark. From high up, maybe it looked like a galaxy. And we'd moved it. Together. We'd tilted a galaxy.

Soon, too soon, it's time to go. I could stay here with Willa for a month but I know not to push.

We're at the van, saying our goodbyes in the dense beach fog. It's early, cold. Willa has made it clear that she has no intention of resurfacing, living like everyone else, no matter how much I beg her to at least visit her old home.

"It's as beautiful as ever, Wills. It's valuable, and it doesn't belong to me. It's yours. If not the land, then the money."

"I don't want it." She says it with complete finality. "Not a penny."

"Then, for your kids. It should be in a trust for them, for when they're twenty-five."

"One thing my dad got right. Growing up with that kind of money isn't any kind of life."

"It hasn't made my father happy. I know that."

Willa doesn't care about how the album does, either—if it gets panned or ignored. She's just satisfied knowing it exists. That we're on there together.

"How will I reach you?" I ask as she climbs into the van. "I can't let you go again." I want details, city names. Dates for visits. She's mentioned a vague itinerary, how they spend winters in Costa Rica or Baja, giving surf lessons up and down the coast.

"I'll send you a letter in Boston. Or…"

"I won't be in Boston for a while. You can mail it to your old address. For now." I didn't decide this until just now, but I need to stay here for a while longer. I can't just find another real estate agent and put the Sandcastle on the market.

She smiles to herself. "Good."

The sound starts out so faint I think it's coming from the ocean. But it's her. Humming "Answers." Softly, but I remember it.

"Promise you'll write? Promise, Willa."

"Promise."

She has trusted me, and I have to trust her, too.

43

Avery

The promised letter didn't come for a month. It arrived only three days after I'd flown back from a quick trip to Boston to get my affairs in order, pack up my apartment, help find the perfect person to take over my music program. A wet-behind-the-ears Berklee College of Music grad who plays bass in a punk band at night and nannies to make ends meet. The kids'll like her.

When the letter came, someone delivered it in person.

Avery.

"This wasn't my idea," Avery says. She hands me the note.

Jackie,

I think our old home has been waiting for you for a long time.

And I wouldn't send my daughter to anyone but you. Remember how I said that she's ready to stay in one place? I can't go back, but you're there, and I have a good feeling about it. You finding me when you did—it was a sign. Even if she cheated a little.

I don't know when I'll be able to come visit. I'm trying to work up the courage, but it may be some time.

Can you take care of her for me? She won't admit it, but she wants one bed, and a teacher. I mean you—not whoever she'll have at school, though I trust you to help her through that. All that junk, like you used to call it.

   She wants to stop moving, and I so want to give those things to her.

   You don't have to do this. But I think maybe you want to.

   I love you.

Your,

W.

I fold up the note and put it in my pocket, smiling at the girl.

She is angry. She is afraid. She asked to come, but now that she's set everything in motion, she's not sure she wants to be here.

I see her defiance and I see struggles ahead and I know nothing about teenagers except what I remember from being one myself. I have no business raising her, but every part of me wants to.

It's a chance to make it right.

"There's just enough daylight left for a tour."

I know the first place I'm going to take her. I've made a new rope ladder and fixed the platform. I've left the walls bare. She can decorate it how she likes.

EPILOGUE

Istand with my back to the waterfall, facing the sea. I have found a kind of peace in coming up here every day, and I understand why this place meant so much to my uncle. But I don't try to write songs here, like he did. I do that alone in my old cabin, or at the beach. I meet Shane at the Rec Room piano after, to try to match the words with the right music.

Then, every afternoon, I come here to relax.

This morning is not about tranquility, though. I have a clipboard in my hands.

Down at the cabins, there's a flurry of activity. Last-minute checking, schedules, repairs. Although we've been ready for weeks.

I glance at my watch: not quite eleven. Shane picked them up at nine thirty, which means the earliest I'd see them is eleven fifteen. He's driving the bus now. A dozen kids, a small group to start. If this summer goes well, next year we'll host three times that. I have a nonprofit business plan and licensing for a two-week winter program, too.

I take a breath. Twelve kids, ten days. We're ready.

I scan the water, looking for Avery. She went surfing before the sun came up. I heard her slipping out before dawn, grabbing her wet suit from the railing. I am trying to be patient with her, to give her space. Each morning that I hear her thump down the stairs from Willa's room, past the parlor, where Shane and I sleep, and onto the front porch is a victory.

"Half-wild," Willa called her. I hope it wasn't a mistake to start all this while Avery is still adjusting. I thought she might be interested in the project, in acting as a sort of counselor-in-train-ing. When our license came, she was the first person I told, but she merely said, "That's nice," and fled to the ocean, as always.

She has withdrawn over the past few weeks, while we have bustled around getting everything ready. I gave her the anni-versary CD, which just came out, and she hasn't said a word about it. It has sat unwrapped, on her dresser, for days, so she can't even see that it is dedicated to her inside the liner booklet. Shane and I thought of that on the same day when they were finalizing the album.

I wish Willa was here. But she still can't set foot on this prop-erty, and I understand. It is enough that she has entrusted me with her daughter.

I wish the sun would come out, but the fog is stubborn this morning.

I don't see Avery out there in the waves. I've been on edge for nearly a year since she moved in, half waiting for her to leave. And now I've piled more kids, more chaos on top of it. For the hundredth time, I hope it's not a mistake.

"Are you nervous?"

I turn. It's Avery. Headphones around her neck, cord lead-ing to the Discman in her back pocket. Her hair is still damp from surfing.

I want to run and hug her, thank her for joining me here. This is a first.

But I restrain myself and instead admit, "I'm terrified."

"You—" In stepping toward me, her headphone cord has

gotten snagged on a branch and she stops, fumbles with it, de-tangling. With torturous slowness, she hooks the headphones in her back pocket.

I what? I want to yell. *Should be terrified? Got myself into this?*

She finishes at last: "You can probably handle it."

This is the height of courtesy, coming from Avery.

"Thank you. That means a lot to me."

"Although some of these kids could be real handfuls. So I'll let you know tonight if I've changed my mind."

"I'll be waiting eagerly for your update."

"Brought you something," she says, pulling it from the back of her waistband and holding it in front of her face: the new *Rolling Stone*, with the review of the album. It even has a cover headline. *Return to the Sandcastle, p. 46.*

Avery peeks out from behind it. "Don't you want to read it?"

"Oh, it's a beautiful album. Who cares what they say?"

"You do."

"I know. But I don't want to."

She holds the magazine flat, like a Frisbee, as if she's going to throw it.

"Do it," I say.

"Seriously?"

I nod, her wrist curls, and she flings the magazine.

"Wait!" I reach out but it's too late. It's sailing. A whirling, flapping, rainbow-colored sphere. Then it's just a dot, and then it falls, splashes. We watch it sink.

Avery and I look at each other for a minute, then burst out laughing.

We stand together, facing the sea.

If the fog burned off, I could show her her mother's trick. How to spot images and letters in the water, the sun's secret messages.

Messages. Avery will only admit to leaving me one within the Sandcastle's fence—placing the diary where I could see it from the treehouse last August. She claims she broke the rope ladder by accident, hurrying down to hide when she heard people heading her way, and insists she was far too careful, lurking around the bowl, for me to ever spot her in the trees. Insists that the golden hair I saw, the flax behind leaves, was my imagination, or a trick of the light. She claims she never set foot inside the house. The album in the Rec Room, the scrap of lace in the hall—she tells me they were just chance. It's possible she's lying.

But I hope she isn't. I'd rather believe it was this place working its magic, helping us. Asking me to stay.

I hear the tinny beat from her headphones, and I wonder if the song is from the tribute album, and which one it is. If it's Graham's, or a song Willa and I wrote together.

She flicks it off before I can make sense of the tune.

I'll choose to believe it is one of the songs her mother and I dreamed up. A secret message from Willa, to tell me she's here with me, that I can do this. That we've found the only way to heal this place.

Avery and I wait, watching, for a long time.

"Look," she says, pointing down at the highway. Silently, we watch the school bus. A bright yellow streak in the distance.

★ ★ ★ ★ ★

ACKNOWLEDGMENTS

Thank you to my superb agent, Stefanie Lieberman, for six years of support, wisdom, and friendship.

Melanie Fried, you're not only an astute editor with a crystal clear eye for structure and pace, your steadiness and optimism are *unearthly*. I'm so proud of us.

Kathleen Carter, huge thanks for working tirelessly to get the word out in these unprecedented times.

To Margaret Marbury, Susan Swinwood, Roxanne Jones, Pamela Osti, and everyone else at Graydon House, I'm honored to be part of the imprint and so grateful for your vision and excellent work. Gigi Lau and Mary Luna, thank you for designing a cover plucked straight from my daydreams.

Molly Steinblatt, Adam Hobbins, and the whole stellar team at Janklow & Nesbit, thanks for seeing promise in my work and giving me precious feedback on my duck-under-the-covers-in-shame-they're-so-raw drafts.

Gratitude and love to Billy Bragg, Wilco, Nora Guthrie, and Woody Guthrie. I got the idea for this novel decades ago from their 1998 album *Mermaid Avenue*—created from a treasure of Woody Guthrie lyrics. If you haven't played it, do so immediately.

Thanks to independent bookstores for keeping the faith and

keeping the lights on—Rakestraw Books, Broadway Books, Powell's, Cloud & Leaf, Books Inc., City Lights, Kepler's, Lido Village, Diesel, The Elliott Bay Book Company, Parnassus Books, Books & Books, E. Shaver, Shakespeare and Co., and hundreds more. You are appreciated, loved, and needed.

Reading sites have been a bright spot for many of us in 2020. Much love to A Mighty Blaze, A Novel Bee, Bookworms Anonymous, Chick Lit Central, Great Thoughts' Great Readers, Linda's Book Obsession, My Book Tribe, Novels N Latte, Readers Coffeehouse, The Romance of Reading, Sue's Reading Neighborhood, and many more.

I took some liberties with the Lilith Fair '99 performer lineup in order to include two of my favorite singer-songwriters, Lucinda Williams and the late Lhasa de Sela, both of whom I was lucky enough to see at other shows. Thank you to Sarah McLachlan and everyone involved in Lilith Fair for the inspiration and the memories.

Professor Susan Rogers at Berklee College of Music was generous with her time and patiently answered my questions about analog recording. Any mistakes are mine.

Wes, you gave me the idea for Novel 4, and Kelsey, I admire your confidence onstage, offstage, and on the way to the stage. Tiff, Dave, Nat, Luke—I miss you. Erin Higgins, I'm so proud to be your aunt. To all the Doans, we may not see each other often, but you're in my heart.

Dad—I still love Willie and George Jones. I miss our KSAN commutes. Mom—I can picture you in 1979 lying on the floor, headphones on, listening to your favorite tunes. Can't wait for a post-pandemic hug.

Mike and Miranda—I may have written most of this in a tent in the backyard, but there's nobody I'd rather be quarantined with than you two. Thank you for putting up with my moods and self-doubt and all that disco on Spotify. Miranda, please keep singing, 'kay?

Carrie—my big sister, my best friend, and forever my role model of a strong woman. You bought me my first 45 record (Melissa Manchester), introduced me to *Solid Gold*, KITS, and KFOG, and I paid you back by stealing your K-Tel albums and mixtapes. Wish we could travel back to '79 for an afternoon and roller-skate to *Grease* and *Xanadu* in the garage. I love you.

LADY SUNSHINE:
THE ALBUM

Side A—Jackie
"On the Radio," Donna Summer
"Heart of Glass," Blondie
"The Hustle," Van McCoy
"Jackie Blue," Ozark Mountain Daredevils
"I Feel Love," Donna Summer
"Sunday Girl," Blondie

Side B—Willa
"California," Joni Mitchell
"Ain't Life a Brook," Ferron
"Suite: Judy Blue Eyes," Crosby, Stills & Nash
"Down to Zero," Joan Armatrading
"Trouble," Yusuf/Cat Stevens
"Who Knows Where the Time Goes," Nina Simone

Find it on Spotify: https://tinyurl.com/yxpxtsmw

THE STORY BEHIND
LADY SUNSHINE

It started with Wilco's song "California Stars."

San Francisco, 1998. I was twenty-five, and the plaintive tune had become my "earworm"—an ugly word for beautiful music. I played it on my red iPod Shuffle in the dingy studio apartment I shared with another girl and her boyfriend, and when I jogged along the foggy Marina. I listened to it when standing on packed buses to and from my dispiriting job as an advertising analyst, and when I couldn't sleep, which was often. I was lonely after a breakup, and the lyrics, about longing to rest one's "heavy head" on a bed of stars, became my lullaby.

A month after I first heard the song, I learned the story behind it from a radio show, and that became as much of an obsession as the song itself. The lyrics were part of a treasure trove of unrecorded Woody Guthrie lines that his daughter Nora had brought to Billy Bragg and Wilco so they could set them to music—which became the album *Mermaid Avenue*.

The gutsy intimacy of this project fascinated me. How brave it was to take a dead genius's words and meld them with your own music. How did Nora Guthrie feel about Bragg and Wilco's interpretations? What secrets of her father's might the lyrics hold? These questions became the seeds of *Lady Sunshine*—about a woman, Jackie, who unexpectedly inherits her folk-singer uncle's iconic estate and the tribute album that a rising producer convinces her to record on the property.

For Jackie, the album further complicates the already-difficult task of preparing her estranged family's estate for sale. She spent just one summer there as a teen in 1979—falling into an intense friendship with her cousin Willa, discovering her own musical talent, and plunging into a free-spirited bohemian lifestyle—but it abruptly ended in a tragedy that changed her forever.

I began to wonder, what if Jackie's legendary uncle wasn't who everyone thought he was? What if excavating his music reminded her of a lost time—and a lost self—she desperately wished she could recapture? Younger Jackie worshipped powerhouse female singers like Donna Summer and Debbie Harry, just as folk-loving Willa revered the brilliant "J singers"—Joni Mitchell, Joan Armatrading, Joan Baez, and Judy Collins. These women were strong and outspoken, like Jackie once was, but she now lives a quiet, safe life as a piano teacher.

As an adult, Jackie discovers a startling clue buried in her uncle's lyrics—and realizes that she may be wrong about what happened that summer long ago. She must choose whether to run from her task, and the truth, or to let the music come to life and provide the answers she's been looking for all these years. *Lady Sunshine* is my tribute to the inescapable tug of the past, the generous spirit and hypnotic bass line of the 1970s, and the endurance of art and music against all odds.

Billy Bragg said that while recording *Mermaid Avenue*, one lyric struck everyone in the studio. It was a line Guthrie wrote about his legacy, how no matter where fate or the fickle winds of popularity might send him, he felt in his heart that one thing would stay: his "scribbling."

I hope *Lady Sunshine* captures a fraction of that joy, and my determination to write novels that stay in readers' hearts for a long, long time.

QUESTIONS FOR DISCUSSION

1. Several characters note the Sandcastle's isolation, describing it as walled off from time or the modern world. How does this affect Jackie's stay there in 1979? In 1999?

2. Voyeurism is a major theme in the novel. Why do Jackie and Willa spy from the treehouse? Is it ultimately constructive or destructive? Who else in the book engages in voyeurism, and why? How are their motives different from or similar to Jackie's and Willa's reasons for spying?

3. Jackie and Willa are opposites in nearly every way, but they idolize each other. Do you think they see each other clearly when they're teenagers? Adults? How do their roles reverse over time?

4. Jackie is obsessed with Debbie Harry and Blondie, while Willa loves folk singers like Joni Mitchell and Joan Armatrading. Who were your favorite musicians when you were a teenager, and why? Have your musical tastes changed over the years?

5. As a teenager, why is Jackie drawn to Graham? What does she find in him that she doesn't find elsewhere in her life? How does this connection impact her reaction to the revelation about his treatment of Angela?

6. How do the following characters approach their musical talent differently?—Graham, Willa, Bree, Jackie, Shane. Why are some people able to handle fame and attention, while others are not?

7. Can you separate a creator from their art? Can you appreciate their work even if they have not behaved appropriately as people?

8. If you left behind unfinished art like Graham did, would you want someone else to complete your work? Why or why not?

9. In 1999, Willa hints that Graham's accident might have been for the best. Do you agree? How are she and Jackie able to look at what happened to him differently as grown women than as teenagers in 1979?

10. Why do Jackie and Avery toss the album review into the ocean? What do you imagine life will be like at the Sandcastle for Jackie and Avery and for future generations? How will it be different or the same?